Garrett P. Serviss'
Science Fiction

Garrett P. Serviss'
Science Fiction

Three Interplanetary Adventures
including the unnauthorised sequel
to H. G. Wells' War of the Worlds

Edison's Conquest of Mars
A Columbus of Space
The Moon Metal

Garrett P. Serviss

LEONAUR

Garrett P. Serviss' Science Fiction: Three Interplanetary Adventures including the unnauthorised sequel to H. G. Wells' War of the Worlds— Edison's Conquest of Mars, A Columbus of Space, The Moon Metal
by Garrett P. Serviss

Published by Leonaur Ltd in 2007

ISBN: 978-1-84677-324-2 (hardcover)
ISBN: 978-1-84677-323-5 (softcover)

http://www.leonaur.com

Publisher's Notes

The opinions expressed in this book are those of the author and are not necessarily those of the publisher.

Contents

Edison's Conquest
of Mars

Chapter 1

It is impossible that the stupendous events which followed the disastrous invasion of the earth by the Martians should go without record, and circumstances having placed the facts at my disposal, I deem it a duty, both to posterity and to those who were witnesses of and participants in the avenging counterstroke that the earth dealt back at its ruthless enemy in the heavens, to write down the story in a connected form.

The Martians had nearly all perished, not through our puny efforts, but in consequence of disease, and the few survivors fled in one of their projectile cars, inflicting their cruellest blow in the act of departure.

They possessed a mysterious explosive, of unimaginable puissance, with whose aid they set their car in motion for Mars from a point in Bergen County, N. J., just back of the Palisades.

The force of the explosion may be imagined when it is recollected that they had to give the car a velocity of more than seven miles per second in order to overcome the attraction of the earth and the resistance of the atmosphere.

The shock destroyed all of New York that had not already fallen a prey, and all the buildings yet standing in the surrounding towns and cities fell in one far-circling ruin.

The Palisades tumbled in vast sheets, starting a tidal wave in the Hudson that drowned the opposite shore.

The victims of this ferocious explosion were numbered by tens of thousands, and the shock, transmitted through the rocky frame of the globe, was recorded by seismographic pendulums in England and on the Continent of Europe.

The terrible results achieved by the invaders had produced everywhere a mingled feeling of consternation and hopelessness. The devastation was widespread. The death-dealing engines which the Martians had brought with them had proved irresistible and the inhabitants of the earth possessed nothing capable of contending against them. There had been no protection for the great cities; no protection even for the open country. Everything had gone down before the savage onslaught of those merciless invaders from space. Savage ruins covered the sites of many formerly flourishing towns and villages, and the broken walls of great cities stared at the heavens like the exhumed skeletons of Pompeii. The awful agencies had extirpated pastures and meadows and dried up the very springs of fertility in the earth where they had touched it. In some parts of the devastated lands pestilence broke out; elsewhere there was famine. Despondency black as night brooded over some of the fairest portions of the globe.

Yet all had not been destroyed, because all had not been reached by the withering hand of the destroyer. The Martians had not had time to complete their work before they themselves fell a prey to the diseases that carried them off at the very culmination of their triumph.

From those lands which had, fortunately, escaped invasion, relief was sent to the sufferers. The outburst of pity and of charity exceeded anything that the world had known. Differences of race and religion were swallowed up in the universal sympathy which was felt for those who had suffered so terribly from an evil that was as unexpected as it was unimaginable in its enormity.

But the worst was not yet. More dreadful than the actual suffering and the scenes of death and devastation which overspread the afflicted lands was the profound mental and moral depression that followed. This was shared even by those who had not seen the Martians and had not witnessed the destructive effects of the frightful engines of war that they had imported for the conquest of the earth. All mankind was sunk deep in this universal despair, and it became tenfold blacker when the astronomers announced from their observatories that strange lights were visible, moving and flashing upon the red surface of the Planet of War. These mysterious appearances could only be interpreted in the light of past experience to mean that the Martians were preparing for another invasion of the earth, and who could doubt that with the invincible powers of destruction at their command they would this time make their work complete and final?

This startling announcement was the more pitiable in its effects because it served to unnerve and discourage those few of stouter hearts and more hopeful temperaments who had already begun the labour of restoration and reconstruction amid the embers of their desolated homes. In New York this feeling of hope and confidence, this determination to rise against disaster and to wipe out the evidences of its dreadful presence as quickly as possible, had especially manifested itself. Already a company had been formed and a large amount of capital subscribed for the reconstruction of the destroyed bridges over the East River. Already architects were busily at work planning new twenty-story hotels and apartment houses; new churches and new cathedrals on a grander scale than before.

Amid this stir of renewed life came the fatal news that Mars was undoubtedly preparing to deal us a death blow. The sudden revulsion of feeling flitted like the shadow of an eclipse over the earth. The scenes that followed were indescribable. Men lost their reason. The faint-hearted ended the suspense with self-destruction, the stout-hearted remained steadfast, but without hope and knowing not what to do.

But there was a gleam of hope of which the general public as yet knew nothing. It was due to a few dauntless men of science, conspicuous among whom were Lord Kelvin, the great English savant; Herr Roentgen, the discoverer of the famous X ray, and especially Thomas A. Edison, the American genius of science. These men and a few others had examined with the utmost care the engines of war, the flying machines, the generators of mysterious destructive forces that the Martians had produced, with the object of discovering, if possible, the sources of their power.

Suddenly from Mr. Edison's laboratory at Orange flashed the startling intelligence that he had not only discovered the manner in which the invaders had been able to produce the mighty energies which they employed with such terrible effect, but that, going further, he had found a way to overcome them.

The glad news was quickly circulated throughout the civilized world. Luckily the Atlantic cables had not been destroyed by the Martians, so that communication between the Eastern and Western continents was uninterrupted. It was a proud day for America. Even while the Martians had been upon the earth, carrying everything before them, demonstrating to the confusion of the most optimistic that there was no possibility of standing against them, a feeling—a confidence had manifested itself in France, to a minor extent in England, and particularly in Russia, that the Americans might discover means to meet and master the invaders.

Now, it seemed, this hope and expectation were to be realized. Too late, it is true, in a certain sense, but not too late to meet the new invasion which the astronomers had announced was impending. The effect was as wonderful and indescribable as that of the despondency which but a little while before had overspread the world. One could almost hear the universal sigh of relief which went up from humanity. To relief succeeded confidence—so quickly does the human spirit recover like an elastic spring, when pressure is released.

"Let them come," was the almost joyous cry. "We shall be ready for them now. The Americans have solved the problem. Edison has placed the means of victory within our power."

Looking back upon that time now, I recall, with a thrill, the pride that stirred me at the thought that, after all, the inhabitants of the Earth were a match for those terrible men from Mars, despite all the advantage which they had gained from their millions of years of prior civilization and science.

As good fortunes, like bad, never come singly, the news of Mr. Edison's discovery was quickly followed by additional glad tidings from that laboratory of marvels in the lap of the Orange mountains. During their career of conquest the Martians had astonished the inhabitants of the earth no less with their flying machines—which navigated our atmosphere as easily as they had that of their native planet—than with their more destructive inventions. These flying machines in themselves had given them an enormous advantage in the contest. High above the desolation that they had caused to reign on the surface of the earth, and, out of the range of our guns, they had hung safe in the upper air. From the clouds they had dropped death upon the earth.

Edison's Flying Machine.

Now, rumour declared that Mr. Edison had invented and perfected a flying machine much more complete and manageable than those of the Martians had been. Wonderful stories quickly found their way into the newspapers concerning what Mr. Edison had already accomplished with the aid of his model electrical balloon. His laboratory was carefully guarded against the invasion of the curious, because he rightly felt that a premature announcement, which should promise more than could be actually fulfilled, would, at this critical juncture, plunge mankind back again into the gulf of despair, out of which it had just begun to emerge.

Nevertheless, inklings of the truth leaked out. The flying machine had been seen by many persons hovering by night high above the Orange hills and disappearing in the faint starlight as if it had gone away into the depths of space, out of which it would re-emerge before the morning light had streaked the east, and be seen settling down again within the walls that surrounded the laboratory of the great inventor. At length the rumour, gradually deepening into a conviction, spread that Edison himself, accompanied by a few scientific friends, had made an experimental trip to the moon. At a time when the spirit of mankind was less profoundly stirred, such a story would have been received with complete incredulity, but now, rising on the wings of the new hope that was buoying up the earth, this extraordinary rumour became a day star of truth to the nations.

And it was true. I had myself been one of the occupants of the car of the flying Ship of Space on that night when it silently left the earth, and rising out of the great shadow of the globe, sped on to the moon. We had landed upon the scarred and desolate face of the earth's satellite, and but that there are greater and more interesting events, the telling of which must not be delayed, I should undertake to describe the particulars of this first visit of men to another world.

But, as I have already intimated, this was only an experimental trip. By visiting this little nearby island in the ocean of space, Mr. Edison simply wished to demonstrate the practicability of his invention, and to convince, first of all, himself and his scientific friends that it was possible for men—mortal men—to quit and to revisit the earth at their will. That aim this experimental trip triumphantly attained.

It would carry me into technical details that would hardly interest the reader to describe the mechanism of Mr. Edison's flying machine. Let it suffice to say that it depended upon the principal of electrical attraction and repulsion. By means of a most ingenious and complicated construction he had mastered the problem of how to produce, in a limited space, electricity of any desired potential and of any polarity, and that without danger to the experimenter or to the material experimented upon. It is gravitation, as everybody knows, that makes man a prisoner on the earth. If he could overcome, or neutralize, gravitation he could float away a free creature of interstellar space. Mr. Edison in his invention had pitted electricity against gravitation. Nature, in fact, had done the same thing long before. Every astronomer knew it, but none had been able to imitate or to reproduce this miracle of nature. When a comet approaches the sun, the orbit in which it travels indicates that it is moving under the impulse of the sun's gravitation. It is in reality falling in a great parabolic or elliptical curve through space. But, while a comet approaches the sun it begins to display—stretching out for millions, and sometimes hundreds of millions of miles on the side away from the sun—an immense luminous train called its tail. This train extends back into that part of space from which the comet is moving. Thus the sun at one and the same time is drawing the comet toward itself and driving off from the comet in an opposite direction minute particles or atoms which, instead of obeying the gravitational force, are plainly compelled to disobey it. That this energy, which the sun exercises against its own gravitation, is electrical in its nature, hardly anybody will doubt. The head of the comet being comparatively heavy and massive, falls on toward the sun, despite the electrical repulsion. But the atoms which form the tail, being almost without weight, yield to the electrical rather than to the gravitational influence, and so fly away from the sun.

Now, what Mr. Edison had done was, in effect, to create an electrified particle which might be compared to one of the atoms composing the tail of a comet, although in reality it was a kind of car, of metal, weighing some hundreds of pounds and capable of bearing some thousands of pounds with it in its flight. By producing, with the aid of the electrical generator contained in this car, an enormous charge of electricity, Mr. Edison was able to counterbalance, and a trifle more than counterbalance, the attraction of the earth, and thus cause the car to fly off from the earth as an electrified pith ball flies from the prime conductor.

As we sat in the brilliantly lighted chamber that formed the interior of the car, and where stores of compressed air had been provided together with chemical apparatus, by means of which fresh supplies of oxygen and nitrogen might be obtained for our consumption during the flight through space, Mr. Edison touched a polished button, thus causing the generation of the required electrical charge on the exterior of the car, and immediately we began to rise.

The moment and direction of our flight had been so timed and prearranged, that the original impulse would carry us straight toward the moon.

When we fell within the sphere of attraction of that orb it only became necessary to so manipulate the electrical charge upon our car as nearly, but not quite, to counterbalance the effect of the moon's attraction in order that we might gradually approach it and with an easy motion, settle, without shock, upon its surface.

We did not remain to examine the wonders of the moon, although we could not fail to observe many curious things therein. Having demonstrated the fact that we could not only leave the earth, but could journey through space and safely land upon the surface of another planet, Mr. Edison's immediate purpose was fulfilled, and we hastened back to the earth, employing in leaving the moon and land-ing again upon our own planet the same means of control over the electrical attraction and repulsion between the respective planets and our car which I have already described.

Telegraphing the News.

When actual experiment had thus demonstrated the practicability of the invention, Mr. Edison no longer withheld the news of what he had been doing from the world. The telegraph lines and the ocean cables laboured with the messages that in endless succession, and bur-dened with an infinity of detail, were sent all over the earth. Every-where the utmost enthusiasm was aroused.

"Let the Martians come," was the cry. "If necessary, we can quit the earth as the Athenians fled from Athens before the advancing host of Xerxes, and like them, take refuge upon our ships—these new ships of space, with which American inventiveness has furnished us."

And then, like a flash, some genius struck out an idea that fired the world.

"Why should we wait? Why should we run the risk of having our cities destroyed and our lands desolated a second time? Let us go to Mars. We have the means. Let us beard the lion in his den. Let us our-selves turn conquerors and take possession of that detestable planet, and if necessary, destroy it in order to relieve the earth of this perpetual threat which now hangs over us like the sword of Damocles."

Chapter 2

This enthusiasm would have had but little justification had Mr. Edison done nothing more than invent a machine which could navigate the atmosphere and the regions of interplanetary space.

He had, however, and this fact was generally known, although the details had not yet leaked out—invented also machines of war intended to meet the utmost that the Martians could do for either offence or defence in the struggle which was now about to ensue.

Acting upon the hint which had been conveyed from various investigations in the domain of physics, and concentrating upon the problem all those unmatched powers of intellect which distinguished him, the great inventor had succeeded in producing a little implement which one could carry in his hand, but which was more powerful than any battleship that ever floated. The details of its mechanism could not be easily explained, without the use of tedious technicalities and the employment of terms, diagrams and mathematical statements, all of which would lie outside the scope of this narrative. But the principle of the thing was simple enough. It was upon the great scientific doctrine, which we have since seen so completely and brilliantly developed, of the law of harmonic vibrations, extending from atoms and molecules at one end of the series up to worlds and suns at the other end, that Mr. Edison based his invention.

Every kind of substance has its own vibratory rhythm. That of iron differs from that of pine wood. The atoms of gold do not vibrate in the same time or through the same range as those of lead, and so on for all known substances, and all the chemical elements. So, on a larger scale, every massive body has its period of vibration. A great suspension bridge vibrates, under the impulse of forces that are applied to it, in long periods. No company of soldiers ever crosses such a bridge without breaking step. If they tramped together, and were followed by other companies keeping the same time with their feet, after a while the vibrations of the bridge would become so great and destructive that it would fall in pieces. So any structure, if its vibration rate is known, could easily be destroyed by a force applied to it in such a way that it should simply increase the swing of those vibrations up to the point of destruction.

Now Mr. Edison had been able to ascertain the vibratory swing of many well-known substances, and to produce, by means of the instrument which he had contrived, pulsations in the ether which were completely under his control, and which could be made long or short, quick or slow, at his will. He could run through the whole gamut from the slow vibrations of sound in air up to the four hundred and twenty-five millions of millions of vibrations per second of the ultra red rays.

Having obtained an instrument of such power, it only remained to concentrate its energy upon a given object in order that the atoms composing that object should be set into violent undulation, sufficient to burst it asunder and to scatter its molecules broadcast. This the inventor effected by the simplest means in the world—simply a parabolic reflector by which the destructive waves could be sent like a beam of light, but invisible, in any direction and focused upon any desired point.

I had the good fortune to be present when this powerful engine of destruction was submitted to its first test. We had gone upon the roof of Mr. Edison's laboratory and the inventor held the little instrument, with its attached mirror, in his hand. We looked about for some object on which to try its powers. On a bare limb of a tree not far away, for it was late in the Fall, sat a disconsolate crow.

"Good," said Mr. Edison, "that will do." He touched a button at the side of the instrument and a soft, whirring noise was heard.

"Feathers," said Mr. Edison, "have a vibration period of three hundred and eighty-six million per second."

He adjusted the index as he spoke. Then, through a sighting tube, he aimed at the bird.

"Now watch," he said.

Another soft whirr in the instrument, a momentary flash of light close around it, and, behold, the crow had turned from black to white!

"Its feathers are gone," said the inventor; "they have been dissipated into their constituent atoms. Now, we will finish the crow."

Instantly there was another adjustment of the index, another out-shooting of vibratory force, a rapid up and down motion of the in-

17

dex to include a certain range of vibrations, and the crow itself was gone—vanished in empty space! There was the bare twig on which a moment before it had stood. Behind, in the sky, was the white cloud against which its black form had been sharply outlined, but there was no more crow.

"That looks bad for the Martians, doesn't it?" said the Wizard. "I have ascertained the vibration rate of all the materials of which their war engines whose remains we have collected together are composed. They can be shattered into nothingness in the fraction of a second. Even if the vibration period were not known, it could quickly be hit upon by simply running through the gamut."

"Hurrah!" cried one of the onlookers. "We have met the Martians and they are ours."

Such in brief was the first of the contrivances which Mr. Edison invented for the approaching war with Mars.

And these facts had become widely known. Additional experiments had completed the demonstration of the inventor's ability, with the aid of his wonderful instrument, to destroy any given object, or any part of an object, provided that that part differed in its atomic constitution, and consequently in its vibratory period, from the other parts.

A most impressive public exhibition of the powers of the little disintegrator was given amid the ruins of New York. On lower Broadway a part of the walls of one of the gigantic buildings, which had been destroyed by the Martians, impended in such a manner that it threatened at any moment to fall upon the heads of the passers-by. The Fire Department did not dare touch it. To blow it up seemed a dangerous expedient, because already new buildings had been erected in its neighbourhood, and their safety would be imperilled by the flying fragments. The fact happened to come to my knowledge.

"Here is an opportunity," I said to Mr. Edison, "to try the powers of your machine on a large scale."

"Capital!" he instantly replied. "I shall go at once."

For the work now in hand it was necessary to employ a battery of disintegrators, since the field of destruction covered by each was comparatively limited. All of the impending portions of the wall must be destroyed at once and together, for otherwise the danger would rather be accentuated than annihilated. The disintegrators were placed upon the roof of a neighbouring building, so adjusted that their fields of destruction overlapped one another upon the wall. Their indexes were all set to correspond with the vibration period of the peculiar kind of brick of which the wall consisted. Then the energy was turned on, and a shout of wonder arose from the multitudes which had assembled at a safe distance to witness the experiment.

The wall did not fall; it did not break asunder; no fragments shot this way and that and high in the air; there was no explosion; no shock or noise disturbed the still atmosphere—only a soft whirr, that seemed to pervade everything and to tingle in the nerves of the spectators; and—what had been was not! The wall was gone! But high above and all around the place where it had hung over the street with its threat of death there appeared, swiftly billowing outward in every direction, a faint, bluish cloud. It was the scattered atoms of the destroyed wall.

And now the cry "On to Mars!" was heard on all sides. But for such an enterprise funds were needed—millions upon millions. Yet some of the fairest and richest portions of the earth had been impoverished by the frightful ravages of those enemies who had dropped down upon them from the skies. Still, the money must be had. The salvation of the planet, as everybody was now convinced, depended upon the successful negotiation of a gigantic war fund, in comparison with which all the expenditures in all of the wars that had been waged by the nations for 2,000 years would be insignificant. The electrical ships and the vibration engines must be constructed by scores and thousands. Only Mr. Edison's immense resources and unrivalled equipment had enabled him to make the models whose powers had been so satisfactorily shown. But to multiply these upon a war scale was not only beyond the resources of any individual—hardly a nation on the globe in the period of its greatest prosperity could have undertaken such a work. All the nations, then, must now conjoin. They must unite their resources, and, if necessary, exhaust all their hoards, in order to raise the needed sum.

Negotiations were at once begun. The United States naturally took the lead, and their leadership was never for a moment questioned abroad.

Washington was selected as the place of meeting for a great congress of the nations. Washington, luckily, had been one of the places which had not been touched by the Martians. But if Washington had been a city composed of hotels alone, and every hotel so great as to be a little city in itself, it would have been utterly insufficient for the accommodation of the innumerable throngs which now flocked to the banks of the Potomac. But when was American enterprise unequal to a crisis? The necessary hotels, lodging houses and restaurants were constructed with astounding rapidity. One could see the city growing and expanding day by day and week after week. It flowed over Georgetown Heights; it leaped the Potomac; it spread east and west, south and north; square mile after square mile of territory was buried under the advancing buildings, until the gigantic city, which had thus grown up like a mushroom in a night, was fully capable of accommodating all its expected guests.

At first it had been intended that the heads of the various governments should in person attend this universal congress, but as the enterprise went on, as the enthusiasm spread, as the necessity for haste became more apparent through the warning notes which were constantly sounded from the observatories where the astronomers were nightly beholding new evidences of threatening preparations in Mars, the kings and queens of the old world felt that they could not remain at home; that their proper place was at the new focus and centre of the whole world—the city of Washington. Without concerted action, without interchange of suggestion, this impulse seemed to seize all the old world monarchs at once. Suddenly cablegrams flashed to the Government at Washington, announcing that Queen Victoria, the Emperor William, the Czar Nicholas, Alphonso of Spain, with his mother, Maria Christina; the old Emperor Francis Joseph and the Empress Elizabeth, of Austria; King Oscar and Queen Sophia, of Sweden and Norway; King Humbert and Queen Margherita, of Italy; King George and Queen Olga, of Greece; Abdul Hamid, of Turkey; Tsait'ien, Emperor of China; Mutsuhito, the Japanese Mikado, with his beautiful Princess Haruko; the President of France, the President of Switzerland, the First Syndic of the little republic of Andorra, perched on the crest of the Pyrenees, and the heads of all the Central and South American republics, were coming to Washington to take part in the deliberations, which, it was felt, were to settle the fate of earth and Mars.

One day, after this announcement had been received, and the additional news had come that nearly all the visiting monarchs had set out, attended by brilliant suites and convoyed by fleets of warships, for their destination, some coming across the Atlantic to the port of New York, others across the Pacific to San Francisco, Mr. Edison said to me:

"This will be a fine spectacle. Would you like to watch it?"

"Certainly," I replied.

The Ship of Space was immediately at our disposal. I think I have not yet mentioned the fact that the inventor's control over the electrical generator carried in the car was so perfect that by varying the potential or changing the polarity he could cause it slowly or swiftly, as might be desired, to approach or recede from any object. The only practical difficulty was presented when the polarity of the electrical charge upon an object in the neighbourhood of the car was unknown to those in the car, and happened to be opposite to that of the charge which the car, at that particular moment, was bearing. In such a case, of course, the car would fly toward the object, whatever it might be, like a pith ball or a feather, attracted to the knob of an electrical machine. In this way, considerable danger was occasionally encountered, and a few accidents could not be avoided. Fortunately, however, such cases were rare. It was only now and then that, owing to some local cause, electrical polarities unknown to or unexpected by the navigators, endangered the safety of the car. As I shall have occasion to relate, however, in the course of the narrative, this danger became more acute and assumed at times a most formidable phase, when we had ventured outside the sphere of the earth and were moving through the unexplored regions beyond.

On this occasion, having embarked, we rose rapidly to a height of some thousands of feet and directed our course over the Atlantic. When half way to Ireland, we beheld, in the distance, steaming westward, the smoke of several fleets. As we drew nearer a marvellous spectacle unfolded itself to our eyes. From the northeast, their great guns flashing in the sunlight and their huge funnels belching black volumes that rested like thunder clouds upon the sea, came the mighty warships of England, with her meteor flag streaming red in the breeze, while the royal insignia, indicating the presence of the ruler of the British Empire, was conspicuously displayed upon the flagship of the squadron.

Following a course more directly westward appeared, under another black cloud of smoke, the hulls and guns and burgeons of another great fleet, carrying the tri-colour of France, and bearing in its midst the head of the magnificent republic of western Europe.

Further south, beating up against the northerly winds, came a third fleet with the gold and red of Spain fluttering from its masthead. This, too, was carrying its King westward, where now, indeed, the star of empire had taken its way.

Rising a little higher, so as to extend our horizon, we saw coming down the English channel, behind the British fleet, the black ships of Russia. Side by side, or following one another's lead, these war fleets were on a peaceful voyage that belied their threatening appearance. There had been no thought of danger to or from the forts and ports of rival nations which they had passed. There was no enmity, and no fear between them when the throats of their ponderous guns yawned at one another across the waves. They were now, in spirit, all one fleet, having one object, bearing against one enemy, ready to defend but one country, and that country was the entire earth.

It was some time before we caught sight of the Emperor William's fleet. It seems that the Kaiser, although at first consenting to the arrangement by which Washington had been selected as the assembling place for the nations, afterwards objected to it.

"I ought to do this thing myself," he had said. "My glorious ancestors would never have consented to allow these upstart Republicans to lead in a warlike enterprise of this kind. What would my grandfather have said to it? I suspect that it is some scheme aimed at the divine right of kings."

But the good sense of the German people would not suffer their ruler to place them in a position so false and so untenable. And swept along by their enthusiasm the Kaiser had at last consented to embark on his flagship at Kiel, and now he was following the other fleets on their great mission to the Western Continent.

Why did they bring their warships when their intentions were peaceable, do you ask? Well, it was partly the effect of ancient habit, and partly due to the fact that such multitudes of officials and members of ruling families wished to embark for Washington that the ordinary means of ocean communications would have been utterly inadequate to convey them.

After we had feasted our eyes on this strange sight, Mr. Edison suddenly exclaimed: "Now let us see the fellows from the rising sun."

The car was immediately directed toward the west. We rapidly approached the American coast, and as we sailed over the Alleghany Mountains and the broad plains of the Ohio and the Mississippi, we saw crawling beneath us from west, south and north, an endless succession of railway trains bearing their multitudes on to Washington. With marvellous speed we rushed westward, rising high to skim over the snow-topped peaks of the Rocky Mountains and then the glittering rim of the Pacific was before us. Half way between the American coast and Hawaii we met the fleets coming from China and Japan. Side by side they were ploughing the main, having forgotten, or laid aside, all the animosities of their former wars.

I well remember how my heart was stirred at this impressive exhibition of the boundless influence which my country had come to exercise over all the people of the world, and I turned to look at the man to whose genius this uprising of the earth was due. But Mr. Edison, after his wont, appeared totally unconscious of the fact that he was personally responsible for what was going on. His mind, seemingly, was entirely absorbed in considering problems, the solution of which might be essential to our success in the terrific struggle which was soon to begin.

"Well, have you seen enough?" he asked. "Then let us go back to Washington."

As we speeded back across the continent we beheld beneath us again the burdened express trains rushing toward the Atlantic, and hundreds of thousands of upturned eyes watched our swift progress, and volleys of cheers reached our ears, for every one knew that this was Edison's electrical warship, on which the hope of the nation, and the hopes of all the nations, depended. These scenes were repeated again and again until the car hovered over the still expanding capital on the Potomac, where the unceasing ring of hammers rose to the clouds.

Chapter 3

The day appointed for the assembling of the nations in Washington opened bright and beautiful. Arrangements had been made for the reception of the distinguished guests at the Capitol. No time was to be wasted, and, having assembled in the Senate Chamber, the business that had called them together was to be immediately begun. The scene in Pennsylvania avenue, when the procession of dignitaries and royalties passed up toward the Capitol, was one never to be forgotten. Bands were playing, magnificent equipages flashed in the morning sunlight, the flags of every nation on the earth fluttered in the breeze. Queen Victoria, with the Prince of Wales escorting her, and riding in an open carriage, was greeted with roars of cheers; the Emperor William, following in another carriage with Empress Victoria at his side, condescended to bow and smile in response to the greetings of a free people. Each of the other monarchs was received in a similar manner. The Czar of Russia proved to be an especial favourite with the multitude on account of the ancient friendship of his house for America. But the greatest applause of all came when the President of France, followed by the President of Switzerland and the First Syndic of the little Republic of Andorra, made their appearance. Equally warm were the greetings extended to the representatives of Mexico and the South American States.

The crowd apparently hardly knew at first how to receive the Sultan of Turkey, but the universal good feeling was in his favour, and finally rounds of hand clapping and cheers greeted his progress along the splendid avenue.

A happy idea had apparently occurred to the Emperor of China and the Mikado of Japan, for, attended by their intermingled suites, they rode together in a single carriage. This object lesson in the unity of international feeling immensely pleased the spectators.

The scene in the Senate Chamber stirred every one profoundly. That it was brilliant and magnificent goes without saying, but there was a seriousness, an intense feeling of expectancy, pervading both those who looked on and those who were to do the work for which these magnates of the earth had assembled, which produced an ineradicable impression. The President of the United States, of course, presided. Representatives of the greater powers occupied the front seats, and some of them were honoured with special chairs near the President.

No time was wasted in preliminaries. The President made a brief speech.

"We have come together," he said, "to consider a question that equally interests the whole earth. I need not remind you that unexpectedly and without provocation on our part the people—the monsters, I should rather say—of Mars, recently came down upon the earth, attacked us in our homes and spread desolation around them. Having the advantage of ages of evolution, which for us are yet in the future, they brought with them engines of death and of destruction against which we found it impossible to contend. It is within the memory of every one in reach of my voice that it was through the entirely unexpected succour which Providence sent us that we were suddenly and effectually freed from the invaders. By our own efforts we could have done nothing."

"But, as you all know, the first feeling of relief which followed the death of our foes was quickly succeeded by the fearful news which came to us from the observatories, that the Martians were undoubtedly preparing for a second invasion of our planet. Against this we should have had no recourse and no hope but for the genius of one of my countrymen, who, as you are all aware, has perfected means which may enable us not only to withstand the attack of those awful enemies, but to meet them, and, let us hope, to conquer them on their own ground."

"Mr. Edison is here to explain to you what those means are. But we have also another object. Whether we send a fleet of interplanetary ships to invade Mars or whether we simply confine our attention to works of defence, in either case it will be necessary to raise a very large sum of money. None of us has yet recovered from the effects of the recent invasion. The earth is poor to-day compared to its position a few years ago; yet we cannot allow our poverty to stand in the way. The money, the means, must be had. It will be part of our business here to raise a gigantic war fund by the aid of which we can construct the equipment and machinery that we shall require. This, I think, is all I need to say. Let us proceed to business."

"Where is Mr. Edison?" cried a voice.

"Will Mr. Edison please step forward?" said the President.

There was a stir in the assembly, and the iron-grey head of the great inventor was seen moving through the crowd. In his hand he carried one of his marvellous disintegrators. He was requested to explain and illustrate its operation. Mr. Edison smiled.

"I can explain its details," he said, "to Lord Kelvin, for instance, but if Their Majesties will excuse me, I doubt whether I can make it plain to the crowned heads."

The Emperor William smiled superciliously. Apparently he thought that another assault had been committed upon the divine right of kings. But the Czar Nicholas appeared to be amused, and the Emperor of China, who had been studying English, laughed in his sleeve, as if he suspected that a joke had been perpetrated.

"I think," said one of the deputies, "that a simple exhibition of the powers of the instrument, without a technical explanation of its method of working, will suffice for our purpose."

This suggestion was immediately approved. In response to it, Mr. Edison, by a few simple experiments, showed how he could quickly and certainly shatter into its constituent atoms any object upon which the vibratory force of the disintegrator should be directed. In this manner he caused an inkstand to disappear under the very nose of the Emperor William without a spot of ink being scattered upon his sacred person, but evidently the odour of the disunited atoms was not agreeable to the nostrils of the Kaiser.

Mr. Edison also explained in general terms the principle on which the instrument worked. He was greeted with round after round of applause, and the spirit of the assembly rose high.

Next the workings of the electrical ship were explained, and it was announced that after the meeting had adjourned an exhibition of the flying powers of the ship would be given in the open air.

These experiments, together with the accompanying explanations, added to what had already been disseminated through the public press, were quite sufficient to convince all the representatives who had assembled in Washington that the problem of how to conquer the Martians had been solved. The means were plainly at hand. It only remained to apply them. For this purpose, as the President had pointed out, it would be necessary to raise a very large sum of money.

"How much will be needed?" asked one of the English representatives.

"At least ten thousand millions of dollars," replied the President.

"It would be safer," said a Senator from the Pacific Coast, "to make it twenty-five thousand millions."

"I suggest," said the King of Italy, "that the nations be called in alphabetical order, and that the representatives of each name a sum which it is ready and able to contribute."

"We want the cash or its equivalent," shouted the Pacific Coast Senator.

"I shall not follow the alphabet strictly," said the President, "but shall begin with the larger nations first. Perhaps, under the circumstances, it is proper that the United States should lead the way. Mr. Secretary," he continued, turning to the Secretary of the Treasury, "how much can we stand?"

An Enormous Sum.

"At least a thousand millions," replied the Secretary of the Treasury.

A roar of applause that shook the room burst from the assembly. Even some of the monarchs threw up their hats. The Emperor Tsait'ten smiled from ear to ear. One of the Roko Tuis, or native chiefs, from Fiji, sprang up and brandished a war club.

The President then proceeded to call the other nations, beginning with Austria-Hungary and ending with Zanzibar, whose Sultan, Hamoud bin Mahomed, had come to the congress in the escort of Queen Victoria. Each contributed liberally.

Germany coming in alphabetical order just before Great Britain, had named, through its Chancellor, the sum of $500,000,000, but when the First Lord of the British Treasury, not wishing to be behind the United States, named double that sum as the contribution of the British Empire, the Emperor William looked displeased. He spoke a word in the ear of the Chancellor, who immediately raised his hand.

"We will give a thousand million dollars," said the Chancellor.

Queen Victoria seemed surprised, though not displeased. The First Lord of the Treasury met her eye, and then, rising in his place, said:

"Make it fifteen hundred million for Great Britain."

Emperor William consulted again with his Chancellor, but evidently concluded not to increase his bid.

But, at any rate, the fund had benefited to the amount of a thousand millions by this little outburst of imperial rivalry.

The greatest surprise of all, however, came when the King of Siam was called upon for his contribution. He had not been given a foremost place in the Congress, but when the name of his country was pronounced he rose by his chair, dressed in a gorgeous specimen of the peculiar attire of his country, then slowly pushed his way to the front, stepped up to the President's desk and deposited upon it a small box.

"This is our contribution," he said, in broken English.

The cover was lifted, and there darted, shimmering in the half gloom of the Chamber, a burst of iridescence from the box.

"My friends of the Western world," continued the King of Siam, "will be interested in seeing this gem. Only once before has the eye of a European been blessed with the sight of it. Your books will tell you that in the seventeenth century a traveller, Tavernier, saw in India an unmatched diamond which afterward disappeared like a meteor, and was thought to have been lost from the earth. You all know the name of that diamond and its history. It is the Great Mogul, and it lies before you. How it came into my possession I shall not explain. At any rate, it is honestly mine, and I freely contribute it here to aid in protecting my native planet against those enemies who appear determined to destroy it."

When the excitement which the appearance of this long lost treasure, that had been the subject of so many romances and of such long and fruitless search, had subsided, the President continued calling the list, until he had completed it.

Upon taking the sum of the contributions (the Great Mogul was reckoned at three millions) it was found to be still one thousand millions short of the required amount.

The Secretary of the Treasury was instantly on his feet.

"Mr. President," he said, "I think we can stand that addition. Let it be added to the contribution of the United States of America."

When the cheers that greeted the conclusion of the business were over, the President announced that the next affair of the Congress was to select a director who should have entire charge of the preparations for the war. It was the universal sentiment that no man could be so well suited for this post as Mr. Edison himself. He was accordingly selected by the unanimous and enthusiastic choice of the great assembly.

"How long a time do you require to put everything in readiness?" asked the President.

"Give me carte blanche," replied Mr. Edison, "and I believe I can have a hundred electric ships and three thousand disintegrators ready within six months."

A tremendous cheer greeted this announcement.

"Your powers are unlimited," said the President, "draw on the fund for as much money as you need," whereupon the Treasurer of the United States was made the disbursing officer of the fund, and the meeting adjourned.

Not less than 5,000,000 people had assembled at Washington from all parts of the world. Every one of this immense multitude had been able to listen to the speeches and the cheers in the Senate chamber, although not personally present there. Wires had been run all over the city, and hundreds of improved telephonic receivers provided, so that every one could hear. Even those who were unable to visit Washington, people living in Baltimore, New York, Boston, and as far away as New Orleans, St. Louis and Chicago, had also listened to the proceedings with the aid of these receivers. Upon the whole, probably not less than 50,000,000 people had heard the deliberations of the great congress of the nations.

The telegraph and the cable had sent the news across the oceans to all the capitols of the earth. The exultation was so great that the people seemed mad with joy.

The promised exhibition of the electrical ship took place the next day. Enormous multitudes witnessed the experiment, and there was a struggle for places in the car. Even Queen Victoria, accompanied by the Prince of Wales, ventured to take a ride in it, and they enjoyed it so much that Mr. Edison prolonged the journey as far as Boston and the Bunker Hill monument.

Most of the other monarchs also took a high ride, but when the turn of the Emperor of China came he repeated a fable which he said had come down from the time of Confucius:

"Once upon a time there was a Chinaman living in the valley of the Hoang-Ho River, who was accustomed frequently to lie on his back, gazing at, and envying, the birds that he saw flying away in the sky. One day he saw a black speck which rapidly grew larger and larger, until as it got near he perceived that it was an enormous bird, which overshadowed the earth with its wings. It was the elephant of birds, the roc. 'Come with me,' said the roc, 'and I will show you the wonders of the kingdom of the birds.' The man caught hold of its claw and nestled among its feathers, and they rapidly rose high in the air, and sailed away to the Kuen-Lun Mountains. Here, as they passed near the top of the peaks, another roc made its appearance. The wings of the two great birds brushed together, and immediately they fell to fighting. In the midst of the melee the man lost his hold and tumbled into the top of a tree, where his pigtail caught on a branch, and he remained suspended. There the unfortunate man hung helpless, until a rat, which had its home in the rocks at the foot of the tree, took compassion upon him, and, climbing up, gnawed off the branch. As the man slowly and painfully wended his weary way homeward, he said: 'This teaches me that creatures to whom nature has given neither feathers nor wings should leave the kingdom of the birds to those who are fitted to inhabit it.'"

Having told this story, Tsait'ien turned his back on the electrical ship.

After the exhibition was finished, and amid the fresh outburst of enthusiasm that followed, it was suggested that a proper way to wind up the Congress and give suitable expression to the festive mood which now possessed mankind would be to have a grand ball. This suggestion met with immediate and universal approval.

But for so gigantic an affair it was, of course, necessary to make special preparations. A convenient place was selected on the Virginia side of the Potomac; a space of ten acres was carefully levelled and covered with a polished floor, rows of columns one hundred feet apart were run across it in every direction, and these were decorated with electric lights, displaying every colour of the spectrum.

Above this immense space, rising in the centre to a height of more than a thousand feet, was anchored a vast number of balloons, all aglow with lights, and forming a tremendous dome, in which brilliant lamps were arranged in such a manner as to exhibit, in an endless succession of combinations, all the national colours, ensigns and insignia of the various countries represented at the Congress. Blazing eagles, lions, unicorns, dragons and other imaginary creatures that the different nations had chosen for their symbols appeared to hover high above the dancers, shedding a brilliant light upon the scene.

Circles of magnificent thrones were placed upon the floor in convenient locations for seeing. A thousand bands of music played, and tens of thousands of couples, gaily dressed and flashing with gems, whirled together upon the polished floor.

The Queen of England led the dance, on the arm of the President of the United States.

The Prince of Wales led forth the fair daughter of the President, universally admired as the most beautiful woman upon the great ballroom floor.

The Emperor William, in his military dress, danced with the beauteous Princess Masaco, the daughter of the Mikado, who wore for the occasion the ancient costume of the women of her country, sparkling with jewels, and glowing with quaint combinations of colour like a gorgeous butterfly.

The Chinese Emperor, with his pigtail flying high as he spun, danced with the Empress of Russia.

The King of Siam essayed a waltz with the Queen Ranavalona, of Madagascar, while the Sultan of Turkey basked in the smiles of a Chicago heiress to a hundred millions.

The Czar choose for his partner a dark-eyed beauty from Peru, but King Malietoa, of Samoa, was suspicious of civilized charmers and, avoiding all of their allurements, expressed his joy and gave vent to his enthusiasm in a *pas seul*. In this he was quickly joined by a band of Sioux Indian chiefs, whose whoops and yells so startled the leader of a German band on their part of the floor that he dropped his baton and, followed by the musicians, took to his heels.

This incident amused the good-natured Emperor of China more than anything else that had occurred.

"Make muchee noisee," he said, indicating the fleeing musicians with his thumb. "Allee same muchee flaid noisee," and then his round face dimpled into another laugh.

The scene from the outside was even more imposing than that which greeted the eye within the brilliantly lighted enclosure. Far away in the night, rising high among the stars, the vast dome of illuminated balloons seemed like some supernatural creation, too grand and glorious to have been constructed by the inhabitants of the earth.

All around it, and from some of the balloons themselves, rose jets and fountains of fire, ceaselessly playing, and blotting out the constellations of the heavens by their splendour.

The Prince of Wales's Toast.

The dance was followed by a grand banquet, at which the Prince of Wales proposed a toast to Mr. Edison:

"It gives me much pleasure," he said, "to offer, in the name of the nations of the Old World, this tribute of our admiration for, and our confidence in, the genius of the New World. Perhaps on such an occasion as this, when all racial differences and prejudices ought to be, and are, buried and forgotten, I should not recall anything that might revive them; yet I cannot refrain from expressing my happiness in knowing that the champion who is to achieve the salvation of the earth has come forth from the bosom of the Anglo-Saxon race."

Several of the great potentates looked grave upon hearing the Prince of Wales's words, and the Czar and the Kaiser exchanged glances; but there was no interruption to the cheers that followed. Mr. Edison, whose modesty and dislike to display and to speechmaking were well known, simply said:

"I think we have got the machine that can whip them. But we ought not to be wasting any time. Probably they are not dancing on Mars, but are getting ready to make us dance."

These words instantly turned the current of feeling in the vast assembly. There was no longer any disposition to expend time in vain boastings and rejoicings. Everywhere the cry now became, "Let us make haste! Let us get ready at once! Who knows but the Martians have already embarked, and are now on their way to destroy us?"

Under the impulse of this new feeling, which, it must be admitted, was very largely inspired by terror, the vast ballroom was quickly deserted. The lights were suddenly put out in the great dome of balloons, for someone had whispered:

"Suppose they should see that from Mars? Would they not guess what we were about, and redouble their preparations to finish us?"

Upon the suggestion of the President of the United States, an executive committee, representing all the principal nations, was appointed, and without delay a meeting of this committee was assembled at the White House. Mr. Edison was summoned before it, and asked to sketch briefly the plan upon which he proposed to work.

I need not enter into the details of what was done at this meeting. Let it suffice to say that when it broke up, in the small hours of the morning, it had been unanimously resolved that as many thousands of men as Mr. Edison might require should be immediately placed at his disposal; that as far as possible all the great manufacturing establishments of the country should be instantly transformed into factories where electrical ships and disintegrators could be built, and upon the suggestion of Professor Sylvanus P. Thompson, the celebrated English electrical expert, seconded by Lord Kelvin, it was resolved that all the leading men of science in the world should place their services at the disposal of Mr. Edison in any capacity in which, in his judgment, they might be useful to him.

The members of this committee were disposed to congratulate one another on the good work which they had so promptly accomplished, when at the moment of their adjournment, a telegraphic dispatch was handed to the President from Professor George E. Hale, the director of the great Yerkes Observatory, in Wisconsin. The telegram read:

What's Happening on Mars?

"Professor Barnard, watching Mars to-night with the forty-inch telescope, saw a sudden outburst of reddish light, which we think indicates that something has been shot from the planet. Spectroscopic observations of this moving light indicated that it was coming earthward, while visible, at the rate of not less than one hundred miles a second."

Hardly had the excitement caused by the reading of this dispatch subsided, when others of a similar import came from the Lick Observatory, in California; from the branch of the Harvard Observatory at Arequipa, in Peru, and from the Royal Observatory, at Potsdam.

When the telegram from this last-named place was read the Emperor William turned to his Chancellor and said:

"I want to go home. If I am to die I prefer to leave my bones among those of my Imperial ancestors, and not in this vulgar country, where no king has ever ruled. I don't like this atmosphere. It makes me feel limp."

And now, whipped on by the lash of alternate hope and fear, the earth sprang to its work of preparation.

Chapter 4

It is not necessary for me to describe the manner in which Mr. Edison performed his tremendous task. He was as good as his word, and within six months from the first stroke of the hammer, a hundred electrical ships, each provided with a full battery of disintegrators, were floating in the air above the harbour and the partially rebuilt city of New York.

It was a wonderful scene. The polished sides of the huge floating cars sparkled in the sunlight, and, as they slowly rose and fell, and swung this way and that, upon the tides of the air, as if held by invisible cables, the brilliant pennons streaming from their peaks waved up and down like the wings of an assemblage of gigantic humming birds.

Not knowing whether the atmosphere of Mars would prove suitable to be breathed by inhabitants of the earth, Mr. Edison had made provision, by means of an abundance of glass-protected openings, to permit the inmates of the electrical ships to survey their surroundings without quitting the interior. It was possible by properly selecting the rate of undulation, to pass the vibratory impulse from the disintegrators through the glass windows of a car, without damage to the glass itself. The windows were so arranged that the disintegrators could sweep around the car on all sides, and could also be directed above or below, as necessity might dictate.

To overcome the destructive forces employed by the Martians no satisfactory plan had yet been devised, because there was no means to experiment with them. The production of those forces was still the secret of our enemies. But Mr. Edison had no doubt that if we could not resist their effects we might at least be able to avoid them by the rapidity of our motions. As he pointed out, the war machines which the Martians had employed in their invasion of the earth, were really very awkward and unmanageable affairs. Mr. Edison's electrical ships, on the other hand, were marvels of speed and of manageability. They could dart about, turn, reverse their course, rise, fall, with the quickness and ease of a fish in the water. Mr. Edison calculated that even if mysterious bolts should fall upon our ships we could diminish their power to cause injury by our rapid evolutions.

We might be deceived in our expectations, and might have overestimated our powers, but at any rate we must take our chances and try.

A multitude, exceeding even that which had assembled during the great congress at Washington, now thronged New York and its neighbourhood to witness the mustering and the departure of the ships bound for Mars. Nothing further had been heard of the mysterious phenomenon reported from the observatories six months before, and which at the time was believed to indicate the departure of another expedition from Mars for the invasion of the earth. If the Martians had set out to attack us they had evidently gone astray; or, perhaps, it was some other world that they were aiming at this time.

The expedition had, of course, profoundly stirred the interest of the scientific world, and representatives of every branch of science, from all the civilized nations, urged their claims to places in the ships. Mr. Edison was compelled, from lack of room, to refuse transportation to more than one in a thousand of those who now, on the plea that they might be able to bring back something of advantage to science, wished to embark for Mars.

On the model of the celebrated corps of literary and scientific men which Napoleon carried with him in his invasion of Egypt, Mr. Edison selected a company of the foremost astronomers, archaeologists, anthropologists, botanists, bacteriologists, chemists, physicists, mathematicians, mechanicians, meteorologists and experts in mining, metallurgy and every other branch of practical science, as well as artists and photographers. It was but reasonable to believe that in another world, and a world so much older than the earth as Mars was, these men would be able to gather materials in comparison with which the discoveries made among the ruins of ancient empires in Egypt and Babylonia would be insignificant indeed.

It was a wonderful undertaking and a strange spectacle. There was a feeling of uncertainty which awed the vast multitude whose eyes were upturned to the ships. The expedition was not large, considering the gigantic character of the undertaking. Each of the electrical ships carried about twenty men, together with an abundant supply of compressed provisions, compressed air, scientific apparatus and so on. In all, there were about 2,000 men, who were going to conquer, if they could, another world!

But though few in numbers, they represented the flower of the earth, the culmination of the genius of the planet. The greatest leaders in science, both theoretical and practical, were there. It was the evolution of the earth against the evolution of Mars. It was a planet in the heyday of its strength matched against an aged and decrepit world which, nevertheless, in consequence of its long ages of existence, had acquired an experience which made it a most dangerous foe. On both sides there was desperation. The earth was desperate because it foresaw destruction unless it could first destroy its enemy. Mars was desperate because nature was gradually depriving it of the means of supporting life, and its teeming population was compelled to swarm like the inmates of an overcrowded hive of bees, and find new homes elsewhere. In this respect the situation on Mars, as we were well aware, resembled what had already been known upon the earth, where the older nations overflowing with population had sought new lands in which to settle, and for that purpose had driven out the native inhabitants, whenever those natives had proven unable to resist the invasion.

No man could foresee the issue of what we were about to undertake, but the tremendous powers which the disintegrators had exhibited and the marvellous efficiency of the electrical ships bred almost universal confidence that we should be successful.

The car in which Mr. Edison travelled was, of course, the flagship of the squadron, and I had the good fortune to be included among its inmates. Here, besides several leading men of science from our own country, were Lord Kelvin, Lord Rayleigh, Professor Roentgen, Dr. Moissan—the man who first made artificial diamonds—and several others whose fame had encircled the world. Each of these men cherished hopes of wonderful discoveries, along his line of investigation, to be made in Mars.

An elaborate system of signals had, of course, to be devised for the control of the squadron. These signals consisted of brilliant electric lights displayed at night and so controlled that by their means long sentences and directions could be easily and quickly transmitted.

The day signals consisted partly of brightly coloured pennons and flags, which were to serve only when, shadowed by clouds or other obstructions, the full sunlight should not fall upon the ships. This could naturally only occur near the surface of the earth or of another planet.

Once out of the shadow of the earth we should have no more clouds and no more night until we arrived at Mars. In open space the sun would be continually shining. It would be perpetual day for us, except as, by artificial means, we furnished ourselves with darkness for the purpose of promoting sleep. In this region of perpetual day, then, the signals were also to be transmitted by flashes of light from mirrors reflecting the rays of the sun.

Yet this perpetual day would be also, in one sense, a perpetual night. There would be no more blue sky for us, because without an atmosphere the sunlight could not be diffused. Objects would be illuminated only on the side toward the sun. Anything that screened off the direct rays of sunlight would produce absolute darkness behind it. There would be no graduation of shadow. The sky would be as black as ink on all sides.

While it was the intention to remain as much as possible within the cars, yet since it was probable that necessity would arise for occasionally quitting the interior of the electrical ships, Mr. Edison had provided for this emergency by inventing an air-tight dress constructed somewhat after the manner of a diver's suit, but of much lighter material. Each ship was provided with several of these suits, by wearing which one could venture outside the car even when it was beyond the atmosphere of the earth.

Provision had been made to meet the terrific cold which we knew would be encountered the moment we had passed beyond the atmosphere—that awful absolute zero which men had measured by anticipation, but never yet experienced—by a simple system of producing within the air-tight suits a temperature sufficiently elevated to counteract the effects of the frigidity without. By means of long, flexible tubes, air could be continually supplied to the wearers of the suits, and by an ingenious contrivance a store of compressed air sufficient to last for several hours was provided for each suit, so that in case of necessity the wearer could throw off the tubes connecting him with the air tanks in the car. Another object which had been kept in view in the preparation of these suits was the possible exploration of an airless planet, such as the moon.

The necessity of some contrivance by means of which we should be enabled to converse with one another when on the outside of the cars in open space, or when in an airless world, like the moon, where there would be no medium by which the waves of sound could be conveyed as they are in the atmosphere of the earth, had been foreseen by our great inventor, and he had not found it difficult to contrive suitable devices for meeting the emergency.

Inside the headpiece of each of the electrical suits was the mouthpiece of a telephone. This was connected with a wire which, when not in use, could be conveniently coiled upon the arm of the wearer. Near the ears, similarly connected with wires, were telephonic receivers.

When two persons wearing the air-tight dresses wished to converse with one another it was only necessary for them to connect themselves by the wires, and conversation could then be easily carried on.

Careful calculations of the precise distance of Mars from the earth at the time when the expedition was to start had been made by a large number of experts in mathematical astronomy. But it was not Mr. Edison's intention to go direct to Mars. With the exception of the first electrical ship, which he had completed, none had yet been tried in a long voyage. It was desirable that the qualities of each of the ships should first be carefully tested, and for this reason the leader of the expedition determined that the moon should be the first port of space at which the squadron would call.

It chanced that the moon was so situated at this time as to be nearly in a line between the earth and Mars, which latter was in opposition to the sun, and consequently as favourably situated as possible for the purposes of the voyage. What would be, then, for 99 out of the 100 ships of the squadron, a trial trip would at the same time be a step of a quarter of a million of miles gained in the direction of our journey, and so no time would be wasted.

The departure from the earth was arranged to occur precisely at midnight. The moon near the full was hanging high over head, and a marvellous spectacle was presented to the eyes of those below as the great squadron of floating ships, with their signal lights ablaze, cast loose and began slowly to move away on their adventurous and unprecedented expedition into the great unknown. A tremendous cheer, billowing up from the throats of millions of excited men and women, seemed to rend the curtain of the night, and made the airships tremble with the atmospheric vibrations that were set in motion.

Instantly magnificent fireworks were displayed in honour of our departure. Rockets by hundreds of thousands shot heaven-ward, and then burst in constellations of fiery drops. The sudden illumination thus produced, overspreading hundreds of square miles of the surface of the earth with a light almost like that of day, must certainly have been visible to the inhabitants of Mars, if they were watching us at the time. They might, or might not, correctly interpret its significance; but, at any rate, we did not care. We were off, and were confident that we could meet our enemy on his own ground before he could attack us again.

And now, as we slowly rose higher, a marvellous scene was disclosed. At first the earth beneath us, buried as it was in night, resembled the hollow of a vast cup of ebony blackness, in the centre of which, like the molten lava run together at the bottom of a volcanic crater, shone the light of the illuminations around New York. But when we got beyond the atmosphere, and the earth still continued to recede below us, its aspect changed. The cup-shaped appearance was gone, and it began to round out beneath our eyes in the form of a vast globe—an enormous ball mysteriously suspended under us, glimmering over most of its surface, with the faint illumination of the moon, and showing toward its eastern edge the oncoming light of the rising sun.

When we were still further away, having slightly varied our course so that the sun was once more entirely hidden behind the centre of the earth, we saw its atmosphere completely illuminated, all around it, with prismatic lights, like a gigantic rainbow in the form of a ring.

Another shift in our course rapidly carried us out of the shadow of the earth and into the all pervading sunshine. Then the great planet beneath us hung unspeakable in its beauty. The outlines of several of the continents were clearly discernible on its surface, streaked and spotted with delicate shades of varying colour, and the sunlight flashed and glowed in long lanes across the convex surface of the oceans. Parallel with the Equator and along the regions of the ever blowing trade winds, were vast belts of clouds, gorgeous with crimson and purple as the sunlight fell upon them. Immense expanses of snow and ice lay like a glittering garment upon both land and sea around the North Pole.

As we gazed upon this magnificent spectacle, our hearts bounded within us. This was our earth—this was the planet we were going to defend—our home in the trackless wilderness of space. And it seemed to us indeed a home for which we might gladly expend our last breath. A new determination to conquer or die sprung up in our hearts, and I saw Lord Kelvin, after gazing at the beauteous scene which the earth presented through his eyeglass, turn about and peer in the direction in which we knew that Mars lay, with a sudden frown that caused the glass to lose its grip and fall dangling from its string upon his breast. Even Mr. Edison seemed moved.

"I am glad I thought of the disintegrator," he said. "I shouldn't like to see that world down there laid waste again."

"And it won't be," said Professor Sylvanus P. Thompson, gripping the handle of an electric machine, "not if we can help it."

Chapter 5

To prevent accidents, it had been arranged that the ships should keep a considerable distance apart. Some of them gradually drifted away, until, on account of the neutral tint of their sides, they were swallowed up in the abyss of space. Still it was possible to know where every member of the squadron was through the constant interchange of signals. These, as I have explained, were effected by means of mirrors flashing back the light of the sun.

But, although it was now unceasing day for us, yet, there being no atmosphere to diffuse the sun's light, the stars were visible to us just as at night upon the earth, and they shone with extraordinary splendour against the intense black background of the firmament. The lights of some of the more distant ships of our squadron were not brighter than the stars in whose neighbourhood they seemed to be. In some cases it was only possible to distinguish between the light of a ship and that of a star by the fact that the former was continually flashing while the star was steady in its radiance.

The most uncanny effect was produced by the absence of atmosphere around us. Inside the car, where there was air, the sunlight, streaming through one or more of the windows, was diffused and produced ordinary daylight.

But when we ventured outside we could only see things by halves. The side of the car that the sun's rays touched was visible, the other side was invisible, the light from the stars not making it bright enough to affect the eye in contrast with the sun-illuminated half.

As I held up my arm before my eyes, half of it seemed to be shaved off lengthwise; a companion on the deck of the ship looked like half a man. So the other electrical ships near us appeared as half ships, only the illuminated sides being visible.

We had now got so far away that the earth had taken on the appearance of a heavenly body like the moon. Its colours had become all blended into a golden-reddish hue, which overspread nearly its entire surface, except at the poles, where there were broad patches of white. It was marvellous to look at this huge orb behind us, while far beyond it shone the blazing sun like an enormous star in the blackest of nights. In the opposite direction appeared the silver orb of the moon, and scattered all around were millions of brilliant stars, amid which, like fireflies, flashed and sparkled the signal lights of the squadron.

A danger that might easily have been anticipated, that perhaps had been anticipated, but against which it would have been difficult, if not impossible, to provide, presently manifested itself.

Looking out of a window toward the right, I suddenly noticed the lights of a distant ship darting about in a curious curve. Instantly afterward another member of the squadron, nearer by, behaved in the same inexplicable manner. Then two or three of the floating cars seemed to be violently drawn from their courses and hurried rapidly in the direction of the flagship. Immediately I perceived a small object, luridly flaming, which seemed to move with immense speed in our direction.

The truth instantly flashed upon my mind, and I shouted to the other occupants of the car:

"A meteor!"

And such indeed it was. We had met this mysterious wanderer in space at a moment when we were moving in a direction at right angles to the path it was pursuing around the sun. Small as it was, and its diameter probably did not exceed a single foot, it was yet an independent little world, and as such a member of the solar system. Its distance from the sun being so near that of the earth, I knew that its velocity, assuming it to be travelling in a nearly circular orbit, must be about eighteen miles in a second. With this velocity, then, it plunged like a projectile shot by some mysterious enemy in space directly through our squadron. It had come and was gone before one could utter a sentence of three words. Its appearance, and the effect it had produced upon the ships in whose neighbourhood it passed, indicated that it bore an intense and tremendous charge of electricity. How it had become thus charged I cannot pretend to say. I simply record the fact. And this charge, it was evident, was opposite in polarity to that which the ships of the squadron bore. It therefore exerted an attractive influence upon them and thus drew them after it.

I had just time to think how lucky it was that the meteor did not strike any of us, when, glancing at a ship just ahead, I perceived that an accident had occurred. The ship swayed violently from its course, dazzling flashes played around it, and two or three of the men forming its crew appeared for an instant on its exterior, wildly gesticulating, but almost instantly falling prone.

It was evident at a glance that the car had been struck by the meteor. How serious the damage might be we could not instantly determine. The course of our ship was immediately altered, the electric polarity was changed, and we rapidly approached the disabled car.

The men who had fallen lay upon its surface. One of the heavy circular glasses covering a window had been smashed to atoms. Through this the meteor had passed, killing two or three men who stood in its course. Then it had crashed through the opposite side of the car, and, passing on, disappeared into space. The store of air contained in the car had immediately rushed out through the openings, and when two or three of us, having donned our air-tight suits as quickly as possible, entered the wrecked car we found all its inmates stretched upon the floor in a condition of asphyxiation. They, as well as those who lay upon the exterior, were immediately removed to the flagship, restoratives were applied, and, fortunately, our aid had come so promptly that the lives of all of them were saved. But life had fled from the mangled bodies of those who had stood directly in the path of the fearful projectile.

This strange accident had been witnessed by several of the members of the fleet, and they quickly drew together, in order to inquire for the particulars. As the flagship was now overcrowded by the addition of so many men to its crew, Mr. Edison had them distributed among the other cars. Fortunately it happened that the disintegrators contained in the wrecked car were not injured. Mr. Edison thought that it would be possible to repair the car itself, and for that purpose he had it attached to the flagship in order that it might be carried on as far as the moon. The bodies of the dead were transported with it, as it was determined, instead of committing them to the fearful deep of space, where they would have wandered forever, or else have fallen like meteors upon the earth, to give them interment in the lunar soil.

As we now rapidly approached the moon the change which the appearance of its surface underwent was no less wonderful than that which the surface of the earth had presented in the reverse order while we were receding from it. From a pale silver orb, shining with comparative faintness among the stars, it slowly assumed the appearance of a vast mountainous desert. As we drew nearer its colours became more pronounced; the great flat regions appeared darker; the mountain peaks shone more brilliantly. The huge chasms seemed bottomless and blacker than midnight. Gradually separate mountains appeared. What seemed like expanses of snow and immense glaciers streaming down their sides sparkled with great brilliancy in the perpendicular rays of the sun. Our motion had now assumed the aspect of falling. We seemed to be dropping from an immeasurable height and with an inconceivable velocity, straight down upon those giant peaks.

Here and there curious lights glowed upon the mysterious surface of the moon. Where the edge of the moon cut the sky behind it, it was broken and jagged with mountain masses. Vast crater rings overspread its surface, and in some of these I imagined I could perceive a lurid illumination coming out of their deepest cavities, and the curling of mephitic vapours around their terrible jaws.

We were approaching that part of the moon which is known to astronomers as the Bay of Rainbows. Here a huge semi-circular region, as smooth almost as the surface of a prairie, lay beneath our eyes, stretching southward into a vast ocean-like expanse, while on the north it was enclosed by an enormous range of mountain cliffs, rising perpendicularly to a height of many thousands of feet, and rent and gashed in every direction by forces which seemed at some remote period to have laboured at tearing this little world in pieces.

The Moon's Strange and Ghastly Surface in Full View of Man.

It was a fearful spectacle; a dead and mangled world, too dreadful to look upon. The idea of the death of the moon was, of course, not a new one to many of us. We had long been aware that the earth's satellite was a body which had passed beyond the stage of life, if indeed it had ever been a life supporting globe; but none of us were prepared for the terrible spectacle which now smote our eyes.

At each end of the semi-circular ridge that encloses the Bay of Rainbows there is a lofty promontory. That at the north-western extremity had long been known to astronomers under the name of Cape Laplace. The other promontory, at the south-eastern termination, is called Cape Heraclides. It was toward the latter that we were approaching, and by interchange of signals all the members of the squadron had been informed that Cape Heraclides was to be our rendezvous upon the moon.

I may say that I had been somewhat familiar with the scenery of this part of the lunar world, for I had often studied it from the earth with a telescope, and I had thought that if there was any part of the moon where one might, with fair expectation of success, look for inhabitants, or if not for inhabitants, at least for relics of life no longer existent there, this would surely be the place. It was, therefore, with no small degree of curiosity, notwithstanding the unexpectedly frightful and repulsive appearance that the surface of the moon presented, that I now saw myself rapidly approaching the region concerning whose secrets my imagination had so often busied itself. When Mr. Edison and I had paid our previous visit to the moon on the first experimental trip of the electrical ship, we had landed at a point on its surface remote from this, and, as I have before explained, we then made no effort to investigate its secrets. But now it was to be different, and we were at length to see something of the wonders of the moon.

I had often on the earth drawn a smile from my friends by showing them Cape Heraclides with a telescope, and calling their attention to the fact that the outline of the peak terminating the cape was such as to present a remarkable resemblance to a human face, unmistakably a feminine countenance, seen in profile, and possessing no small degree of beauty. To my astonishment, this curious human semblance still remained when we had approached so close to the moon that the mountains forming the cape filled nearly the whole field of view of the window from which I was watching it. The resemblance, indeed, was most startling.

"Can this indeed be Diana herself?" I said half aloud, but instantly afterward I was laughing at my fancy, for Mr. Edison had overheard me and exclaimed, "Where is she?"

"Who?"

"Diana."

"Why, there," I said, pointing to the moon. But lo! the appearance was gone even while I spoke. A swift change had taken place in the line of sight by which we were viewing it, and the likeness had disappeared in consequence.

A few moments later my astonishment was revived, but the cause this time was a very different one. We had been dropping rapidly toward the mountains, and the electrician in charge of the car was swiftly and constantly changing his potential, and, like a pilot who feels his way into an unknown harbour, endeavouring to approach the moon in such a manner that no hidden peril should surprise us. As we thus approached I suddenly perceived, crowning the very apex of the lofty peak near the termination of the cape, the ruins of what appeared to be an ancient watch tower. It was evidently composed of Cyclopean blocks larger than any that I had ever seen even among the ruins of Greece, Egypt and Asia Minor.

Here, then, was visible proof that the moon had been inhabited, although probably it was not inhabited now. I cannot describe the exultant feeling which took possession of me at this discovery. It settled so much that learned men had been disputing about for centuries.

"What will they say," I exclaimed, "when I show them a photograph of that?"

Below the peak, stretching far to right and left, lay a barren beach which had evidently once been washed by sea waves, because it was marked by long curved ridges such as the advancing and retiring tide leaves upon the shore of the ocean.

This beach sloped rapidly outward and downward toward a profound abyss, which had once, evidently, been the bed of a sea, but which now appeared to us simply as the empty, yawning shell of an ocean that had long vanished.

It was with no small difficulty, and only after the expenditure of considerable time, that all the floating ships of the squadron were gradually brought to rest on this lone mountain top of the moon. In accordance with my request, Mr. Edison had the flagship moored in the interior of the great ruined watch tower that I have described. The other ships rested upon the slope of the mountain around us.

Although time pressed, for we knew that the safety of the earth depended upon our promptness in attacking Mars, yet it was determined to remain here at least two or three days in order that the wrecked car might be repaired. It was found also that the passage of the highly electrified meteor had disarranged the electrical machinery in some of the other cars, so that there were many repairs to be made besides those needed to restore the wreck.

Moreover, we must bury our unfortunate companions who had been killed by the meteor. This, in fact, was the first work that we performed. Strange was the sight, and stranger our feelings, as here on the surface of a world distant from the earth, and on soil which had never before been pressed by the foot of man, we performed that last ceremony of respect which mortals pay to mortality. In the ancient beach at the foot of the peak we made a deep opening, and there covered forever the faces of our friends, leaving them to sleep among the ruins of empires, and among the graves of races which had vanished probably ages before Adam and Eve appeared in Paradise.

While the repairs were being made several scientific expeditions were sent out in various directions across the moon. One went westward to investigate the great ring plain of Plato, and the lunar Alps. Another crossed the ancient Sea of Showers toward the lunar Apennines.

One started to explore the immense crater of Copernicus, which, yawning fifty miles across, presents a wonderful appearance even from the distance of the earth. The ship in which I, myself, had the good fortune to embark, was bound for the mysterious lunar mountain Aristarchus.

Before these expeditions started, a careful exploration had been made in the neighbourhood of Cape Heraclides. But, except that the broken walls of the watch tower on the peak, composed of blocks of enormous size, had evidently been the work of creatures endowed with human intelligence, no remains were found indicating the former presence of inhabitants upon this part of the moon.

But along the shore of the old sea, just where the so-called Bay of Rainbows separates itself from the abyss of the Sea of Showers, there were found some stratified rocks in which the fascinated eyes of the explorer beheld the clear imprint of a gigantic human foot, measuring five feet in length from toe to heel.

The most minute search failed to reveal another trace of the presence of the ancient giant, who had left the impress of his foot in the wet sands of the beach here so many millions of years ago that even the imagination of the geologists shrank from the task of attempting to fix the precise period.

Around this gigantic footprint gathered most of the scientific members of the expedition, wearing their oddly shaped air-tight suits, connected with telephonic wires, and the spectacle, but for the impressiveness of the discovery, would have been laughable in the extreme. Bending over the mark in the rock, nodding their heads together, pointing with their awkwardly accoutred arms, they looked like an assemblage of antediluvian monsters collected around their prey. Their disappointment over the fact that no other marks of anything resembling human habitation could be discovered was very great.

Still this footprint in itself was quite sufficient, as they all declared, to settle the question of the former inhabitation of the moon, and it would serve for the production of many a learned volume after their return to the earth, even if no further discoveries should be made in other parts of the lunar world.

It was the hope of making such other discoveries that led to the dispatch of the other various expeditions which I have already named. I had chosen to accompany the car that was going to Aristarchus, because, as every one who had viewed the moon from the earth was aware, there was something very mysterious about that mountain. I knew that it was a crater nearly thirty miles in diameter and very deep, although its floor was plainly visible.

What rendered it remarkable was the fact that the floor and the walls of the crater, particularly on the inner side, glowed with a marvellous brightness which rendered them almost blinding when viewed with a powerful telescope.

So bright were they, indeed, that the eye was unable to see many of the details which the telescope would have made visible but for the flood of light which poured from the mountains. Sir William Herschel had been so completely misled by this appearance that he supposed he was watching a lunar volcano in eruption.

It had always been a difficult question what caused the extraordinary luminosity of Aristarchus. No end of hypotheses had been invented to account for it. Now I was to assist in settling these questions forever.

From Cape Heraclides to Aristarchus the distance in an air line was something over 300 miles. Our course lay across the north-eastern part of the Sea of Showers, with enormous cliffs, mountain masses and peaks shining on the right, while in the other direction the view was bounded by the distant range of the lunar Apennines, some of whose towering peaks, when viewed from our immense elevation, appeared as sharp as the Swiss Matterhorn.

When we had arrived within about a hundred miles of our destination we found ourselves floating directly over the so-called Harbinger Mountains. The serrated peaks of Aristarchus then appeared ahead of us, fairly blazing in the sunshine.

It seemed as if a gigantic string of diamonds, every one as great as a mountain peak, had been cast down upon the barren surface of the moon and left to waste their brilliance upon the desert air of this abandoned world.

As we rapidly approached, the dazzling splendour of the mountain became almost unbearable to our eyes, and we were compelled to resort to the device, practiced by all climbers of lofty mountains, where the glare of sunlight upon snow surfaces is liable to cause temporary blindness, of protecting our eyes with neutral-tinted glasses.

Professor Moissan, the great French chemist and maker of artificial diamonds, fairly danced with delight.

"Voila! Voila! Voila!" was all that he could say.

When we were comparatively near, the mountain no longer seemed to glow with a uniform radiance, evenly distributed over its entire surface, but now innumerable points of light, all as bright as so many little suns, blazed away at us. It was evident that we had before us a mountain composed of, or at least covered with, crystals.

Without stopping to alight on the outer slopes of the great ring-shaped range of peaks which composed Aristarchus, we sailed over their rim and looked down into the interior. Here the splendour of the crystals was greater than on the outer slopes, and the broad floor of the crater, thousands of feet beneath us, shone and sparkled with overwhelming radiance, as if it were an immense bin of diamonds, while a peak in the centre flamed like a stupendous tiara incrusted with selected gems.

Eager to see what these crystals were, the car was now allowed rapidly to drop into the interior of the crater. With great caution we brought it to rest upon the blazing ground, for the sharp edges of the crystals would certainly have torn the metallic sides of the car if it had come into violent contact with them.

Donning our air-tight suits and stepping carefully out upon this wonderful footing we attempted to detach some of the crystals. Many of them were firmly fastened, but a few—some of astonishing size— were readily loosened.

A moment's inspection showed that we had stumbled upon the most marvellous work of the forces of crystallization that human eyes had ever rested upon. Some time in the past history of the moon there had been an enormous outflow of molten material from the crater. This had overspread the walls and partially filled up the interior, and later its surface had flowered into gems, as thick as blossoms in a bed of pansies.

The whole mass flashed prismatic rays of indescribable beauty and intensity. We gazed at first speechless with amazement.

"It cannot be, surely it cannot be," said Professor Moissan at length.

"But it is," said another member of the party.

"Are these diamonds?" asked a third.

"I cannot yet tell," replied the Professor. "They have the brilliancy of diamonds, but they may be something else."

"Moon jewels," suggested a third.

"And worth untold millions, whatever they are," remarked another.

These magnificent crystals, some of which appeared to be almost flawless, varied in size from the dimensions of a hazelnut to geometrical solids several inches in diameter. We carefully selected as many as it was convenient to carry and placed them in the car for future examination. We had solved another long standing lunar problem and had, perhaps, opened up an inexhaustible mine of wealth which might eventually go far toward reimbursing the earth for the damage which it had suffered from the invasion of the Martians.

On returning to Cape Heraclides we found that the other expeditions had arrived at the rendezvous ahead of us. Their members had wonderful stories to tell of what they had seen, but nothing caused quite so much astonishment as that which we had to tell and to show.

The party which had gone to visit Plato and the lunar Alps brought back, however, information which, in a scientific sense, was no less interesting than what we had been able to gather.

They had found within this curious ring of Plato, which is a circle of mountains sixty miles in diameter, enclosing a level plain remarkably smooth over most of its surface, unmistakable evidences of former inhabitation. A gigantic city had evidently at one time existed near the centre of this great plain. The outlines of its walls and the foundation marks of some of its immense buildings were plainly made out, and elaborate plans of this vanished capital of the moon were prepared by several members of the party.

One of them was fortunate enough to discover an even more precious relic of the ancient lunarians. It was a piece of petrified skullbone, representing but a small portion of the head to which it had belonged, but yet sufficient to enable the anthropologists, who immediately fell to examining it, to draw ideal representations of the head as it must have been in life—the head of a giant of enormous size, which, if it had possessed a highly organized brain, of proportionate magnitude, must have given to its possessor intellectual powers immensely greater than any of the descendants of Adam have ever been endowed with.

Indeed, one of the professors was certain that some little concretions found on the interior of the piece of skull were petrified portions of the brain matter itself, and he set to work with the microscope to examine its organic quality.

In the mean time, the repairs to the electrical ships had been completed, and, although these discoveries upon the moon had created a most profound sensation among the members of the expedition, and aroused an almost irresistible desire to continue the explorations thus happily begun, yet everybody knew that these things were aside from the main purpose in view, and that we should be false to our duty in wasting a moment more upon the moon than was absolutely necessary to put the ships in proper condition to proceed on their warlike voyage.

Everything being prepared then, we left the moon with great regret, just forty-eight hours after we had landed upon its surface, carrying with us a determination to revisit it and to learn more of its wonderful secrets in case we should survive the dangers which we were now going to face.

Chapter 6

A day or two after leaving the moon we had another adventure with a wandering inhabitant of space which brought us into far greater peril than had our encounter with the meteor.

The airships had been partitioned off so that a portion of the interior could be darkened in order to serve as a sleeping chamber, wherein, according to the regulations prescribed by the commander of the squadron each member of the expedition in his turn passed eight out of every twenty-four hours—sleeping if he could, if not, meditating, in a more or less dazed way, upon the wonderful things that he was seeing and doing—things far more incredible than the creations of a dream.

One morning, if I may call by the name morning the time of my periodical emergence from the darkened chamber, glancing from one of the windows, I was startled to see in the black sky a brilliant comet.

No periodical comet, as I knew, was at this time approaching the neighbourhood of the sun, and no stranger of that kind had been detected from the observatories making its way sunward before we left the earth. Here, however, was unmistakably a comet rushing toward the sun, flinging out a great gleaming tail behind it and so close to us that I wondered to see it remaining almost motionless in the sky. This phenomenon was soon explained to me, and the explanation was of a most disquieting character.

The stranger had already been perceived, not only from the flagship, but from the other members of the squadron, and, as I now learned, efforts had been made to get out of the neighbourhood, but for some reason the electrical apparatus did not work perfectly—some mysterious disturbing force acting upon it—and so it had been found impossible to avoid an encounter with the comet, not an actual coming into contact with it, but a falling into the sphere of its influence.

In fact, I was informed that for several hours the squadron had been dragging along in the wake of a comet, very much as boats are sometimes towed off by a wounded whale. Every effort had been made to so adjust the electric charge upon the ships that they would be repelled from the cometic mass, but, owing apparently to eccentric changes continually going on in the electric charge affecting the clashing mass of meteoric bodies which constituted the head of the comet, we found it impossible to escape from its influence.

At one instant the ships would be repelled; immediately afterward they would be attracted again, and thus they were dragged hither and thither, but never able to break from the invisible leash which the comet had cast upon them. The latter was moving with enormous velocity toward the sun, and, consequently, we were being carried back again, away from the object of our expedition, with a fair prospect of being dissipated in blazing vapours when the comet had dragged us, unwilling prisoners, into the immediate neighbourhood of the solar furnace.

Even the most cool-headed lost his self-control in this terrible emergency. Every kind of device that experience or the imagination could suggest was tried, but nothing would do. Still on we rushed with the electrified atoms composing the tail of the comet sweeping to and fro over the members of the squadron, as they shifted their position, like the plume of smoke from a gigantic steamer, drifting over the sea birds that follow in its course.

Was this to end it all, then? Was this the fate that Providence had in store for us? Were the hopes of the earth thus to perish? Was the expedition to be wrecked and its fate to remain forever unknown to the planet from which it had set forth? And was our beloved globe, which had seemed so fair to us when we last looked upon it near by, and in whose defence we had resolved to spend our last breath, to be left helpless and at the mercy of its implacable foe in the sky?

At length we gave ourselves up for lost. There seemed to be no possible way to free ourselves from the baleful grip of this terrible and unlooked-for enemy.

As the comet approached the sun its electric energy rapidly increased, and watching it with telescopes, for we could not withdraw our fascinated eyes from it, we could clearly behold the fearful things that went on in its nucleus.

This consisted of an immense number of separate meteors of no very great size individually, but which were in constant motion among one another, darting to and fro, clashing and smashing together, while fountains of blazing metallic particles and hot mineral vapours poured out in every direction.

As I watched it, unable to withdraw my eyes, I saw imaginary forms revealing themselves amid the flaming meteors. They seemed like creatures in agony, tossing their arms, bewailing in their attitudes the awful fate that had overtaken them, and fairly chilling my blood with the pantomime of torture which they exhibited. I thought of an old superstition which I had often heard about the earth, and exclaimed: "Yes, surely, this is a flying hell!"

As the electric activity of the comet increased, its continued changes of potential and polarity became more frequent, and the electrical ships darted about with even greater confusion than before. Occasionally one of them, seized with a sudden impulse, would spring forward toward the nucleus of the comet with a sudden access of velocity that would fling every one of its crew from his feet, and all would lie sprawling on the floor of the car while it rushed, as it seemed, to inevitable and instant destruction.

Then, either through the frantic efforts of the electrician struggling with the controller or through another change in the polarity of the comet, the ship would be saved on the very brink of ruin and stagger away out of immediate danger.

Thus the captured squadron was swept, swaying and darting hither and thither, but never able to get sufficiently far from the comet to break the bond of its fatal attraction.

So great was our excitement and so complete our absorption in the fearful peril that we had not noticed the precise direction in which the comet was carrying us. It was enough to know that the goal of the journey was the furnace of the sun. But presently someone in the flagship recalled us to a more accurate sense of our situation in space by exclaiming:

"Why, there is the earth!"

And there, indeed, it was, its great globe rolling under our eyes, with the contrasted colours of the continents and clouds and the watery gleam of the ocean spread beneath us.

"We are going to strike it!" exclaimed somebody. "The comet is going to dash into the earth."

Such a collision at first seemed inevitable, but presently it was noticed that the direction of the comet's motion was such that while it might graze the earth it would not actually strike it.

And so, like a swarm of giant insects circling about an electric light from whose magic influence they cannot escape, our ships went on, to be whipped against the earth in passing and then to continue their swift journey to destruction.

"Thank God, this saves us," suddenly cried Mr. Edison.

"What—what?"

"Why, the earth, of course. Do you not see that as the comet sweeps close to the great planet the superior attraction of the latter will snatch us from its grasp, and that thus we shall be able to escape?"

And it was indeed as Mr. Edison had predicted. In a blaze of falling meteors the comet swept the outer limits of the earth's atmosphere and passed on, while the swaying ships, having been instructed by signals what to do, desperately applied their electrical machinery to reverse the attraction and threw themselves into the arms of their mother earth.

In another instant we were all free, settling down through the quiet atmosphere with the Atlantic Ocean sparkling in the morning sun far below.

We looked at one another in amazement. So this was the end of our voyage! This was the completion of our warlike enterprise. We had started out to conquer a world, and we had come back ignominiously dragged in the train of a comet.

The earth which we were going to defend and protect had herself turned protector, and reaching out her strong arm had snatched her foolish children from the destruction which they had invited.

It would be impossible to describe the chagrin of every member of the expedition.

The electric ships rapidly assembled and hovered high in the air, while their commanders consulted about what should be done. A universal feeling of shame almost drove them to a decision not to land upon the surface of the planet, and if possible not to let its inhabitants know what had occurred.

But it was too late for that. Looking carefully beneath us, we saw that fate had brought us back to our very starting point, and signals displayed in the neighbourhood of New York indicated that we had already been recognized. There was nothing for us then but to drop down and explain the situation.

I shall not delay my narrative by undertaking to describe the astonishment and the disappointment of the inhabitants of the earth when, within a fortnight from our departure, they saw us back again, with no laurels of victory crowning our brows.

At first they had hoped that we were returning in triumph, and we were overwhelmed with questions the moment we had dropped within speaking distance.

"Have you whipped them?"

"How many are lost?"

"Is there any more danger?"

"Faix, have ye got one of thim men from Mars?"

But their rejoicings and their facetiousness were turned into wailing when the truth was imparted.

We made a short story of it, for we had not the heart to go into details. We told of our unfortunate comrades whom we had buried on the moon, and there was one gleam of satisfaction when we exhibited the wonderful crystals we had collected in the crater of Aristarchus.

Mr. Edison determined to stop only long enough to test the electrical machinery of the cars, which had been more or less seriously deranged during our wild chase after the comet, and then to start straight back for Mars—this time on a through trip.

The astronomers, who had been watching Mars, since our departure, with their telescopes, reported that mysterious lights continued to be visible, but that nothing indicating the starting of another expedition for the earth had been seen.

Within twenty-four hours we were ready for our second start.

The moon was now no longer in a position to help us on our way. It had moved out of the line between Mars and the earth.

High above us, in the centre of the heavens, glowed the red planet which was the goal of our journey.

The needed computations of velocity and direction of flight having been repeated, and the ships being all in readiness, we started direct for Mars.

An enormous charge of electricity was imparted to each member of the squadron, in order that as soon as we had reached the upper limits of the atmosphere, where the ships could move swiftly, without danger of being consumed by the heat developed by the friction of their passage through the air, a very great initial velocity could be imparted.

Once started off by this tremendous electrical kick, and with no atmosphere to resist our motion, we should be able to retain the same velocity, barring incidental encounters, until we arrived near the surface of Mars.

When we were free of the atmosphere, and the ships were moving away from the earth, with the highest velocity which we were able to impart to them, observations on the stars were made in order to determine the rate of our speed.

This was found to be ten miles in a second, or 864,000 miles in a day, a very much greater speed than that with which we had travelled on starting to touch at the moon. Supposing this velocity to remain uniform, and, with no known resistance, it might reasonably be expected to do so, we should arrive at Mars in a little less than forty-two days, the distance of the planet from the earth being, at this time, about thirty-six million miles.

Nothing occurred for many days to interrupt our journey. We became accustomed to our strange surroundings, and many entertainments were provided to while away the time. The astronomers in the expedition found plenty of occupation in studying the aspects of the stars and the other heavenly bodies from their new point of view.

At the expiration of about thirty-five days we had drawn so near to Mars that with our telescopes, which, though small, were of immense power, we could discern upon its surface features and details which no one had been able to glimpse from the earth.

As the surface of this world, that we were approaching as a tiger hunter draws near the jungle, gradually unfolded itself to our inspection, there was hardly one of us willing to devote to sleep or idleness the prescribed eight hours that had been fixed as the time during which each member of the expedition must remain in the darkened chamber. We were too eager to watch for every new revelation upon Mars.

But something was in store that we had not expected. We were to meet the Martians before arriving at the world they dwelt in.

Among the stars which shone in that quarter of the heavens where Mars appeared as the master orb, there was one, lying directly in our path, which, to our astonishment, as we continued on, altered from the aspect of a star, underwent a gradual magnification, and soon presented itself in the form of a little planet.

"It is an asteroid," said somebody.

"Yes, evidently; but how does it come inside the orbit of Mars?"

"Oh, there are several asteroids," said one of the astronomers, "which travel inside the orbit of Mars, along a part of their course, and, for aught we can tell, there may be many which have not yet been caught sight of from the earth, that are nearer to the sun than Mars is."

"This must be one of them."

"Manifestly so."

As we drew nearer the mysterious little planet revealed itself to us as a perfectly formed globe not more than five miles in diameter.

"What is that upon it?" asked Lord Kelvin, squinting intently at the little world through his glass. "As I live, it moves."

"Yes, yes!" exclaimed several others, "there are inhabitants upon it, but what giants!"

"What monsters!"

"Don't you see?" exclaimed an excited savant. "They are the Martians!"

The startling truth burst upon the minds of all. Here upon this little planetoid were several of the gigantic inhabitants of the world that we were going to attack. There was more than one man in the flagship who recognized them well, and who shuddered at the recognition, instinctively recalling the recent terrible experience of the earth.

Around these monstrous enemies we saw several of their engines of war. Some of these appeared to have been wrecked, but at least one, as far as we could see, was still in a proper condition for use.

How had these creatures got there?

"Why, that is easy enough to account for," I said, as a sudden recollection flashed into my mind. "Don't you remember the report of the astronomers more than six months ago, at the end of the conference in Washington, that something would seem to indicate the departure of a new expedition from Mars had been noticed by them? We have heard nothing of that expedition since. We know that it did not reach the earth. It must have fallen foul of this asteroid, run upon this rock in the ocean of space and been wrecked here."

"We've got 'em, then," shouted our electric steersman, who had been a workman in Mr. Edison's laboratory and had unlimited confidence in his chief.

The electrical ships were immediately instructed by signal to slow down, an operation that was easily affected through the electrical repulsion of the asteroid.

The nearer we got the more terrifying was the appearance of the gigantic creatures who were riding upon the little world before us like castaway sailors upon a block of ice. Like men, and yet not like men, combining the human and the beast in their appearance, it required a steady nerve to look at them. If we had not known their malignity and their power to work evil, it would have been different, but in our eyes their moral character shone through their physical aspect and thus rendered them more terrible than they would otherwise have been.

When we first saw them their appearance was most forlorn, and their attitudes indicated only despair and desperation, but as they caught sight of us their malign power of intellect instantly penetrated the mystery, and they recognized us for what we were.

Their despair immediately gave place to reawakened malevolence. On the instant they were astir, with such heart-chilling movements as those that characterize a venomous serpent preparing to strike.

Not imagining that they would be in a position to make serious resistance, we had been somewhat incautious in approaching.

Suddenly there was a quicker movement than usual among the Martians, a swift adjustment of that one of their engines of war which, as already noticed, seemed to be practically uninjured, and then there darted from it and alighted upon one of the foremost ships a dazzling lightning stroke a mile in length, at whose touch the metallic sides of the car curled and withered and, licked for a moment by what seemed lambent flames, collapsed into a mere cinder.

For an instant not a word was spoken, so sudden and unexpected was the blow.

We knew that every soul in the stricken car had perished.

"Back! Back!" was the signal instantaneously flashed from the flagship, and reversing their polarities the members of the squadron sprang away from the little planet as rapidly as the electrical impulse could drive them.

But before we were out of reach a second flaming tongue of death shot from the fearful engine, and another of our ships, with all its crew, was destroyed.

It was an inauspicious beginning for us. Two of our electrical ships, with their entire crews, had been wiped out of existence, and this appalling blow had been dealt by a few stranded and disabled enemies floating on an asteroid.

What hope would there be for us when we came to encounter the millions of Mars itself on their own ground and prepared for war?

However, it would not do to despond. We had been incautious, and we should take good care not to commit the same fault again.

The first thing to do was to avenge the death of our comrades. The question whether we were able to meet these Martians and overcome them might as well be settled right here and now. They had proved what they could do, even when disabled and at a disadvantage. Now it was our turn.

Chapter 7

The squadron had been rapidly withdrawn to a very considerable distance from the asteroid. The range of the mysterious artillery employed by the Martians was unknown to us. We did not even know the limit of the effective range of our own disintegrators. If it should prove that the Martians were able to deal their strokes at a distance greater than any we could reach, then they would of course have an insuperable advantage.

On the other hand, if it should turn out that our range was greater than theirs, the advantage would be on our side. Or—which was perhaps most probable—there might be practically no difference in the effective range of the engines.

Anyhow, we were going to find out how the case stood, and that without delay.

Everything being in readiness, the disintegrators all in working order, and the men who were able to handle them, most of whom were experienced marksmen, chosen from among the officers of the regular army of the United States, and accustomed to the straight shooting and the sure hits of the West, standing at their posts, the squadron again advanced.

In order to distract the attention of the Martians, the electrical ships had been distributed over a wide space. Some dropped straight down toward the asteroid; others approached it by flank attack, from this side and that. The flagship moved straight in toward the point where the first disaster occurred. Its intrepid commander felt that his post should be that of the greatest danger, and where the severest blows would be given and received.

The approach of the ships was made with great caution. Watching the Martians with our telescopes we could clearly see that they were disconcerted by the scattered order of our attack. Even if all of their engines of war had been in proper condition for use it would have been impossible for them to meet the simultaneous assault of so many enemies dropping down upon them from the sky.

But they were made of fighting metal, as we knew from old experience. It was no question of surrender. They did not know how to surrender, and we did not know how to demand a surrender. Besides, the destruction of the two electrical ships with the forty men, many of whom bore names widely known upon the earth, had excited a kind of fury among the members of the squadron which called for vengeance.

Suddenly a repetition of the quick movement by the Martians, which had been the forerunner of the former coup, was observed; again a blinding flash burst from their war engine and instantaneously a shiver ran through the frame of the flagship; the air within quivered with strange pulsations and seemed suddenly to have assumed the temperature of a blast furnace.

We all gasped for breath. Our throats and lungs seemed scorched in the act of breathing. Some fell unconscious upon the floor. The marksmen, carrying the disintegrators ready for use, staggered, and one of them dropped his instrument.

But we had not been destroyed like our comrades before us. In a moment the wave of heat passed; those who had fallen recovered from their momentary stupor and staggered to their feet.

The electrical steersman stood hesitating at his post.

"Move on," said Mr. Edison sternly, his features set with determination and his eyes afire. "We are still beyond their effective range. Let us get closer in order to make sure work when we strike."

The ship moved on. One could hear the heartbeats of its inmates. The other members of the squadron, thinking for the moment that disaster had overtaken the flagship, had paused and seemed to be meditating flight.

"Signal them to move on," said Mr. Edison.

The signal was given, and the circle of electrical ships closed in upon the asteroid.

In the meantime Mr. Edison had been donning his air-tight suit. Before we could clearly comprehend his intention he had passed through the double-trapped door which gave access to the exterior of the car without permitting the loss of air, and was standing upon what served as the deck of the ship.

In his hand he carried a disintegrator. With a quick motion he sighted it.

As quickly as possible I sprang to his side. I was just in time to note the familiar blue gleam about the instrument, which indicated that its terrific energies were at work. The whirring sound was absent, because here, in open space, where there was no atmosphere, there could be no sound.

My eyes were fixed upon the Martians' engine, which had just dealt us a staggering, but not fatal, blow, and particularly I noticed a polished knob projecting from it, which seemed to have been the focus from which its destructive bolt emanated.

A moment later the knob disappeared. The irresistible vibrations darted from the electrical disintegrator and had fallen upon it and instantaneously shattered it into atoms.

"That fixes them," said Mr. Edison, turning to me with a smile.

And indeed it did fix them. We had most effectually spiked their gun. It would deal no more death blows.

The doings of the flagship had been closely watched throughout the squadron. The effect of its blow had been evident to all, and a moment later we saw, on some of the nearer ships, men dressed in their air suits, appearing upon the deck, swinging their arms and sending forth noiseless cheers into empty space.

The stroke that we had dealt was taken by several of the electrical ships as a signal for a common assault, and we saw two of the Martians fall beside the ruin of their engine, their heads having been blown from their bodies.

"Signal them to stop firing," commanded Mr. Edison. "We have got them down, and we are not going to murder them without necessity."

"Besides," he added, "I want to capture some of them alive."

The signal was given as he had ordered. The flagship then alone dropped slowly toward the place on the asteroid where the prostrate Martians were.

As we got near them a terrible scene unfolded itself to our eyes. There had evidently been not more than half a dozen of the monsters in the beginning. Two of these were stretched headless upon the ground. Three others had suffered horrible injuries where the invisible vibratory beams from the disintegrators had grazed them, and they could not long survive. One only remained apparently uninjured.

It is impossible for me to describe the appearance of this creature in terms that would be readily understood. Was he like a man? Yes and no. He possessed many human characteristics, but they were exaggerated and monstrous in scale and in detail. His head was of enormous size, and his huge projecting eyes gleamed with a strange fire of intelligence. His face was like a caricature, but not one to make the beholder laugh. Drawing himself up, he towered to a height of at least fifteen feet.

But let the reader not suppose from this inadequate description that the Martians stirred in the beholder precisely the sensation that would be caused by the sight of a gorilla, or other repulsive inhabitant of one of our terrestrial jungles, suddenly confronting him in its native wilds.

With all his horrible characteristics, and all his suggestions of beast and monster, nevertheless the Martian produced the impression of being a person and not a mere animal.

I have already referred to the enormous size of his head, and to the fact that his countenance bore considerable resemblance to that of a man. There was something in this face that sent a shiver through the soul of the beholder. One could feel in looking upon it that here was intellect, intelligence developed to the highest degree, but in the direction of evil instead of good.

The sensations of one who had stood face to face with Satan, when he was driven from the battlements of heaven by the swords of his fellow archangels, and had beheld him transformed from Lucifer, the Son of the Morning, into the Prince of Night and Hell, might not have been unlike those which we now experienced as we gazed upon this dreadful personage, who seemed to combine the intellectual powers of a man, raised to their highest pitch, with some of the physical features of a beast, and all the moral depravity of a fiend.

The appearance of the Martian was indeed so threatening and repellent that we paused at the height of fifty feet above the ground, hesitating to approach nearer. A grin of rage and hate overspread his face. If he had been a man I should say he shook his fist at us. What he did was to express in even more telling pantomime his hatred and defiance, and his determination to grind us to shreds if he could once get us within his clutches.

Mr. Edison and I still stood upon the deck of the ship, where several others had gathered around us. The atmosphere of the little asteroid was so rare that it practically amounted to nothing, and we could not possibly have survived if we had not continued to wear our air-tight suits. How the Martians contrived to live here was a mystery to us. It was another of their secrets which we were yet to learn.

Mr. Edison retained his disintegrator in his hand.

"Kill him," said someone. "He is too horrible to live."

"If we do not kill him we shall never be able to land upon the asteroid," said another.

"No," said Mr. Edison, "I shall not kill him. We have got another use for him. Tom," he continued, turning to one of his assistants, whom he had brought from his laboratory, "bring me the anaesthetizer."

This was something entirely new to nearly all the members of the expedition. Mr. Edison, however, had confided to me before we left the earth the fact that he had invented a little instrument by means of which a bubble, strongly charged with a powerful anaesthetic agent, could be driven to a considerable distance into the face of an enemy, where, exploding without other damage, it would instantly put him to sleep.

When Tom had placed the instrument in his hands Mr. Edison ordered the electrical ship to forge slightly ahead and drop a little lower toward the Martian, who, with watchful eyes and threatening gestures, noted our approach in the attitude of a wild beast on the spring. Suddenly Mr. Edison discharged from the instrument in his hand a little gaseous globe, which glittered like a ball of tangled rainbows in the sunshine, and darted with astonishing velocity straight into the upturned face of the Martian. It burst as it touched and the monster fell back senseless upon the ground.

"You have killed him!" exclaimed all.

"No," said Mr. Edison, "he is not dead, only asleep. Now we shall drop down and bind him tight before he can awake."

When we came to bind our prisoner with strong ropes we were more than ever impressed with his gigantic stature and strength. Evidently in single combat with equal weapons he would have been a match for twenty of us.

All that I had read of giants had failed to produce upon my mind the impression of enormous size and tremendous physical energy which the sleeping body of this immense Martian produced. He had fallen on his back, and was in a most profound slumber. All his features were relaxed, and yet even in that condition there was a devilishness about him that made the beholders instinctively shudder.

So powerful was the effect of the anaesthetic which Mr. Edison had discharged into his face that he remained perfectly unconscious while we turned him half over in order the more securely to bind his muscular limbs.

In the meantime the other electrical ships approached, and several of them made a landing upon the asteroid. Everybody was eager to see this wonderful little world, which, as I have already remarked, was only five miles in diameter.

Several of us from the flagship started out hastily to explore the miniature planet. And now our attention was recalled to an intensely interesting phenomenon which had engaged our thoughts not only when we were upon the moon, but during our flight through space. This was the almost entire absence of weight.

On the moon, where the force of gravitation is one-sixth as great as upon the earth, we had found ourselves astonishingly light. Five-sixths of our own weight, and of the weight of the air-tight suits in which we were encased, had magically dropped from us. It was therefore comparatively easy for us, encumbered as we were, to make our way about on the moon.

But when we were far from both the earth and the moon, the loss of weight was more astonishing still—not astonishing because we had not known that it would be so, but nevertheless a surprising phenomenon in contrast with our lifelong experience on the earth.

In open space we were practically without weight. Only the mass of the electrical car in which we were enclosed attracted us, and inside that we could place ourselves in any position without falling. We could float in the air. There were no up and no down, no top and no bottom for us. Stepping outside the car, it would have been easy for us to spring away from it and leave it forever.

One of the most startling experiences that I have ever had was one day when we were navigating space about half way between the earth and Mars. I had stepped outside the car with Lord Kelvin, both of us, of course, wearing our air-tight suits. We were perfectly well aware what would be the consequence of detaching ourselves from the car as we moved along. We should still retain the forward motion of the car, and of course accompany it in its flight. There would be no falling one way or the other. The car would have a tendency to draw us back again by its attraction, but this tendency would be very slight, and practically inappreciable at a distance.

"I am going to step off," I suddenly said to Lord Kelvin. "Of course I shall keep right along with the car, and step aboard again when I am ready."

"Quite right on general principles, young man," replied the great savant, "but beware in what manner you step off. Remember, if you give your body an impulse sufficient to carry it away from the car to any considerable distance, you will be unable to get back again, unless we can catch you with a boathook or a fishline. Out there in empty space you will have nothing to kick against, and you will be unable to propel yourself in the direction of the car, and its attraction is so feeble that we should probably arrive at Mars before it had drawn you back again."

All this was, of course, perfectly self-evident, yet I believe that but for the warning word of Lord Kelvin, I should have been rash enough to step out into empty space with sufficient force to have separated myself hopelessly from the electrical ship.

As it was, I took good care to retain a hold upon a projecting portion of the car. Occasionally cautiously releasing my grip, I experienced for a few minutes the delicious, indescribable pleasure of being a little planet swinging through space, with nothing to hold me up and nothing to interfere with my motion.

Mr. Edison, happening to come upon the deck of the ship at this time, and seeing what we were about, at once said:

"I must provide against this danger. If I do not, there is a chance that we shall arrive at Mars with the ships half empty and the crews floating helplessly around us."

Mr. Edison's way of guarding against the danger was by contriving a little apparatus, modelled after that which was the governing force of the electrical ships themselves, and which, being enclosed in the airtight suits, enabled their wearers to manipulate the electrical charge upon them in such a way that they could make excursions from the cars into open space like steam launches from a ship, going and returning at their will.

These little machines being rapidly manufactured, for Mr. Edison had a miniature laboratory aboard, were distributed about the squadron, and henceforth we had the pleasure of paying and receiving visits among the various members of the fleet.

But to return from this digression to our experience of the asteroid. The latter being a body of some mass was, of course, able to impart to us a measurable degree of weight. Being five miles in diameter, on the assumption that its mean density was the same as that of the earth, the weight of bodies on its surface should have borne the same ratio to their weight upon the earth that the radius of the asteroid bore to the radius of the earth; in other words, as 1 to 1,600.

Having made this mental calculation, I knew that my weight, being 150 pounds on the earth, should on this asteroid be an ounce and a half.

Curious to see whether fact would bear out theory, I had myself weighed with a spring balance. Mr. Edison, Lord Kelvin and the other distinguished scientists stood by watching the operation with great interest.

To our complete surprise, my weight, instead of coming out an ounce and a half, as it should have done, on the supposition that the mean density of the asteroid resembled that of the earth—a very liberal supposition on the side of the asteroid, by the way—actually came out five ounces and a quarter!

"What in the world makes me so heavy?" I asked.

"Yes, indeed, what an elephant you have become," said Mr. Edison.

Lord Kelvin screwed his eyeglass in his eye, and carefully inspected the balance.

Weight, Five and a Quarter Ounces.

"It's quite right," he said. "You do indeed weigh five ounces and a quarter. Too much; altogether too much," he added. "You shouldn't do it, you know."

"Perhaps the fault is in the asteroid," suggested Professor Sylvanus P. Thompson.

"Quite so," exclaimed Lord Kelvin, a look of sudden comprehension overspreading his features. "No doubt it is the internal constitution of the asteroid which is the cause of the anomaly. We must look into that. Let me see? This gentleman's weight is three and one-half times as great as it ought to be. What element is there whose density exceeds the mean density of the earth in about that proportion?"

"Gold," exclaimed one of the party.

For a moment we were startled beyond expression. The truth had flashed upon us.

This must be a golden planet—this little asteroid. If it were not composed internally of gold it could never have made me weigh three times more than I ought to weigh.

"But where is the gold?" cried one.

"Covered up, of course," said Lord Kelvin. "Buried in star dust. This asteroid could not have continued to travel for millions of years through regions of space strewn with meteoric particles without becoming covered with the inevitable dust and grime of such a journey. We must dig down, and then doubtless we shall find the metal."

This hint was instantly acted upon. Something that would serve for a spade was seized by one of the men, and in a few minutes a hole had been dug in the comparatively light soil of the asteroid.

I shall never forget the sight, nor the exclamations of wonder that broke forth from all of us standing around, when the yellow gleam of the precious metal appeared under the "star dust." Collected in huge masses it reflected the light of the sun from its hiding place.

Evidently the planet was not a solid ball of gold, formed like a bullet run in a mould, but was composed of nuggets of various sizes, which had come together here under the influence of their mutual gravitation, and formed a little metallic planet.

Judging by the test of weight which we had already tried, and which had led to the discovery of the gold, the composition of the asteroid must be the same to its very centre.

In an assemblage of famous scientific men such as this the discovery of course immediately led to questions as to the origin of this incredible phenomenon.

How did these masses of gold come together? How did it chance that, with the exception of the thin crust of the asteroid, nearly all its substance was composed of the precious metal?

One asserted that it was quite impossible that there should be so much gold at so great a distance from the sun.

"It is the general law," he said, "that the planets increase in density toward the sun. There is every reason to think that the inner planets possess the greater amount of dense elements, while the outer ones are comparatively light."

But another referred to the old theory that there was once in this part of the solar system a planet which had been burst in pieces by some mysterious explosion, the fragments forming what we know as the asteroids. In his opinion, this planet might have contained a large quantity of gold, and in the course of ages the gold, having, in consequence of its superior atomic weight, not being so widely scattered by the explosion as some of the other elements of the planet, had collected itself together in this body.

But I observed that Lord Kelvin and the other more distinguished men of science said nothing during this discussion. The truly learned man is the truly wise man. They were not going to set up theories without sufficient facts to sustain them. The one fact that the gold was here was all they had at present. Until they could learn more they were not prepared to theorize as to how the gold got there.

And in truth, it must be confessed, the greater number of us really cared less for the explanation of the wonderful fact than we did for the fact itself.

Gold is a thing which may make its appearance anywhere and at any time without offering any excuses or explanations.

"Phew! Won't we be rich?" exclaimed a voice.

"How are we going to dig it and get it back to earth?" asked another.

"Carry it in your pockets," said one.

"No need of staking claims here," remarked another. "There is enough for everybody."

Mr. Edison suddenly turned the current of talk.

"What do you suppose those Martians were doing here?"

"Why, they were wrecked here."

"Not a bit of it," said Mr. Edison. "According to your own showing they could not have been wrecked here. This planet hasn't gravitation enough to wreck them by a fall, and besides I have been looking at their machines and I know there has been a fight."

"A fight?" exclaimed several, pricking up their ears.

"Yes," said Mr. Edison; "those machines bear the marks of the lightning of the Martians. They have been disabled, but they are made of some metal or some alloy of metals unknown to me, and consequently they have withstood the destructive force applied to them, as our electric ships were unable to withstand it. It is perfectly plain to me that they have been disabled in a battle. The Martians must have been fighting among themselves."

"About the gold!" exclaimed one.

"Of course. What else was there to fight about?"

At this instant one of our men came running from a considerable distance, waving his arms excitedly, but unable to give voice to his story, in the inappreciable atmosphere of the asteroid, until he had come up and made telephonic connection with us.

"There is a lot of dead Martians over there," he said. "They've been cleaning one another out."

"That's it," said Mr. Edison. "I knew it when I saw the condition of those machines."

"Then this is not a wrecked expedition, directed against the earth?"

"Not at all."

"This must be the great gold mine of Mars," said the president of an Australian mining company, opening both his eyes and his mouth as he spoke.

"Yes, evidently that's it. Here's where they come to get their wealth."

"And this," I said, "must be their harvest time. You notice that this asteroid, being several million miles nearer to the sun than Mars is, must have an appreciably shorter period of revolution. When it is in conjunction with Mars, or nearly so, as it is at present, the distance between the two is not very great, whereas when it is in the opposite part of its orbit they are separated by an enormous gap of space and the sun is between them."

"Manifestly in the latter case it would be perilous if not entirely impossible for the Martians to visit the golden asteroid, but when it is near Mars, as it is at present, and as it must be periodically for several years at a time, then is their opportunity."

"With their projectile cars sent forth with the aid of the mysterious explosives which they possess, it is easy for them under such circumstances, to make visits to the asteroid."

"Having obtained all the gold they need, or all that they can carry, a comparatively slight impulse given to their car, the direction of which is carefully calculated, will carry them back again to Mars."

"If that's so," exclaimed a voice, "we had better look out for ourselves! We have got into a very hornet's nest! If this is the place where the Martians come to dig gold, and if this is the height of their season, as you say, they are not likely to leave us here long undisturbed."

"These fellows must have been pirates that they had the fight with," said another.

"But what's become of the regulars, then?"

"Gone back to Mars for help, probably, and they'll be here again pretty quick, I am afraid!"

Considerable alarm was caused by this view of the case, and orders were sent to several of the electrical ships to cruise out to a safe distance in the direction of Mars and keep a sharp outlook for the approach of enemies.

Meanwhile our prisoner awoke. He turned his eyes upon those standing about him, without any appearance of fear, but rather with a look of contempt, like that which Gulliver must have felt for the Lilliputians who had bound him under similar circumstances.

There were both hatred and defiance in his glance. He attempted to free himself, and the ropes strained with the tremendous pressure that he put upon them, but he could not break loose.

Satisfied that the Martian was safely bound, we left him where he lay, and, while awaiting news from the ships which had been sent to reconnoitre, continued the exploration of the little planet.

At a point nearly opposite to that where we had landed we came upon the mine which the Martians had been working. They had removed the thin coating of soil, laying bare the rich stores of gold beneath, and large quantities of the latter had been removed. Some of it was so solidly packed that the strokes of the instruments by means of which they had detached it were visible like the streaks left by a knife cutting cheese.

The more we saw of this golden planet the greater became our astonishment. What the Martians had removed was a mere nothing in comparison with the entire bulk of the asteroid. Had the celestial mine been easier to reach, perhaps they would have removed more, or, possibly, their political economists perfectly understood the necessity of properly controlling the amount of precious metal in circulation. Very likely, we thought, the mining operations were under government control in Mars and it might be that the majority of the people there knew nothing of this store of wealth floating in the firmament. That would account for the battle with the supposed pirates, who, no doubt, had organized a secret expedition to the asteroid and been caught red-handed at the mine.

There were many detached masses of gold scattered about, and some of the men, on picking them up, exclaimed with astonishment at their lack of weight, forgetting for the moment that the same law which caused their own bodies to weigh so little must necessarily affect everything else in like degree.

A mass of gold that on the earth no man would have been able to lift could here be tossed about like a hollow rubber ball.

While we were examining the mine, one of the men left to guard the Martian came running to inform us that the latter evidently wished to make some communication. Mr. Edison and others hurried to the side of the prisoner. He still lay on his back, from which position he was not able to move, notwithstanding all his efforts. But by the motion of his eyes, aided by a pantomime with his fingers, he made us understand that there was something in a metallic box fastened at his side which he wished to reach.

With some difficulty we succeeded in opening the box and in it there appeared a number of bright red pellets, as large as an ordinary egg.

When the Martian saw these in our hands he gave us to understand by the motion of his lips that he wished to swallow one of them. A pellet was accordingly placed in his mouth, and he instantly and with great eagerness swallowed it.

While trying to communicate his wishes to us, the prisoner had seemed to be in no little distress. He exhibited spasmodic movements which led some of the bystanders to think that he was on the point of dying, but within a few seconds after he had swallowed the pellet he appeared to be completely restored. All evidences of distress vanished, and a look of content came over his ugly face.

"It must be a powerful medicine," said one of the bystanders. "I wonder what it is."

"I will explain to you my notion," said Professor Moissan, the great French chemist. "I think it was a pill of the air, which he has taken."

"What do you mean by that?"

"My meaning is," said Professor Moissan, "that the Martian must have, for that he may live, the nitrogen and the oxygen. These can he not obtain here, where there is not the atmosphere. Therefore must he get them in some other manner. This has he managed to do by combining in these pills the oxygen and the nitrogen in the proportions which make atmospheric air. Doubtless upon Mars there are the very great chemists. They have discovered how this may be done. When the Martian has swallowed his little pill, the oxygen and the nitrogen are rendered to his blood as if he had breathed them, and so he can live with that air which has been distributed to him with the aid of his stomach in the place of his lungs."

If Monsieur Moissan's explanation was not correct, at any rate it seemed the only one that would fit the facts before us. Certainly the Martian could not breathe where there was practically no air, yet just as certainly after he had swallowed his pill he seemed as comfortable as any of us.

Suddenly, while we were gathered around the prisoner, and interested in this fresh evidence of the wonderful ingenuity of the Martians, and of their control over the processes of nature, one of the electrical ships that had been sent off in the direction of Mars was seen rapidly returning and displaying signals.

It reported that the Martians were coming!

Chapter 8

The alarm was spread instantly among those upon the planet and through the remainder of the fleet.

One of the men from the returning electrical ship dropped down upon the asteroid and gave a more detailed account of what they had seen.

His ship had been the one which had gone to the greatest distance in the direction of Mars. While cruising there, with all eyes intent, they had suddenly perceived a glittering object moving from the direction of the ruddy planet, and manifestly approaching them. A little inspection with the telescope had shown that it was one of the projectile cars used by the Martians.

Our ship had ventured so far from the asteroid that for a moment it seemed doubtful whether it would be able to return in time to give warning, because the electrical influence of the asteroid was comparatively slight at such a distance, and, after they had reversed their polarity, and applied their intensifier, so as to make that influence effective, their motion was at first exceedingly slow.

Fortunately after a time they got under way with sufficient velocity to bring them back to us before the approaching Martians could overtake them.

The latter were not moving with great velocity, having evidently projected themselves from Mars with only just sufficient force to throw them within the feeble sphere of gravitation of the asteroid, so that they should very gently land upon its surface.

Indeed, looking out behind the electrical ship which had brought us the warning, we immediately saw the projectile of the Martians approaching. It sparkled like a star in the black sky as the sunlight fell upon it.

The ships of the squadron whose crews had not landed upon the planet were signalled to prepare for action, while those who were upon the asteroid made ready for battle there. A number of disintegrators were trained upon the approaching Martians, but Mr. Edison gave strict orders that no attempt should be made to discharge the vibratory force at random.

"They do not know that we are here," he said, "and I am convinced that they are unable to control their motions as we can do with our electrical ships. They depend simply upon the force of gravitation. Having passed the limit of the attraction of Mars, they have now fallen within the attraction of the asteroid, and they must slowly sink to its surface."

"Having, as I am convinced, no means of producing or controlling electrical attraction and repulsion, they cannot stop themselves, but must come down upon the asteroid. Having got here they could never get away again, except as we know the survivors got away from earth, by propelling their projectile against gravitation with the aid of an explosive."

"Therefore, to a certain extent they will be at our mercy. Let us allow them quietly to land upon the planet, and then I think, if it becomes necessary, we can master them."

Notwithstanding Mr. Edison's reassuring words and manner, the company upon the asteroid experienced a dreadful suspense while the projectile which seemed very formidable as it drew near, sank with a slow and graceful motion toward the surface of the ground. Evidently it was about to land very near the spot where we stood awaiting it.

Its inmates had apparently just caught sight of us. They evinced signs of astonishment, and seemed at a loss exactly what to do. We could see projecting from the fore part of their car at least two of the polished knobs, whose fearful use and power we well comprehended.

Several of our men cried out to Mr. Edison in an extremity of terror:

"Why do you not destroy them? Be quick, or we shall all perish."

"No," said Mr. Edison, "there is no danger. You can see that they are not prepared. They will not attempt to attack us until they have made their landing."

And Mr. Edison was right. With gradually accelerated velocity, and yet very, very slowly in comparison with the speed they would have exhibited in falling upon such a planet as the earth, the Martians and their car came down to the ground.

We stood at a distance of perhaps three hundred feet from the point where they touched the asteroid. Instantly a dozen of the giants sprang from the car and gazed about for a moment with a look of intense surprise. At first it was doubtful whether they meant to attack us at all.

We stood on our guard, several carrying disintegrators in our hands, while a score more of these terrible engines were turned upon the Martians from the electrical ships which hovered near.

Suddenly he who seemed to be the leader of the Martians began to speak to them in pantomime, using his fingers after the manner in which they are used for conversation by deaf and dumb people.

Of course, we did not know what he was saying, but his meaning became perfectly evident a minute later. Clearly they did not comprehend the powers of the insignificant-looking strangers with whom they had to deal. Instead of turning their destructive engines upon us, they advanced on a run, with the evident purpose of making us prisoners or crushing us by main force.

The soft whirr of the disintegrator in the hands of Mr. Edison standing near me came to my ears through the telephonic wire. He quickly swept the concentrating mirror a little up and down, and instantly the foremost Martian vanished! Part of some metallic dress that he wore fell upon the ground where he had stood, its vibratory rate not having been included in the range imparted to the disintegrator.

His followers paused for a moment, amazed, stared about as if looking for their leader, and then hurried back to their projectile and disappeared within it.

"Now we've got business on our hands," said Mr. Edison. "Look out for yourselves."

As he spoke, I saw the death-dealing knob of the war engine contained in the car of the Martians moving around toward us. In another instant it would have launched its destroying bolt.

Before that could occur, however, it had been dissipated into space by a vibratory stream from a disintegrator.

But we were not to get the victory quite so easily. There was another of the war engines in the car, and before we could concentrate our fire upon it, its awful flash shot forth, and a dozen of our comrades perished before our eyes.

"Quick! Quick!" shouted Mr. Edison to one of his electrical experts standing near. "There is something the matter with this disintegrator, and I cannot make it work. Aim at the knob, and don't miss it."

But the aim was not well taken, and the vibratory force fell upon a portion of the car at a considerable distance from the knob, making a great breach, but leaving the engine uninjured.

A section of the side of the car had been destroyed, and the vibratory energy had spread no further. To have attempted to sweep the car from end to end would have been futile, because the period of action of the disintegrators during each discharge did not exceed one second, and distributing the energy over so great a space would have seriously weakened its power to shatter apart the atoms of the resisting substance. The disintegrators were like firearms, in that after each discharge they must be readjusted before they could be used again.

Through the breach we saw the Martians inside making desperate efforts to train their engine upon us, for after their first disastrous stroke we had rapidly shifted our position. Swiftly the polished knob, which gleamed like an evil eye, moved round to sweep over us. Instinctively, though incautiously, we had collected in a group.

A single discharge would sweep us all into eternity.

"Will no one fire upon them?" exclaimed Mr. Edison, struggling with the disintegrator in his hands, which still refused to work.

At this fearful moment I glanced around upon our company, and was astonished at the spectacle. In the presence of the danger many of them had lost all self-command. A half dozen had dropped their disintegrators upon the ground. Others stood as if frozen fast in their tracks. The expert electrician, whose poor aim had had such disastrous results, held in his hand an instrument which was in perfect condition, yet with mouth agape, he stood trembling like a captured bird.

It was a disgraceful exhibition. Mr. Edison, however, had not lost his head. Again and again he sighted at the dreadful knob with his disintegrator, but the vibratory force refused to respond.

The means of safety were in our hands, and yet through a combination of ill luck and paralyzing terror we seemed unable to use them.

In a second more it would be all over with us.

The suspense in reality lasted only during the twinkling of an eye, though it seemed ages long.

Unable to endure it, I sharply struck the shoulder of the paralyzed electrician. To have attempted to seize the disintegrator from his hands would have been a fatal waste of time. Luckily the blow either roused him from his stupor or caused an instinctive movement of his hand that set the little engine in operation.

I am sure he took no aim, but providentially the vibratory force fell upon the desired point, and the knob disappeared.

We were saved!

Instantly half a dozen rushed toward the car of the Martians. We bitterly repented their haste; they did not live to repent.

Unknown to us the Martians carried hand engines, capable of launching bolts of death of the same character as those which emanated from the knobs of their larger machines. With these they fired, so to speak, through the breach in their car, and four of our men who were rushing upon them fell in heaps of cinders. The effect of the terrible fire was like that which the most powerful strokes of lightning occasionally produce on earth.

The destruction of the threatening knob had instantaneously relieved the pressure upon the terror-stricken nerves of our company, and they had all regained their composure and self-command. But this new and unexpected disaster, following so close upon the fear which had recently overpowered them, produced a second panic, the effect of which was not to stiffen them in their tracks as before, but to send them scurrying in every direction in search of hiding places.

And now a most curious effect of the smallness of the planet we were on began to play a conspicuous part in our adventures. Standing on a globe only five miles in diameter was like being on the summit of a mountain whose sides sloped rapidly off in every direction, disappearing in the black sky on all sides, as if it were some stupendous peak rising out of an unfathomable abyss.

In consequence of the quick rounding off of the sides of this globe, the line of the horizon was close at hand, and by running a distance of less than 250 yards the fugitives disappeared down the sides of the asteroid, and behind the horizon, even from the elevation of about fifteen feet from which the Martians were able to watch them. From our sight they disappeared much sooner.

The slight attraction of the planet and their consequent almost entire lack of weight enabled the men to run with immense speed. The result, as I subsequently learned, was that after they had disappeared from our view they quitted the planet entirely, the force being sufficient to partially free them from its gravitation, so that they sailed out into space, whirling helplessly end over end, until the elliptical orbits in which they travelled eventually brought them back again to the planet on the side nearly opposite to that from which they had departed.

But several of us, with Mr. Edison, stood fast, watching for an opportunity to get the Martians within range of the disintegrators. Luckily we were enabled, by shifting our position a little to the left, to get out of the line of sight of our enemies concealed in the car.

"If we cannot catch sight of them," said Mr. Edison, "we shall have to riddle the car on the chance of hitting them."

"It will be like firing into a bush to kill a hidden bear," said one of the party.

But help came from a quarter which was unexpected to us, although it should not have been so. Several of the electric ships had been hovering above us during the fight, their commanders being apparently uncertain how to act—fearful, perhaps, of injuring us in the attempt to smite our enemy.

But now the situation apparently lightened for them. They saw that we were at an immense disadvantage, and several of them immediately turned their batteries upon the car of the Martians.

They riddled it far more quickly and effectively than we could have done. Every stroke of the vibratory emanation made a gap in the side of the car, and we could perceive from the commotion within that our enemies were being rapidly massacred in their fortification.

So overwhelming was the force and the advantage of the ships that in a little while it was all over. Mr. Edison signalled them to stop firing because it was plain that all resistance had ceased and probably not one of the Martians remained alive.

We now approached the car, which had been transpierced in every direction, and whose remaining portions were glowing with heat in consequence of the spreading of the atomic vibrations. Immediately we discovered that all our anticipations were correct and that all of our enemies had perished.

The effect of the disintegrators upon them had been awful—too repulsive, indeed, to be described in detail. Some of the bodies had evidently entirely vanished; only certain metal articles which they had worn remaining, as in the case of the first Martian killed, to indicate that such beings had ever existed. The nature of the metal composing these articles was unknown to us. Evidently its vibratory rhythm did not correspond with any included in the ordinary range of the disintegrators.

Some of the giants had been only partially destroyed, the vibratory current having grazed them, in such a manner that the shattering undulations had not acted upon the entire body.

One thing that lends a peculiar horror to a terrestrial battlefield was absent; there was no bloodshed. The vibratory energy, not only completely destroyed whatever it fell upon but it seared the veins and arteries of the dismembered bodies so that there was no sanguinary exhibition connected with its murderous work.

All this time the shackled Martian had lain on his back where we had left him bound. What his feeling must have been may be imagined. At times, I caught a glimpse of his eyes, wildly rolling and exhibiting, when he saw that the victory was in our hands, the first indications of fear and terror shaking his soul that had yet appeared.

"That fellow is afraid at last," I said to Mr. Edison.

"Well, I should think he ought to be afraid," was the reply.

"So he ought, but if I am not mistaken this fear of his may be the beginning of a new discovery for us."

"How so?" asked Mr. Edison.

"In this way. When once he fears our power, and perceives that there would be no hope of contending against us, even if he were at liberty, he will respect us. This change in his mental attitude may tend to make him communicative. I do not see why we should despair of learning his language from him, and having done that, he will serve as our guide and interpreter, and will be of incalculable advantage to us when we have arrived at Mars."

"Capital! Capital!" said Mr. Edison. "We must concentrate the linguistic genius of our company upon that problem at once."

In the meantime some of the skulkers whose flight I have referred to began to return, chapfallen, but rejoicing in the disappearance of the danger. Several of them, I am ashamed to say, had been army officers. Yet possibly some excuse could be made for the terror by which they had been overcome. No man has a right to hold his fellow beings to account for the line of conduct they may pursue under circumstances which are not only entirely unexampled in their experience, but almost beyond the power of the imagination to picture.

Paralyzing terror had evidently seized them with the sudden comprehension of the unprecedented singularity of their situation. Millions of miles away from the earth, confronted on an asteroid by these diabolical monsters from a maleficent planet, who were on the point of destroying them with a strange torment of death—perhaps it was really more than human nature, deprived of the support of human surroundings, could have been expected to bear.

Those who, as already described, had run with so great a speed that they were projected, all unwilling, into space, rising in elliptical orbits from the surface of the planet, describing great curves in what might be denominated its sky, and then coming back again to the little globe on another side, were so filled with the wonders of their remarkable adventure that they had almost forgotten the terror which had inspired it.

There was nothing surprising in what had occurred to them the moment one considered the laws of gravitation on the asteroid, but their stories aroused an intense interest among all who listened to them.

Lord Kelvin was particularly interested, and while Mr. Edison was hastening preparations to quit the asteroid and resume our voyage to Mars, Lord Kelvin and a number of other scientific men instituted a series of remarkable experiments.

It was one of the most laughable things imaginable to see Lord Kelvin, dressed in his air-tight suit, making tremendous jumps into empty space. It reminded me forcibly of what Lord Kelvin, then plain William Thompson, and Professor Blackburn had done when spending a Summer vacation at the seaside, while they were under-graduates of Cambridge University. They had spent all their time, to the surprise of onlookers, in spinning rounded stones on the beach, their object being to obtain a practical solution of the mathematical problem of "precession."

Immediately Lord Kelvin was imitated by a dozen others. With what seemed very slight effort they projected themselves straight up-ward, rising to a height of four hundred feet or more, and then slowly settling back again to the surface of the asteroid. The time of rise and fall combined was between three and four minutes.

On this little planet the acceleration of gravity or the velocity ac-quired by a falling body in one second was only four-fifths of an inch. A body required an entire minute to fall a distance of only 120 feet. Consequently, it was more like gradually settling than falling. The figures of these men of science, rising and sinking in this manner, ap-peared like so many gigantic marionettes bobbing up and down in a pneumatic bottle.

"Let us try that," said Mr. Edison, very much interested in the experiments.

Both of us jumped together. At first, with great swiftness, but gradually losing speed, we rose to an immense height straight from the ground. When we had reached the utmost limit of our flight we seemed to come to rest for a moment, and then began slowly, but with accelerated velocity, to sink back again to the planet. It was not only a peculiar but a delicious sensation, and but for strict orders which were issued that the electrical ships should be immediately prepared for departure, our entire company might have remained for an indefinite period enjoying this new kind of athletic exercise in a world where gravitation had become so humble that it could be trifled with.

While the final preparations for departure were being made, Lord

Kelvin instituted other experiments that were no less unique in their results. The experience of those who had taken unpremeditated flights in elliptical orbits when they had run from the vicinity of the Martians suggested the throwing of solid objects in various directions from the surface of the planet in order to determine the distance that they would go and the curves they would describe in returning.

For these experiments there was nothing more convenient or abundant than chunks of gold from the Martians' mine. These, accordingly, were hurled in various directions, and with every degree of velocity. A little calculation had shown that an initial velocity of thirty feet per second imparted to one of these chunks, moving at right angles to the radius of the asteroid, would, if the resistance of an almost inappreciable atmosphere were neglected, suffice to turn the piece of gold into a little satellite that would describe an orbit around the asteroid, and continue to do so forever, or at least until the slight atmospheric resistance should eventually bring it down to the surface.

But a less velocity than thirty feet per second would cause the golden missile to fly only part way around, while a greater velocity would give it an elliptical instead of a circular orbit, and in this ellipse it would continue to revolve around the asteroid in the character of a satellite.

If the direction of the original impulse were at more than a right angle to the radius of the asteroid, then the flying body would pass out to a greater or less distance in space in an elliptical orbit, eventually coming back again and falling upon the asteroid, but not at the same spot from which it had departed.

So many took part in these singular experiments, which assumed rather the appearance of outdoor sports than of scientific demonstrations, that in a short time we had provided the asteroid with a very large number of little moons, or satellites, of gold, which revolved around it in orbits of various degrees of ellipticity, taking, on the average, about three-quarters of an hour to complete a circuit. Since, on completing a revolution, they must necessarily pass through the point from which they started, they kept us constantly on the qui vive to avoid being knocked over by them as they swept around in their orbits.

Finally the signal was given for all to embark, and with great regret the savants quitted their scientific games and prepared to return to the electric ships.

Just on the moment of departure, the fact was announced by one, who had been making a little calculation on a bit of paper, that the velocity with which a body must be thrown in order to escape forever the attraction of the asteroid, and to pass on to an infinite distance in any direction, was only about forty-two feet in a second.

Manifestly it would be quite easy to impart such a speed as that to the chunks of gold that we held in our hands.

"Hurrah!" exclaimed one. "Let's send some of this back to the earth."

"Where is the earth?" asked another.

Being appealed to, several astronomers turned their eyes in the direction of the sun, where the black firmament was ablaze with stars, and in a moment recognized the earth-star shining there, with the moon attending close at hand.

"There," said one, "is the earth. Can you throw straight enough to hit it?"

"We'll try," was the reply, and immediately several threw huge golden nuggets in the direction of our far-away world, endeavouring to impart to them at least the required velocity of forty-two feet in a second, which would insure their passing beyond the attraction of the asteroid, and if there should be no disturbance on the way, and the aim were accurate, their eventual arrival upon the earth.

"Here's for you, Old Earth," said one of the throwers, "good luck, and more gold to you!"

If these precious missiles ever reached the earth we knew that they would plunge into the atmosphere like meteors and that probably the heat developed by their passage would melt and dissipate them in golden vapours before they could touch the ground.

Yet, there was a chance that some of them—if the aim were true— might survive the fiery passage through the atmosphere and fall upon the surface of our planet where, perhaps, they would afterward be picked up by a prospector and lead him to believe that he had struck a new bonanza.

But until we returned to the earth it would be impossible for us to tell what had become of the golden gifts which we had launched into space for our mother planet.

Chapter 9

"All aboard!" was the signal, and the squadron having assembled under the lead of the flagship, we started again for Mars.

This time, as it proved, there was to be no further interruption, and when next we paused it was in the presence of the world inhabited by our enemies, and facing their frowning batteries.

We did not find it so easy to start from the asteroid as it had been to start from the earth; that is to say, we could not so readily generate a very high velocity.

In consequence of the comparatively small size of the asteroid, its electric influence was very much less than that of the earth, and notwithstanding the appliances which we possessed for intensifying the electrical effect, it was not possible to produce a sufficient repulsion to start us off for Mars with anything like the impulse which we had received from the earth on our original departure.

The utmost velocity that we could generate did not exceed three miles in a second, and to get this required our utmost efforts. In fact, it had not seemed possible that we should attain even so great a speed as that. It was far more than we could have expected, and even Mr. Edison was surprised, as well as greatly gratified, when he found that we were moving with the velocity that I have named.

We were still about 6,000,000 miles from Mars, so that, travelling three miles in a second, we should require at least twenty-three days to reach the immediate neighbourhood of the planet.

Meanwhile we had a plenty of occupation to make the time pass quickly. Our prisoner was transported along with us, and we now began our attempts to ascertain what his language was, and, if possible, to master it ourselves.

Before quitting the asteroid we had found that it was necessary for him to swallow one of his "air pills," as Prof. Moissan called them, at least three times in the course of every twenty-four hours. One of us supplied him regularly and I thought that I could detect evidences of a certain degree of gratitude in his expression. This was encouraging, because it gave additional promise of the possibility of our being able to communicate with him in some more effective way than by mere signs. But once inside the car, where we had a supply of air kept at the ordinary pressure experienced on the earth, he could breathe like the rest of us.

The best linguists in the expedition, as Mr. Edison had suggested, were now assembled in the flagship, where the prisoner was, and they set to work to devise some means of ascertaining the manner in which he was accustomed to express his thoughts.

We had not heard him speak, because until we carried him into our car there was no atmosphere capable of conveying any sounds he might attempt to utter.

It seemed a fair assumption that the language of the Martians would be scientific in its structure. We had so much evidence of the practical bent of their minds, and of the immense progress which they had made in the direction of the scientific conquest of nature, that it was not to be supposed their medium of communication with one another would be lacking in clearness, or would possess any of the puzzling and unnecessary ambiguities that characterized the languages spoken on the earth.

"We shall not find them making he's and she's of stones, sticks and other inanimate objects," said one of the American linguists. "They must certainly have gotten rid of all that nonsense long ago."

"Ah," said a French professor from the Sorbonne, one of the makers of the never-to-be-finished dictionary. "It will be like the language of my country. Transparent, similar to the diamond, and sparkling as is the fountain."

"I think," said a German enthusiast, "that it will be a universal language, the Volapuk of Mars, spoken by all the inhabitants of that planet."

"But all these speculations," broke in Mr. Edison, "do not help you much. Why not begin in a practical manner by finding out what the Martian calls himself, for instance."

This seemed a good suggestion, and accordingly several of the bystanders began an expressive pantomime, intended to indicate to the giant, who was following all their motions with his eyes, that they wished to know by what name he called himself. Pointing their fingers to their own breasts they repeated, one after the other, the word "man."

If our prisoner had been a stupid savage, of course any such attempt as this to make him understand would have been idle. But it must be remembered that we were dealing with a personage who had presumably inherited from hundreds of generations the results of a civilization, and an intellectual advance, measured by the constant progress of millions of years.

Accordingly we were not very much astonished, when, after a few repetitions of the experiment, the Martian—one of whose arms had been partially released from its bonds in order to give him a little freedom of motion—imitated the action of his interrogators by pressing his finger over his heart.

Then, opening his mouth, he gave utterance to a sound which shook the air of the car like the hoarse roar of a lion. He seemed himself surprised by the noise he made, for he had not been used to speak in so dense an atmosphere.

Our ears were deafened and confused, and we recoiled in astonishment, not to say, half in terror.

With an ugly grin distorting his face as if he enjoyed our discomfiture, the Martian repeated the motion and the sound.

"R-r-r-r-r-h!"

It was not articulate to our ears, and not to be represented by any combination of letters.

"Faith," exclaimed a Dublin University professor, "if that's what they call themselves, how shall we ever translate their names when we come to write the history of the conquest?"

"Whist, mon," replied a professor from the University of Aberdeen, "let us whip the gillravaging villains first, and then we can describe than by any intitulation that may suit our deesposition."

The beginning of our linguistic conquest was certainly not promising, at least if measured by our acquirement of words, but from another point of view it was very gratifying, inasmuch as it was plain that the Martian understood what we were trying to do, and was, for the present, at least, disposed to aid us.

These efforts to learn the language of Mars were renewed and repeated every few hours, all the experience, learning and genius of the squadron being concentrated upon the work, and the result was that in the course of a few days we had actually succeeded in learning a dozen or more of the Martian's words and were able to make him understand us when we pronounced them, as well as to understand him when our ears had become accustomed to the growling of his voice.

Finally, one day the prisoner, who seemed to be in an unusually cheerful frame of mind, indicated that he carried in his breast some object which he wished us to see.

With our assistance he pulled out a book!

Actually, it was a book, not very unlike the books which we have upon the earth, but printed, of course, in characters that were entirely strange and unknown to us. Yet these characters evidently gave expression to a highly intellectual language. All those who were standing by at the moment uttered a shout of wonder and of delight, and the cry of "A book! a book!" ran around the circle, and the good news was even promptly communicated to some of the neighbouring electric ships of the squadron. Several other learned men were summoned in haste from them to examine our new treasure.

The Martian, whose good nature had manifestly been growing day after day, watched our inspection of his book with evidences of great interest, not unmingled with amusement. Finally he beckoned the holder of the book to his side, and placing his broad finger upon one of the huge letters—if letters they were, for they more nearly resembled the characters employed by the Chinese printer—he uttered a sound which we, of course, took to be a word, but which was different from any we had yet heard. Then he pointed to one after another of us standing around.

"Ah," explained everybody, the truth being apparent, "that is the word by which the Martians designate us. They have a name, then, for the inhabitants of the earth."

"Or, perhaps, it is rather the name for the earth itself," said one.

But this could not, of course, be at once determined. Anyhow, the word, whatever its precise meaning might be, had now been added to our vocabulary, although as yet our organs of speech proved unable to reproduce it in a recognizable form.

This promising and unexpected discovery of the Martian's book lent added enthusiasm to those who were engaged in the work of trying to master the language of our prisoner, and the progress that they made in the course of the next few days was truly astonishing. If the prisoner had been unwilling to aid them, of course, it would have been impossible to proceed, but, fortunately for us, he seemed more and more to enter into the spirit of the undertaking, and actually to enjoy it himself. So bright and quick was his understanding that he was even able to indicate to us methods of mastering his language that would otherwise, probably, never have occurred to our minds.

In fact, in a very short time he had turned teacher and all these learned men, pressing around him with eager attention, had become his pupils.

I cannot undertake to say precisely how much of the Martian language had been acquired by the chief linguists of the expedition before the time when we arrived so near to Mars that it became necessary for most of us to abandon our studies in order to make ready for the more serious business which now confronted us.

But, at any rate, the acquisition was so considerable as to allow of the interchange of ordinary ideas with our prisoner, and there was no longer any doubt that he would be able to give us much information when we landed on his native planet.

At the end of twenty-three days as measured by terrestrial time, since our departure from the asteroid, we arrived in the sky of Mars.

For a long time the ruddy planet had been growing larger and more formidable, gradually turning from a huge star into a great red moon, and then expanding more and more until it began to shut out from sight the constellations behind it. The curious markings on its surface, which from the earth can only be dimly glimpsed with a powerful telescope, began to reveal themselves clearly to our naked eyes.

I have related how even before we had reached the asteroid, Mars began to present a most imposing appearance as we saw it with our telescopes. Now, however, that it was close at hand, the naked eye view of the planet was more wonderful than anything we had been able to see with telescopes when at a greater distance.

We were approaching the southern hemisphere of Mars in about latitude 45 degrees south. It was near the time of the vernal equinox in that hemisphere of the planet, and under the stimulating influence of the Spring sun, rising higher and higher every day, some such awakening of life and activity upon its surface as occurs on the earth under similar circumstances was evidently going on.

Around the South Pole were spread immense fields of snow and ice, gleaming with great brilliance. Cutting deep into the borders of these ice fields, we could see broad channels of open water, indicating the rapid breaking of the grip of the frost.

Almost directly beneath us was a broad oval region, light red in colour, to which terrestrial astronomers had given the name of Hellas. Toward the south, between Hellas and the borders of the polar ice, was a great belt of darkness that astronomers had always been inclined to regard as a sea. Looking toward the north, we could perceive the immense red expanses of the continents of Mars, with the long curved line of the Syrtis Major, or "The Hour Glass Sea," sweeping through the midst of them toward the north until it disappeared under the horizon.

Crossing and re-crossing the red continents, in every direction, were the canals of Schiaparelli.

Plentifully sprinkled over the surface we could see brilliant points, some of dazzling brightness, outshining the daylight. There was also an astonishing variety in the colours of the broad expanses beneath us. Activity, vivacity and beauty, such as we were utterly unprepared to behold, expressed their presence on all sides.

The excitement on the flagship and among the other members of the squadron was immense. It was certainly a thrilling scene. Here, right under our feet, lay the world we had come to do battle with. Its appearances, while recalling in some of their broader aspects those which it had presented when viewed from our observatories, were far more strange, complex and wonderful than any astronomer had ever dreamed of. Suppose all of our anticipations about Mars should prove to have been wrong, after all?

There could be no longer any question that it was a world which, if not absolutely teeming with inhabitants, like a gigantic ant-hill, at any rate bore on every side the marks of their presence and of their incredible undertakings and achievements.

Here and there clouds of smoke arose and spread slowly through the atmosphere beneath us. Floating higher above the surface of the planet were clouds of vapour, assuming the familiar forms of stratus and cumulus with which we were acquainted upon the earth.

These clouds, however, seemed upon the whole to be much less dense than those to which we were accustomed at home. They had, too, a peculiar iridescent beauty as if there was something in their composition or their texture which split up the chromatic elements of the sunlight and thus produced internal rainbow effects that caused some of the heavier cloud masses to resemble immense collections of opals, alive with the play of ever-changing colours and magically suspended above the planet.

As we continued to study the phenomena that was gradually unfolded beneath us we thought that we could detect in many places evidences of the existence of strong fortifications. The planet of war appeared to be prepared for the attacks of enemies. Since, as our own experience had shown, it sometimes waged war with distant planets, it was but natural that it should be found prepared to resist foes who might be disposed to revenge themselves for injuries suffered at its hands.

As had been expected, our prisoner now proved to be of very great assistance to us. Apparently he took a certain pride in exhibiting to strangers from a distant world the beauties and wonders of his own planet.

We could not understand by any means all that he said, but we could readily comprehend, from his gestures, and from the manner in which his features lighted up at the recognition of familiar scenes and objects, what his sentiments in regard to them were, and, in a general way, what part they played in the life of the planet.

He confirmed our opinion that certain of the works which we saw beneath us were fortifications, intended for the protection of the planet against invaders from outer space. A cunning and almost diabolical look came into his eyes as he pointed to one of these strongholds.

His confidence and his mocking looks were not reassuring to us. He knew what his planet was capable of, and we did not. He had seen, on the asteroid, the extent of our power, and while its display served to intimidate him there, yet now that he and we together were facing the world of his birth, his fear had evidently fallen from him, and he had the manner of one who feels that the shield of an all-powerful protector had been extended over him.

But it could not be long now before we should ascertain, by the irrevocable test of actual experience, whether the Martians possessed the power to annihilate us or not.

How shall I describe our feelings as we gazed at the scene spread beneath us? They were not quite the same as those of the discoverer of new lands upon the earth. This was a whole new world that we had discovered, and it was filled, as we could see, with inhabitants.

But that was not all. We had not come with peaceful intentions.

We were to make war on this new world.

Deducting our losses we had not more than 940 men left. With these we were to undertake the conquest of a world containing we could not say how many millions!

Our enemies, instead of being below us in the scale of intelligence were, we had every reason to believe, greatly our superiors. They had proved that they possessed a command over the powers of nature such as we, up to the time when Mr. Edison made his inventions, had not even dreamed that it was possible for us to obtain.

It was true that at present we appeared to have the advantage, both in our electrical ships and in our means of offence. The disintegrator was at least as powerful an engine of destruction as any that the Martians had yet shown that they possessed. It did not seem that in that respect they could possibly excel us.

During the brief war with the Martians upon the earth it had been gunpowder against a mysterious force as much stronger than gunpowder as the latter was superior to the bows and arrows that preceded it.

There had been no comparison whatever between the offensive means employed by the two parties in the struggle on the earth.

But the genius of one man had suddenly put us on the level of our enemies in regard to fighting capacity.

Then, too, our electrical ships were far more effective for their purpose than the projectile cars used by the Martians. In fact, the principle upon which they were based was, at bottom, so simple that it seemed astonishing the Martians had not hit upon it.

Mr. Edison himself was never tired of saying in reference to this matter:

"I cannot understand why the Martians did not invent these things. They have given ample proof that they understand electricity better than we do. Why should they have resorted to the comparatively awkward and bungling means of getting from one planet to another that they have employed when they might have ridden through the solar system in such conveyances as ours with perfect ease?"

"And besides," Mr. Edison would add, "I cannot understand why they did not employ the principle of harmonic vibrations in the construction of their engines of war. The lightning-like strokes that they deal from their machines are no doubt equally powerful, but I think the range of destruction covered by the disintegrators is greater."

However, these questions must remain open until we could effect a landing on Mars, and learn something of the condition of things there.

The thing that gave us the most uneasiness was the fact that we did not yet know what powers the Martians might have in reserve. It was but natural to suppose that here, on their own ground, they would possess means of defence even more effective than the offensive engines they had employed in attacking enemies so many millions of miles from home.

It was important that we should waste no time, and it was equally important that we should select the most vulnerable point for attack. It was self-evident, therefore, that our first duty would be to reconnoitre the surface of the planet and determine its weakest point of defence.

At first Mr. Edison contemplated sending the various ships in different directions around the planet in order that the work of exploration might be quickly accomplished. But upon second thought it seemed wiser to keep the squadron together, thus diminishing the chance of disaster.

Besides, the commander wished to see with his own eyes the exact situation of the various parts of the planet, where it might appear advisable for us to begin our assault.

Thus far we had remained suspended at so great a height above the planet that we had hardly entered into the perceptible limits of its atmosphere and there was no evidence that we had been seen by the inhabitants of Mars; but before starting on our voyage of exploration it was determined to drop down closer to the surface in order that we might the more certainly identify the localities over which we passed.

When we had arrived within a distance of three miles from the surface of Mars we suddenly perceived approaching from the eastward a large airship which was navigating the Martian atmosphere at a height of perhaps half a mile above the ground.

This airship moved rapidly on to a point nearly beneath us, when it suddenly paused, reversed its course, and evidently made signals, the purpose of which was not at first evident to us.

But in a short time their meaning became perfectly plain, when we found ourselves surrounded by at least twenty similar aerostats approaching swiftly from different sides.

It was a great mystery to us where so many airships had been concealed previous to their sudden appearance in answer to the signals.

But the mystery was quickly solved when we saw detaching itself from the surface of the planet beneath us, where, while it remained immovable, its colour had blended with that of the soil so as to render it invisible, another of the mysterious ships.

Then our startled eyes beheld on all sides these formidable-looking enemies rising from the ground beneath us like so many gigantic insects, disturbed by a sudden alarm.

In a short time the atmosphere a mile or two below us, and to a distance of perhaps twenty miles around in every direction, was alive with airships of various sizes, and some of most extraordinary forms, exchanging signals, rushing to and fro, but all finally concentrating beneath the place where our squadron was suspended.

We had poked the hornet's nest with a vengeance!

As yet there had been no sting, but we might quickly expect to feel it if we did not get out of range.

Quickly instructions were flashed throughout the squadron to instantly reverse polarities and rise as swiftly as possible to a great height.

It was evident that this manoeuvre would save us from danger if it were quickly effected, because the airships of the Martians were simply airships and nothing more. They could only float in the atmosphere, and had no means of rising above it, or of navigating empty space.

To have turned our disintegrators upon them, and to have begun a battle then and there, would have been folly.

They overwhelmingly outnumbered us, the majority of them were yet at a considerable distance and we could not have done battle, even with our entire squadron acting together, with more than one-quarter of them simultaneously. In the meantime the others would have surrounded and might have destroyed us. We must first get some idea of the planet's means of defence before we ventured to assail it.

Having risen rapidly to a height of twenty-five or thirty miles, so that we could feel confident that our ships had vanished at least from the naked eye view of our enemies beneath, a brief consultation was held.

It was determined to adhere to our original programme and to circumnavigate Mars in every direction before proceeding to open the war.

The overwhelming forces shown by the enemy had intimidated even some of the most courageous of our men, but still it was universally felt that it would not do to retreat without a blow struck.

The more we saw of the power of the Martians, the more we became convinced that there would be no hope for the earth, if these enemies ever again effected a landing upon its surface, the more especially since our squadron contained nearly all of the earth's force that would be effective in such a contest.

With Mr. Edison and the other men of science away, they would not be able at home to construct such engines as we possessed, or to manage them even if they were constructed.

Our planet had staked everything on a single throw.

These considerations again steeled our hearts, and made us bear up as bravely as possible in the face of the terrible odds that confronted us.

Turning the noses of our electrical ships toward the west, we began our circumnavigation.

Chapter 10

At first we rose to a still greater height, in order more effectually to escape the watchful eyes of our enemies, and then, after having moved rapidly several hundred miles toward the west, we dropped down again within easy eyeshot of the surface of the planet, and commenced our inspection.

When we originally reached Mars, as I have related, it was at a point in its southern hemisphere, in latitude 45 degrees south, and longitude 75 degrees east, that we first closely approached its surface. Underneath us was the land called "Hellas," and it was over this land of Hellas that the Martian air fleet had suddenly made its appearance.

Our westward motion, while at a great height above the planet, had brought us over another oval-shaped land called "Noachia," surrounded by the dark ocean, the "Mare Erytraeum." Now approaching nearer the surface our course was changed so as to carry us toward the equator of Mars.

We passed over the curious, half-drowned continent known to terrestrial astronomers as the Region of Deucalion, then across another sea, or gulf, until we found ourselves floating, at a height of perhaps five miles, above a great continental land, at least three thousand miles broad from east to west, and which I immediately recognized as that to which astronomers had given the various names of "Aeria," "Edom," "Arabia," and "Eden."

Here the spectacle became of breathless interest.

"Wonderful! Wonderful!"

"Who could have believed it!"

Such were the exclamations heard on all sides.

When at first we were suspended above Hellas, looking toward the north, the northeast and the northwest, we had seen at a distance some of these great red regions, and had perceived the curious network of canals by which they were intersected. But that was a far-off and imperfect view.

Now, when we were near at hand and straight above one of these singular lands, the magnificence of the panorama surpassed belief.

From the earth about a dozen of the principal canals crossing the continent beneath us had been perceived, but we saw hundreds, nay, thousands of them!

It was a double system, intended both for irrigation and for protection, and far more marvellous in its completeness than the boldest speculative minds among our astronomers had ever dared to imagine.

"Ha! that's what I always said," exclaimed a veteran from one of our great observatories. "Mars is red because its soil and vegetation are red."

And certainly appearances indicated that he was right.

There were no green trees, and there was no green grass. Both were red, not of a uniform red tint, but presenting an immense variety of shades which produced a most brilliant effect, fairly dazzling our eyes.

But what trees! And what grass! And what flowers!

Our telescopes showed that even the smaller trees must be 200 or 300 feet in height, and there were forests of giants, whose average height was evidently at least 1,000 feet.

"That's all right," exclaimed the enthusiast I have just quoted. "I knew it would be so. The trees are big, for the same reason that the men are, because the planet is small, and they can grow big without becoming too heavy to stand."

Flashing in the sun on all sides were the roofs of metallic buildings, which were evidently the only kind of edifices that Mars possessed. At any rate, if stone or wood were employed in their construction both were completely covered with metallic plates.

This added immensely to the warlike aspect of the planet. For warlike it was. Everywhere we recognized fortified stations, glittering with an array of the polished knobs of the lightning machines, such as we had seen in the land of Hellas.

From the land of Edom, directly over the equator of the planet, we turned our faces westward, and, skirting the Mare Erytraeum, arrived above the place where the broad canal known as the Indus empties into the sea.

Before us, and stretching away toward the northwest, now lay the continent of Chryse, a vast red land, oval in outline, and surrounded and crossed by innumerable canals. Chryse was not less than 1,600 miles across, and it, too, evidently swarmed with giant inhabitants.

But the shadow of night lay upon the greater portion of the land of Chryse. In our rapid motion westward we had out-stripped the sun and had now arrived at a point where day and night met upon the surface of the planet beneath us.

Behind all was brilliant with sunshine, but before us the face of Mars gradually disappeared in the deepening gloom. Through the darkness, far away, we could behold magnificent beams of electric light darting across the curtain of night, and evidently serving to illuminate towns and cities that lay beneath.

We pushed on into the night for two or three hundred miles over that part of the continent of Chryse whose inhabitants were doubtless enjoying the deep sleep that accompanies the dark hours immediately preceding the dawn. Still everywhere splendid clusters of light lay like fallen constellations upon the ground, indicating the sites of great towns, which, like those of the earth, never sleep.

But this scene, although weird and beautiful, could give us little of the kind of information we were in search of.

Accordingly it was resolved to turn back eastward until we had arrived in the twilight space separating day and night, and then hover over the planet at that point, allowing it to turn beneath us so that, as we looked down, we should see in succession the entire circuit of the globe of Mars while it rolled under our eyes.

The rotation of Mars on its axis is performed in a period very little longer than that of the earth's rotation, so that the length of the day and night in the world of Mars is only some forty minutes longer than their length upon the earth.

In thus remaining suspended over the planet, on the line of daybreak, so to speak, we believed that we should be peculiarly safe from detection by the eyes of the inhabitants. Even astronomers are not likely to be wide awake just at the peep of dawn. Almost all of the inhabitants, we confidently believed, would still be sound asleep upon that part of the planet passing directly beneath us, and those who were awake would not be likely to watch for unexpected appearances in the sky.

Besides, our height was so great that notwithstanding the numbers of the squadron, we could not easily be seen from the surface of the planet, and if seen at all we might be mistaken for high-flying birds.

Here we remained then through the entire course of twenty-four hours and saw in succession as they passed from night into day beneath our feet the land of Chryse, the great continent of Tharsis, the curious region of intersecting canals which puzzled astronomers on the earth had named the "Gordian Knot," the continental lands of Memnonia, Amazonia and Aeolia, the mysterious centre where hundreds of vast canals came together from every direction, called the Trivium Charontis; the vast circle of Elysium, a thousand miles across, and completely surrounded by a broad green canal; the continent of Libya, which, as I remembered, had been half covered by a tremendous inundation whose effects were visible from the earth in the year 1889, and finally the long, dark sea of the Syrtis Major, lying directly south of the land of Hellas.

The excitement and interest which we all experienced were so great that not one of us took a wink of sleep during the entire twenty-four hours of our marvellous watch.

There are one or two things of special interest amid the multitude of wonderful observations that we made which I must mention here on account of their connection with the important events that followed soon after.

Just west of the land of Chryse we saw the smaller land of Ophir, in the midst of which is a singular spot called the Juventae Fons, and this Fountain of Youth, as our astronomers, by a sort of prophetic inspiration, had named it, proved later to be one of the most incredible marvels on the planet Mars.

Further to the west, and north from the great continent of Tharsis, we beheld the immense oval-shaped land of Thaumasia containing in its centre the celebrated "Lake of the Sun," a circular body of water not less than 500 miles in diameter, with dozens of great canals running away from it like the spokes of a wheel in every direction, thus connecting it with the ocean which surrounds it on the south and east, and with the still larger canals that encircle it toward the north and west.

This Lake of the Sun came to play a great part in our subsequent adventures. It was evident to us from the beginning that it was the chief centre of population on the planet. It lies in latitude 25 degrees South and longitude about 90 degrees west.

Having completed the circuit of the Martian globe, we were moved by the same feeling which every discoverer of new lands experiences, and immediately returned to our original place above the land of Hellas, because since that was the first part of Mars that we had seen, we felt a greater degree of familiarity with it than with any other portion of the planet, and there, in a certain sense, we felt "at home."

But, as it proved, our enemies were on the watch for us there. We had almost forgotten them, so absorbed were we by the great spectacles that had been unrolling themselves beneath our feet.

We ought, of course, to have been a little more cautious in approaching the place where they first caught sight of us, since we might have known that they would remain on the watch near that spot.

But at any rate they had seen us, and it was now too late to think of taking them again by surprise.

They on their part had a surprise in store for us, which was greater than any we had yet experienced.

We saw their ships assembling once more far down in the atmosphere beneath us, and we thought we could detect evidences of something unusual going on upon the surface of the planet.

Suddenly from the ships, and from various points on the ground beneath, there rose high in the air, and carried by invisible currents in every direction, immense volumes of black smoke, or vapour, which blotted out of sight everything below them!

South, north, west and east, the curtain of blackness rapidly spread, until the whole face of the planet as far as our eyes could reach, and the airships thronging under us, were all concealed from sight!

Mars had played the game of the cuttlefish, which, when pursued by its enemies, darkens the water behind it by a sudden outgush of inky fluid, and thus escapes the eye of its foe.

The eyes of man had never beheld such a spectacle!

Where a few minutes before the sunny face of a beautiful and populous planet had been shining beneath us, there was now to be seen nothing but black, billowing clouds, swelling up everywhere like the mouse-coloured smoke that pours from a great transatlantic liner when fresh coal has just been heaped upon her fires.

In some places the smoke spouted upward in huge jets to the height of several miles; elsewhere it eddied in vast whirlpools of inky blackness.

Not a glimpse of the hidden world beneath was anywhere to be seen.

Mars had put on its war mask, and fearful indeed was the aspect of it!

After the first pause of surprise the squadron quickly backed away into the sky, rising rapidly, because, from one of the swirling eddies beneath us the smoke began suddenly to pile itself up in an enormous aerial mountain, whose peaks shot higher and higher, with apparently increasing velocity, until they seemed about to engulf us with their tumbling ebon masses.

Unaware what the nature of this mysterious smoke might be, and fearing it was something more than a shield for the planet, and might be destructive to life, we fled before it, as before the onward sweep of a pestilence.

Directly underneath the flagship, one of the aspiring smoke peaks grew with most portentous swiftness, and, notwithstanding all our efforts, in a little while it had enveloped us.

Several of us were standing on the deck of the electrical ship. We were almost stifled by the smoke, and were compelled to take refuge within the car, where, until the electric lights had been turned on, darkness so black that it oppressed the strained eyeballs prevailed.

But in this brief experience, terrifying though it was, we had learned one thing. The smoke would kill by strangulation, but evidently there was nothing especially poisonous in its nature. This fact might be of use to us in our subsequent proceedings.

"This spoils our plans," said the commander. "There is no use of remaining here for the present; let us see how far this thing extends."

At first we rose straight away to a height of 200 or 300 miles, thus passing entirely beyond the sensible limits of the atmosphere, and far above the highest point that the smoke could reach.

From this commanding point of view our line of sight extended to an immense distance over the surface of Mars in all directions. Everywhere the same appearance; the whole planet was evidently covered with the smoke.

A complete telegraphic system evidently connected all the strategic points upon Mars, so that, at a signal from the central station, the wonderful curtain could be instantaneously drawn over the entire face of the planet.

In order to make certain that no part of Mars remained uncovered, we dropped down again nearer to the upper level of the smoke clouds, and then completely circumnavigated the planet. It was thought possible that on the night side no smoke would be found and that it would be practicable for us to make a descent there.

But when we had arrived on that side of Mars which was turned away from the sun, we no longer saw beneath us, as we had done on our previous visit to the night hemisphere of the planet, brilliant groups and clusters of electric lights beneath us. All was dark.

In fact, so completely did the great shell of smoke conceal the planet that the place occupied by the latter seemed to be simply a vast black hole in the firmament.

The sun was hidden behind it, and so dense was the smoke that even the solar rays were unable to penetrate it, and consequently there was no atmospheric halo visible around the concealed planet.

All the sky around was filled with stars, but their countless host suddenly disappeared when our eyes turned in the direction of Mars. The great black globe blotted them out without being visible itself.

"Apparently we can do nothing here," said Mr. Edison. "Let us return to the daylight side."

When we had arrived near the point where we had been when the wonderful phenomenon first made its appearance, we paused, and then, at the suggestion of one of the chemists, dropped close to the surface of the smoke curtain which had now settled down into comparative quiescence, in order that we might examine it a little more critically.

The flagship was driven into the smoke cloud so deeply that for a minute we were again enveloped in night. A quantity of the smoke was entrapped in a glass jar.

Rising again into the sunlight, the chemists began an examination of the constitution of the smoke. They were unable to determine its precise character, but they found that its density was astonishingly slight. This accounted for the rapidity with which it had risen, and the great height which it had attained in the comparatively light atmosphere of Mars.

"It is evident," said one of the chemists, "that this smoke does not extend down to the surface of the planet. From what the astronomers say as to the density of the air on Mars, it is probable that a clear space of at least a mile in height exists between the surface of Mars and the lower limit of the smoke curtain. Just how deep the latter is we can only determine by experiment, but it would not be surprising if the thickness of this great blanket which Mars has thrown around itself should prove to be a quarter or half a mile."

"Anyhow," said one of the United States army officers, "they have dodged out of sight, and I don't see why we should not dodge in and get at them. If there is clear air under the smoke, as you think, why couldn't the ships dart down through the curtain and come to a close tackle with the Martians?"

"It would not do at all," said the commander. "We might simply run ourselves into an ambush. No; we must stay outside, and if possible fight them from here."

"They can't keep this thing up forever," said the officer. "Perhaps the smoke will clear off after a while, and then we will have a chance."

"Not much hope of that, I am afraid," said the chemist who had originally spoken. "This smoke could remain floating in the atmosphere for weeks, and the only wonder to me is how they ever expect to get rid of it, when they think their enemies have gone and they want some sunshine again."

"All that is mere speculation," said Mr. Edison; "let us get at something practical. We must do one of two things: either attack them shielded as they are, or wait until the smoke has cleared away. The only other alternative, that of plunging blindly down through the curtain, is at present not to be thought of."

"I am afraid we couldn't stand a very long siege ourselves," suddenly remarked the chief commissary of the expedition, who was one of the members of the flagship's company.

"What do you mean by that?" asked Mr. Edison sharply, turning to him.

"Well, sir, you see," said the commissary, stammering, "our provisions wouldn't hold out."

"Wouldn't hold out?" exclaimed Mr. Edison, in astonishment, "why, we have compressed and prepared provisions enough to last this squadron for three years."

"We had, sir, when we left the earth," said the commissary, in apparent distress, "but I am sorry to say that something has happened."

"Something has happened! Explain yourself!"

"I don't know what it is, but on inspecting some of the compressed stores, a short time ago, I found that a large number of them were destroyed, whether through leakage of air, or what, I am unable to say. I sent to inquire as to the condition of the stores in the other ships in the squadron and I found that a similar condition of things prevailed there."

"The fact is," continued the commissary, "we have only provisions enough, in proper condition, for about ten days' consumption."

"After that we shall have to forage on the country, then," said the army officer.

"Why did you not report this before?" demanded Mr. Edison.

"Because, sir," was the reply, "the discovery was not made until after we arrived close to Mars, and since then there has been so much excitement that I have hardly had time to make an investigation and find out what the precise condition of affairs is; besides, I thought we should land upon the planet and then we would be able to renew our supplies."

I closely watched Mr. Edison's expression in order to see how this most alarming news would affect him. Although he fully comprehended its fearful significance, he did not lose his self-command.

"Well, well," he said, "then it will become necessary for us to act quickly. Evidently we cannot wait for the smoke to clear off, even if there were any hope of its clearing. We must get down on Mars now, having conquered it first if possible, but anyway we must get down there, in order to avoid starvation."

"It is very lucky," he continued, "that we have ten days' supply left. A great deal can be done in ten days."

A few hours after this the commander called me aside, and said:

"I have thought it all out. I am going to reconstruct some of our disintegrators, so as to increase their range and their power. Then I am going to have some of the astronomers of the expedition locate for me the most vulnerable points upon the planet, where the population is densest and a hard blow would have the most effect, and I am going to pound away at them, through the smoke, and see whether we cannot draw them out of their shell."

With his expert assistants Mr. Edison set to work at once to transform a number of the disintegrators into still more formidable engines of the same description. One of these new weapons having been distributed to each of the members of the squadron, the next problem was to decide where to strike.

When we first examined the surface of the planet it will be remembered that we had regarded the Lake of the Sun and its environs as being the very focus of the planet. While it might also be a strong point of defence, yet an effective blow struck there would go to the enemy's heart and be more likely to bring the Martians promptly to terms than anything else.

The first thing, then, was to locate the Lake of the Sun on the smoke-hidden surface of the planet beneath us. This was a problem that the astronomers could readily solve.

Fortunately, in the flagship itself there was one of the star-gazing gentlemen who had made a specialty of the study of Mars. That planet, as I have already explained, was now in opposition to the earth. The astronomer had records in his pocket which enabled him, by a brief calculation, to say just when the Lake of the Sun would be on the meridian of Mars as seen from the earth. Our chronometers still kept terrestrial time; we knew the exact number of days and hours that had elapsed since we had departed, and so it was possible by placing ourselves in a line between the earth and Mars to be practically in the situation of an astronomer in his observatory at home.

Then it was only necessary to wait for the hour when the Lake of the Sun would be upon the meridian of Mars in order to be certain what the true direction of the latter from the flagship was.

Having thus located the heart of our foe behind its shield of darkness, we prepared to strike.

"I have ascertained," said Mr. Edison, "the vibration period of the smoke, so that it will be easy for us to shatter it into invisible atoms. You will see that every stroke of the disintegrators will open a hole through the black curtain. If their field of destruction could be made wide enough, we might in that manner clear away the entire covering of smoke, but all that we shall really be able to do will be to puncture it with holes, which will, perhaps, enable us to catch glimpses of the surface beneath. In that manner we may be able more effectually to concentrate our fire upon the most vulnerable points."

Everything being prepared, and the entire squadron having assembled to watch the effect of the opening blow and be ready to follow it up, Mr. Edison himself poised one of the new disintegrators, which was too large to be carried in the hand, and, following the direction indicated by the calculations of the astronomers, launched the vibratory discharge into the ocean of blackness beneath.

Instantly there opened beneath us a huge well-shaped hole, from which the black clouds rolled violently back in every direction.

Through this opening we saw the gleam of brilliant lights beneath. We had made a hit.

"It is the Lake of the Sun!" shouted the astronomer who furnished the calculation by means of which its position had been discovered.

And, indeed, it was the Lake of the Sun. While the opening in the clouds made by the discharge was not wide, yet it sufficed to give us a view of a portion of the curving shore of the lake, which was ablaze with electric lights.

Whether our shot had done any damage, beyond making the circular opening in the cloud curtain, we could not tell, for almost immediately the surrounding black smoke masses billowed in to fill up the hole.

But in the brief glimpse we had caught sight of two or three large air ships hovering in space above that part of the Lake of the Sun and its bordering city which we had beheld. It seemed to me in the brief glance I had that one ship had been touched by the discharge and was wandering in an erratic manner. But the clouds closed in so rapidly that I not be certain.

Anyhow, we had demonstrated one thing, and that was that we could penetrate the cloud shield and reach the Martians in their hiding place.

It had been prearranged that the first discharge from the flagship should be a signal for the concentration of the fire of all the other ships upon the same spot.

A little hesitation, however, occurred, and a half a minute had elapsed before the disintegrators from the other members of the squadron were got into play.

Then, suddenly we saw an immense commotion in the cloud beneath us. It seemed to be beaten and hurled in every direction and punctured like a sieve with nearly a hundred great circular holes. Through these gaps we could see clearly a large region of the planet's surface, with many airships floating above it, and the blaze of innumerable electric lights illuminating it. The Martians had created an artificial day under the curtain.

This time there was no question that the blow had been effective. Four or five of the airships, partially destroyed, tumbled headlong toward the ground, while even from our great distance there was unmistakable evidence that fearful execution had been done among the crowded structures along the shore of the Lake.

As each of our ships possessed but one of the new disintegrators, and since a minute or so was required to adjust them for a fresh discharge, we remained for a little while inactive after delivering the blow. Meanwhile the cloud curtain, though rent to shreds by the concentrated discharge of the disintegrators, quickly became a uniform black sheet again, hiding everything.

We had just had time to congratulate ourselves on the successful opening of our bombardment, and the disintegrator of the flagship was poised for another discharge, when suddenly out of the black expanse beneath, quivered immense electric beams, clear cut and straight as bars of steel, but dazzling our eyes with unendurable brilliance.

It was the reply of the Martians to our attack.

Three or four of the electrical ships were seriously damaged, and one, close beside the flagship, changed colour, withered and collapsed, with the same sickening phenomena that had made our hearts shudder when the first disaster of this kind occurred during our brief battle over the asteroid.

Another score of our comrades were gone, and yet we had hardly begun the fight.

Glancing at the other ships, which had been injured, I saw that the damage to them was not so serious, although they were evidently hors de combat for the present.

Our fighting blood was now boiling and we did not stop long to count our losses.

"Into the smoke!" was the signal, and the ninety and more electric ships which still remained in condition for action immediately shot downward.

101

Chapter 11

It was a wild plunge. We kept off the decks while rushing through the blinding smoke, but the instant we emerged below, where we found ourselves still a mile above the ground, we were out again, ready to strike.

I have simply a confused recollection of flashing lights beneath, and a great, dark arch of clouds above, out of which our ships seemed dropping on all sides, and then the fray burst upon and around us, and no man could see or notice anything except by half-comprehended glances.

Almost in an instant, it seemed, a swarm of airships surrounded us, while from what, for lack of a more descriptive name, I shall call the forts about the Lake of the Sun, leaped tongues of electric fire, before which some of our ships were driven like bits of flaming paper in a high wind, gleaming for a moment, then curling up and gone forever!

It was an awful sight; but the battle fever was raging in us, and we, on our part, were not idle.

Every man carried a disintegrator, and these hand instruments, together with those of heavier calibre on the ships poured their resistless vibrations in every direction through the quivering air.

The airships of the Martians were destroyed by the score, but yet they flocked upon us thicker and faster.

We dropped lower and our blows fell upon the forts, and upon the widespread city bordering the Lake of the Sun. We almost entirely silenced the fire of one of the forts; but there were forty more in full action within reach of our eyes!

Some of the metallic buildings were partly unroofed by the disintegrators and some had their walls riddled and fell with thundering crashes, whose sound rose to our ears above the hellish din of battle. I caught glimpses of giant forms struggling in the ruins and rushing wildly through the streets, but there was no time to see anything clearly.

Our flagship seemed charmed. A crowd of airships hung upon it like a swarm of angry bees, and, at times, one could not see for the lightning strokes—yet we escaped destruction, while ourselves dealing death on every hand.

It was a glorious fight, but it was not war; no, it was not war. We really had no more chance of ultimate success amid that multitude of enemies than a prisoner running the gauntlet in a crowd of savages has of escape.

A conviction of the hopelessness of the contest finally forced itself upon our minds, and the shattered squadron, which had kept well together amid the storm of death, was signalled to retreat.

Shaking off their pursuers, as a hunted bear shakes off the dogs, sixty of the electrical ships rose up through the clouds where more than ninety had gone down!

Madly we rushed upward through the vast curtain and continued our flight to a great elevation, far beyond the reach of the awful artillery of the enemy.

Looking back it seemed the very mouth of hell that we had escaped from.

The Martians did not for an instant cease their fire, even when we were far beyond their reach. With furious persistence they blazed away through the cloud curtains, and the vivid spikes of lightning shuddered so swiftly on one another's track that they were like a flaming halo of electric lances around the frowning helmet of the War Planet.

But after a while they stopped their terrific sparring, and once more the immense globe assumed the appearance of a vast ball of black smoke, still wildly agitated by the recent disturbance, but exhibiting no opening through which we could discern what was going on beneath.

Evidently the Martians believed they had finished us.

At no time since the beginning of our adventure had it appeared to me quite so hopeless, reckless and mad as it seemed at present.

We had suffered fearful losses, and yet what had we accomplished? We had won two fights on the asteroid, it is true, but then we had overwhelming numbers on our side.

Now we were facing millions on their own ground, and our very first assault had resulted in a disastrous repulse, with the loss of at least thirty electric ships and 600 men!

Evidently we could not endure this sort of thing. We must find some other means of assailing Mars or else give up the attempt.

But the latter was not to be thought of. It was no mere question of self-pride, however, and no consideration of the tremendous interests at stake, which would compel us to continue our apparently vain attempt.

Our provisions could last only a few days longer. The supply would not carry us one-quarter of the way back to the earth, and we must therefore remain here and literally conquer or die.

In this extremity a consultation of the principal officers was called upon the deck of the flagship.

Here the suggestion was made that we should attempt to effect by strategy what we had failed to do by force.

An old army officer who had served in many wars against the cunning Indians of the West, Colonel Alonzo Jefferson Smith, was the author of this suggestion.

"Let us circumvent them," he said. "We can do it in this way. The chances are that all of the available fighting force of the planet Mars is now concentrated on this side and in the neighbourhood of the Lake of the Sun."

"Possibly, by some kind of X-ray business, they can only see us dimly through the clouds, and if we get a little further away they will not be able to see us at all."

"Now, I suggest that a certain number of the electrical ships be withdrawn from the squadron to a great distance, while the remainder stay here; or, better still, approach to a point just beyond the reach of those streaks of lightning, and begin a bombardment of the clouds without paying any attention to whether the strokes reach through the clouds and do any damage or not."

"This will induce the Martians to believe that we are determined to press our attack at this point."

"In the meantime, while these ships are raising a hullabaloo on this side of the planet, and drawing their fire, as much as possible, without running into any actual danger, let the others which have been selected for the purpose, sail rapidly around to the other side of Mars and take them in the rear."

It was not perfectly clear what Colonel Smith intended to do after the landing had been effected in the rear of the Martians, but still there seemed a good deal to be said for his suggestion, and it would, at any rate, if carried out, enable us to learn something about the condition of things on the planet, and perhaps furnish us with a hint as to how we could best proceed in the further prosecution of the siege.

Accordingly it was resolved that about twenty ships should be told off for this movement, and Colonel Smith himself was placed in command.

At my desire I accompanied the new commander in his flagship.

Rising to a considerable elevation in order that there might be no risk of being seen, we began our flank movement while the remaining ships, in accordance with the understanding, dropped nearer the curtain of cloud and commenced a bombardment with the disintegrators, which caused a tremendous commotion in the clouds, opening vast gaps in them, and occasionally revealing a glimpse of the electric lights on the planet, although it was evident that the vibratory currents did not reach the ground. The Martians immediately replied to this renewed attack, and again the cloud-covered globe bristled with lightning, which flashed so fiercely out of the blackness below that the stoutest hearts among us quailed, although we were situated well beyond the danger.

But this sublime spectacle rapidly vanished from our eyes when, having attained a proper elevation, we began our course toward the opposite hemisphere of the planet.

We guided our flight by the stars, and from our knowledge of the rotation period of Mars, and the position which the principal points on its surface must occupy at certain hours, we were able to tell what part of the planet lay beneath us.

Having completed our semi-circuit, we found ourselves on the night side of Mars, and determined to lose no time in executing our coup. But it was deemed best that an exploration should first be made by a single electrical ship, and Colonel Smith naturally wished to undertake the adventure with his own vessel.

We dropped rapidly through the black cloud curtain, which proved to be at least half a mile in thickness, and then suddenly emerged, as if suspended at the apex of an enormous dome, arching above the surface of the planet a mile beneath us, which sparkled on all sides with innumerable lights.

These lights were so numerous and so brilliant as to produce a faint imitation of daylight, even at our immense height above the ground, and the dome of cloud out of which we had emerged assumed a soft fawn colour that produced an indescribably beautiful effect.

For a moment we recoiled from our undertaking, and arrested the motion of the electric ship.

But on closely examining the surface beneath us we found that there was a broad region, where comparatively few bright lights were to be seen. From my knowledge of the geography of Mars I knew that this was a part of the Land of Ausonia, situated a few hundred miles northeast of Hellas, where we had first seen the planet.

Evidently it was not so thickly populated as some of the other parts of Mars, and its comparative darkness was an attraction to us. We determined to approach within a few hundred feet of the ground with the electric ship, and then, in case no enemies appeared, to visit the soil itself.

"Perhaps we shall see or hear something that will be of use to us," said Colonel Smith, "and for the purposes of this first reconnaissance it is better that we should be few in number. The other ships will await our return, and at any rate we shall not be gone long."

As our car approached the ground we found ourselves near the tops of some lofty trees.

"This will do," said Colonel Smith, to the electrical steersman. "Stay right here."

He and I then lowered ourselves into the branches of the trees, each carrying a small disintegrator, and cautiously clambered down to the ground.

We believed we were the first of the descendants of Adam to set foot on the planet of Mars.

At first we suffered somewhat from the effects of the rare atmosphere. It was so lacking in density that it resembled the air on the summits of the loftiest terrestrial mountains.

Having reached the foot of the tree in safety, we lay down for a moment on the ground to recover ourselves and to become accustomed to our new surroundings.

A thrill, born half of wonder, half of incredulity, ran through me at the touch of the soil of Mars. Here was I, actually on that planet, which had seemed so far away, so inaccessible, and so full of mysteries when viewed from the earth. And yet, surrounding me, were things— gigantic, it is true—but still resembling and recalling the familiar sights of my own world.

After a little while our lungs became accustomed to the rarity of the atmosphere and we experienced a certain stimulation in breathing.

We then got upon our feet and stepped out from under the shadow of the gigantic tree. High above we could faintly see our electrical ship, gently swaying in the air close to the treetop.

There were no electric lights in our immediate neighbourhood, but we noticed that the whole surface of the planet around us was gleaming with them, producing an effect like the glow of a great city seen from a distance at night. The glare was faintly reflected from the vast dome of clouds above, producing the general impression of a moonlight night upon the earth.

It was a wonderfully quiet and beautiful spot where we had come down. The air had a delicate feel and a bracing temperature, while a soft breeze soughed through the leaves of the tree above our heads.

Not far away was the bank of a canal, bordered by a magnificent avenue shaded by a double row of immense umbrageous trees.

We approached the canal, and, getting upon the road, turned to the left to make an exploration in that direction. The shadow of the trees falling upon the roadway produced a dense gloom, in the midst of which we felt that we should be safe, unless the Martians had eyes like those of cats.

As we pushed along, our hearts, I confess, beating a little quickly, a shadow stirred in front of us.

Something darker than the night itself approached.

As it drew near it assumed the appearance of an enormous dog, as tall as an ox, which ran swiftly our way with a threatening motion of its head. But before it could even utter a snarl the whirr of Colonel Smith's disintegrator was heard and the creature vanished in the shadow.

"Gracious, did you ever see such a beast?" said the Colonel. "Why, he was as big as a grizzly."

"The people he belonged to must be near by," I said. "Very likely he was a watch on guard."

"But I see no signs of a habitation."

"True, but you observe there is a thick hedge on the side of the road opposite the canal. If we get through that perhaps we shall catch sight of something."

Cautiously we pushed our way through the hedge, which was composed of shrubs as large as small trees, and very thick at the bottom, and, having traversed it, found ourselves in a great meadow-like expanse which might have been a lawn. At a considerable distance, in the midst of a clump of trees, a large building towered skyward, its walls of some red metal, gleaming like polished copper in the soft light that fell from the cloud dome.

There were no lights around the building itself, and we saw nothing corresponding to windows on that side which faced us, but toward the right a door was evidently open, and out of this streamed a brilliant shaft of illumination, which lay bright upon the lawn, then crossed the highway through an opening in the hedge, and gleamed on the water of the canal beyond.

Where we stood the ground had evidently been recently cleared, and there was no obstruction, but as we crept closer to the house—for our curiosity had now become irresistible—we found ourselves crawling through grass so tall that if we had stood erect it would have risen well above our heads.

"This affords good protection," said Colonel Smith, recalling his adventures on the Western plains. "We can get close in to the Indians—I beg pardon, I mean the Martians—without being seen."

Heavens, what an adventure was this! To be crawling about in the night on the face of another world and venturing, perhaps, into the jaws of a danger which human experience could not measure!

But on we went, and in a little while we had emerged from the tall grass and were somewhat startled by the discovery that we had got close to the wall of the building.

Carefully we crept around toward the open door.

As we neared it we suddenly stopped as if we had been stricken with instantaneous paralysis.

Out of the door floated, on the soft night air, the sweetest music I have ever listened to.

It carried me back in an instant to my own world. It was the music of the earth. It was the melodious expression of a human soul. It thrilled us both to the heart's core.

"My God!" exclaimed Colonel Smith. "What can that be? Are we dreaming, or where in heaven's name are we?"

Still the enchanting harmony floated out upon the air.

What the instrument was I could not tell; but the sound seemed more nearly to resemble that of a violin than of anything else I could think of.

When we first heard it the strains were gentle, sweet, caressing and full of an infinite depth of feeling, but in a little while its tone changed, and it became a magnificent march, throbbing upon the air in stirring notes that set our hearts beating in unison with its stride and inspiring in us a courage that we had not felt before.

Then it drifted into a wild fantasia, still inexpressibly sweet, and from that changed again into a requiem or lament, whose mellifluous tide of harmony swept our thoughts back again to the earth.

"I can endure this no longer," I said. "I must see who it is that makes that music. It is the product of a human heart and must come from the touch of human fingers."

We carefully shifted our position until we stood in the blaze of light that poured out of the door.

The doorway was an immense arched opening, magnificently ornamented, rising to a height of, I should say, not less than twenty or twenty-five feet and broad in proportion. The door itself stood widely open and it, together with all of its fittings and surroundings, was composed of the same beautiful red metal.

Stepping out a little way into the light I could see within the door an immense apartment, glittering on all sides with metallic ornaments and gems and lighted from the centre by a great chandelier of electric candles.

In the middle of the great floor, holding the instrument delicately poised, and still awaking its ravishing voice, stood a figure, the sight of which almost stopped my breath.

It was a slender sylph of a girl!

A girl of my own race: a human being here upon the planet Mars!

Her hair was loosely coiled and she was attired in graceful white drapery.

"By ——!" cried Colonel Smith, "she's human!"

Chapter 12

Still the bewildering strains of the music came to our ears, and yet we stood there unperceived, though in the full glare of the chandelier.

The girl's face was presented in profile. It was exquisite in beauty, pale, delicate with a certain pleading sadness which stirred us to the heart.

An element of romance and a touch of personal interest such as we had not looked for suddenly entered into our adventure.

Colonel Smith's mind still ran back to the perils of the plains.

"She is a prisoner," he said, "and by the Seven Devils of Dona Ana we'll not leave her here. But where are the hellhounds themselves?"

Our attention had been so absorbed by the sight of the girl that we had scarcely thought of looking to see if there was any one else in the room.

Glancing beyond her, I now perceived sitting in richly decorated chairs three or four gigantic Martians. They were listening to the music as if charmed.

The whole story told itself. This girl, if not their slave, was at any rate under their control, and she was furnishing entertainment for them by her musical skill. The fact that they could find pleasure in music so beautiful was, perhaps, an indication that they were not really as savage as they seemed.

Yet our hearts went out to the girl, and were turned against them with an uncontrollable hatred.

They were of the same remorseless race with those who so lately had lain waste our fair earth and who would have completed its destruction had not Providence interfered in our behalf.

Singularly enough, although we stood full in the light, they had not yet seen us.

Suddenly the girl, moved by what impulse I know not, turned her face in our direction. Her eyes fell upon us. She paused abruptly in her playing, and her instrument dropped to the floor. Then she uttered a cry, and with extended arms ran toward us.

But when she was near she stopped abruptly, the glad look fading from her face, and started back with terror-stricken eyes, as if, after all, she had found us not what she expected.

Then for an instant she looked more intently at us, her countenance cleared once more, and, overcome by some strange emotion, her eyes filled with tears, and, drawing a little nearer, she stretched forth her hands to us appealingly.

Meanwhile the Martians had started to their feet. They looked down upon us in astonishment. We were like pigmies to them; like little gnomes which had sprung out of the ground at their feet.

One of the giants seized some kind of a weapon and started forward with a threatening gesture.

The girl sprang to my side and grasped my arm with a cry of fear.

This seemed to throw the Martian into a sudden frenzy, and he raised his arms to strike.

But the disintegrator was in my hand.

My rage was equal to his.

I felt the concentrated vengeance of the earth quivering through me as I pressed the button of the disintegrator and, sweeping it rapidly up and down, saw the gigantic form that confronted me melt into nothingness.

There were three other giants in the room, and they had been on the point of following up the attack of their comrade. But when he disappeared from before their eyes, they paused, staring in amazement at the place where, but a moment before, he had stood, but where now only the metal weapon he had wielded lay on the floor.

At first they started back, and seemed on the point of fleeing; then, with a second glance, perceiving again how small and insignificant we were, all three together advanced upon us.

The girl sank trembling on her knees.

In the meantime I had readjusted my disintegrator for another discharge, and Colonel Smith stood by me with the light of battle upon his face.

"Sweep the discharge across the three," I exclaimed. "Otherwise there will be one left and before we can fire again he will crush us."

The whirr of the two instruments sounded simultaneously, and with a quick, horizontal motion we swept the lines of force around in such a manner that all three of the Martians were caught by the vibratory streams and actually cut in two.

Long gaps were opened in the wall of the room behind them, where the destroying currents had passed, for with wrathful fierceness, we had run the vibrations through half a gamut on the index.

The victory was ours. There were no other enemies, that we could see, in the house.

Yet at any moment others might make their appearance, and what more we did must be done quickly.

The girl evidently was as much amazed as the Martians had been by the effects which we had produced. Still she was not terrified, and continued to cling to us and to glance beseechingly into our faces, expressing in her every look and gesture the fact that she knew we were of her own race.

But clearly she could not speak our tongue, for the words she uttered were unintelligible.

Colonel Smith, whose long experience in Indian warfare had made him intensely practical, did not lose his military instincts, even in the midst of events so strange.

"It occurs to me," he said, "that we have got a chance at the enemies' supplies. Suppose we begin foraging right here. Let's see if this girl can't show us the commissary department."

He immediately began to make signs to the girl to indicate that he was hungry.

A look of comprehension flitted over her features, and, seizing our hands, she led us into an adjoining apartment and pointed to a number of metallic boxes. One of these she opened, taking out of it a kind of cake, which she placed between her teeth, breaking off a very small portion and then handing it to us, motioning that we should eat, but at the same time showing us that we ought to take only a small quantity.

"Thank God! It's compressed food," said Colonel Smith. "I thought these Martians with their wonderful civilization would be up to that. And it's mighty lucky for us, because, without overburdening ourselves, if we can find one or two more caches like this we shall be able to re-provision the entire fleet. But we must get reinforcements before we can take possession of the fodder."

Accordingly we hurried out into the night, passed into the roadway, and, taking the girl with us, ran as rapidly as possible to the foot of the tree where we had made our descent. Then we signalled to the electric ship to drop down to the level of the ground.

This was quickly done, the girl was taken aboard, and a dozen men, under our guidance, hastened back to the house, where we loaded ourselves with the compressed provisions and conveyed them to the ship.

On this second trip to the mysterious house we had discovered another apartment containing a very large number of the metallic boxes, filled with compressed food.

"By Jove, it is a store house," said Colonel Smith. "We must get more force and carry it all off. Gracious, but this is a lucky night. We can re-provision the whole fleet from this room."

"I thought it singular," I said, "that with the exception of the girl whom we have rescued no women were seen in the house. Evidently the lights over yonder indicate the location of a considerable town, and it is quite probable that this building, without windows, and so strongly constructed, is the common storehouse, where the provisions for the town are kept. The fellows we killed must have been the watchmen in charge of the storehouse, and they were treating themselves to a little music from the slave girl when we happened to come upon them."

With the utmost haste several of the other electrical ships, waiting above the cloud curtain, were summoned to descend, and, with more than a hundred men, we returned to the building, and this time almost entirely exhausted its stores, each man carrying as much as he could stagger under.

Fortunately our proceedings had been conducted without much noise, and the storehouse being situated at a considerable distance from other buildings, none of the Martians, except those who would never tell the story, had known of our arrival or of our doings on the planet.

"Now, we'll return and surprise Edison with the news," said Colonel Smith.

Our ship was the last to pass up through the clouds, and it was a strange sight to watch the others as one after another they rose toward the great dome, entered it, though from below it resembled a solid vault of greyish-pink marble, and disappeared.

We quickly followed them, and having penetrated the enormous curtain, were considerably surprised on emerging at the upper side to find that the sun was shining brilliantly upon us. It will be remembered that it was night on this side of Mars when we went down, but our adventure had occupied several hours, and now Mars had so far turned upon its axis that the portion of its surface over which we were had come around into the sunlight.

We knew that the squadron which we had left besieging the Lake of the Sun must also have been carried around in a similar manner, passing into the night while the side of the planet where we were was emerging into day.

Our shortest way back would be by travelling westward, because then we should be moving in a direction opposite to that in which the planet rotated, and the main squadron, sharing that rotation, would be continually moving in our direction.

But to travel westward was to penetrate once more into the night side of the planet.

The prows, if I may so call them, of our ships were accordingly turned in the direction of the vast shadow which Mars was invisibly projecting into space behind it, and on entering that shadow the sun disappeared from our eyes, and once more the huge hidden globe beneath us became a black chasm among the stars.

Now that we were in the neighbourhood of a globe capable of imparting considerable weight to all things under the influence of its attraction that peculiar condition which I have before described as existing in the midst of space, where there was neither up nor down for us, had ceased. Here where we had weight "up" and "down" had resumed their old meanings. "Down" was toward the centre of Mars, and "up" was away from that centre.

Standing on the deck, and looking overhead as we swiftly ploughed our smooth way at a great height through the now imperceptible atmosphere of the planet, I saw the two moons of Mars meeting in the sky exactly above us.

Before our arrival at Mars, there had been considerable discussion among the learned men as to the advisability of touching at one of their moons, and when the discovery was made that our provisions were nearly exhausted, it had been suggested that the Martian satellites might furnish us with an additional supply.

But it had appeared a sufficient reply to this suggestion that the moons of Mars are both insignificant bodies, not much larger than the asteroid we had fallen in with, and that there could not possibly be any form of vegetation or other edible products upon them.

This view having prevailed, we had ceased to take an interest in the satellites, further than to regard them as objects of great curiosity on account of their motions.

The nearer of these moons, Phobos, is only 3,700 miles from the surface of Mars, and we watched it travelling around the planet three times in the course of every day. The more distant one, Deimos, 12,500 miles away, required considerably more than one day to make its circuit.

It now happened that the two had come into conjunction, as I have said, just over our heads, and, throwing myself down on my back on the deck of the electrical ship, for a long time I watched the race between the two satellites, until Phobos, rapidly gaining upon the other, had left its rival far behind.

Suddenly Colonel Smith, who took very little interest in these astronomical curiosities, touched me, and pointing ahead, said:

"There they are."

I looked, and sure enough there were the signal lights of the principal squadron, and as we gazed we occasionally saw, darting up from the vast cloud mass beneath, an electric bayonet, fiercely thrust into the sky, which showed that the siege was still actively going on, and that the Martians were jabbing away at their invisible enemies outside the curtain.

In a short time the two fleets had joined, and Colonel Smith and I immediately transferred ourselves to the flagship.

"Well, what have you done?" asked Mr. Edison, while others crowded around with eager attention.

"If we have not captured their provision train," said Colonel Smith, "we have done something just about as good. We have foraged on the country, and have collected a supply that I reckon will last this fleet for at least a month."

"What's that? What's that?"

"It's just what I say," and Colonel Smith brought out of his pocket one of the square cakes of compressed food. "Set your teeth in that, and see what you think of it, but don't take too much, for it's powerful strong."

"I say," he continued, "we have got enough of that stuff to last us all for a month, but we've done more than that; we have got a surprise for you that will make you open your eyes. Just wait a minute."

Colonel Smith made a signal to the electrical ship which we had just quitted to draw near. It came alongside, so that one could step from its deck onto the flagship. Colonel Smith disappeared for a minute in the interior of his ship, then re-emerged, leading the girl whom we had found upon the planet.

"Take her inside, quick," he said, "for she is not used to this thin air."

In fact, we were at so great an elevation that the rarity of the atmosphere now compelled us all to wear our air-tight suits, and the girl, not being thus attired, would have fallen unconscious on the deck if we had not instantly removed her to the interior of the car.

There she quickly recovered from the effects of the deprivation of air and looked about her, pale, astonished, but yet apparently without fear.

Every motion of this girl convinced me that she not only recognized us as members of her own race, but that she felt that her only hope lay in our aid. Therefore, strange as we were to her in many respects, nevertheless she did not think that she was in danger while among us.

The circumstances under which we had found her were quickly explained. Her beauty, her strange fate and the impenetrable mystery which surrounded her excited universal admiration and wonder.

"How did she get on Mars?" was the question that everybody asked, and that nobody could answer.

But while all were crowding around and overwhelming the poor girl with their staring, suddenly she burst into tears, and then, with arms outstretched in the same appealing manner which had so stirred our sympathies when we first saw her in the house of the Martians, she broke forth in a wild recitation, which was half a song and half a wail.

As she went on I noticed that a learned professor of languages from the University of Heidelberg was listening to her with intense attention. Several times he appeared to be on the point of breaking in with an exclamation. I could plainly see that he was becoming more and more excited as the words poured from the girl's lips. Occasionally he nodded and muttered, smiling to himself. Her song finished, the girl sank half-exhausted upon the floor. She was lifted and placed in a reclining position at the side of the car.

Then the Heidelberg professor stepped to the centre of the car, in the sight of all, and in a most impressive manner said:

"Gentlemen, our sister."

"I have her tongue recognized! The language that she speaks, the roots of the great Indo-European, or Aryan stock, contains."

"This girl, gentlemen, to the oldest family of the human race belongs. Her language every tongue that now upon the earth is spoken antedates. Convinced am I that it that great original speech is from which have all the languages of the civilized world sprung."

"How she here came, so many millions of miles from the earth, a great mystery is. But it shall be penetrated, and it is from her own lips that we the truth shall learn, because not difficult to us shall it be the language that she speaks to acquire since to our own it is akin."

This announcement of the Heidelberg professor stirred us all most profoundly. It not only deepened our interest in the beautiful girl whom we had rescued, but, in a dim way, it gave us reason to hope that we should yet discover some means of mastering the Martians by dealing them a blow from within.

It had been expected, the reader will remember, that the Martian whom we had made prisoner on the asteroid, might be of use to us in a similar way, and for that reason great efforts had been made to acquire his language, and considerable progress had been effected in that direction.

But from the moment of our arrival at Mars itself, and especially after the battles began, the prisoner had resumed his savage and uncommunicative disposition, and had seemed continually to be expecting that we would fall victims to the prowess of his fellow beings, and that he would be released. How an outlaw, such as he evidently was, who had been caught in the act of robbing the Martian gold mines, could expect to escape punishment on returning to his native planet it was difficult to see. Nevertheless, so strong are the ties of race we could plainly perceive that all his sympathies were for his own people.

In fact, in consequence of his surly manner, and his attempts to escape, he had been more strictly bound than before and to get him out of the way had been removed from the flagship, which was already overcrowded, and placed in one of the other electric ships, and this ship—as it happened—was one of those which were lost in the great battle beneath the clouds. So after all, the Martian had perished, by a vengeful stroke launched from his native globe.

But Providence had placed in our hands a far better interpreter than he could ever have been. This girl of our own race would need no urging, or coercion, on our part in order to induce her to reveal any secrets of the Martians that might be useful in our further proceedings.

But one thing was first necessary to be done.

We must learn to talk with her.

But for the discovery of the store of provisions it would have been impossible for us to spare the time needed to acquire the language of the girl, but now that we had been saved from the danger of starvation, we could prolong the siege for several weeks, employing the intervening time to the best advantage.

The terrible disaster which we had suffered in the great battle above the Lake of the Sun, wherein we had lost nearly a third of our entire force, had been quite sufficient to convince us that our only hope of victory lay in dealing the Martians some paralyzing stroke that at one blow would deprive them of the power of resistance. A victory that cost us the loss of a single ship would be too dearly purchased now.

How to deal that blow, and first of all, how to discover the means of dealing it, were at present the uppermost problems in our minds.

The only hope for us lay in the girl.

If, as there was every reason to believe, she was familiar with the ways and secrets of the Martians, then she might be able to direct our efforts in such a manner as to render them effective.

"We can spare two weeks for this," said Mr. Edison. "Can you fellows of many tongues learn to talk with the girl in that time?"

"We'll try it," said several.

"It shall we do," cried the Heidelberg professor more confidently.

"Then there is no use of staying here," continued the commander. "If we withdraw the Martians will think that we have either given up the contest or been destroyed. Perhaps they will then pull off their blanket and let us see their face once more. That will give us a better opportunity to strike effectively when we are again ready."

"Why not rendezvous at one of the moons?" said an astronomer. "Neither of the two moons is of much consequence, as far as size goes, but still it would serve as a sort of anchorage ground, and while there, if we were careful to keep on the side away from Mars, we should escape detection."

This suggestion was immediately accepted, and the squadron having been signalled to assemble quickly bore off in the direction of the more distant moon of Mars, Deimos. We knew that it was slightly smaller than Phobos but its greater distance gave promise that it would better serve our purpose of temporary concealment. The moons of Mars, like the earth's moon, always keep the same face toward their master. By hiding behind Deimos we should escape the prying eyes of the Martians, even when they employed telescopes, and thus be able to remain comparatively close at hand, ready to pounce down upon them again after we had obtained, as we now had good hope of doing, information that would make us masters of the situation.

Chapter 13

Deimos proved to be, as we had expected, about six miles in diameter. Its mean density is not very great so that the acceleration of gravity did not exceed one two-thousandths of the earth's. Consequently the weight of a man turning the scales at 150 pounds at home was here only about one ounce.

The result was that we could move about with greater ease than on the golden asteroid, and some of the scientific men eagerly resumed their interrupted experiments.

But the attraction of this little satellite was so slight that we had to be very careful not to move too swiftly in going about lest we should involuntarily leave the ground and sail out into space, as, it will be remembered, happened to the fugitives during the fight on the asteroid.

Not only would such an adventure have been an uncomfortable experience, but it might have endangered the success of our scheme. Our present distance from the surface of Mars did not exceed 12,500 miles, and we had reason to believe that Martians possessed telescopes powerful enough to enable them not merely to see the electrical ships at such a distance, but to also catch sight of us individually. Although the cloud curtain still rested on the planet it was probable that the Martians would send some of their airships up to its surface in order to determine what our fate had been. From that point of vantage, with their exceedingly powerful glasses, we feared that they might be able to detect anything unusual upon or in the neighbourhood of Deimos.

Accordingly strict orders were given, not only that the ships should be moored on that side of the satellite which is perpetually turned away from Mars, but that, without orders, no one should venture around on the other side of the little globe, or even on the edge of it, where he might be seen in profile against the sky.

Still, of course, it was essential that we, on our part, should keep a close watch, and so a number of sentinels were selected, whose duty it was to place themselves at the edge of Deimos, where they could peep over the horizon, so to speak, and catch sight of the globe of our enemies.

The distance of Mars from us was only about three times its own diameter, consequently it shut off a large part of the sky, as viewed from our position.

But in order to see its whole surface it was necessary to go a little beyond the edge of the satellite, on that side which faced Mars. At the suggestion of Colonel Smith, who had so frequently stalked Indians that devices of this kind readily occurred to his mind, the sentinels all wore garments corresponding in colour to that of the soil of the asteroid, which was of a dark, reddish brown hue. This would tend to conceal them from the prying eyes of the Martians.

The commander himself frequently went around the edge of the planet in order to take a look at Mars, and I often accompanied him.

I shall never forget one occasion, when, lying flat on the ground, and cautiously worming our way around on the side toward Mars, we had just begun to observe it with our telescopes, when I perceived, against the vast curtain of smoke, a small, glinting object, which I instantly suspected to be an airship.

I called Mr. Edison's attention to it, and we both agreed that it was, undoubtedly, one of the Martians' aerial vessels, probably on the lookout for us.

A short time afterward a large number of airships made their appearance at the upper surface of the clouds, moving to and fro, and although, with our glasses, we could only make out the general form of the ships, without being able to discern the Martians upon them, yet we had not the least doubt but they were sweeping the sky in every direction in order to determine whether we had been completely destroyed or had retreated to a distance from the planet.

Even when that side of Mars on which we were looking had passed into night, we could still see the guard-ships circling above the clouds, their presence being betrayed by the faint twinkling of the electric lights that they bore.

Finally, after about a week had passed, the Martians evidently made up their minds that they had annihilated us, and that there was no longer danger to be feared. Convincing evidence that they believed we should not be heard from again was furnished when the withdrawal of the great curtain of cloud began.

This phenomenon first manifested itself by a gradual thinning of the vaporous shield, until, at length, we began to perceive the red surface of the planet dimly shining through it. Thinner and rarer it became, and, after the lapse of about eighteen hours, it had completely disappeared, and the huge globe shone out again, reflecting the light of the sun from its continents and oceans with a brightness that, in contrast with the all-enveloping night to which we had so long been subjected, seemed unbearable to our eyes.

Indeed, so brilliant was the illumination which fell upon the surface of Deimos that the number of persons who had been permitted to pass around upon the exposed side of the satellite was carefully restricted. In the blaze of light which had been suddenly poured upon us we felt somewhat like malefactors unexpectedly enveloped in the illumination of a policeman's dark lantern.

Meanwhile, the object which we had in view in retreating to the satellite was not lost sight of, and the services of the chief linguists of the expedition were again called into use for the purpose of acquiring a new language. The experiment was conducted in the flagship. The fact that this time it was not a monster belonging to an utterly alien race upon whom we were to experiment, but a beautiful daughter of our common Mother Eve, added zest and interest as well as the most confident hopes of success to the efforts of those who were striving to understand the accents of her tongue.

Still the difficulty was very great, notwithstanding the conviction of the professors that her language would turn out to be a form of the great Indo-European speech from which the many tongues of civilized men upon the earth had been derived.

The learned men, to tell the truth, gave the poor girl no rest. For hours at a time they would ply her with interrogations by voice and by gesture, until, at length, wearied beyond endurance, she would fall asleep before their faces.

Then she would be left undisturbed for a little while, but the moment her eyes opened again the merciless professors flocked about her once more, and resumed the tedious iteration of their experiments.

Our Heidelberg professor was the chief inquisitor, and he revealed himself to us in a new and entirely unexpected light. No one could have anticipated the depth and variety of his resources. He placed himself in front of the girl and gestured and gesticulated, bowed, nodded, shrugged his shoulders, screwed his face into an infinite variety of expressions, smiled, laughed, scowled and accompanied all these dumb shows with posturings, exclamations, queries, only half expressed in words, and cadences which, by some ingenious manipulation of the tones of the voice, he managed to make as marvellous expressive of his desires.

He was a universal actor—comedian, tragedian, buffoon—all in one. There was no shade of human emotion which he did not seem capable of giving expression to.

His every attitude was a symbol, and all his features became in quick succession types of thought and exponents of hidden feelings, while his inquisitive nose stood forth in the midst of their ceaseless play like a perpetual interrogation point that would have electrified the Sphinx into life, and set its stone lips gabbling answers and explanations.

The girl looked on, partly astonished, partly amused, and partly comprehending. Sometimes she smiled, and then the beauty of her face became most captivating. Occasionally she burst into a cheery laugh when the professor was executing some of his extraordinary gyrations before her.

It was a marvellous exhibition of what the human intellect, when all its powers are concentrated upon a single object, is capable of achieving. It seemed to me, as I looked at the performance, that if all the races of men, who had been stricken asunder at the foot of the Tower of Babel by the miracle which made the tongues of each to speak a language unknown to the others, could be brought together again at the foot of the same tower, with all the advantages which thousands of years of education had in the meantime imparted to them, they would be able, without any miracle, to make themselves mutually understood.

And it was evident that an understanding was actually growing between the girl and the professor. Their minds were plainly meeting, and when both had become focused upon the same point, it was perfectly certain that the object of the experiment would be attained.

Whenever the professor got from the girl an intelligent reply to his pantomimic inquiries, or whenever he believed that he got such a reply, it was immediately jotted down in the ever open notebook which he carried in his hand.

And then he would turn to us standing by, and with one hand on his heart, and the other sweeping grandly through the air, would make a profound bow and say:

"The young lady and I great progress make already. I have her words comprehended. We shall wondrous mysteries solve. *Jawohl! Wunderlich!* Make yourselves gentlemen easy. Of the human race the ancestral stem have I here discovered."

Once I glanced over a page of his notebook, and there I read this:

"Mars—*Zahmor.*"

"Copper—*Hayez.*"

"Sword—*Anz.*"

"I jump—*Altesna.*"

"I slay—*Amoutha.*"

"I cut off a head—*Ksutaskofa.*"

"I sleep—*Zlcha.*"

"I love—*Levza.*"

When I saw this last entry I looked suspiciously at the professor.

Was he trying to make love without our knowing it to the beautiful captive from Mars?

If so, I felt certain that he would get himself into difficulty. She had made a deep impression upon every man in the flagship, and I knew that there was more than one of the younger men who would have promptly called him to account if they had suspected him of trying to learn from those beautiful lips the words, "I love."

I pictured to myself the state of mind of Colonel Alonzo Jefferson Smith if, in my place, he had glanced over the notebook and read what I had read.

And then I thought of another handsome young fellow in the flagship—Sidney Phillips—who, if mere actions and looks could make him so, had become exceedingly devoted to this long lost and happily recovered daughter of Eve.

In fact, I had already questioned within my own mind whether the peace would be strictly kept between Colonel Smith and Mr. Phillips, for the former had, to my knowledge, noticed the young fellow's adoring glances, and had begun to regard him out of the corners of his eyes as if he considered him no better than an Apache or a Mexican greaser.

"But what," I asked myself, "would be the vengeance that Colonel Smith would take upon this skinny professor from Heidelberg if he thought that he, taking advantage of his linguistic powers, had stepped in between him and the damsel whom he had rescued?"

However, when I took a second look at the professor, I became convinced that he was innocent of any such amorous intention, and that he had learned, or believed he had learned, the word for "love" simply in pursuance of the method by which he meant to acquire the language of the girl.

There was one thing which gave some of us considerable misgiving, and that was the question whether, after all, the language the professor was acquiring was really the girl's own tongue or one that she had learned from the Martians.

But the professor bade us rest easy on that point. He assured us, in the first place, that this girl could not be the only human being living upon Mars, but that she must have friends and relatives there. That being so, they unquestionably had a language of their own, which they spoke when they were among themselves. Here finding herself among beings belonging to her own race, she would naturally speak her own tongue and not that which she had acquired from the Martians.

"Moreover, gentlemen," he added, "I have in her speech many roots of the great Aryan tongue already recognized."

We were greatly relieved by this explanation, which seemed to all of us perfectly satisfactory.

Yet, really, there was no reason why one language should be any better than the other for our present purpose. In fact, it might be more useful to us to know the language of the Martians themselves. Still, we all felt that we should prefer to know her language rather than that of the monsters among whom she had lived.

Colonel Smith expressed what was in all our minds when, after listening to the reasoning of the Professor, he blurted out:

"Thank God, she doesn't speak any of their blamed lingo! By Jove, it would soil her pretty lips."

"But also that she speaks, too," said the man from Heidelberg, turning to Colonel Smith with a grin. "We shall both of them eventually learn."

Three entire weeks were passed in this manner. After the first week the girl herself materially assisted the linguists in their efforts to acquire her speech.

At length the task was so far advanced that we could, in a certain sense, regard it as practically completed. The Heidelberg Professor declared that he had mastered the tongue of the ancient Aryans. His delight was unbounded. With prodigious industry he set to work, scarcely stopping to eat or sleep, to form a grammar of the language.

"You shall see," he said, "it will the speculations of my countrymen vindicate."

No doubt the Professor had an exaggerated opinion of the extent of his acquirements, but the fact remained that enough had been learned of the girl's language to enable him and several others to converse with her quite as readily as a person of good capacity who has studied under the instructions of a native teacher during a period of six months can converse in a foreign tongue.

Immediately almost every man in the squadron set vigorously at work to learn the language of this fair creature for himself. Colonel Smith and Sidney Phillips were neck and neck in the linguistic race.

One of the first bits of information which the Professor had given out was the name of the girl.

It was Aina (pronounced *Ah-ee-na*).

This news was flashed throughout the squadron, and the name of our beautiful captive was on the lips of all.

After that came her story. It was a marvellous narrative. Translated into our tongue it ran as follows:

> The traditions of my fathers, handed down for generations so many that no one can number them, declare that the planet of Mars was not the place of our origin.
>
> Ages and ages ago our forefathers dwelt on another and distant world that was nearer to the sun than this one is, and enjoyed brighter daylight than we have here.
>
> They dwelt—as I have often heard the story from my father, who had learned it by heart from his father, and he from his—in a beautiful valley that was surrounded by enormous mountains towering into the clouds and white about their tops with snow that never melted. In the valley were lakes, around which clustered the dwellings of our race.
>
> It was, the traditions say, a land wonderful for its fertility, filled with all things that the heart could desire, splendid with flowers and rich with luscious fruits.
>
> It was a land of music, and the people who dwelt in it were very happy.

While the girl was telling this part of her story the Heidelberg Professor became visibly more and more excited. Presently he could keep quiet no longer, and suddenly exclaimed, turning to us who were listening, as the words of the girl were interpreted for us by one of the other linguists:

"Gentlemen, it is the Vale of Cashmere! Has not my great countryman, Adelung, so declared? Has he not said that the Valley of Cashmere was the cradle of the human race already?"

"From the Valley of Cashmere to the planet Mars—what a romance!" exclaimed one of the bystanders.

Colonel Smith appeared to be particularly moved, and I heard him humming under his breath, greatly to my astonishment, for this rough soldier was not much given to poetry or music:

"Who has not heard of the Vale of Cashmere, With its roses the brightest that earth ever gave; Its temples, its grottoes, its fountains as clear, As the love-lighted eyes that hang over the wave."

Mr. Sidney Phillips, standing by, and also catching the murmur of Colonel Smith's words, showed in his handsome countenance some indications of distress, as if he wished he had thought of those lines himself.

The girl resumed her narrative:

Suddenly there dropped down out of the sky strange gigantic enemies, armed with mysterious weapons, and began to slay and burn and make desolate. Our forefathers could not withstand them. They seemed like demons, who had been sent from the abodes of evil to destroy our race.

Some of the wise men said that this thing had come upon our people because they had been very wicked, and the gods in Heaven were angry. Some said they came from the moon, and some from the far-away stars. But of these things my forefathers knew nothing for a certainty.

The destroyers showed no mercy to the inhabitants of the beautiful valley. Not content with making it a desert, they swept over other parts of the earth.

The tradition says that they carried off from the valley, which was our native land, a large number of our people, taking them first into a strange country, where there were oceans of sand, but where a great river, flowing through the midst of the sands, created a narrow land of fertility. Here, after having slain and driven out the native inhabitants, they remained for many years, keeping our people, whom they had carried into captivity, as slaves.

And in this Land of Sand, it is said, they did many wonderful works.

They had been astonished at the sight of the great mountains which surrounded our valley, for on Mars there are no mountains, and after they came into the Land of Sand they built there with huge blocks of stone mountains in imitation of what they had seen, and used them for purposes that our people did not understand.

Then, too, it is said they left there at the foot of these mountains that they had made a gigantic image of the great chief who led them in their conquest of our world.

At this point in the story the Heidelberg Professor again broke in, fairly trembling with excitement:

The Wonders of the Martians!

"Gentlemen, gentlemen," he cried, "is it that you do not understand? This Land of Sand and of a wonderful fertilizing river—what can it be? Gentlemen, it is Egypt! These mountains of rock that the Martians have erected, what are they? Gentlemen, they are the great mystery of the land of the Nile, the Pyramids. The gigantic statue of their leader that they at the foot of their artificial mountains have set up—gentlemen, what is that? It is the Sphinx!"

The Professor's agitation was so great that he could go no further. And indeed there was not one of us who did not fully share his excitement. To think that we should have come to the planet Mars to solve one of the standing mysteries of the earth, which had puzzled mankind and defied all their efforts at solution for so many centuries! Here, then, was the explanation of how those gigantic blocks that constitute the great Pyramid of Cheops had been swung to their lofty elevation. It was not the work of puny man, as many an engineer had declared that it could not be, but the work of these giants of Mars.

Aina resumed her story.

At length, our traditions say, a great pestilence broke out in the Land of Sand, and a partial vengeance was granted to us in the destruction of the larger number of our enemies. At last the giants who remained, fleeing before this scourge of the gods, used the mysterious means at their command, and, carrying our ancestors with them, returned to their own world, in which we have ever since lived.

Then there are more of your people in Mars? said one of the professors.

Alas, no, replied Aina, her eyes filling with tears, I alone am left.

For a few minutes she was unable to speak. Then she continued:

What fury possessed them I do not know, but not long ago an expedition departed from the planet, the purpose of which, as it was noised about over Mars, was the conquest of a distant world. After a time a few survivors of that expedition returned. The story they told caused great excitement among our masters. They had been successful in their battles with the inhabitants of the world they had invaded, but as in the days of

127

our forefathers, in the Land of Sand, a pestilence smote them, and but few survivors escaped.

Not long after that, you, with your mysterious ships, appeared in the sky of Mars. Our masters studied you with their telescopes, and those who had returned from the unfortunate expedition declared that you were inhabitants of the world which they had invaded, come, doubtless, to take vengeance upon them.

Some of my people who were permitted to look through the telescopes of the Martians, saw you also, and recognized you as members of their own race. There were several thousand of us, altogether, and we were kept by the Martians to serve them as slaves, and particularly to delight their ears with music, for our people have always been especially skilful in the playing of musical instruments, and in songs, and while the Martians have but little musical skill themselves, they are exceedingly fond of these things.

Although Mars had completed not less than five thousand circuits about the sun since our ancestors were brought as prisoners to its surface, yet the memory of our distant home had never perished from the hearts of our race, and when we recognized you, as we believed, our own brothers, come to rescue us from long imprisonment, there was great rejoicing. The news spread from mouth to mouth, wherever we were in the houses and families of our masters. We seemed to be powerless to aid you or to communicate with you in any manner. Yet our hearts went out to you, as in your ships you hung above the planet, and preparations were secretly made by all the members of our race for your reception when, as we believed, would occur, you should effect a landing upon the planet and destroy our enemies.

But in some manner the fact that we had recognized you, and were preparing to welcome you, came to the ears of the Martians.

At this point the girl suddenly covered her eyes with her hands, shuddering and falling back in her seat.

"Oh, you do not know them as I do!" at length she exclaimed. "The monsters! Their vengeance was too terrible! Instantly the order went forth that we should all be butchered, and that awful command was executed!"

"How, then, did you escape?" asked the Heidelberg Professor.

Aina seemed unable to speak for a while. Finally mastering her emotion, she replied:

"One of the chief officers of the Martians wished me to remain alive. He, with his aides, carried me to one of the military depot of supplies, where I was found and rescued," and as she said this she turned toward Colonel Smith with a smile that reflected on his ruddy face and made it glow like a Chinese lantern.

"By ——!" muttered Colonel Smith, "that was the fellow we blew into nothing! Blast him, he got off too easy!"

The remainder of Aina's story may be briefly told.

When Colonel Smith and I entered the mysterious building which, as it now proved, was not a storehouse belonging to a village, as we had supposed, but one of the military depots of the Martians, the girl, on catching sight of us, immediately recognized us as belonging to the strange squadron in the sky. As such she felt that we must be her friends, and saw in us her only possible hope of escape. For that reason she had instantly thrown herself under our protection. This accounted for the singular confidence which she had manifested in us from the beginning.

Her wonderful story had so captivated our imaginations that for a long time after it was finished we could not recover from the spell. It was told over and over again from mouth to mouth, and repeated from ship to ship, everywhere exciting the utmost astonishment.

Destiny seemed to have sent us on this expedition into space for the purpose of clearing off mysteries that had long puzzled the minds of men. When on the moon we had unexpectedly to ourselves settled the question that had been debated from the beginning of astronomical history of the former habitability of that globe.

Now, on Mars, we had put to rest no less mysterious questions relating to the past history of our own planet. Adelung, as the Heidelberg Professor asserted, had named the Vale of Cashmere as the probable site of the Garden of Eden, and the place of origin of the human race, but later investigators had taken issue with this opinion, and the question where the Aryans originated upon the earth had long been one of the most puzzling that science presented.

This question seemed now to have been settled.

Aina had said that Mars had completed 5,000 circuits about the sun since her people were brought to it as captives. One circuit of Mars occupies 687 days. More than 9,000 years had therefore elapsed since the first invasion of the earth by the Martians.

Another great mystery—that of the origin of those gigantic and inexplicable monuments, the great pyramids and the Sphinx, on the banks of the Nile, had also apparently been solved by us, although these Egyptian wonders had been the furthest things from our thoughts when we set out for the planet Mars.

We had travelled more than thirty millions of miles in order to get answers to questions which could not be solved at home.

But from these speculations and retrospects we were recalled by the commander of the expedition.

"This is all very interesting and very romantic, gentlemen," he said, "but now let us get at the practical side of it. We have learned Aina's language and have heard her story. Let us next ascertain whether she cannot place in our hands some key which will place Mars at our mercy. Remember what we came here for, and remember that the earth expects every man of us to do his duty."

This Nelson-like summons again changed the current of our thoughts, and we instantly set to work to learn from Aina if Mars, like Achilles, had not some vulnerable point where a blow would be mortal.

Chapter 14

It was a curious scene when the momentous interview which was to determine our fate and that of Mars began. Aina had been warned of what was coming. We in the flagship had all learned to speak her language with more or less ease, but it was deemed best that the Heidelberg Professor, assisted by one of his colleagues, should act as interpreter.

The girl, flushed with excitement of the novel situation, fully appreciating the importance of what was about to occur, and looking more charming than before, stood at one side of the principal apartment. Directly facing her were the interpreters, and the rest of us, all with ears intent and eyes focused upon Aina, stood in a double row behind them.

As heretofore, I am setting down her words translated into our own tongue, having taken only so much liberty as to connect the sentences into a stricter sequence than they had when falling from her lips in reply to the questions that were showered upon her.

"You will never be victorious," she said, "if you attack them openly as you have been doing. They are too strong and too numerous. They are well prepared for such attacks, because they have had to resist them before."

"They have waged war with the inhabitants of the asteroid Ceres, whose people are giants greater than themselves. Their enemies from Ceres have attacked them here. Hence these fortifications, with weapons pointing skyward, and the great air fleets which you have encountered."

"But there must be some point," said Mr. Edison, "where we can."

"Yes, yes," interrupted the girl quickly, "there is one blow you can deal them which they could not withstand."

"What is that?" eagerly inquired the commander.

"You can drown them out."

"How? With the canals?"

"Yes, I will explain to you. I have already told you, and, in fact, you must have seen it for yourselves, that there are almost no mountains on Mars. A very learned man of my race used to say that the reason was because Mars is so very old a world that the mountains it once had have been almost completely levelled, and the entire surface of the planet had become a great plain. There are depressions, however, most of which are occupied by the seas. The greater part of the land lies below the level of the oceans. In order at the same time to irrigate the soil and make it fruitful, and to protect themselves from overflows by the ocean breaking in upon them, the Martians have constructed the immense and innumerable canals which you see running in all directions over the continents."

"There is one period in the year, and that period has now arrived, when there is special danger of a great deluge. Most of the oceans of Mars lie in the southern hemisphere. When it is Summer in that hemisphere, the great masses of ice and snow collected around the south pole melt rapidly away."

"Yes, that is so," broke in one of our astronomers, who was listening attentively. "Many a time I have seen the vast snow fields around the southern pole of Mars completely disappear as the Summer sun rose high upon them."

"With the melting of these snows," continued Aina, "a rapid rise in the level of the water in the southern oceans occurs. On the side facing these oceans the continents of Mars are sufficiently elevated to prevent an overflow, but nearer the equator the level of the land sinks lower."

"With your telescopes you have no doubt noticed that there is a great bending sea connecting the oceans of the south with those of the north and running through the midst of the continents."

"Quite so," said the astronomer who had spoken before, "we call it the Syrtis Major."

"That long narrow sea," Aina went on, "forms a great channel through which the flood of waters caused by the melting of the southern polar snows flows swiftly toward the equator and then on toward the north until it reaches the sea basins which exist there. At that point it is rapidly turned into ice and snow, because, of course, while it is Summer in the southern hemisphere it is Winter in the northern."

"The Syrtis Major (I am giving our name to the channel of communication in place of that by which the girl called it) is like a great safety valve, which, by permitting the waters to flow northward, saves the continents from inundation."

"But when mid-Summer arrives, the snows around the pole having been completely melted away, the flood ceases and the water begins to recede. At this time, but for a device which the Martians have employed, the canals connected with the oceans would run dry, and the vegetation, left without moisture under the Summer sun, would quickly perish."

"To prevent this they have built a series of enormous gates extending completely across the Syrtis Major at its narrowest point (latitude 25 degrees south). These gates are all controlled by machinery collected at a single point on the shore of the strait. As soon as the flood in the Syrtis Major begins to recede, the gates are closed, and, the water being thus restrained, the irrigating canals are kept full long enough to mature the harvests."

"The clew! The clew at last!" exclaimed Mr. Edison. "That is the place where we shall nip them. If we can close those gates now at the moment of high tide we shall flood the country. Did you say," he continued, turning to Aina, "that the movement of the gates was all controlled from a single point?"

"Yes," said the girl. "There is a great building (power house) full of tremendous machinery which I once entered when my father was taken there by his master, and where I saw one Martian, by turning a little handle, cause the great line of gates, stretching a hundred miles across the sea, to slowly shut in, edge to edge, until the flow of the water toward the north had been stopped."

"How is the building protected?"

"So completely," replied Aina, "that my only fear is that you may not be able to reach it. On account of the danger from their enemies on Ceres, the Martians have fortified it strongly on all sides, and have even surrounded it and covered it overhead with a great electrical network, to touch which would be instant death."

"Ah," said Mr. Edison, "they have got an electric shield, have they? Well, I think we shall be able to manage that."

"Anyhow," he continued, "we have got to get into that power house, and we have got to close those gates, and we must not lose much time in making up our minds how it is to be done. Evidently this is our only chance. We have not force enough to contend in open battle with the Martians, but if we can flood them out, and thereby render the engines contained in their fortifications useless, perhaps we shall be able to deal with the airships, which will be all the means of defence that will then remain to them."

This idea commended itself to all the leaders of the expedition. It was determined to make a reconnaissance at once.

But it would not do for us to approach the planet too hastily, and we certainly could not think of landing upon it in broad daylight. Still, as long as we were yet at a considerable distance from Mars, we felt that we should be safe from observation, because so much time had elapsed while we were hidden behind Deimos that the Martians had undoubtedly concluded that we were no longer in existence.

So we boldly quitted the little satellite with our entire squadron and once more rapidly approached the red planet of war. This time it was to be a death grapple and our chances of victory still seemed good.

As soon as we arrived so near the planet that there was danger of our being actually seen, we took pains to keep continually in the shadow of Mars, and the more surely to conceal our presence all lights upon the ships were extinguished. The precaution of the commander even went so far as to have the smooth metallic sides of the cars blackened over so that they should not reflect light, and thus become visible to the Martians as shining specks, moving suspiciously among the stars.

The precise location of the great power house on the shores of the Syrtis Major having been carefully ascertained, the squadron dropped down one night into the upper limits of the Martian atmosphere, directly over the gulf.

Then a consultation was called on the flagship and a plan of campaign was quickly devised.

It was deemed wise that the attempt should be made with a single electrical ship, but that the others should be kept hovering near, ready to respond on the instant to any signal for aid which might come from below. It was thought that, notwithstanding the wonderful defences, which, according to Aina's account surrounded the building, a small party would have a better chance of success than a large one.

Mr. Edison was certain that the electrical network which was described as covering the power house would not prove a serious obstruction to us, because by carefully sweeping the space where we intended to pass with the disintegrators before quitting the ship, the netting could be sufficiently cleared away to give us uninterrupted passage.

At first the intention was to have twenty men, each armed with two disintegrators (that being the largest number that one person could carry to advantage) descend from the electrical ship and make the venture. But, after further discussion, this number was reduced; first to a dozen, and finally, to only four. These four consisted of Mr. Edison, Colonel Smith, Mr. Sidney Phillips and myself.

Both by her own request and because we could not help feeling that her knowledge of the locality would be indispensable to us, Aina was also included in our party, but not, of course, as a fighting member of it.

It was about an hour after midnight when the ship in which we were to make the venture parted from the remainder of the squadron and dropped cautiously down. The blaze of electric lights running away in various directions indicated the lines of innumerable canals with habitations crowded along their banks, which came to a focus at a point on the continent of Aeria, westward from the Syrtis Major.

We stopped the electrical ship at an elevation of perhaps three hundred feet above the vast roof of a structure which Aina assured us was the building we were in search of.

Here we remained for a few minutes, cautiously reconnoitring. On that side of the power house which was opposite to the shore of the Syrtis Major there was a thick grove of trees, lighted beneath, as was apparent from the illumination which here and there streamed up through the cover of leaves, but, nevertheless, dark and gloomy above the tree tops.

"The electric network extends over the grove as well as over the building," said Aina.

This was lucky for us, because we wished to descend among the trees, and, by destroying part of the network over the tree tops, we could reach the shelter we desired and at the same time pass within the line of electric defences.

With increased caution, and almost holding our breath lest we should make some noise that might reach the ears of the sentinels beneath, we caused the car to settle gently down until we caught sight of a metallic net stretched in the air between us and the trees.

After our first encounter with the Martians on the asteroid, where, as I have related, some metal which was included in their dress resisted the action of the disintegrators, Mr. Edison had readjusted the range of vibrations covered by the instruments, and since then we had found nothing that did not yield to them. Consequently, we had no fear that the metal of the network would not be destroyed.

There was danger, however, of arousing attention by shattering holes through the tree tops. This could be avoided by first carefully ascertaining how far away the network was, and then with the adjustable mirrors attached to the disintegrators focusing the vibratory discharge at that distance.

So successful were we that we opened a considerable gap in the network without doing any perceptible damage to the trees beneath.

The ship was cautiously lowered through the opening and brought to rest among the upper branches of one of the tallest trees. Colonel Smith, Mr. Phillips, Mr. Edison and myself at once clambered out upon a strong limb.

For a moment I feared our arrival had been betrayed on account of the altogether too noisy contest that arose between Colonel Smith and Mr. Phillips as to which of them should assist Aina. To settle the dispute I took charge of her myself.

At length we were all safely in the tree.

Then followed the still more dangerous undertaking of descending from this great height to the ground. Fortunately, the branches were very close together and they extended down within a short distance of the soil. So the actual difficulties of the descent were not very great after all. The one thing that we had particularly to bear in mind was the absolute necessity of making no noise.

At length the descent was successfully accomplished, and we all five stood together in the shadow at the foot of the great tree. The grove was so thick around that while there was an abundance of electric lights among the trees, their illumination did not fall upon us where we stood.

Peering cautiously through the vistas in various directions, we ascertained our location with respect to the wall of the building. Like all the structures that we had seen on Mars, it was composed of polished red metal.

"Where is the entrance?" inquired Mr. Edison, in a whisper.

"Come softly this way, and look out for the sentinel," replied Aina.

Gripping our disintegrators firmly, and screwing up our courage, with noiseless steps we followed the girl among the shadows of the trees.

We had one very great advantage. The Martians had evidently placed so much confidence in the electric network which surrounded the power house that they never dreamed of enemies being able to penetrate it—at least, without giving warning of their coming.

But the hole which we had blown in this network with the disintegrators had been made noiselessly, and Mr. Edison believed, since no enemies had appeared, that our operations had not been betrayed by any automatic signal to watchers inside the building.

Consequently, we had every reason to think that we now stood within the line of defence, in which they reposed the greatest confidence, without their having the least suspicion of our presence.

Aina assured us that on the occasion of her former visit to the power house there had been but two sentinels on guard at the entrance. At the inner end of a long passage leading to the interior, she said, there were two more. Besides these there were three or four Martian engineers watching the machinery in the interior of the building.

A number of air ships were supposed to be on guard around the structure, but possibly their vigilance had been relaxed, because not long ago the Martians had sent an expedition against Ceres which had been so successful that the power of that planet to make an attack upon Mars had for the present been destroyed.

Supposing us to have been annihilated in the recent battle among the clouds, they would have no fear or cause for vigilance on our account.

The entrance to the great structure was low—at least, when measured by the stature of the Martians. Evidently the intention was that only one person at a time should find room to pass through it.

Drawing cautiously near, we discerned the outlines of two gigantic forms, standing in the darkness, one on either side of the door. Colonel Smith whispered to me:

"If you will take the fellow on the right, I will attend to the other one."

Adjusting our aim as carefully as was possible in the gloom, Colonel Smith and I simultaneously discharged our disintegrators, sweeping them rapidly up and down in the manner which had become familiar to us when endeavouring to destroy one of the gigantic Martians with a single stroke. And so successful were we that the two sentinels disappeared as if they had been ghosts of the night.

Instantly we all hurried forward and entered the door. Before us extended a long, straight passage, brightly illuminated by a number of electric candles. Its polished sides gleamed with blood-red reflections, and the gallery terminated, at a distance of two or three hundred feet, with an opening into a large chamber beyond, on the further side of which we could see part of a gigantic and complicated mass of machinery.

Making as little noise as possible, we pushed ahead along the passage, but when we had arrived within a distance of a dozen paces from the inner end, we stopped, and Colonel Smith, getting down upon his knees, crept forward until he had reached the inner end of the passage. There he peered cautiously around the edge into the chamber, and, turning his head a moment later, beckoned us to come forward. We crept to his side, and, looking out into the vast apartment, could perceive no enemies.

What had become of the sentinels supposed to stand at the inner end of the passage we could not imagine. At any rate, they were not at their posts.

The chamber was an immense square room at least a hundred feet in height and 400 feet on a side, and almost filling the wall opposite to us was an intricate display of machinery, wheels, levers, rods and polished plates. This we had no doubt was one end of the great engine which opened and shut the great gates that could dam an ocean.

"There is no one in sight," said Colonel Smith.

"Then we must act quickly," said Mr. Edison.

"Where," he said, turning to Aina, "is the handle by turning which you saw the Martian close the gates?"

Aina looked about in bewilderment. The mechanism before us was so complicated that even an expert mechanician would have been excusable for finding himself unable to understand it. There were scores of knobs and handles, all glistening in the electric light, any one of which, so far as the uninstructed could tell, might have been the master key that controlled the whole complex apparatus.

"Quick," said Mr. Edison, "where is it?"

The girl in her confusion ran this way and that, gazing hopelessly upon the machinery, but evidently utterly unable to help us.

To remain here inactive was not merely to invite destruction for ourselves, but was sure to bring certain failure upon the purpose of the expedition. All of us began instantly to look about in search of the proper handle, seizing every crank and wheel in sight and striving to turn it.

"Stop that!" shouted Mr. Edison, "you may set the whole thing wrong. Don't touch anything until we have found the right lever."

But to find that seemed to most of us now utterly beyond the power of man.

It was at this critical moment that the wonderful depth and reach of Mr. Edison's mechanical genius displayed itself. He stepped back, ran his eye quickly over the whole immense mass of wheels, handles, bolts, bars and levers, paused for an instant, as if making up his mind, then said decidedly, "There it is," and, stepping quickly forward, selected a small wheel amid a dozen others, all furnished at the circumference with handles like those of a pilot's wheel, and, giving it a quick wrench, turned it half way around.

At this instant, a startling shout fell upon our ears. There was a thunderous clatter behind us, and, turning, we saw three gigantic Martians rushing forward.

Chapter 15

"Sweep them! Sweep them!" cried Colonel Smith, as he brought his disintegrator to bear. Mr. Phillips and I instantly followed his example, and thus we swept the Martians into eternity, while Mr. Edison coolly continued his manipulations of the wheel.

The effect of what he was doing became apparent in less than half a minute. A shiver ran through the mass of machinery and shook the entire building.

"Look! look!" cried Sidney Phillips, who had stepped a little apart from the others.

We all ran to his side and found ourselves in front of a great window which opened through the side of the engine, giving a view of what lay in front of it. There, gleaming in the electric lights, we saw the Syrtis Major, its waters washing high against the walls of the vast power house. Running directly out from the shore, there was an immense metallic gate at least 400 yards in length and rising 300 feet above the present level of the water.

This great gate was slowly swinging upon an invisible hinge in such a manner that in a few minutes it would evidently stand across the current of the Syrtis Major at right angles.

Beyond was a second gate, which was moving in the same manner. Further on was a third gate, and then another, and another, as far as the eye could reach, evidently extending in an unbroken series completely across the great strait.

As the gates, with accelerated motion when the current caught them, clanged together, we beheld a spectacle that almost stopped the beating of our hearts.

The great Syrtis seemed to gather itself for a moment, and then it leaped upon the obstruction and hurled its waters into one vast foaming geyser that seemed to shoot a thousand feet skyward.

But the metal gates withstood the shock, though buried from our sight in the seething white mass, and the baffled waters instantly swirled round in ten thousand gigantic eddies, rising to the level of our window and beginning to inundate the power house before we fairly comprehended our peril.

"We have done the work," said Mr. Edison, smiling grimly. "Now we had better get out of this before the flood bursts upon us."

The warning came none too soon. It was necessary to act upon it at once if we would save our lives. Even before we could reach the entrance to the long passage through which we had come into the great engine room, the water had risen half way to our knees. Colonel Smith, catching Aina under his arm, led the way. The roar of the maddened torrent behind deafened us.

As we ran through the passage, the water followed us, with a wicked swishing sound, and within five seconds it was above our knees; in ten seconds up to our waists.

The great danger now was that we should be swept from our feet, and once down in that torrent there would have been little chance of our ever getting our heads above its level. Supporting ourselves as best we could with the aid of the walls, we partly ran, and were partly swept along, until, when we reached the outer end of the passage and emerged into the open air, the flood was swirling about our shoulders.

Here there was an opportunity to clutch some of the ornamental work surrounding the doorway, and thus we managed to stay our mad progress, and gradually to work out of the current until we found that the water, having now an abundance of room to spread, had fallen again as low as our knees.

But suddenly we heard the thunder of the banks tumbling behind us, and to the right and left, and the savage growl of the released water as it sprang through the breaches.

To my dying day, I think, I shall not forget the sight of a great fluid column that burst through the dyke at the edge of the grove of trees, and, by the tremendous impetus of its rush, seemed turned into a solid thing.

Like an enormous ram, it ploughed the soil to a depth of twenty feet, uprooting acres of the immense trees like stubble turned over by the ploughshare.

The uproar was so awful that for an instant the coolest of us lost our self-control. Yet we knew that we had not the fraction of a second to waste. The breaking of the banks had caused the water again rapidly to rise about us. In a little while it was once more as high as our waists.

In the excitement and confusion, deafened by the noise and blinded by the flying foam, we were in danger of becoming separated in the flood. We no longer knew certainly in what direction was the tree by whose aid we had ascended from the electrical ship. We pushed first one way and then another, staggering through the rushing waters in search of it. Finally we succeeded in locating it, and with all our strength hurried toward it.

Then there came a noise as if the globe of Mars had been split asunder, and another great head of water hurled itself down upon the soil before us, and, without taking time to spread, bored a vast cavity in the ground, and scooped out the whole of the grove before our eyes as easily as a gardener lifts a sod with his spade.

Our last hope was gone. For a moment the level of the water around us sank again, as it poured into the immense excavation where the grove had stood, but in an instant it was reinforced from all sides and began once more rapidly to rise.

We gave ourselves up for lost, and, indeed, there did not seem any possible hope of salvation.

Even in the extremity I saw Colonel Smith lifting the form of Aina, who had fainted, above the surface of the surging water, while Sidney Phillips stood by his side and aided him in supporting the unconscious girl.

"We stayed a little too long," was the only sound I heard from Mr. Edison.

The huge bulk of the power house partially protected us against the force of the current, and the water spun around us in great eddies. These swept us this way and that, but yet we managed to cling together, determined not to be separated in death if we could avoid it.

Suddenly a cry rang out directly above our heads:

"Jump for your lives, and be quick!"

At the same instant the ends of several ropes splashed into the water.

We glanced upward, and there, within three or four yards of our heads, hung the electrical ship, which we had left moored at the top of the tree.

Tom, the expert electrician from Mr. Edison's shop, who had remained in charge of the ship, had never once dreamed of such a thing as deserting us. The moment he saw the water bursting over the dam, and evidently flooding the building which we had entered, he cast off his moorings, as we subsequently learned, and hovered over the entrance to the power house, getting as low down as possible and keeping a sharp watch for us.

But most of the electric lights in the vicinity had been carried down by the first rush of water, and in the darkness he did not see us when we emerged from the entrance. It was only after the sweeping away of the grove of trees had allowed a flood of light to stream upon the scene from a cluster of electric lamps on a distant portion of the bank on the Syrtis that had not yet given way that he caught sight of us.

Immediately he began to shout to attract our attention, but in the awful uproar we could not hear him. Getting together all the ropes that he could lay his hands on, he steered the ship to a point directly over us, and then dropped down within a few yards of the boiling flood.

Now as he hung over our heads, and saw the water up to our very necks and still swiftly rising, he shouted again:

"Catch hold, for God's sake!"

The three men who were with him in the ship seconded his cries.

But by the time we had fairly grasped the ropes, so rapidly was the flood rising, we were already afloat. With the assistance of Tom and his men we were rapidly drawn up, and immediately Tom reversed the electric polarity, and the ship began to rise.

At that same instant, with a crash that shivered the air, the immense metallic power house gave way and was swept tumbling, like a hill torn loose from its base, over the very spot where a moment before we had stood. One second's hesitation on the part of Tom, and the electrical ship would have been battered into a shapeless wad of metal by the careening mass.

When we had attained a considerable height, so that we could see to a great distance on either side, the spectacle became even more fearful than it was when we were close to the surface.

On all sides banks and dykes were going down; trees were being uprooted; buildings were tumbling, and the ocean was achieving that victory over the land which had long been its due, but which the ingenuity of the inhabitants of Mars had postponed for ages.

Far away we could see the front of the advancing wave crested with foam that sparkled in the electric lights, and as it swept on it changed the entire aspect of the planet—in front of it all life, behind it all death.

Eastward our view extended across the Syrtis Major toward the land of Libya and the region of Isidis. On that side also the dykes were giving way under the tremendous pressure, and the floods were rushing toward the sunrise, which had just begun to streak the eastern sky.

The continents that were being overwhelmed on the western side of the Syrtis were Meroe, Aeria, Arabia, Edom and Eden.

The water beneath us continually deepened. The current from the melting snows around the southern pole was at its strongest, and one could hardly have believed that any obstruction put in its path would have been able to arrest it and turn it into these two all-swallowing deluges, sweeping east and west. But, as we now perceived, the level of the land over a large part of its surface was hundreds of feet below the ocean, so that the latter, when once the barriers were broken, rushed into depressions that yawned to receive it.

The point where we had dealt our blow was far removed from the great capital of Mars, around the Lake of the Sun, and we knew that we should have to wait for the floods to reach that point before the desired effect could be produced. By the nearest way, the water had at least 5,000 miles to travel. We estimated that its speed where we hung above it was as much as a hundred miles an hour. Even if that speed were maintained, more than two days and nights would be required for the floods to reach the Lake of the Sun.

But as the water rushed on it would break the banks of all the canals intersecting the country, and these, being also elevated above the surface, would add the impetus of their escaping waters to hasten the advance of the flood. We calculated, therefore, that about two days would suffice to place the planet at our mercy.

Half way from the Syrtis Major to the Lake of the Sun another great connecting link between the Southern and Northern ocean basins, called on our maps of Mars the Indus, existed, and through this channel we knew that another great current must be setting from the south toward the north. The flood that we had started would reach and break the banks of the Indus within one day.

The flood travelling in the other direction, towards the east, would have considerably further to go before reaching the neighbourhood of the Lake of the Sun. It, too, would involve hundreds of great canals as it advanced and would come plunging upon the Lake of the Sun and its surrounding forts and cities, probably about half a day later than the arrival of the deluge that travelled towards the west.

Now that we had let the awful destroyer loose we almost shrank from the thought of the consequences which we had produced. How many millions would perish as the result of our deed we could not even guess. Many of the victims, so far as we knew, might be entirely innocent of enmity toward us, or of the evil which had been done to our native planet. But this was a case in which the good—if they existed—must suffer with the bad on account of the wicked deeds of the latter.

I have already remarked that the continents of Mars were higher on their northern and southern borders where they faced the great oceans. These natural barriers bore to the main mass of the land somewhat the relation of the edge of a shallow dish to its bottom. Their rise on the land side was too gradual to give them the appearance of hills, but on the side toward the sea they broke down in steep banks and cliffs several hundred feet in height. We guessed that it would be in the direction of these elevations that the inhabitants would flee, and those who had timely warning might thus be able to escape in case the flood did not—as it seemed possible it might in its first mad rush—overtop the highest elevations on Mars.

As day broke and the sun slowly rose upon the dreadful scene beneath us, we began to catch sight of some of the fleeing inhabitants. We had shifted the position of the fleet toward the south, and were now suspended above the south-eastern corner of Aeria. Here a high bank of reddish rock confronted the sea, whose waters ran lashing and roaring along the bluffs to supply the rapid draught produced by the emptying of the Syrtis Major. Along the shore there was a narrow line of land, hundreds of miles in length, but less than a quarter of a mile broad, which still rose slightly above the surface of the water, and this land of refuge was absolutely packed with the monstrous inhabitants of the planet who had fled hither on the first warning that the water was coming.

In some places it was so crowded that the later comers could not find standing ground on dry land, but were continually slipping back and falling into the water. It was an awful sight to look at them. It reminded me of pictures that I had seen of the deluge in the days of Noah, when the waters had risen to the mountain tops, and men, women and children were fighting for a foothold upon the last dry spots that the earth contained.

We were all moved by a desire to help our enemies, for we were overwhelmed with feelings of pity and remorse, but to aid them was now utterly beyond our power. The mighty floods were out, and the end was in the hands of God.

Fortunately, we had little time for these thoughts, because no sooner had the day begun to dawn around us than the airships of the Martians appeared. Evidently the people in them were dazed by the disaster and uncertain what to do. It is doubtful whether at first they comprehended the fact that we were the agents who had produced the cataclysm.

But as the morning advanced the airships came flocking in greater and greater numbers from every direction, many swooping down close to the flood in order to rescue those who were drowning. Hundreds gathered along the slip of land which was crowded as I have described, with refugees, while other hundreds rapidly assembled about us, evidently preparing for an attack.

We had learned in our previous contests with the airships of the Martians that our electrical ships had a great advantage over them, not merely in rapidity and facility of movement, but in the fact that our disintegrators could sweep in every direction, while it was only with much difficulty that the Martian airships could discharge their electrical strokes at an enemy poised directly above their heads.

Accordingly, orders were instantly flashed to all the squadron to rise vertically to an elevation so great that the rarity of the atmosphere would prevent the airships from attaining the same level.

This manoeuvre was executed so quickly that the Martians were unable to deal us a blow before we were poised above them in such a position that they could not easily reach us. Still they did not mean to give up the conflict.

Presently we saw one of the largest of their ships manoeuvring in a very peculiar manner, the purpose of which we did not at first comprehend. Its forward portion commenced slowly to rise, until it pointed upward like the nose of a fish approaching the surface of the water. The moment it was in this position, an electrical bolt was darted from its prow, and one of our ships received a shock which, although it did not prove fatal to the vessel itself, killed two or three men aboard it, disarranged its apparatus, and rendered it for the time being useless.

"Ah, that's their trick, is it?" said Mr. Edison. "We must look out for that. Whenever you see one of the airships beginning to stick its nose up after that fashion blaze away at it."

An order to this effect was transmitted throughout the squadron. At the same time several of the most powerful disintegrators were directed upon the ship which had executed the stratagem and, reduced to a wreck, it dropped, whirling like a broken kite until it fell into the flood beneath.

Still the Martians' ships came flocking in ever greater numbers from all directions. They made desperate attempts to attain the level at which we hung above them. This was impossible, but many, getting an impetus by a swift run in the denser portion of the atmosphere beneath, succeeded in rising so high that they could discharge their electric artillery with considerable effect. Others, with more or less success, repeated the manoeuvre of the ship which had first attacked us, and thus the battle became gradually more general and more fierce, until, in the course of an hour or two, our squadron found itself engaged with probably a thousand airships, which blazed with incessant lightning strokes, and were able, all too frequently, to do us serious damage.

But on our part the battle was waged with a cool determination and a consciousness of insuperable advantage which boded ill for the enemy. Only three or four of our sixty electrical ships were seriously damaged, while the work of the disintegrators upon the crowded fleet that floated beneath us was terrible to look upon.

Our strokes fell thick and fast on all sides. It was like firing into a flock of birds that could not get away. Notwithstanding all their efforts they were practically at our mercy. Shattered into unrecognizable fragments, hundreds of the airships continually dropped from their great height to be swallowed up in the boiling waters.

Yet they were game to the last. They made every effort to get at us, and in their frenzy they seemed to discharge their bolts without much regard to whether friends or foes were injured. Our eyes were nearly blinded by the ceaseless glare beneath us, and the uproar was indescribable.

At length, after this fearful contest had lasted for at least three hours, it became evident that the strength of the enemy was rapidly weakening. Nearly the whole of their immense fleet of airships had been destroyed, or so far damaged that they were barely able to float. Just so long, however, as they showed signs of resistance we continued to pour our merciless fire upon them, and the signal to cease was not given until the airships which had escaped serious damage began to flee in every direction.

"Thank God, the thing is over," said Mr. Edison. "We have got the victory at last, but how we shall make use of it is something that at present I do not see."

"But will they not renew the attack," asked someone.

"I do not think they can," was the reply. "We have destroyed the very flower of their fleet."

"And better than that," said Colonel Smith, "we have destroyed their *elan*; we have made them afraid. Their discipline is gone."

But this was only the beginning of our victory. The floods below were achieving a still greater triumph, and now that we had conquered the airships we dropped within a few hundred feet of the surface of the water and then turned our faces westward in order to follow the advance of the deluge and see whether, as we had hoped, it would overwhelm our enemies in the very centre of their power.

In a little while we had overtaken the front wave, which was still devouring everything. We saw it bursting the banks of the canals, sweeping away forests of gigantic trees, and swallowing cities and villages, leaving nothing but a broad expanse of swirling and eddying waters, which, in consequence of the prevailing red hue of the vegetation and the soil, looked, as shuddering we gazed down upon it, like an ocean of blood flecked with foam and steaming with the escaping life of the planet from whose veins it gushed.

As we skirted the southern borders of the continent the same dreadful scenes which we had beheld on the coast of Aeria presented themselves. Crowds of refugees thronged the high border of the land and struggled with one another for a foothold against the continually rising flood.

We saw, too, flitting in every direction, but rapidly fleeing before our approach, many airships, evidently crowded with Martians, but not armed either for offence or defence. These, of course, we did not disturb, for merciless as our proceedings seemed even to ourselves, we had no intention of making war upon the innocent, or upon those who had no means to resist. What we had done it had seemed to us necessary to do, but henceforth we were resolved to take no more lives if it could be avoided.

Thus, during the remainder of that day, all of the following night and all of the next day, we continued upon the heels of the advancing flood.

Chapter 16

The second night we could perceive ahead of us the electric lights covering the land of Thaumasia, in the midst of which lay the Lake of the Sun. The flood would be upon it by daybreak, and, assuming that the demoralization produced by the news of the coming of the waters, which we were aware had hours before been flashed to the capital of Mars, would prevent the Martians from effectively manning their forts, we thought it safe to hasten on with the flagship, and one or two others, in advance of the water, and to hover over the Lake of the Sun in the darkness, in order that we might watch the deluge perform its awful work in the morning.

Thaumasia, as I have before remarked, was a broad, oval land, about 1,800 miles across, having the Lake of the Sun exactly in its centre. From this lake, which was four or five hundred miles in diameter, and circular in outline, many canals radiated, as straight as the spokes of a wheel, in every direction, and connected it with the surrounding seas.

Like all the other Martian continents, Thaumasia lay below the level of the sea, except toward the south, where it fronted the ocean.

Completely surrounding the lake was a great ring of cities constituting the capital of Mars. Here the genius of the Martians had displayed itself to the full. The surrounding country was irrigated until it fairly bloomed with gigantic vegetation and flowers; the canals were carefully regulated with locks so that the supply of water was under complete control; the display of magnificent metallic buildings of all kinds and sizes produced a most dazzling effect, and the protection against enemies afforded by the innumerable fortifications surrounding the ringed city, and guarding the neighbouring lands, seemed complete.

Suspended at a height of perhaps two miles from the surface, near the southern edge of the lake, we waited for the oncoming flood. With the dawn of day we began to perceive more clearly the effects which the news of the drowning of the planet had produced. It was evident that many of the inhabitants of the cities had already fled. Airships on which the fugitives hung as thick as swarms of bees were seen, elevated but a short distance above the ground, and making their way rapidly toward the south.

The Martians knew that their only hope of escape lay in reaching the high southern border of the land before the floods were upon them. But they must have known also that that narrow beach would not suffice to contain one in ten of those who sought refuge there. The density of the population around the Lake of the Sun seemed to us incredible. Again our hearts sank within us at the sight of the fearful destruction of life for which we were responsible. Yet we comforted ourselves with the reflection that it was unavoidable. As Colonel Smith put it:

"You couldn't trust these coyotes. The only thing to do was to drown them out. I am sorry for them, but I guess there will be as many left as will be good for us, anyhow."

We had not long to wait for the flood. As the dawn began to streak the east we saw its awful crest moving out of the darkness, bursting across the canals and ploughing its way in the direction of the crowded shores of the Lake of the Sun. The supply of water behind that great wave seemed inexhaustible. Five thousand miles it had travelled, and yet its power was as great as when it started from the Syrtis Major.

We caught sight of the oncoming water before it was visible to the Martians beneath us. But while it was yet many miles away, the roar of it reached them, and then arose a chorus of terrified cries, the effect of which, coming to our ears out of the half gloom of the morning, was most uncanny and horrible. Thousands upon thousands of the Martians still remained here to become the victims of the deluge. Some, perhaps, had doubted the truth of the reports that the banks were down and the floods were out; others, for one reason or another had been unable to get away; others, like the inhabitants of Pompeii, had lingered too long, or had returned after beginning their flight to secure abandoned treasures, and now it was too late to get away.

With a roar that shook the planet the white wall rushed upon the great city beneath our feet, and in an instant it had been engulfed. On went the flood, swallowing up the Lake of the Sun itself, and in a little while, as far as our eyes could range, the land of Thaumasia had been turned into a raging sea.

We now turned our ships toward the southern border of the land, following the direction of the airships carrying the fugitives, a few of which were still navigating the atmosphere a mile beneath us. In their excitement and terror the Martians paid little attention to us, although, as the morning brightened, they must have been aware of our presence over their heads. But, apparently, they no longer thought of resistance; their only object was escape from the immediate and appalling danger.

When we had progressed to a point about half way from the Lake of the Sun to the border of the sea, having dropped down within a few hundred feet of the surface, there suddenly appeared, in the midst of the raging waters, a sight so remarkable that at first I rubbed my eyes in astonishment, not crediting their report of what they beheld.

Standing on the apex of a sandy elevation, which still rose a few feet above the gathering flood, was the figure of a woman, as perfect in form and in classic beauty of feature as the Venus of Milo—a magnified human being not less than forty feet in height!

But for her swaying and the wild motions of her arms, we should have mistaken her for a marble statue.

Aina, who happened to be looking, instantly exclaimed:

"It is the woman from Ceres. She was taken prisoner by the Martians during their last invasion of that world, and since then has been a slave in the palace of the Emperor."

Apparently her great stature had enabled her to escape, while her masters had been drowned. She had fled like the others, toward the south, but being finally surrounded by the rising waters, had taken refuge on the hillock of sand, where we saw her. This was fast giving way under the assault of the waves, and even while we watched the water rose to her knees.

"Drop lower," was the order of the electrical steersman of the flagship, and as quickly as possible we approached the place where the towering figure stood.

She had realized the hopelessness of her situation, and quickly ceased those appalling and despairing gestures, which at first served to convince us that it was indeed a living being on whom we were looking.

There she stood, with a light, white garment thrown about her, erect, half-defiant, half yielding to her fear, more graceful than any Greek statue, her arms outstretched, yet motionless, and her eyes upcast, as if praying to her God to protect her. Her hair, which shone like gold in the increasing light of day, streamed over her shoulders, and her great eyes were astare between terror and supplication. So wildly beautiful a sight not one of us had ever beheld. For a moment sympathy was absorbed in admiration. Then:

"Save her! Save her!" was the cry that arose throughout the ship.

Ropes were instantly thrown out, and one or two men prepared to let themselves down in order better to aid her.

But when we were almost within reach, and so close that we could see the very expression of her eyes, which appeared to take no note of us, but to be fixed, with a far-away look upon something beyond human ken, suddenly the undermined bank on which she stood gave way, the blood-red flood swirled in from right to left, and then:

"The waters closed above her face With many a ring."

"If but for that woman's sake, I am sorry we drowned the planet," exclaimed Sidney Phillips. But a moment afterward I saw that he regretted what he had said, for Aina's eyes were fixed upon him. Perhaps, however, she did not understand his remark, and perhaps if she did it gave her no offence.

After this episode we pursued our way rapidly until we arrived at the shore of the Southern Ocean. There, as we had expected, was to be seen a narrow strip of land with the ocean on one side and the raging flood seeking to destroy it on the other. In some places it had been already broken through, so that the ocean was flowing in to assist in the drowning of Thaumasia.

But some parts of the coast were evidently so elevated that no matter how high the flood might rise it would not completely cover them. Here the fugitives had gathered in dense throngs and above them hovered most of the airships, loaded down with others who were unable to find room upon the dry land.

On one of the loftiest and broadest of these elevations we noticed indications of military order in the alignment of the crowds and the shore all around was guarded by gigantic pickets, who mercilessly shoved back into the flood all the later comers, and thus prevented too great crowding upon the land. In the centre of this elevation rose a palatial structure of red metal which Aina informed us was one of the residences of the Emperor, and we concluded that the monarch himself was now present there.

The absence of any signs of resistance on the part of the airships, and the complete drowning of all of the formidable fortifications on the surface of the planet, convinced us that all we now had to do in order to complete our conquest was to get possession of the person of the chief ruler.

The fleet was, accordingly, concentrated, and we rapidly approached the great Martian palace. As we came down within a hundred feet of them and boldly made our way among their airships, which retreated at our approach, the Martians gazed at us with mingled fear and astonishment.

We were their conquerors and they knew it. We were coming to demand their surrender, and they evidently understood that also. As we approached the palace signals were made from it with brilliant coloured banners which Aina informed us were intended as a token of truce.

"We shall have to go down and have a confab with them, I suppose," said Mr. Edison. "We can't kill them off now that they are helpless, but we must manage somehow to make them understand that unconditional surrender is their only chance."

"Let us take Aina with us," I suggested, "and since she can speak the language of the Martians we shall probably have no difficulty in arriving at an understanding."

Accordingly the flagship was carefully brought further down in front of the entrance to the palace, which had been kept clear by the Martian guards, and while the remainder of the squadron assembled within a few feet directly over our heads with the disintegrators turned upon the palace and the crowd below. Mr. Edison and myself, accompanied by Aina, stepped out upon the ground.

There was a forward movement in the immense crowd, but the guards sternly kept everybody back. A party of a dozen giants, preceded by one who seemed to be their commander, gorgeously attired in jewelled garments, advanced from the entrance of the palace to meet us. Aina addressed a few words to the leader, who replied sternly, and then, beckoning us to follow, retraced his steps into the palace.

Notwithstanding our confidence that all resistance had ceased, we did not deem it wise actually to venture into the lion's den without having taken every precaution against a surprise. Accordingly, before following the Martian into the palace, we had twenty of the electrical ships moored around it in such a position that they commanded not only the entrance but all of the principal windows, and then a party of forty picked men, each doubly armed with powerful disintegrators, were selected to attend us into the building. This party was placed under the command of Colonel Smith, and Sidney Phillips insisted on being a member of it.

In the meantime the Martian with his attendants who had first invited us to enter, finding that we did not follow him, had returned to the front of the palace. He saw the disposition that we had made of our forces, and instantly comprehended its significance, for his manner changed somewhat, and he seemed more desirous than before to conciliate us.

When he again beckoned us to enter, we unhesitatingly followed him, and, passing through the magnificent entrance, found ourselves in a vast ante-chamber, adorned after the manner of the Martians in the most expensive manner. Thence we passed into a great circular apartment, with a dome painted in imitation of the sky, and so lofty that to our eyes it seemed like the firmament itself. Here we found ourselves approaching an elevated throne situated in the centre of the apartment, while long rows of brilliantly armoured guards flanked us on either side, and, grouped around the throne, some standing and others reclining upon the flights of steps which appeared to be of solid gold, was an array of Martian woman, beautifully and becomingly attired, all of whom greatly astonished us by the singular charm of their faces and bearing, so different from the aspect of most of the Martians, whom we had already encountered.

Despite their stature—for these women averaged twelve or thirteen feet in height—the beauty of their complexions—of a dark, olive tint—was no less brilliant than that of the women of Italy or Spain.

At the top of the steps on a magnificent golden throne, sat the Emperor himself. There are some busts of Caracalla which I have seen that are almost as ugly as the face of the Martian ruler. He was of gigantic stature, larger than the majority of his subjects, and as near as I could judge must have been between fifteen and sixteen feet in height.

As I looked at him I understood a remark which had been made by Aina to the effect that the Martians were not all alike, and that the peculiarities of their minds were imprinted on their faces and expressed in their forms in a very wonderful, and sometimes terrible manner.

I had also learned from her that Mars was under a military government, and that the military class had absolute control of the planet. I was somewhat startled, then, in looking at the head and centre of the great military system of Mars, to find in his appearance a striking confirmation of the speculations of our terrestrial phrenologists. His broad, misshapen head bulged in those parts where they had placed the so-called organs of combativeness, destructiveness, etc.

Plainly, this was an effect of his training and education. His very brain had become a military engine; and the aspect of his face, the pitiless lines of his mouth and chin, the evil glare of his eyes, the attitude and carriage of his muscular body, all tended to complete the warlike ensemble.

He was magnificently dressed in some vesture that had the lustre of a polished plate of gold, with the suppleness of velvet. As we approached he fixed his immense, deep-set eyes sternly upon our faces.

The contrast between his truly terrible countenance and the Eve-like features of the women who surrounded his throne was as great as if Satan after his fall had here re-enthroned himself in the midst of angels.

Mr. Edison, Colonel Smith, Sidney Phillips, Aina and myself advanced at the head of the procession, our guard following in close order behind us. It had been evident from the moment that we entered the palace that Aina was regarded with aversion by all of the Martians. Even the women about the throne gazed scowlingly at her as we drew near. Apparently, the bitterness of feeling which had led to the awful massacre of all her race had not yet vanished. And, indeed, since the fact that she remained alive could have been known only to the Martian who had abducted her and to his immediate companions, her reappearance with us must have been a great surprise to all those who now looked upon her.

It was clear to me that the feeling aroused by her appearance was every moment becoming more intense. Still, the thought of a violent outbreak did not occur to me, because our recent triumph had seemed so complete that I believed the Martians would be awed by our presence, and would not undertake actually to injure the girl.

I think we all had the same impression, but as the event proved, we were mistaken.

Suddenly one of the gigantic guards, as if actuated by a fit of ungovernable hatred, lifted his foot and kicked Aina. With a loud shriek, she fell to the floor.

The blow was so unexpected that for a second we all remained riveted to the spot. Then I saw Colonel Smith's face turn livid, and at the same instant heard the whirr of his disintegrator, while Sidney Phillips, forgetting the deadly instrument that he carried in his hand, sprung madly toward the brute who had kicked Aina, as if he intended to throttle him, colossus as he was.

But Colonel Smith's aim, though instantaneously taken, as he had been accustomed to shoot on the plains, was true, and Phillips, plunging madly forward, seemed wreathed in a faint blue mist—all that the disintegrator had left of the gigantic Martian.

Who could adequately describe the scene that followed?

I remember that the Martian Emperor sprang to his feet, looking tenfold more terrible than before. I remember that there instantly burst from the line of guards on either side crinkling beams of death-fire that seemed to sear the eyeballs. I saw a half a dozen of our men fall in heaps of ashes, and even at that terrible moment I had time to wonder that a single one of us remained alive.

Rather by instinct than in consequence of any order given, we formed ourselves in a hollow square, with Aina lying apparently lifeless in the centre, and then with gritted teeth we did our work.

The lines of guards melted before the disintegrators like rows of snow men before a licking flame.

The discharge of the lightning engines in the hands of the Martians in that confined space made an uproar so tremendous that it seemed to pass the bounds of human sense.

More of our men fell before their awful fire, and for the second time since our arrival on this dreadful planet of war our annihilation seemed inevitable.

But in a moment the whole scene changed. Suddenly there was a discharge into the room which I knew came from one of the disintegrators of the electrical ships. It swept through the crowded throng like a destroying blast. Instantly from another side swished a second discharge, no less destructive, and this was quickly followed by a third. Our ships were firing through the windows.

Almost at the same moment I saw the flagship, which had been moored in the air close to the entrance and floating only three or four feet above the ground, pushing its way through the gigantic doorway from the ante-room, with its great disintegrators pointed upon the crowd like the muzzles of a cruiser's guns.

And now the Martians saw that the contest was hopeless for them, and their mad struggle to get out of the range of the disintegrators and to escape from the death chamber was more appalling to look upon than anything that had yet occurred.

It was a panic of giants. They trod one another under foot; they yelled and screamed in their terror; they tore each other with their claw-like fingers. They no longer thought of resistance. The battle spirit had been blown out of them by a breath of terror that shivered their marrow.

Still the pitiless disintegrators played upon them until Mr. Edison, making himself heard, now that the thunder of their engines had ceased to reverberate through the chamber, commanded that our fire should cease.

In the meantime the armed Martians outside the palace, hearing the uproar within, seeing our men pouring their fire through the windows, and supposing that we were guilty at once of treachery and assassination, had attempted an attack upon the electrical ships stationed round the building. But fortunately they had none of their larger engines at hand, and with their hand arms alone they had not been able to stand up against the disintegrators. They were blown away before the withering fire of the ships by the hundred until, fleeing from destruction, they rushed madly, driving their unarmed companions before them into the seething waters of the flood close at hand.

Chapter 17

Through all this terrible contest the emperor of the Martians had remained standing upon his throne, gazing at the awful spectacle, and not moving from the spot. Neither he nor the frightened woman gathered upon the steps of the throne had been injured by the disintegrators. Their immunity was due to the fact that the position and elevation of the throne were such that it was not within the range of fire of the electrical ships which had poured their vibratory discharges through the windows, and we inside had only directed our fire toward the warriors who had attacked us.

Now that the struggle was over we turned our attention to Aina. Fortunately the girl had not been seriously injured and she was quickly restored to consciousness. Had she been killed, we would have been practically helpless in attempting further negotiations, because the knowledge which we had acquired of the language of the Martians from the prisoner captured on the golden asteroid, was not sufficient to meet the requirements of the occasion.

When the Martian monarch saw that we had ceased the work of death, he sank upon his throne. There he remained, leaning his chin upon his two hands and staring straight before him like that terrible doomed creature who fascinates the eyes of every beholder standing in the Sistine Chapel and gazing at Michael Angelo's dreadful painting of "The Last Judgement."

This wicked Martian also felt that he was in the grasp of pitiless and irresistible fate, and that a punishment too well deserved, and from which there was no possible escape, now confronted him.

There he remained in a hopelessness which almost compelled our sympathy, until Aina had so far recovered that she was once more able to act as our interpreter. Then we made short work of the negotiations. Speaking through Aina, the commander said:

"You know who we are. We have come from the earth, which, by your command, was laid waste. Our commission was not revenge, but self-protection. What we have done has been accomplished with that in view. You have just witnessed an example of our power, the exercise of which was not dictated by our wish, but compelled by the attack wantonly made upon a helpless member of our own race under our protection."

"We have laid waste your planet, but it is simply a just retribution for what you did with ours. We are prepared to complete the destruction, leaving not a living being in this world of yours, or to grant you peace, at your choice. Our condition of peace is simply this: 'All resistance must cease absolutely.'"

"Quite right," broke in Colonel Smith; "let the scorpion pull out his sting or we'll do it for him."

"Nothing that we could now do," continued the commander, "would in my opinion save you from ultimate destruction. The forces of nature which we have been compelled to let loose upon you will complete their own victory. But we do not wish, unnecessarily, to stain our hands further with your blood. We shall leave you in possession of your lives. Preserve them if you can. But, in case the flood recedes before you have all perished from starvation, remember that you here take an oath, solemnly binding yourself and your descendants forever never again to make war upon the earth."

"That's really the best we can do," said Mr. Edison, turning to us. "We can't possibly murder these people in cold blood. The probability is that the flood has hopelessly ruined all their engines of war. I do not believe that there is one chance in ten that the waters will drain off in time to enable them to get at their stores of provisions before they have perished from starvation."

"It is my opinion," said Lord Kelvin, who had joined us (his pair of disintegrators hanging by his side, attached to a strap running over the back of his neck, very much as a farmer sometimes carries his big mittens), "it is my opinion that the flood will recede more rapidly than you think, and that the majority of these people will survive. But I quite agree with your merciful view of the matter. We must be guilty of no wanton destruction. Probably more than nine-tenths of the inhabitants of Mars have perished in the deluge. Even if all the others survived ages would elapse before they could regain the power to injure us."

I need not describe in detail how our propositions were received by the Martian monarch. He knew, and his advisers, some of whom he had called in consultation, also knew, that everything was in our hands to do as we pleased. They readily agreed, therefore, that they would make no more resistance and that we and our electrical ships should be undisturbed while we remained upon Mars. The monarch took the oath prescribed after the manner of his race: thus the business was completed. But through it all there had been the shadow of a sneer on the emperor's face which I did not like. But I said nothing.

And now we began to think of our return home, and of the pleasure we should have in recounting our adventures to our friends on the earth, who were doubtless eagerly waiting for news from us. We knew they had been watching Mars with powerful telescopes, and we were also eager to learn how much they had seen and how much they had been able to guess of our proceedings.

But a day or two at least would be required to overhaul the electrical ships and to examine the state of our provisions. Those which we had brought from the earth, it will be remembered, had been spoiled and we had been compelled to replace them from the compressed provisions found in the Martians' storehouse. This compressed food had proved not only exceedingly agreeable to the taste, but very nourishing, and all of us had grown extremely fond of it. A new supply, however, would be needed in order to carry us back to the earth. At least sixty days would be required for the homeward journey, because we could hardly expect to start from Mars with the same initial velocity which we had been able to generate on leaving home.

In considering the matter of provisioning the fleet it finally became necessary to take an account of our losses. This was a thing that we had all shrunk from, because they had seemed to us almost too terrible to be borne. But now the facts had to be faced. Out of the 100 ships, carrying something more than two thousand souls, with which we had quitted the earth, there remained only fifty-five ships and 1,085 men! All the others had been lost in our terrific encounters with the Martians, and particularly in our first disastrous battle beneath the clouds.

Among the lost were many men whose names were famous upon the earth, and whose death would be widely deplored when the news of it was received upon their native planet. Fortunately this number did not include any of those whom I have had occasion to mention in the course of this narrative. The venerable Lord Kelvin, who, notwithstanding his age, and his pacific disposition, proper to a man of science, had behaved with the courage and coolness of a veteran in every crisis; Monsieur Moissan, the eminent chemist; Prof. Sylvanus P. Thompson, and the Heidelberg Professor, to whom we all felt under special obligations because he had opened to our comprehension the charming lips of Aina—all these had survived, and were about to return with us to the earth.

It seemed to some of us almost heartless to deprive the Martians who still remained alive of any of the provisions which they themselves would require to tide them over the long period which must elapse before the recession of the flood should enable them to discover the sites of their ruined homes, and to find the means of sustenance. But necessity was now our only law. We learned from Aina that there must be stores of provisions in the neighbourhood of the palace, because it was the custom of the Martians to lay up such stores during the harvest time in each Martian year in order to provide against the contingency of an extraordinary drought.

It was not with very good grace that the Martian Emperor acceded to our demands that one of the storehouses should be opened, but resistance was useless, and of course we had our way.

The supplies of water which we brought from the earth, owing to a peculiar process invented by Monsieur Moissan, had been kept in exceedingly good condition, but they were now running low and it became necessary to replenish them also. This was easily done from the Southern Ocean, for on Mars, since the levelling of the continental elevations, brought about many years ago, there is comparatively little salinity in the sea waters.

While these preparations were going on Lord Kelvin and the other men of science entered with the utmost eagerness upon those studies, the prosecution of which had been the principal inducement leading them to embark on the expedition. But, almost all of the face of the planet being covered with the flood, there was comparatively little that they could do. Much, however, could be learned with the aid of Aina from the Martians, now crowded on the land about the palace.

The results of these discoveries will in due time appear, fully elaborated in learned and authoritative treatises prepared by these savants themselves. I shall only call attention to one, which seemed to me very remarkable. I have already said that there were astonishing differences in the personal appearance of the Martians, evidently arising from differences of character and education, which had impressed themselves in the physical aspect of the individuals.

We now learned that these differences were more completely the result of education than we had at first supposed.

Looking about among the Martians by whom we were surrounded, it soon became easy for us to tell who were the soldiers and who were the civilians, simply by the appearance of their bodies, and particularly of their heads. All members of the military class resembled, to a greater or less extent, the monarch himself, in that those parts of their skulls which our phrenologists had designated as the bumps of destructiveness, combativeness and so on were enormously and disproportionately developed.

And all this, as we were assured, was completely under the control of the Martians themselves. They had learned, or invented, methods by which the brain itself could be manipulated, so to speak, and any desired portions of it could be specially developed, while the other parts of it were left to their normal growth. The consequence was that in the Martian schools and colleges there was no teaching in our sense of the word. It was all brain culture.

A Martian youth selected to be a soldier had his fighting faculties especially developed, together with those parts of the brain which impart courage and steadiness of nerve. He who was intended for scientific investigation had his brain developed into a mathematical machine, or an instrument of observation. Poets and literary men had their heads bulging with the imaginative faculties. The heads of inventors were developed into a still different shape.

"And so," said Aina, translating for us the words of a professor in the Imperial University of Mars, from whom we derived the greater part of our information on this subject, "the Martian boys do not study a subject; they do not have to learn it, but, when their brains have been sufficiently developed in the proper direction, they comprehend it instantly, by a kind of divine instinct."

But among the women of Mars, we saw none of these curious, and to our eyes monstrous, differences of development. While the men received, in addition to their special education, a broad general culture also, with the women there was no special education. It was all general in its character, yet thorough enough in that way. The consequence was that only female brains upon Mars were entirely well balanced. This was the reason why we invariably found the Martian women to be remarkably charming creatures, with none of those physical exaggerations and uncouth developments which disfigured their masculine companions.

All the books of the Martians, we ascertained, were books of history and of poetry. For scientific treatises they had no need, because, as I have explained, when the brains of those intended for scientific pursuits had been developed in the proper way the knowledge of nature's laws came to them without effort, as a spring bubbles from the rocks.

One word of explanation may be needed concerning the failure of the Martians, with all their marvellous powers, to invent electrical ships like those of Mr. Edison and engines of destruction comparable with our disintegrators. This failure was simply due to the fact that on Mars there did not exist the peculiar metals by the combination of which Mr. Edison had been able to effect his wonders. The theory involved in our inventions was perfectly understood by them, and had they possessed the means, doubtless they would have been able to carry it into practice even more effectively than we had done.

After two or three days all the preparations having been completed, the signal was given for our departure. The men of science were still unwilling to leave this strange world, but Mr. Edison decided that we could linger no longer.

At the moment of starting a most tragic event occurred. Our fleet was assembled around the palace, and the signal was given to rise slowly to a considerable height before imparting a great velocity to the electrical ships. As we slowly rose we saw the immense crowd of giants beneath us, with upturned faces, watching our departure. The Martian monarch and all his suite had come out upon the terrace of the palace to look at us. At a moment when he probably supposed himself to be unwatched he shook his fist at the retreating fleet. My eyes and those of several others in the flagship chanced to be fixed upon him. Just as he made the gesture one of the women of his suite, in her eagerness to watch us, apparently lost her balance and stumbled against him. Without a moment's hesitation, with a tremendous blow, he felled her like an ox at his feet.

A fearful oath broke from the lips of Colonel Smith, who was one of those looking on. It chanced that he stood near the principal disintegrator of the flagship. Before anybody could interfere he had sighted and discharged it. The entire force of the terrible engine, almost capable of destroying a fort, fell upon the Martian Emperor, and not merely blew him into a cloud of atoms, but opened a great cavity in the ground on the spot where he had stood.

A shout arose from the Martians, but they were too much astounded at what had occurred to make any hostile demonstrations, and, anyhow, they knew well that they were completely at our mercy.

Mr. Edison was on the point of rebuking Colonel Smith for what he had done, but Aina interposed.

"I am glad it was done," said she, "for now only can you be safe. That monster was more directly responsible than any other inhabitant of Mars for all the wickedness of which they have been guilty."

"The expedition against the earth was inspired solely by him. There is a tradition among the Martians—which my people, however, could never credit—that he possessed a kind of immortality. They declared that it was he who led the former expedition against the earth when my ancestors were brought away prisoners from their happy home, and that it was his image which they had set up in stone in the midst of the Land of Sand. He prolonged his existence, according to this legend, by drinking the waters of a wonderful fountain, the secret of whose precise location was known to him alone, but which was situated at that point where in your maps of Mars the name of the Fons Juventae occurs. He was personified wickedness, that I know; and he never would have kept his oath if power had returned to him again to injure the earth. In destroying him, you have made your victory secure."

Chapter 18

When at length we once more saw our native planet, with its well-remembered features of land and sea, rolling beneath our eyes, the feeling of joy that came over us transcended all powers of expression.

In order that all the nations which had united in sending out the expedition should have visual evidence of its triumphant return, it was decided to make the entire circuit of the earth before seeking our starting point and disembarking. Brief accounts in all known languages, telling the story of what we had done were accordingly prepared, and then we dropped down through the air until again we saw the well-loved blue dome over our heads, and found ourselves suspended directly above the white-topped cone of Fujiyama, the sacred mountain of Japan. Shifting our place toward the northeast, we hung above the city of Tokyo and dropped down into the crowds that had assembled to watch us, the prepared accounts of our journey, which, the moment they had been read and comprehended, led to such an outburst of rejoicing as it would be quite impossible to describe.

One of the ships containing the Japanese members of the expedition dropped to the ground, and we left them in the midst of their rejoicing countrymen. Before we started—and we remained but a short time suspended above the Japanese capital—millions had assembled to greet us with their cheers.

We now repeated what we had done during our first examination of the surface of Mars. We simply remained suspended in the atmosphere, allowing the earth to turn beneath us. As Japan receded in the distance we found China beginning to appear. Shifting our position a little toward the south we again came to rest over the city of Peking, where once more we parted with some of our companions, and where the outburst of universal rejoicing was repeated.

From Asia, crossing the Caspian Sea, we passed over Russia, visiting in turn Moscow and St. Petersburg.

Still the great globe rolled steadily beneath, and still we kept the sun with us. Now Germany appeared, and now Italy, and then France, and England, as we shifted our position, first North then South, in order to give all the world the opportunity to see that its warriors had returned victorious from their far conquest. And in each country as it passed beneath our feet, we left some of the comrades who had shared our perils and our adventures.

At length the Atlantic had rolled away under us, and we saw the spires of the new New York.

The news of our coming had been flashed ahead from Europe, and our countrymen were prepared to welcome us. We had originally started, it will be remembered, at midnight, and now again as we approached the new capital of the world the curtain of night was just beginning to be drawn over it. But our signal lights were ablaze, and through these they were aware of our approach.

Again the air was filled with bursting rockets and shaken with the roar of cannon, and with volleying cheers, poured from millions of throats, as we came to rest directly above the city.

Three days after the landing of the fleet, and when the first enthusiasm of our reception had a little passed, I received a beautifully engraved card inviting me to be present in Trinity Church at the wedding of Aina and Sidney Phillips.

When I arrived at the church, which had been splendidly decorated, I found there Mr. Edison, Lord Kelvin, and all the other members of the crew of the flagship, and, considerably to my surprise, Colonel Smith, appropriately attired, and with a grace for the possession of which I had not given him credit, gave away the beautiful bride.

But Alonzo Jefferson Smith was a man and a soldier, every inch of him.

"I asked her for myself," he whispered to me after the ceremony, swallowing a great lump in his throat, "but she has had the desire of her heart. I am going back to the plains. I can get a command again, and I still know how to fight."

And thus was united, for all future time, the first stem of the Aryan race, which had been long lost, but not destroyed, with the latest offspring of that great family, and the link which had served to bring them together was the far-away planet of Mars.

A Columbus of Space

CHAPTER 1

A Marvellous Invention

I am a hero worshiper; an insatiable devourer of biographies; and I say that no man in all the splendid list ever equalled Edmund Stonewall. You smile because you have never heard his name, for, until now, his biography has not been written. And this is not truly a biography; it is only the story of the crowning event in Stonewall's career.

Really it humbles one's pride of race to see how ignorant the world is of its true heroes. Many a man who cuts a great figure in history is, after all, a poor specimen of humanity, slavishly following old ruts, destitute of any real originality, and remarkable only for some exaggeration of the commonplace. But in the case of Edmund Stonewall the world cannot be blamed for its ignorance, because, as I have already said, his story remains to be written, and hitherto it has been guarded as a profound secret.

I do not wish to exaggerate; yet I cannot avoid seeming to do so in simply telling the facts. If Stonewall's proceedings had become matter of common knowledge the world would have been—I must speak plainly—revolutionized. He held in his hands the means of realizing the wildest dreams of power, wealth, and human mastery over the forces of nature, that any enthusiast ever treasured in his prophetic soul. It was a part of his originality that he never entertained the thought of employing his advantage in any such way. His character was entirely free from the ordinary forms of avidity. He cared nothing for wealth in itself, and as little for fame. All his energies were concentrated upon the attainment of ends which nobody but himself would have regarded as of any practical importance. Thus it happened that, having made an invention which would have put every human industry upon a new footing, and multiplied beyond the limits of calculation the activities and achievements of mankind, this extraordinary person turned his back upon the colossal fortune which he had

169

but to stretch forth his hand and grasp, refused to seize the unlimited power which his genius had laid at his feet, and used his unparalleled discovery for a purpose so eccentric, so wildly unpractical, so utterly beyond the pale of waking life, that to any ordinary man he must have seemed a lunatic lost in an endless dream of bedlam. And to this day I cannot, without a nervous thrill, think how the desire of all the ages, the ideal that has been the loadstar for thousands of philosophers, savants, inventors, prophets, and dreamers, was actually realized upon the earth; and yet of all its fifteen hundred million inhabitants but a single one knew it, possessed it, controlled it—and he would not reveal it, but hoarded and used his knowledge for the accomplishment of the craziest design that ever took shape in a human brain.

Now, to be more specific. Of Stonewall's antecedents I know very little. I only know that, in a moderate way, he was wealthy, and that he had no immediate family ties. He was somewhere near thirty years of age, and held the diploma of one of our oldest universities. But he was not, in a general way, sociable, and I never knew him to attend any of the reunions of his former classmates, or to show the slightest interest in any of the events or functions of society, although its doors were open to him through some distant relatives who were widely connected in New York, and who at times tried to draw him into their circle. He would certainly have adorned it, but it had no attraction for him. Nevertheless he was a member of the Olympus Club, where he frequently spent his evenings. But he made very few acquaintances even there, and I believe that except myself, Jack Ashton, Henry Darton, and Will Church, he had no intimates. And we knew him only at the club. There, when he was alone with us, he sometimes partly opened up his mind, and we were charmed by his variety of knowledge and the singularity of his conversation. I shall not disguise the fact that we thought him extremely eccentric, although the idea of anything in the nature of insanity never entered our heads. We knew that he was engaged in recondite researches of a scientific nature, and that he possessed a private laboratory, although none of us had ever entered it. Occasionally he would speak of some new advance of science, throwing a flood of light by his clear expositions upon things of which we should otherwise have remained profoundly ignorant. His imagination flashed like lightning over the subject of his talk, revealing it at the most unexpected angles, and often he roused us to real enthusiasm for things the very names of which we almost forgot amidst the next day's occupations.

There was one subject on which he was particularly eloquent—radioactivity; that most strange property of matter whose discovery had been the crowning glory of science in the closing decade of the nineteenth century. None of us really knew anything about it except what Stonewall taught us. If some new incomprehensible announcement appeared in the newspapers we skipped it, being sure that Edmund would make it all clear at the club in the evening. He made us understand, in a dim way, that some vast, tremendous secret lay behind it all. I recall his saying, on one occasion, not long before the blow fell:

"Listen to this! Here's Professor Thomson declaring that a single grain of radium contains in its padlocked atoms energy enough to lift a million tons three hundred yards high. Professor Thomson is too modest in his estimates, and he hasn't the ghost of an idea how to get at that energy. Neither has Professor Rutherford, nor Lord Kelvin; *but somebody will get at it, just the same.*"

He positively thrilled us when he spoke thus, for there was a look in his eyes which seemed to penetrate depths unfathomable to our intelligence. Yet we had not the faintest conception of what was really passing in his mind. If we had understood it, if we had caught a single clear glimpse of the workings of his intellect, we should have been appalled. And if we had known how close we stood to the verge of an abyss of mystery about to be lighted by such a gleam as had never before been emitted from the human spirit, I believe that we would have started from our chairs and fled in dismay.

But we understood nothing, except that Edmund was indulging in one of his eccentric dreams, and Jack, in his large, careless, good-natured way broke in with:

"Well, Edmund, suppose *you* could 'get at it,' as you say; what would you do with it?"

Stonewall's eyes gleamed for a moment, and then he replied, with a curious emphasis:

"I might do what Archimedes dreamed of."

None of us happened to remember what it was that Archimedes had dreamed, and the subject was dropped.

For a considerable time afterwards we saw nothing of Stonewall. He did not come to the club, and we were beginning to think of looking him up, when one evening, quite unexpectedly, he dropped in, wearing an unusually cheerful expression. We had greatly missed him, and we now greeted him with effusion. His animation impressed us all, and he had no sooner shaken hands than he said, with suppressed excitement in his voice:

"Well, I've 'got at it.'"

"Got at what?" drawled Jack.

"The inter-atomic energy. I've got it under control."

"The deuce you have!" said Jack.

"Yes, I've arrived where a certain professor dreamed of being when he averred that 'when man knows that every breath of air he draws has contained within itself force enough to drive the workshops of the world he will find out some day, somehow, some way of tapping that energy.' The thing is done, for I've tapped it!"

We stared at one another, not knowing what to say, except Jack, who, inspired by the spirit of mischief, drawled out:

"Ah, yes, I remember. Well then, Edmund, as I asked you before, what are you going to do with it?"

There was not really any thought among us of poking fun at Edmund; we respected and admired him far too much for that; nevertheless, catching the infection of banter from Jack, we united in demanding, in a manner which I can now see must have appeared most provoking:

"Why, yes, Edmund, tell us what you are going to do with it."

And then Jack added fuel by mockingly, though with perfectly good-natured intention, taking Edmund by the hand and swinging him in front of us with:

"Gentlemen, Archimedes junior."

Stonewall's eyes flashed and his cheek darkened, but for a moment he said nothing. Presently, with a return of his former affability, he said:

"I wish you would come over to the laboratory and let me show you what I am going to do."

Of course we instantly assented. Nothing could have pleased us better than this invitation, for we had long been dying to see the inside of Edmund's laboratory. We all got our hats and started out with him. We knew where he lived, occupying a whole house though he was a bachelor, but none of us had ever seen the inside of it, and our curiosity was on the *qui vive*. He led us through a handsome hallway and a rear apartment directly into the back yard, half of which we were surprised to find enclosed and roofed over, forming a huge shanty, like a workshop. Edmund opened the door of the shanty and ushered us in.

A remarkable object at once concentrated our attention. In the centre of the place was the queerest-looking thing that you can well imagine. I can hardly describe it. It was round and elongated like a boiler, with bulging ends, and seemed to be made of polished steel. Its total length was about eighteen feet, and its width ten feet. Edmund approached it and opened a door in the end, which was wide and high enough for us to enter without stooping or crowding.

"Step in, gentlemen," he said, and unhesitatingly we obeyed him, all except Church, who for some unknown reason remained outside, and when we looked for him had disappeared.

Edmund turned on a bright light, and we found ourselves in an oblong chamber, beautifully fitted up with polished woodwork, and leather-cushioned seats running round the sides. Many metallic knobs and handles shone on the walls.

"Sit down," said Edmund, "and I will tell you what I have got here."

He stepped to the door and called again for Church but there was no answer. We concluded that, thinking the thing would be too deep to be interesting, he had gone back to the club. That was not what he had done, as you will learn later, but he never regretted what he did do. Getting no response from Church, Edmund finally sat down with us on one of the leather-covered benches, and began his explanation.

"As I was telling you at the club," he said, "I've solved the mystery of the atoms. I'm sure you'll excuse me from explaining my method" (there was a little raillery in his manner), "but at least you can understand the plain statement that I've got unlimited power at my command. These knobs and handles that you see are my keys for turning it on and off, and controlling it as I wish. Mark you, this power comes right out of the heart of what we call matter; the world is chock full of it. We have known that it was there at least ever since radioactivity was discovered, but it looked as though human intelligence would never be able to set it free from its prison. Nevertheless I have not only set it free, but I am able to control it as perfectly as if it were steam from a boiler, or an electric current from a dynamo."

Jack, who was as unscientific a person as ever lived, yawned, and Edmund noticed it. But he showed no irritation, merely smiling, and saying, with a wink at me and Henry:

"Even this seems to be rather too deep, so perhaps I had better show you, instead of telling you, what I mean. Excuse me a moment."

He stepped out of the door, and we remained seated. We heard a noise outside like the opening of a barn door, and immediately Edmund reappeared and closed the door of the chamber in which we were. We watched him with growing curiosity. With a singular smile he pressed a knob on the wall, and instantly we felt that the chamber was rising in the air. It rocked a little like a boat in wavy water. We were startled, of course, but not alarmed.

"Hello!" exclaimed Jack. "What kind of a balloon is this?"

"It's something more than a balloon," was Edmund's reply, and as he spoke he touched another knob, and we felt the car, as I must now call it, come to rest. Then Edmund opened a shutter at one side, and we all sprang up to look out. Below us we saw roofs and the tops of two trees standing at the side of the street.

"We're about a hundred feet up," said Edmund quietly. "What do you think of it now?"

"Wonderful! wonderful!" we exclaimed in a breath. And I continued:

"And do you say that it is inter-atomic energy that does this?"

"Nothing else in the world," returned Edmund.

But bantering Jack must have his quip:

"By the way, Edmund," he demanded, "what was it that Archimedes dreamed? But no matter; you've knocked him silly. Now, what are you going to do with your atomic balloon?"

Edmund's eyes flashed:

"You'll see in a minute."

The scene out of the window was beautiful, and for a moment we all remained watching it. The city lights were nearly all below our level, and away off over the New Jersey horizon I noticed the planet Venus, near to setting, but as brilliant as a diamond. I am fond of star-gazing, and I called Edmund's attention to the planet as he happened to be standing next to me.

"Lovely, isn't she?" he said with enthusiasm. "The finest world in the solar system, and what a strange thing that she should have one side always day and the other always night."

I was surprised by his exhibition of astronomic lore, for I had never known that he had given any attention to the subject, but a minute later the incident was forgotten as Edmund suddenly pushed us back from the window and closed the shutter.

"Going down again so soon?" asked Jack.

Edmund smiled. "Going," he said simply, and put his hand to one of the knobs. Immediately we felt ourselves moving very slowly.

"That's right, Edmund," put in Jack again, "let us down easy; I don't like bumps."

We expected at each instant to feel the car touch the cradle in which it had evidently rested, but never were three mortals so mistaken. What really did happen can better be described in the words of Will Church, who, you will remember, had disappeared at the beginning of our singular adventure. I got the account from him long afterwards. He had written it out carefully and put it away in a safe, as a sort of historic document. Here is Church's narrative, omitting the introduction, which read like a law paper:

"When we went over from the club to Stonewall's house, I dropped behind the others, because the four of them took up the whole width of the sidewalk. Stonewall was talking to them, and my attention was attracted by something uncommon in his manner. He had an indefinable carriage of the head which suggested to me the suspicion that everything was not just as it should be. I don't mean that I thought him crazy, or anything of that kind, but I felt that he had some scheme in his mind to fool us.

"I bitterly repented, after things turned out as they did, that I had not whispered a word to the others. But that would have been difficult, and, besides, I had no idea of the seriousness of the affair. Nevertheless, I determined to stay out of it, so that the laugh should not be on me at any rate. Accordingly when the others entered the car I stayed outside, and when Stonewall called me I did not answer.

"When he came out to open the roof of the shed, he did not see me in the shadow where I stood. The opening of the roof revealed the whole scheme in a flash. I had had no suspicion that the car was any kind of a balloon, and even after he had so significantly thrown the roof open, and then entered the car and closed the door, I was fairly amazed to see the thing began to rise without the slightest noise, and as if it were enchanted. It really looked diabolical as it floated silently upward and passed through the opening, and the sight gave me a shiver.

"But I was greatly relieved when it stopped at a height of a hundred feet or so, and then I said to myself that I should have been less of a fool if I had stayed with the others, for now they would have the laugh on me alone. Suddenly, while I watched, expecting every moment to see them drop down again, for I supposed that it was merely an experiment to show that the thing would float, the car started upward, very slowly at first, but increasing its speed until it had attained an elevation of perhaps five hundred feet. There it hung for a moment, like some mail-clad monster glinting in the quavering light of the street arcs, and then, without warning, made a dart skyward. For a minute it circled like a strange bird taking its bearings, and finally rushed off westward until I lost sight of it behind some tall buildings. I ran into the house to reach the street, but found the outer door locked, and not a person visible. I called but nobody came. Returning to the yard I discovered a place where I could get over the fence, and so I escaped into the street. Immediately I searched the sky for the mysterious car, but could see no sign of it. They were gone! I almost sank upon the pavement in a state of helpless excitement, which I could not have explained to myself if I had stopped to reason; for why, after all, should I take the thing so tragically. But something within me said that all was wrong. A policeman happened to pass.

"'Officer! officer!' I shouted, 'have you seen it?'

"'Seen what?' asked the blue-coat, twirling his club.

"'The car—the balloon,' I stammered.

"'Balloon in your head! You're drunk. Get long out o' here!'

"I realized the impossibility of explaining the matter to him, and running back to the place where I had got over the fence I climbed into the yard and entered the shed. Fortunately the policeman paid no further attention to my movements after I left him. I sat down on the empty cradle and stared up through the opening in the roof, hoping against hope to see them coming back. It must have been midnight before I gave up my vigil in despair, and went home, sorely puzzled, and blaming myself for having kept my suspicions unuttered. I finally got to sleep, but I had horrible dreams.

"The next day I was up early looking through all the papers in the hope of finding something about the car. But there was not a word. I watched the news columns for several days without result. Whenever the coast was clear I haunted Stonewall's yard, but the fatal shed yawned empty, and there was not a soul about the house. I cannot describe my feelings. My friends seemed to have been snatched away by some mysterious agency, and the horror of the thing almost drove me crazy. I felt that I was, in a manner, responsible for their disappearance.

"One day my heart sank at the sight of a cousin of Jack Ashton's motioning to me in the street. He approached, with a troubled look. 'Mr. Church,' he said, 'I think you know me; can you tell me what has become of Jack? I haven't seen him for several days.' What could I say? Still believing that they would soon come back, I invented, on the spur of the moment, a story that Jack, with a couple of intimate friends, had gone off on a hunting expedition. I took a little comfort in the reflection that my friends, like myself, were bachelors, and consequently at liberty to disappear if they chose.

"But when more than a week had passed with out any news of them I was thrown into despair. I had to give up all hope. Remembering how near we were to the coast, I concluded that they had drifted out over the sea and gone down. It was hard for me, after the lie I had told, to let out the truth to such of their friends as I knew, but I had to do it. Then the police took the matter in hand and ransacked Stonewall's laboratory and the shanty without finding anything to throw light on the mystery. It was a newspaper sensation for a few days, but as nothing came of it everybody soon forgot all about it—all except me. I was left to my loneliness and my regrets.

"A year has now passed with no news from them. I write this on the anniversary of their departure. My friends, I know, are dead—somewhere! Oh, what an experience it has been! When your friends die and are buried it is hard enough but when they disappear in a flash and leave no token—! It is almost beyond endurance!"

CHAPTER 2
A Trip of Terror

I take up the story at the point where I dropped it to introduce Church's narrative.

As minute after minute elapsed and we continued in motion we changed our minds about the descent, and concluded that the inventor was going to give us a much longer ride than we had anticipated. We were startled and puzzled but not really alarmed, for the car travelled so smoothly that it gave one a sense of confidence. On the other hand, we felt a little indignation that Edmund should treat us like a lot of boys, without wills of our own. No doubt we had provoked him, though unintentionally, but this was going too far on his part. I am sure we were all hot with this feeling and presently Jack flamed out:

"Look here, Edmund," he exclaimed, dropping his customary good-natured manner, "this is carrying things with a pretty high hand. It's a good deal like kidnapping, it seems to me. I didn't give you permission to carry me off in this way, and I want to know what you mean by it and what you are about. I've no objection to making a little trip in your car, which is certainly mighty comfortable, but first I'd like to be asked whether I want to go or no."

Edmund shrugged his shoulders and made no reply. He was very busy just then with the metallic knobs. Suddenly we were jerked off our feet as if we had been in a trolley driven by a green motorman. Edmund also would have fallen if he had not clung to one of the handles. We felt that we were spinning through the air at a fearful speed. Still Edmund uttered not a word, but while we staggered upon our feet, and steadied ourselves with hands and knees on the leather-cushioned benches like so many drunken men, he continued pulling and pushing at his knobs. Finally the motion became more regular and it was evident that the car had slowed down from its wild rush.

"Excuse me," said Edmund, then, quite in his natural manner, "the thing is new yet and I've got to learn the stops by experience. But there's no occasion for alarm."

But our indignation had grown hotter with the shake-up that we had just had, and as usual Jack was spokesman for it:

"Maybe there is no occasion for alarm," he said excitedly, "but will you be kind enough to answer my question, and tell us what you're about and where we are going?"

And Henry, too, who was ordinarily as mute as a clam, broke out still more hotly:

"See here! I've had enough of this thing! Just go down and let me out. I won't be carried off so, against my will and knowledge."

By this time Edmund appeared to have got things in the shape he wanted, and he turned to face us. He always had a magnetism that was inexplicable, and now we felt it as never before. His features were perfectly calm, but there was a light in his eyes that seemed electric. As if disdaining to make a direct reply to the heated words of Jack and Henry he began in a quiet voice:

"It was my first intention to invite you to accompany me on a very interesting expedition. I knew that none of you had any ties of family or business to detain you, and I felt sure that you would readily consent. In case you should not, however, I had made up my mind to go alone. But you provoked me more than you knew, probably, at the club, and after we had entered the car, and, being myself hot-tempered, I determined to teach you a lesson. I have no intention, however, of abducting you. It is true that you are in my power at present, but if you now say that you do not wish to be concerned in what I assure you will prove the most wonderful enterprise ever undertaken by human beings, I will go back to the shed and let you out."

We looked at one another, in doubt what to reply until Jack, who, with all his impulsiveness had more of the milk of human kindness in his heart than anyone else I ever knew, seized Edmund's hand and exclaimed:

"All right, old boy, bygones are bygones; I'm with you. Now what do you fellows say?"

"I'm with you, too," I cried, yielding to the spur of Jack's enthusiasm and moved also by an intense curiosity. "I say go ahead."

Henry was more backward. But his curiosity, too, was aroused, and at length he gave in his voice with the others.

Jack swung his hat.

"Three cheers, then, for the modern Archimedes! You won't take that amiss now Edmund."

We gave the cheers, and I could see that Edmund was immensely pleased.

"And now," Jack continued, "tell us all about it. Where are we going?"

"Pardon me, Jack," was Edmund's reply, "but I'd rather keep that for a surprise. You shall know everything in good time; or at least everything that you can understand," he added, with a slightly malicious smile.

Feeling a little more interest than the others, perhaps, in the scientific aspects of the business, I asked Edmund to tell us something more about the nature of his wonderful invention. He responded with great good humour, but rather in the manner of a schoolmaster addressing pupils who, he knows, cannot entirely follow him.

"These knobs and handles on the walls," he said, "control the driving power, which, as I have told you, comes from the atoms of matter which I have persuaded to unlock their hidden forces. I push or turn one way and we go ahead, or we rise; I push or turn another way and we stop, or go back. So I concentrate the atomic force just as I choose. It makes us go, or it carries us back to earth, or it holds us motionless, according to the way I apply it. The earth is what I kick against at present, and what I hold fast by; but any other sufficiently massive body would serve the same purpose. As to the machinery, you'd need a special education in order to understand it. You'd have to study the whole subject from the bottom up, and go through all the experiments that I have tried. I confess that there are some things the fundamental reason of which I don't understand myself. But I know how to apply and control the power, and if I had Professor Thomson and Professor Rutherford here, I'd make them open their eyes. I wish I had been able to kidnap them."

"That's a confession that, after all, you've kidnapped us," put in Jack, smiling.

"If you insist upon stating it in that way—yes," replied Edmund, smiling also. "But you know that now you've consented."

"Perhaps you'll treat us to a trip to Paris," Jack persisted.

"Better than that," was the reply. "Paris is only an ant-hill in comparison with what you are going to see."

And so, indeed, it turned out!

Finally all got out their pipes, and we began to make ourselves at home, for truly, as far as luxurious furniture was concerned, we were as comfortable as at the Olympus Club, and the motion of the strange craft was so smooth and regular that it soothed us like an anodyne. It was only those unnamed, subtle senses which man possesses almost without being aware of their existence that assured us that we were in motion at all.

After we had smoked for an hour or so, talking and telling stories quite in the manner of the club, Edmund suddenly asked, with a peculiar smile:

"Aren't you a little surprised that this small room is not choking full of smoke? You know that the shutters are tightly closed."

"By Jo," exclaimed Jack, "that's so! Why here we've been pouring out clouds like old Vesuvius for an hour with no windows open, and yet the air is as clear as a bell."

"The smoke," said Edmund impressively, "has been turned into atomic energy to speed us on our way. I'm glad you're all good smokers, for that saves me fuel. Look," he continued, while we, amazed, stared at him, "those fellows there have been swallowing your smoke, and glad to get it."

He pointed at a row of what seemed to be grinning steel mouths, barred with innumerable black teeth, and half concealed by a projecting ledge at the bottom of the wall opposite the entrance, and as I looked I was thrilled by the sight of faint curls of smoke disappearing within their gaping jaws.

"They are omnivorous beasts," said Edmund. "They feed on the carbon from your breath, too. Rather remarkable, isn't it, that every time you expel the air from your lungs you help this car to go?"

None of us knew what to say; our astonishment was beyond speech. We began to look askance at Edmund, with creeping sensations about the spine. A formless, unacknowledged fear of him entered our souls. It never occurred to us to doubt the truth of what he had said. We knew him too well for that; and, then, were we not here, flying mysteriously through the air in a heavy metallic car that had no apparent motive power? For my part, instead of demanding any further explanations, I fell into a hazy reverie on the marvel of it all; and Jack and Henry must have been seized the same way, for not one of us spoke a word, or asked a question; while Edmund, satisfied, perhaps, with the impression he had made, kept equally quiet.

Thus another hour passed, and all of us, I think, had fallen into a doze, when Edmund aroused us by saying:

"I'll have to keep the first watch, and all the others, too, this night."

"So then we're not going to land to-night?"

"No, not to-night, and you may as well turn in. You see that I have prepared good, comfortable bunks, and I think you'll make out very well."

As Edmund spoke he lifted the tops from some of the benches along the walls, and revealed excellent beds, ready for occupancy.

"I believe that I have forgotten nothing that we shall really need," he added. "Beds, arms, instruments, books, clothing, furs, and good things to eat."

Again we looked at one another in surprise, but nobody spoke, although the same thought probably occurred to each—that this promised to be a pretty long trip, judging from the preparations. Arms! What in the world should we need of arms? Was he going to the Rocky Mountains for a bear hunt? And clothing, and furs!

But we were really sleepy, and none of us was very long in taking Edmund at his word and leaving him to watch alone. He considerately drew a shade over the light, and then noiselessly opened a shutter and looked out. When I saw that, I was strongly tempted to rise and take a look myself, but instead I fell asleep. My dreams were disturbed by visions of the grinning nondescripts at the foot of the wall, which transformed themselves into winged dragons, and remorselessly pursued me through the measureless abysses of space.

When I woke, windows were open on both sides of the car, and brilliant sunshine was streaming in through one of them. Henry was still asleep, Jack was yawning in his bunk, and Edmund stood at one of the windows staring out. I made a quick toilet, and hastened to Edmund's side.

"Good morning," he said heartily, taking my hand. "Look out here, and tell me what you think of the prospect."

As I put my face close to the thick but very transparent glass covering the window, my heart jumped into my mouth!

"In Heaven's name, where are we?" I cried out.

Jack, hearing my agitated exclamation, jumped out of his bunk and ran to the window also. He gasped as he gazed out, and truly it was enough to take away one's breath!

We appeared to be at an infinite elevation, and the sky, as black as ink, was ablaze with stars, although the bright sunlight was streaming into the opposite window behind us. I could see nothing of the earth. Evidently we were too high for that.

"It must lie away down under our feet," I murmured half aloud, "so that even the horizon has sunk out of sight. Heavens, what a height!"

I had that queer uncontrollable qualm that comes to every one who finds himself suddenly on the edge of a soundless deep.

Presently I became aware that straight before us, but afar off, was a most singular appearance in the sky. At first glance I thought that it was a cloud, round and mottled, But it was strangely changeless in form, and it had an unvapourous look.

"Phew!" whistled Jack, suddenly catching sight of it and fixing his eyes in a stare, "what's *that?*"

"That's the earth!"

It was Edmund who spoke, looking at us with a quizzical smile. A shock ran through my nerves, and for an instant my brain whirled. I saw that it was the truth that he had uttered, for, as sure as I sit here, his words had hardly struck my ears when the great cloud rounded out and hardened, the deception vanished, and I recognized, as clearly as ever I saw them on a school globe, the outlines of Asia and the Pacific Ocean!

In a second I had become too weak to stand, and I sank trembling upon a bench. But Jack, whose eyes had not accommodated themselves as rapidly as mine to the gigantic perspective, remained at the window, exclaiming:

"Fiddlesticks! What are you trying to give us? The earth is down below, I reckon."

But in another minute he, too, saw it as it really was, and his astonishment equalled mine. In fact he made so much noise about it that he awoke Henry, who, jumping out of bed, came running to see, and when we had explained to him where we were, sank upon a seat with a despairing groan and covered his face. Our astonishment and dismay were too great to permit us quickly to recover our self-command, but after a while Jack seized Edmund's arm, and demanded:

"For God's sake, tell us what you've been doing."

"Nothing that ought to appear very extraordinary," answered Edmund, with uncommon warmth. "If men had not been fools for so many ages they might have done this, and more than this long ago. It's enough to make one ashamed of his race! For countless centuries, instead of grasping the power that nature had placed at the disposal of their intelligence, they have idled away their time gabbling about nothing. And even since, at last, they have begun to do something, look at the time that they have wasted upon such petty forces as steam and 'electricity,' burning whole mines of coal and whole lakes of oil, and childishly calling upon winds and tides and waterfalls to help them, when they had under their thumbs the limitless energy of the atoms, and no more understood it than a baby understands what makes its whistle scream! It's inter-atomic force that has brought us out here, and that is going to carry us a great deal farther."

We simply listened in silence; for what could we say? The facts were more eloquent than any words, and called for no commentary.

Here we *were*, out in the middle of space; and *there* was the earth, hanging on nothing, like a summer cloud. At least we knew where we were if we didn't quite understand how we had got there.

Seeing us speechless, Edmund resumed in a different tone:

"We made a fairly good run during the night. You must be hungry by this time, for you've slept late; suppose we have breakfast."

So saying, he opened a locker, took out a folding table, covered it with a white cloth, turned on something resembling a little electric range, and in a few minutes had ready as appetizing a breakfast of eggs and as good a cup of coffee as I ever tasted. It is one of the compensations of human nature that it is able to adjust itself to the most unheard-of conditions provided only that the inner man is not neglected. The smell of breakfast would almost reconcile a man to purgatory—anyhow it reconciled us for the time being to our unparalleled situation, and we ate and drank, and indulged in as cheerful good comradeship as that of a fishing party in the wilderness after a big morning's catch.

When the breakfast was finished we began to chat and smoke, which reminded me of those gulping mouths under the wainscot, and I leaned down to catch a glimpse of their rows of black fangs, thinking to ask Edmund for further explanation about them; but the sight gave me a shiver, and I felt the hopelessness of trying to understand their function.

Then we took a turn at looking out of the window to see the earth. Edmund furnished us with binoculars which enabled us to recognize many geographical features of our planet. The western shore of the Pacific was now in plain sight, and a few small spots, near the edge of the ocean, we knew to be Japan and the Philippines. The snowy Himalayas showed as a crinkling line, and a huge white smudge over the China Sea indicated where a storm was raging and where good ships, no doubt, were battling with the tossing waves.

After a time I noticed that Edmund was continually going from one window to the other and looking out with an air of anxiety. He seemed to be watching for something, and there was a look of mingled expectation and apprehension in his eyes. He had a peephole at the forward end of the car and another in the floor, and these he frequently visited. I now recalled that even while we were at breakfast he had seemed uneasy and occasionally left his seat to look out. At last I asked him:

"What are you looking for, Edmund?"

"Meteors."

"Meteors, out here!"

"Of course. You're something of an astronomer; don't you know that they hang about all the planets? They didn't give me any rest last night. I was on tender hooks all the time while you were sleeping. I was half inclined to call one of you to help me. We passed some pretty ugly fellows while you slept, I can tell you! You know that this is an unexplored sea that we are navigating, and I don't want to run on the rocks."

"But we seem to be a good way off from the earth now," I remarked, "and there ought not to be much danger."

"It's not as dangerous as it was, but there may be some of them yet around here. I'll feel safer when we have put a few more million miles behind us."

A few more million miles! We all stood aghast when we heard the words. We had, indeed, imagined that the earth looked as if it might be a million miles away, but, then, it was merely a passing impression, which had given us no sense of reality; but now when we heard Edmund say that we actually had travelled such a distance, the idea struck us with overwhelming force.

"In the name of all that's good, Edmund," cried Jack, "at what rate are we travelling, then?"

"Just at present," Edmund replied, glancing at an indicator, "we're making twenty miles a second."

Twenty miles a second! Our excited nerves had another shock.

"Why," I exclaimed, "that's faster than the earth moves in its orbit!"

"Yes, a trifle faster; but I'll probably have to work up to a little better speed in order to get where I want to go before our goal begins to run away from us."

"Ah, there you are," said Jack. "That's what I wanted to know. What is our goal? Where are we going?"

Before Edmund could reply we all sprang to our feet in affright. A loud grating noise had broken upon our ears. At the same instant the car gave a lurch, and a blaze of the most vicious lightning streamed through a window.

"Confound the things!" shouted Edmund, springing to the window, and then darting to one of his knobs and beginning to twist it with all his force.

In a second we were sprawling on the floor—all except Edmund, who kept his hold on the knob. Our course had been changed with amazing quickness, and our startled eyes beheld a huge misshapen object darting past the window.

"Here comes another!" cried Edmund, again seizing the knob.

I had managed to get my face to the window, and I certainly thought that we were done for. Apparently only a few rods away, and rushing straight at the car, was a vast black mass, shaped something like a dumb-bell, with ends as big as houses, tumbling over and over, and threatening us with annihilation. If it hit us, as it seemed sure that it would do, I knew that we should never return to the earth, unless in the form of pulverized ashes!

CHAPTER 3

The Planetary Limited

But Edmund had seen the meteor sooner than I, and as quick as thought he swerved the car, and threw us all off our feet once more. But we should have been thankful if he had broken our heads, since he had saved us from instant destruction.

The danger, however, was not yet passed. Scarcely had the immense dumb-bell (which Edmund declared must have been composed of solid iron, so great was its effect on his needles) disappeared, before there came from outside a blaze so fierce that it fairly slapped our lids shut.

"A collision!" Edmund exclaimed. "The thing has struck another big meteor, and they are exchanging fiery compliments."

He threw himself flat on the floor, and stared out of the peephole. Then he jumped to his feet and gave us another tumble.

"They're all about us," he faltered, breathless with exertion; then, having drawn a deep inspiration, he continued: "We're like a boat in a raging freshet, with rocks, tree trunks, and cakes of ice threatening it on all sides. But we'll get out of it. The car obeys its helm as if it appreciated the danger. Why, I got away from that last fellow by setting up atomic reaction against it, as a boatman pushes with his pole."

Even in the midst of our terror we could not but admire our leader. His resources seemed boundless, and our confidence in him grew with every escape. While he kept guard at the peepholes we watched for meteors from the windows. We must have come almost within striking distance of a thousand in the course of an hour, but Edmund decided not to diminish our speed, for he said that he could control the car quicker when it was under full headway.

So on we rushed, dodging the things like a crow in a flock of pestering jays, and we really enjoyed the excitement. It was more fascinating sport than shooting rapids in a careening skiff, and at last we grew so confident in the powers of our car and its commander that we were rather sorry when the last meteor passed, and we found ourselves once more in open, unimpeded space.

After that the time passed quietly. We ate our meals and went to bed and rose as regularly as if we had been at home. In one respect, however, things were very different from what they were on the earth. We had no night! The sun shone continually, although the sky was black and always glittering with stars. None of us needed to be told by our conductor that this was due to the fact that we no longer had the shadow of the earth to make night for us when the sun was behind it. The sun was now never behind the earth, or any other great opaque body, and when we wished to sleep we made an artificial night, for our special use, by closing all the shutters. And there was no atmosphere about us to diffuse the sunlight, and so to hide the stars. We kept count of the days by the aid of a calendar clock; there seemed to be nothing that Edmund had forgotten. And it was a delightful experience, the wonder of which grew upon us hour by hour. It was too marvellous, too incredible, to be believed, and yet—*there we were!*

Once the idea suddenly came to me that it was astonishing that we had not long ago perished for lack of oxygen. I understood, of course, from what Edmund had said, that the mysterious machines along the wall absorbed the carbonic acid, but we must be constantly using up the oxygen. When I put my difficulty before Edmund he laughed.

"That's the easiest thing of all," he said. "Look here."

He threw open a little grating.

"In there," he continued, "there's an apparatus which manufactures just enough oxygen to keep the air in good condition. It is supplied with materials to last a month, which will be much longer than this expedition will take."

"There you are again," exclaimed Jack. "I was asking you about that when we ran into those pesky meteors. What *is* this expedition? Where are we going, anyway?"

"Well," Edmund replied, "since we have become pretty good shipmates, I don't see any objection to telling you. We are going to Venus."

"Going to Venus!" we all cried in a breath.

"To be sure. Why not? We've got the proper sort of conveyance, haven't we?"

There was no denying that. Our conveyance had already brought us some millions of miles out into space; why, indeed, should it not be able to carry us to Venus, or any other planet?

"How far is it to Venus?" asked Jack.

"When we quit the earth," Edmund answered, "Venus was rapidly approaching inferior conjunction. You know what that is," addressing me, "it's when the planet comes between the sun and the earth. The distance from the earth is not always the same at such a conjunction, but I figured out that on this occasion, after allowing for the circuit we should have to make, there would be just twenty-seven million miles to travel. At an average speed of twenty miles a second we could do that distance in fifteen days, fourteen and one half hours. But, of course, I had to lose some time going slow through the earth's atmosphere, for otherwise the car would have taken fire, like a meteor, on account of the friction. Then, too, I shall have to slow up on entering the atmosphere of Venus, which appears to be very deep and dense; so, upon the whole, I don't count on landing upon Venus in less than sixteen days from the time of our departure. We've already been out five days, and within eleven more I expect to introduce you to the inhabitants of another world."

The inhabitants of another world! Again Edmund had thrown out an idea which took us all aback.

"Do you believe there are any inhabitants on Venus?" I asked at length.

"Certainly. I know there are."

"For sure," put in Jack, stretching out his legs and pulling at his pipe. "Who'd go twenty-seven million miles to pay a visit if he didn't know there was somebody at home?"

"Then that's what you put the arms aboard for," I remarked.

"Yes, but I hope we shall not have to use them."

"Strikes me that this is a sort of pirate ship," said Jack. "But what kind of arms have you got, Edmund?"

For answer Edmund threw open a locker and showed us a gleaming array of automatic guns and pistols and even some cutlasses.

"Decidedly piratical!" exclaimed the incorrigible Jack. "You'd better hoist the black flag. But, see here, Edmund, with all this interatomic energy that you talk about, why in the world didn't you invent something new—something that would just knock the Venusians silly, and blow their old planet up if necessary? Automatic arms are pretty good at home, on that unprogressive earth that you have spurned with your heels, but they'll likely be rather small pumpkins on Venus."

"I didn't prepare anything else," Edmund replied, "because, in the first place, I was too busy with more important things, and in the second place because I don't really anticipate that we shall have any use for arms. I only took these as a precaution."

189

"You mean to try moral suasion, I suppose," drawled Jack. "Well, anyhow, I hope they'll be glad to see us, and since it is Venus that we are going to visit, I don't look for much fighting. I'm glad you made it Venus instead of Mars, Edmund, for, from all I've heard of Mars with its fourteen-foot giants, I don't think I should like to try the pirate business in that direction."

We all laughed at Jack's fancies; but there was something tremendously thrilling in the idea. Think of landing on another world! Think of meeting inhabitants there! Really, it made one's head spin.

"Confound it, this is all a dream," I said to myself. "I'm on my back in bed with a nightmare. I'll kick myself awake."

But do what I would I could make no dream of it. On the contrary, I felt that I had never been quite so much awake in all my life before.

After a while we all settled down to take the thing in earnest. And then the charm of it began to master our imaginations. We talked over the prospects in all their aspects. Edmund said little, and Henry nothing, but Jack and I were stirred to the bottom of our romantic souls. Henry was different. He had no romance in his make-up. He always looked at the money in a thing. To his mind, going to Venus was playing the fool, when we had at our command the means of owning the earth.

"Edmund," he said, after mumbling for a while under his breath, "this is the most utter tomfoolery that ever I heard of. Here you've got an invention that would revolutionize mechanics, and instead of utilizing it you rush off into space on a harebrained adventure. You might have been twenty times a billionaire inside of a year if you had stayed at home and developed the thing. Why, it's folly; pure, beastly folly! Going to Venus! What can you make on Venus?"

Edmund only smiled. After a little he said:

"Well, I'm sorry for you, Henry. But then you're cut out on the ordinary pattern. But cheer up. When we go back, perhaps I'll let you take out a patent, and you can make the billions. For my part, Venus is more interesting to me than all the money you could pile up between the Atlantic Ocean and the Rocky Mountains. Why," he continued, warming up, and straightening with a certain pride which he had, "am I not the Columbus of Space?—And you my lieutenants," he added, with a smile.

"Right you are," cried Jack enthusiastically. "The Columbus of Space, that's the ticket! Where's old Archimedes now? Buried, by Jo! *He* couldn't go to Venus! And what need we care for your billionaires?"

Edmund patted Jack on the back, and I rather sympathized with his enthusiasm myself.

The time ran on, and we watched anxiously the day-hand of the calendar clock. Soon it had marked a week; then ten days; then a fortnight. We knew we must be getting very close to our goal, yet up to this time neither Jack, nor Henry, nor I had caught a glimpse of Venus. Edmund, however, had seen it, but he told us that in order to do so he had been obliged to alter our course because the planet was directly in the eye of the sun. In consequence of the change of course we were now approaching Venus from the east—flanking her, so to speak—and Edmund described her appearance as that of an enormous crescent. Finally he invited us to take a look for ourselves.

I shall never forget that first view! It was only a glimpse, for Edmund was nervous about meteors again, and would allow us only a moment at the peephole because he wished to be continually on the watch himself. But, brief as was the view, that vast gleaming sickle hanging in the black sky was the most tremendous thing I ever looked upon!

Soon afterwards Edmund changed the course again, and then we saw her no more. We had not come upon the swarms of meteors that Edmund had expected to find lurking about the planet, and he said that he now felt safe in running into her shadow, and making a landing on her night hemisphere. You will allow me to remind you that Schiaparelli had long before found out that Venus doesn't turn on her axis once every twenty-four hours, like the earth, but keeps always the same face to the sun; the consequence being that she has perpetual day on one side and perpetual night on the other. I asked Edmund why he should not rather land on the daylight side; but he replied that his plan was safer, and that we could easily go from one side to the other whenever we chose. It didn't turn out to be so easy after all, but that is another part of the story.

"I hardly expect to find any inhabitants on the night side," Edmund remarked, "for it must be fearfully cold there—too cold for life to exist, perhaps; but I have provided against that as far as we are concerned. Still, one can never tell. There *may* be inhabitants there, and at any rate I am going to find out. If there are none, we'll just stop long enough to take a look at things, and then the car will quickly transport us to the daylight hemisphere, where life certainly exists. By landing on the uninhabited side, you see, we shall have a chance to reconnoitre a little, and can approach the inhabitants on the other side so much the more safely."

"That sounds all right enough," said Jack, "but if Venus is correctly named, I'm for getting where the inhabitants are as quick as possible."

When we swung round into the shadow of the planet we got her between the sun and ourselves, and as she completely hid the sun, we now had perpetual night about the car. Out of the peephole she looked like a stupendous black circle, blacker than the sky itself, but round the rim was a beautiful ring of light.

"That's her atmosphere," Edmund explained, "lighted up by the sun from behind. But, for the life of me, I cannot tell what those immense flames mean."

He referred to a vast circle of many-coloured spires that blazed and flickered like a burning rainbow at the inner edge of the ring of light. It was one of the most awful, and yet beautiful, sights that I had ever gazed upon.

"That's something altogether outside my calculations," Edmund added. "I can't account for it at all."

"Perhaps they are already celebrating our arrival with fireworks," suggested Jack, always ready to take the humorous view of everything.

"That's not fire," Edmund responded earnestly. "But what it is I confess I can't imagine. We'll find out, however, for I haven't come all this distance to be scared off."

And here I must try to explain a very curious thing which had puzzled our senses, though not our understanding (because Edmund had promptly explained it), throughout the voyage, and that was—levitation. On our first day out from the earth, we began to notice the remarkable ease with which we handled things, and the strange tendency we had to bump into one another because we seemed to be all the time employing more strength than was necessary and almost to be able to walk on air. Jack declared that he felt as if his head had become a toy balloon.

"It's the lack of weight," said Edmund. "Every time we double our distance from the earth we lose another three quarters of our weight. If I had thought to bring along a spring dynamometer, I could have shown you, Jack, that when we were 4,000 miles above the earth's surface the 200 good pounds with which you depress the scales at home had diminished to 50, and that when we had passed about 150,000 miles into space you weighed no more than a couple of ounces. From that point on, it has been the attraction of the sun to which we have owed whatever weight we had, and the floor of the car has been toward the sun, because, at that distance from the earth, the latter ceases to exercise the master force, and the pull of the sun becomes greater than the earth's. But as we approach Venus the latter begins to restore our weight, and when we arrive on her surface we shall weigh about four fifths as much as when we started from the earth."

"But I don't look as if I had lost any avoirdupois," said Jack, glancing at his round limbs. "And when you give us a fling I seem to strike pretty hard, though in other respects I confess I do feel a good deal like an angel."

"Ah," said Edmund, laughing, "that's the *inertia of mass*. Your mass is the same, although your weight has almost disappeared. Weight depends upon the distance from the attracting body, but mass is independent of everything."

"Do you mean to say that angels are massive?"

"They may be as massive as they like provided they keep well away from great centres of gravitation."

"But Venus is such a centre—then there can't be any angels there."

"I hope to find something better than angels," was Edmund's smiling reply.

Now, as we drew near to Venus, the truth of Edmund's statements became apparent. We felt that our weight was returning, and our muscular activity sinking back to the normal again. We imagined that every minute we could feel our feet pressing more heavily upon the floor.

Our approach was so rapid that the immense black circle grew visibly minute by minute. Soon it was so large that we could no longer see its boundaries through the peephole in the floor.

"We're now within a thousand miles," said Edmund, "and must be close to the upper limits of the atmosphere. I'll have to slow down, or else we'll be burnt up by the heat of friction."

He proceeded to slow down a little more rapidly than was comfortable. It was jerk after jerk, as he dropped off the power, and put on the brakes, but at last we got down to the speed of a fast express train. Soon we were so close that the surface of the planet became dimly visible, simply from the starlight. We were now settling down very cautiously, and presently we began to notice curious shafts of light which appeared to issue from the ground, as if the surface beneath us had been sprinkled with iron foundries.

"Aha!" cried Edmund, "I believe there *are* inhabitants on this side after all. Those lights don't come from volcanoes. I'm going to make for the nearest one, and we'll soon know what they are."

Accordingly we steered for one of the gleaming shafts. It was a thrilling moment, I can tell you—that when we first saw another world than ours under our feet! As we approached the light it threw a pale illumination on the ground around. Everything appeared to be perfectly flat and level. It was like dropping down at night upon a vast prairie. But the features of the landscape were indistinguishable in the gloom. Edmund boldly continued to approach until we were within a hundred feet of the shaft of light, which we could now perceive issued directly from the ground. Suddenly, with the slightest perceptible bump, we touched the soil, and the car came to rest. We had landed on Venus!

"It's unquestionably frightfully cold outside," said Edmund, "and we'll now put on these things."

He dragged out of one of his many lockers four suits of thick fur garments, and as many pairs of fur gloves, together with caps and shields for the face, leaving only narrow openings for the eyes. When we had got them on we looked like so many Eskimo. Finally Edmund handed each of us a pair of small automatic pistols, telling us to put them where they would be handy in our side pockets.

"Boarders all!" cried the irrepressible Jack. "Pirates, do your duty!"

Our preparations being made, we opened the door. The air that rushed in almost hardened us into icicles!

"It won't hurt you," said Edmund in a whisper. "It can't be down to absolute zero on account of the dense atmosphere. You'll get used to it in a few minutes. Come on."

His whispering gave us a sense of imminent danger, but nevertheless we followed as he led the way straight toward the shaft of light. On nearing it we saw that it came out of an irregularly round hole in the ground. When we got yet nearer we were astonished to see rough steps which led down into the pit. The next instant we were frozen in our tracks! For a moment my heart stopped beating.

Standing on the steps, just below the level of the ground, and intently watching us, with eyes as big and luminous as moons, was a creature shaped like a man, but more savage than a gorilla!

CHAPTER 4

The Caverns of Venus

For two or three minutes the creature continued to stare at us, motionless; and we stared at him. It was so dramatic that it makes my nerves tingle now when I think of it. His eyes alone were enough to harrow up your soul. Huge beyond belief, round and luminous as full moons, they were filled with the phosphorescent greenish-yellow glare that sometimes appears in the expanded pupils of a cat or a wild beast. The great hairy head was black, but the stocky body was as white as a polar bear. The arms were apelike and very long and muscular, and the entire aspect of the creature betokened immense strength and activity.

Edmund was the first to recover from the stupor of surprise, and instantly he did a thing so apparently absurd but so marvellous in its calculated effect that no brain but his could have conceived it. It shakes me at once with laughter and recollected terror when I recall it.

"WELL, HELLO YOU!" he called out in a voice of such stentorian power that we jumped as at a thunderclap. The effect on the strange brute was electric. A film shot across the big eyes, he leaped into the air, uttering a squeak that was ridiculous, coming from an animal of such size and strength, and instantly disappeared, tumbling down the steps.

But we were as much frightened as the ugly monster himself. We stared at Edmund, speechless in our amazement. Never could I have believed it possible for such a voice to issue from the human throat. It was not the voice of our friend, nor the voice of a man at all, but an indescribable clangour; and the words I have quoted had been scarcely distinguishable, so shattered were they by the crash of sound that whirled them into our astonished ears. Edmund, seeing us gaping in speechless wonder, laughed with such an appearance of hearty enjoyment as I had never known him to exhibit—and his merriment produced another thunderous explosion that shook the air.

Then the truth burst upon me, and I exclaimed:

"It's the atmosphere!"

I had not spoken very loudly, but the words seemed to reverberate in my mouth, as if to testify to the correctness of my explanation.

"Yes," said Edmund, taking pains to moderate his voice, "you've hit it, it's the atmosphere. I had calculated on an effect of the kind, but the reality exceeds all that I had anticipated. Spectroscopic analysis as well as telescopic appearances demonstrated long ago that the atmosphere of Venus was extraordinarily extensive and dense, from which fact I inferred that we should encounter some wonderful acoustic phenomena here, and this was in my mind when, on stepping out of the car, I addressed you in a whisper. The reaction even of the whisper on my organs of speech told me that I was right, and showed me what to expect if the full power of the voice were used. When we caught sight of the creature at the top of the pit I had no desire to shoot him, and I saw that he was too powerful to be captured alive. In a second I had decided what to do. It ran through my mind that, in a world where the density, and probably something also in the peculiar constitution of the air, had the effect of vastly magnifying sound, the phonetic and acoustic organs of the inhabitants would be modified, and that the sounds uttered by them would be much fainter than those that we are accustomed to hear from living creatures on the earth. That being so, I argued that a very great and heavy sound coming from a strange animal would produce in the creature before us a paralyzing terror. You have seen that it did so. I expect that this will give us an immense advantage to begin with. We have already inspired so great a fear that I believe that we can now safely follow the creature into its habitation, and encounter without danger any of its congeners that may be there. Nevertheless, I shall not ask you to run any risks, and I will alone descend into the pit."

"If you do, may I be hanged for sheep stealing!"

You will guess at once that it was Jack who had spoken thus.

"No, sir," he continued, "if you go, we all go. Isn't that so, boys?"

In answer to an appeal thus put, neither Henry nor myself could have hung back even if we had had the disposition to do so. But I believe that we all instinctively felt that our place was by Edmund's side, wherever he might choose to go.

"Go ahead, then, Edmund," Jack added, seeing that we consented, "we're with you." And then his enthusiasm taking fire, as usual, he exclaimed: "Hurrah! Columbus forever! We've conquered a hemisphere with a blank shot."

And so we began our descent into the mysterious pit. The strange light that came from it, and formed a shaft in the dense atmosphere above like sunlight in a haymow, was accompanied by a considerable degree of heat, which was very grateful to our lungs after the frigid plunge that we had taken from the comfortable car. As we descended, the temperature continually rose until we were glad to throw off our Arctic togs, and leave them on a shelf of rock to await our return. But, fortunately, we did not forget to take the pistols from the pockets before leaving the garments. I am very uncertain what would have been the future course of our history if we had neglected this precaution.

It was an awful hole for depth. The steps, rudely cut, wound round and round the sides like those in a cathedral tower, but the pit was not perfectly circular. It looked like a natural formation, such as the vertical entrance to a limestone cavern, or the throat of a sleeping volcano. But whatever the nature of the pit might be, I was convinced that the steps were of artificial origin. They were reasonably regular in height and broad enough for two, or even three, persons to go abreast.

When we had descended perhaps as much as two hundred feet, we suddenly found ourselves in a broad cavern with a surprisingly level floor. The temperature had been steadily rising all the time, and here it was as warm as in an ordinary living room. The cavern appeared to be about twenty yards broad and eight or ten feet in height, with a flat roof of rock. It was dimly illuminated by a small heap of what seemed to be hard coal, burning in a very roughly constructed brazier, which, as far as looks went, one would have said was constructed of iron.

You will imagine our surprise upon seeing these things. The appearance of the gorilla-like beast with the awful eyes had certainly not led us to anticipate the finding in his lair of any such evidences of human intelligence, and we stood fast in our tracks for a minute or two, nobody speaking a word. Then Edmund said:

"This is far better than I hoped. I had not thought about caverns, though I ought to have foreseen the probability of something of the kind. It is hard to drive out life as long as a world has solid foundations, and air for breathing. I shall be greatly surprised now if these creatures do not turn out to be at least as intelligent as our African or Australian savages."

"But," said I, "the fellow that we saw surely cannot have more intelligence than a beast. There must be some more highly developed creatures living here."

"I'm not so sure of that," Edmund responded. "Looks go for nothing in such a case. He had arms and hands, and his brain may be well organized."

"If his brain is as big as his eyes," Jack put in, "he ought to be able to give odds to old Solomon and beat him easy. My, but I'd like to see their spectacles—if they ever wear any!"

Jack's humour recalled us from our meditation, and we began to look about more carefully. There was not a living creature in sight, but over in a corner I detected a broad hole, down which the steps continued to descend.

"Here's the way," said Edmund, discovering the steps at the same moment. "Down we go."

He again led the way, and we resumed the descent. As we stumbled along downward we began to talk of a strange but agreeable odour which we had noticed in the cavern. Edmund said that it was due, perhaps, to some peculiar quality of the atmosphere.

"I think," he continued, "that it is heavily charged with oxygen. You have noticed that none of us feels the slightest fatigue, notwithstanding the precipitancy of our long descent."

I reflected that this might also be the cause of our rising courage, for I was sure that not one of us felt the slightest fear in thus pushing on toward dangers of whose nature we could form no idea. The steps, precisely like those above, wound round and round and led us down I should say as much as three hundred feet before we entered another cavern, larger and loftier than the first.

And there we found them!

There was never another such sight! It made our blood run cold once more, rather with surprise than fear, though the latter quickly followed.

Ranged along the farther side of the cavern, and visible in the light of another glowing heap in the centre, were as many as thirty of those huge hairy creatures, standing shoulder to shoulder, their great eyes glaring like bull's-eye lanterns. But the thing that filled us with terror was their motions.

You have read, with thrilling nerves, how a huge cobra, reared on his coils, sways his terrible head from side to side before striking. Well, all those black heads before us were swaying in unison, but with a sickening circular movement, which was regularly reversed in direction. Three times by the right and then three times by the left those heads circled, in rhythmic cadence, while the luminous eyes seemed to leave phosphorescent rings in the air, intersecting one another in consequence of the rapidity of the motion.

It was such a spectacle as I had never beheld in the wildest dream. It was baleful. It was the charm of the serpent fascinating his terrified prey. In an instant I felt my brain turning, and I staggered in spite of my utmost efforts. A kind of paralysis stiffened my limbs.

Presently, all moving together, and uttering a hissing, whistling sound, they began slowly to approach us, keeping in line, each shaggy leg lifted at the same moment, like so many soldiers on parade, while the heads continued to swing, and the glowing eyes to cut linked circles in the air. But for Edmund we should certainly have been lost. Standing a little to the fore, he spoke to us over his shoulder, in a low voice:

"Take out your pistols, but don't shoot unless they make a rush. Then kill as many as you can. I'll knock over the leader in the centre, and I think that will be enough."

We could as easily have stirred our arms if we had been marble statues, but he promptly raised his pistol, and the explosion followed on the instant. The report was like an earthquake. It shocked us into our senses and almost out of them again. The weight of the air and the confinement of the cavern magnified and concentrated the sound so that it was awful beyond belief. The fellow in the centre was hurled back as if shot from a catapult, and the others fell at flat as he, and lay there grovelling, their big eyes filming and swaying, but no longer in unison.

The charm was broken, and as we saw our fearful enemies prostrate, our courage returned at a bound.

"I thought as much," said Edmund coolly. "But I'm sorry now that I aimed at that fellow; the sound alone would have sufficed. It was not necessary to take life. However, we should probably have had to come to it eventually, and now we have them thoroughly cowed. Our safety consists in keeping them terrified."

Thus speaking, Edmund boldly approached the grovelling row, and pushed with his foot the furry body of the one he had shot. The bullet had gone through his head. At Edmund's approach the creatures sank lower on the rocky floor, and those nearest him turned up their moon eyes with an expression of submission and supplication that was grotesque. He motioned us to join him and, imitating him, we began to pat and smooth the shrinking bodies until, understanding that we would not hurt them, they gradually acquired confidence.

In the meantime the crowd in the cavern increased, others coming in through side passages, and exhibiting the utmost astonishment at the spectacle which greeted them. It was clear that those who had taken part in the opening scene imparted to the newcomers a knowledge of the situation of affairs, and we could see that our prestige was thoroughly established. It remained to utilize our advantage, and we looked to Edmund to show how it should be done. He was equal to the undertaking, but I shall not trouble you with the details of his diplomacy. Let it suffice to say that by a combination of gentleness and firmness he quickly reduced almost the entire population of the caverns (for, as we afterwards discovered, there were a dozen or more of these underground dwellings connected by horizontal passages through the rocks) into subjection to his will. I say "almost," because, as you will see in a little while, there were certain members of this extraordinary community who possessed a spirit of independence too strong to be so easily subdued.

As we became better acquainted with the cave dwellers we found that they were by no means as savage as they looked. Their appearance was certainly grotesque, and even unaccountable. Why, for instance, should their heads have been covered with coarse black disordered hair while their bodies, from the neck down, were almost beautiful with a natural raiment of golden white, as soft as silk and as brilliant as floss? I never could explain it, and Edmund was no less puzzled by this peculiarity. The immense size of their eyes did not seem astonishing after we began to reflect upon the consequences of the relative lack of light in their world. It was but a natural adjustment to their environment; with such eyes they could see in the dark better than cats. Their feet were bare and covered on the soles with thick soft skin, while the insides of their long hands were almost as white and delicate as those of a human being.

Their intelligence was sufficiently demonstrated by the construction of the hundreds of rocky steps leading from the caverns to the surface of the ground, and by their employment of fire, and manufacture of the metallic braziers which contained it. But this was not all. We found that in some of the winding passages connecting the caverns they cultivated food. It consisted entirely of vegetables of various kinds, and all unlike any that I ever saw on the earth. Water dripped from the roofs of these particular passages, and the almost colourless vegetation thrived there with astonishing luxuriance. They had many simple ways of cooking their food, and it was evident that they possessed some form of salt, though we did not discover the deposit from which they must have drawn it. They collected water in cisterns hollowed in the rock.

Although we still had abundance of food in the car, Edmund insisted on trying theirs, and it proved to be very palatable.

"This is fortunate, though hardly surprising," said Edmund. "If we had found the food on Venus uneatable, we should indeed have been in a fine fix. While we remain here we will eat as the natives eat, and save our own supplies for future need."

The only brute animals that we saw in the caverns were some dog-like creatures, about as large as terriers, but very furry, which showed the utmost terror whenever we appeared.

One of the first things that we discovered outside the main cavern where we had made our debut was the burial ground of the community. This happened when they came to dispose of the fellow that Edmund had shot. They formed a regular procession, which greatly impressed us, and we followed them as they bore the body through several winding ways into a large cavern, at a considerable distance from any of the others. Here they had dug a grave, and, to our astonishment, there appeared to be something resembling a religious ceremony connected with the interment. And then, for the first time, we distinguished the females from the others. But a still greater surprise awaited us. It was no less than plain evidence of regular family relationship.

As the body was lowered into the grave one of the females approached with every sign of distress and sorrow. Jack declared that he saw tears running down her hairy cheeks. She held two little ones by the hand, and this spectacle produced an astonishing effect upon Edmund, revealing an entirely new side of his character. I have told you that he expressed regret for having killed the fellow in the cavern, but now, at the sight before him, he seemed filled with remorse.

"I wish I had never come here!" he said bitterly. "The first thing I have done is to kill an inoffensive and intelligent creature."

"Intelligent, perhaps," said Jack, "but inoffensive—not by a long shot! Where'd we have been if you hadn't killed him? They'd have made mincemeat of us."

"No," replied Edmund, sorrowfully shaking his head, "it wasn't necessary. The noise would have sufficed; and I ought to have known it."

"Why didn't you shout, then? That scared the first one," put in Henry, whose soul, it must be said, was not overflowing with sympathy.

"I did what I thought was best at the moment," Edmund replied, with a broken voice. "They were so many and so threatening that I imagined my voice alone might not be effective. But I'm sorry, sorry!"

"Henry, you're a fool!" cried the sympathetic Jack. "Come now, Edmund," he continued, kindly laying a hand on his shoulder, "what you did was the only thing under heaven that could have been done. You're wrong to blame yourself. By Jo, if you hadn't done it I would!"

But Edmund only shook his head, as if refusing to be comforted. It was the first sign of weakness that we had seen in our incomparable leader, but I am sure it only increased our respect for him—at least that's true of Jack and me. After that I noticed that Edmund was far more gentle than before in his relations with the people of the caverns.

Not long after this painful incident we made a discovery of extreme interest. It was nothing less than a big smithy! Edmund had foretold that we should find something of the kind.

"Those braziers and cooking pots," he had said, "and the tools that must have been needed to build the steps and to dig their graves, prove that they know how to work in iron. If it is not done in these caverns, then they get it from some other similar community. But I think it likely that we shall come upon some signs of the work hereabouts."

"Maybe they import it from Pittsburgh," was the remark that fun-loving Jack could not refrain from making.

"Well, you'll see," said Edmund.

And, as I have already told you, he was right. We did find the smithy, with several stout fellows pounding out rude tools with equally rude hammers of iron. Of course we could ask them no questions, for their language was only a kind of squeak, and they seemed to converse mostly by means of expressive signs. But Edmund was not long in drawing his conclusions.

"This," he said, after closely examining the metal, "is native iron. There's nothing remarkable in the fact that it should be here. All the solid planets, as you know" (turning to me), "are very largely composed of iron, and Venus, being nearer the centre of the system, may have proportionally more of it than the earth. And these fellows have found out its usefulness, and how to work it. There's nothing surprising in that, either, for some of our savages have done as much on the earth. Now I'll make another prediction—we are going to find coal here. That is inevitable, since we know that they burn it in the caverns. I shouldn't wonder if it were close at hand, from the look of these rocks."

He approached the wall of the cavern containing the smithy, and immediately exclaimed:

"Look here! Here it is!"

And sure enough, on joining him we saw a seam of as fine anthracite as Pennsylvania ever produced.

"A Carboniferous Age on Venus!" Edmund continued. "What do you think of that? But, of course, it was sure to be so; all the planets that are old enough have been through practically the same stages. Think of it! The plants that gave origin to this coal must have flourished here when Venus still rotated on her axis rapidly enough to have day and night succeeding one another on all sides of her, for now no vegetation except the insignificant plants that grow in these caverns can live on this hemisphere. And think, too, of the countless ages that must have been consumed in slowing down her rotation by the friction of her ocean tides."

"Has Venus got any oceans?" asked Jack.

"I haven't a doubt of it; but we shall find none on this side, although they must once have been here."

We all mused for a time on the subject that Edmund had started, when suddenly his face lighted up with the greatest animation, and he exclaimed, but as if speaking to himself rather than to us:

"Capital! It couldn't have happened better!"

"What's capital?" drawled Jack.

"Why, this smithy, and these Tubal Cains here. Unconsciously they have solved for me a problem that has given me considerable trouble. Almost as soon as we got acquainted with the people of the caverns the idea occurred to me that I should like to take some of them with us when we visit the other hemisphere. There are many interesting observations that their presence on that side of Venus would give rise to, and, besides, they might be of great use to us. Of course I meant to bring them back to their home. But the puzzling question has been how to transport them. The car has a full load already."

"They've got good legs; make 'em walk," said Jack.

Edmund burst into a laugh.

"Why, Jack," he asked, "how far do you think it is to the other side of Venus?"

"I don't know," said Jack, "but I suppose it's not very far round her. How far is it?"

"Five thousand miles, at least, to the edge of the sunlit hemisphere."

Jack whistled.

"By Jo! I wouldn't have believed it."

"Well, it's a fact," said Edmund, "and of course I don't propose to take several months to make the journey. Now the sight of these fellows at work has shown me just how it can be done in short order. It's this way: I'll have iron sleds made, put the natives that I propose to take along upon them, hitch them by wire cables, which luckily I've got, to the car, and away we'll spin. The power of the car is practically unlimited, and, as you have observed, the ground is as flat and smooth as a prairie, and, moreover, is coated with an icy covering."

Jack glowed with enthusiasm over this project, and was about to indulge in one of his characteristic outbreaks, when there came an interruption which ended in a drama that put silver streaks among my coal-black locks! Some one came in where we were and called off the workmen, who went out with the others in great haste. Of course we followed at their heels. On reaching the principal cavern, we found a singular scene. Two natives, whom we had never seen before, were evidently in charge of some kind of a ceremony. They wore tall, conical hats made of polished metal and covered with hieroglyphics, and carried staves of iron in their hands.

"Priests," Edmund immediately whispered. "Now we'll see something interesting."

The "priests" marshalled all the others, numbering several hundreds, into a long column, and then began a slow, solemn march up the steps. The leaders produced a squeaking music by blowing into the ends of their staves. Women were mingled with men, and even the children were there, too. We followed at the tail of the procession, our curiosity at the highest pitch. At the rate we went it must have taken nearly an hour to mount the steps, but at last all emerged in the open air, where the cold struck to our marrow. The natives didn't seem to mind it, but we ran back and donned our furs. Then we re-ascended and stepped out into the Arctic night, finding the crowd assembled not far from the entrance to the cavern. The frosty sky was ablaze with stars, and directly overhead shone a planet of amazing size and splendour with a little one beside it.

"The earth and the moon!" exclaimed Edmund.

I cannot describe the flood of feeling that went over me at that sight! But in a moment Edmund interrupted my meditation by saying, in a quick, nervous way:

"Look at that!"

The natives had formed themselves in a circle with the two priests standing alone in the centre. All but these two had dropped on their knees, while the leaders, elevating their long arms toward the zenith, gazed upward, uttering a kind of chant in their queer, squeaking voices.

"Don't you see what they're about?" demanded Edmund, twitching me irritably by the sleeve. "They're worshipping the earth!"

It was the truth—the amazing truth! They were worshipping our planet in the sky! And, indeed, she looked worth worshipping. Never have I seen so splendid a star. She was twenty times as bright as the most brilliant planet that any terrestrial astronomer ever beheld; and the moon, glowing beside her like an attendant, redoubled the beauty of the sight.

"It's just the moment of the conjunction," said Edmund. "This is their religion; the earth is their goddess, and when she is nearest and brightest they perform this ceremony in her honour. I wouldn't have missed this for a world."

Suddenly the two priests began to pirouette, and as they whirled more and more rapidly, their huge glowing eyes made phosphorescent circles in the gloom like those that had so alarmed and fascinated us in the cavern. They gyrated round the ring of worshipers with accelerated speed, and all those poor creatures fell under the fascination and drooped with heads to the ground. Now for the first time I caught sight of an oblong object rising a couple of feet above the ground in the centre of the circle. I was wondering what it might be when the spinning priests, who had gradually drawn closer to the ring of worshipers, dived into the circle, and, catching each a native in his arms, ran with their captives to the curious object that I have just described.

"It's a sacrificial stone!" exclaimed Edmund. "They're going to kill them as an offering to the earth and her child the moon."

I was frozen with horror at the sight, but just as the second priest reached the altar, where the first victim had already been pinned with the sharp point of the sacrificial staff, his captive, suddenly recovering his senses, and terrified by the awful fate confronting him, uttered a cry, wrenched himself loose, and, running like the wind, leaped over the circle and disappeared in the darkness. The fugitive passed close by us, and Jack shouted as he darted past:

"Good boy!"

The enraged priest was after him like lightning, and as he came near us his awful eyes seemed to emit actual flames. But the runner had vanished. Without an instant's hesitation the priest shot out his great arm and caught *me* by the throat! In another second I felt myself carried in a bound, as if a tiger had seized me, over the drooping heads of the worshipers and toward the horrible altar.

Chapter 5

Off for the Sun Lands

Dreadful as the moment was, I did not lose my senses. On the contrary, my mind was fearfully clear and active. There was not a horror that I missed. The strength and agility of my captor were astounding. I could no more have struggled with him than with a lion. Only one thing flashed upon me to do; I yelled with all the strength of my lungs. But they had become accustomed to our voices now, and the maddened creature was so intent upon his fell purpose that a cannon-shot would not have diverted him from it.

He got me to the altar, where the preceding victim already lay with his heart torn out, and, pressing me against it with all his bestial force, raised the pointed staff to transfix me. With dying eyes I saw the earth gleaming, magnificent, directly over my head, and my heart bounded with unreasoning hope at the sight. It was my mother planet, powerful to save!

All this passed in a second, while the dreadful spear was poised for its work. Even in that fraction of time I noticed the bunching muscles of the murderer's hairy arm, and then I pressed my eyes shut.

Bang!

Something touched me, and I felt the warm blood gushing. Then I knew no more.

* * * * * * *

In the midst of a dream of boyhood scenes a murmur of familiar voices awoke me. I opened my eyes, but as I could not make out where I was, closed them again.

Then I heard Edmund saying:

"He's coming out all right."

Thereupon, I reopened my eyes, but still the scene puzzled me. I saw Edmund's face, and behind those of Jack and Henry, wearing anxious looks. But this was not my room! It seemed to be a cave, with faint firelight reflections on the walls.

"Where am I?" I asked.

"Back in the cavern, and coming along all right," said Edmund.

Back in the cavern! What did he mean? Then, suddenly, memory returned.

"So he didn't sacrifice me!" I cried.

"Not on your life!" Jack's hearty voice responded. "Edmund was too quick for that."

"But only by a fraction of a second!" said Edmund, smiling.

"What happened, then?" I asked, my recollections coming back stronger and stronger.

"A mighty good shot happened," said Jack. "The best I ever saw."

I looked inquiringly at Edmund. He saw that I could bear it, and he began:

"When that fellow snatched you up and leaped inside the circle I had my furs wrapped so closely around me, not anticipating any danger, that for quite ten seconds I was unable to get out my pistol. I tore the garment open just in time, for already he was pressing you against the accursed altar with his spear poised. I didn't waste any time finding my aim, but even as it was the iron point had touched you when the bullet crashed through his brain. The shock swerved the weapon a little and you were only wounded in the shoulder. You got a scratch which might have been serious but for your Arctic coat. The fellow fell dead beside you, and under the circumstances I felt compelled to shoot the other one also, for he was insane with the delirium of their bloody rite, and I knew that our lives would never be safe if he remained ready for mischief.

"I'm sorry to have had to begin killing right and left again, but I guess that's the lot of all invaders, wherever they may go. It's the second lesson for these savages, and I believe it will prove final. When their priests were dead and the others had no fight in them, even if they had intended any harm to us. Nobody knows to what those chaps might have led them, and my conscience is easy this time."

"How long have I been here?" I asked.

"Two days by the calendar clock?" replied Jack.

"Yes, two days," Edmund assented. "I never saw a man so knocked out by a shock, for the wound wasn't much; I fixed that up in five minutes. But I don't blame you. In your place I should have been scared to the bottom of my soul also. But look at yourself."

He held a pocket mirror before me, and then I saw that my hair was streaked with grey!

"But we haven't been idle in the meanwhile," Edmund went on. "I've got two sleds nearly completed, and to-morrow at midnight—earth time—I mean to set out for the sunny lands of Venus."

"How in the world could you have worked so fast?" I asked in surprise.

"Because I had certain tools in the car which vastly facilitated the operation; but I must admit that the savage blacksmiths worked well, too, and showed surprising intelligence in comprehending my directions. Perhaps that was because I had learned their language."

"Learned their language!" I exclaimed, staring in amazement.

"Well, perhaps that's putting it a little too strong; but I have learned enough to establish a pretty good understanding with them. There's nothing like working together to make intelligent creatures comprehend one another."

"But what kind of a language is it, then?" I asked.

"A language to make your hair stand on end," put in Jack. "The language that ghosts speak, I reckon! Not that I understand the least little bit of it, but I judge from what Edmund says."

With increasing bewilderment I looked at our leader. He smiled, and then looked thoughtful for a moment before again speaking. At last he said:

"It's a subject that I may be better able to discuss after I have learned more about it. All I can say at present is that it appears to be a kind of telepathy. You know that their voices seem hardly more cultivated, or capable of regular articulation, than those of mere brutes; and, besides, they have a certain horror of sound. These smiths wear coverings over their ears to minify the noise of their hammering. Yet they are able to converse, partly by physical signs, but more, I am sure, by some means which they possess of transferring thought without the mediation of any senses familiar to us. Sometimes I imagine that their extraordinary eyes play a large part in the phenomenon. But, however that may be, they certainly are able to read some of my thoughts, when we are in close relations and working together. One of them is especially gifted in this way, and what do you think? I have discovered his name!"

"Now, Edmund—" I began incredulously.

"Yes," he persisted, "it's a fact. You are to remember that they do interchange some of their ideas by means of sounds, and they have certain words, among which I am disposed to think are their individual designations. One of these words particularly attracted my attention because I observed that it was always addressed to the person I have just spoken of, and I finally concluded that it was his name. As near as I can imitate it, it sounds something like 'Juba.' So that's what I call him, and he's going to be the chief of the party that I propose to take with us. His services may be invaluable to us."

A great deal more was said on this curious subject, but since we did not arrive at a complete understanding of it until after we had reached the other side of the planet, I shall postpone any further explanation to the chapters which will be devoted to our astonishing adventures on that part of Venus.

My wound, as Edmund had said, was very slight, and the effects of the shock having passed off during the period of my unconsciousness, I was soon busy with the others in making the final preparations for our departure. The sleds were, of course, very rude affairs, but they were also very strong. Among the innumerable stores which Edmund's foresight had led him to put into the car were a number of exceedingly strong but light metallic cables. With these the two sleds were hitched, one behind the other, and a line about a hundred feet long connected them with the car. The latter could thus rise to a considerable height without lifting the sleds from the ground.

The sleds were provisioned from the stores of the natives, and we also took some of their food in the car, not only to eke out our own but because we had come to like it.

Edmund had already chosen the fellows who were to accompany us, and among them were two of the smiths besides Juba. In all they were eight. How he succeeded in persuading them I do not know, but not the slightest objection was apparent on their part, or on the part of their compatriots in the caverns. We were all ready at the predetermined time, and the scene at our departure was a strange one.

At least five hundred natives had assembled in a furry crowd around the entrance to the caverns to see us off. When we started, the fellows on the sleds, being unused to the motion, clung together like so many awkward white bears taking a ride in the circus. Their friends stood about the ill-omened sacrificial altar, waving their long arms, while their huge eyes goggled in the starlight.

Jack, in a burst of enthusiasm, fired four or five parting shots from his pistol. As the reports crashed through the heavy air, you should have seen the crowd vanish down the hole! The sight made me wince, for they must have gone down like a cataract, all heaped together. But they were tough, and I trust no heads were broken. The effect on the eight fellows on the sleds came near being disastrous. I expected to see them leap off and run, which no doubt they would have done if Edmund had not taken, for other reasons, the precaution to tie them fast. But they strained at their bonds, and squealed in terror.

"Give me your pistol!" commanded Edmund, in a voice of thunder, and with blazing eyes.

Jack was almost twice his size, but he handed over the pistol with the air of a rebuked schoolboy.

"When you learn how to use it, I'll give it back to you," said Edmund sternly, and that closed the incident.

Then we began gradually to put on speed, and as the ground was icy smooth and entirely unobstructed, we were soon travelling at the rate of sixty miles an hour. The plan of the sleds worked like magic, and after their first terror had passed away it was plain to be seen that the natives enjoyed the new sensation immensely. And, indeed, it was a glorious spin!

But in a little while a danger developed which we had not thought of. It arose from the existence of other caverns whose mouths opened upon the plain. To have precipitated the sleds into these would have been fatal. Luckily, shafts of light issued from all of them, and warned by these, we managed to avoid the danger. But it was not entirely passed before we had travelled at least a hundred miles. It was like an immense city of prairie dogs without mounds. The cavern that we had discovered on our arrival was evidently situated on the outskirts of the group, and now we were passing through the centre of it. Occasionally we saw a huge white form disappear in one of the holes as we swiftly approached, but that was all we beheld of the inhabitants. But the spectacle of the shafts of light rising all around us was amazing. When we were in the midst of it Edmund hesitated for a moment, muttering that we had been too hasty and should have remained longer to study the peculiarities of this wonderful world of night; but finally he decided to keep on, and soon afterwards we saw the last of the caverns. Then, as there appeared to be no obstructions of any kind, the speed was worked up to a hundred miles an hour. Going straight ahead as we did, there was no danger of the sleds being overturned.

Having, as Edmund had calculated, about five thousand miles to go before reaching the edge of the sun-illuminated hemisphere, it was evident that, at our present rate of progress, we should arrive there in a little over two days by the calendar clock. We guided our course by the stars, and for me one of the most interesting things was to see the earth sinking toward the horizon, accompanied by the stars, as if the heavens were revolving in a direction opposed to our line of travel. We smoked and talked and ate and slept in the old way, while the marvellous mouths in the wall resumed their strange deglutition. Thus the time passed, without ennui, until, unexpectedly, a new phenomenon captured our attention.

Ahead, through the peephole, Edmund had descried again the flaming spires which had so astonished us on our approach to Venus. But now their appearance was splendid and imposing beyond words. Above them rose an arc of pearly light which grew higher every hour. And with the arc of light rose the flames also. At the same time they seemed to spread to the right and the left, until they were simultaneously visible from both of the side windows of the car. Their colours were wonderful—red, green, purple, orange—all the hues of the prism.

"There is the old mystery again," exclaimed Edmund, "and I can no more explain it now than I could when we first saw it on nearing the planet. The arc of light above is natural enough; it's simply the dawn. The sun never rises on this side of Venus, but it will rise for us because we are approaching it, and the light is the first indication that we are getting near enough to the border between day and night for some of the sun's rays to be bent over the horizon by refraction. But those flames! See how steady they are as a whole, and yet how they change colour like a slowly turning prism."

"Don't, for God's sake, run us into a conflagration," said Jack. "I'm ready to believe anything of this topsy-turvy old planet, and I shouldn't be surprised if the other side is all fire as this one is all frost. I can stand these hairy beasts, but I'll be hanged if I want to be introduced among salamanders."

"That's not real fire," said Edmund. "When we get a little nearer we can see what it is. In the meantime I'll try to think it out."

The result of Edmund's meditations, when he announced it to us, an hour later, awoke as much amazement in our minds as anything that had yet occurred. He had been sitting silent in his corner, occasionally taking a glimpse through the peephole, or one of the windows, when suddenly he slapped his thigh, and springing to his feet, exclaimed:

"They're mountains of crystal!"

"Mountains of crystal!" we echoed.

"Nothing else in the world, and I am ashamed not to have foreseen the thing. It's plain enough when you come to think about it. Remember that Venus being a world lying half in the daylight and half in the night, is necessarily as hot on one side as it is cold on the other. All of the clouds and floating vapours are on the day side, where the sunbeams act. The heated air charged with moisture rises over the sunward hemisphere, and flows off above, on all sides, toward the night side, while from the latter cold air flows in beneath to take its place. Along the junction of the two hemispheres the clouds and moisture are condensed by the intense cold, and fall in ceaseless snowstorms. This snow descending for ages has piled up in mountainous masses whose height may be increased in some places by real mountain ranges buried beneath. The atmospheric moisture cannot pass very far into the night hemisphere without being condensed, and so it is all arrested within a ring, or band, extending completely around the planet, and marking the division between perpetual day and perpetual night. The appearance of gigantic flames is produced by the sunbeams striking these mountains of ice and snow from behind and breaking into prismatic fire."

We listened to this explanation, so simple and yet so wonderful, with mingled feelings of astonishment and admiration. And then we turned again to regard the phenomenon, which now, with our nearer approach, had become splendid and awful beyond description.

In a few minutes Edmund addressed us again. "I foresee now," he said, "considerable trouble for us. There has been a warning of that, too, if I had but heeded it. I've noticed for some time that a wind, getting gradually stronger, has been following us, sometimes dying out and then coming on again stronger than before. It is likely that this wind gets to be a perfect hurricane in the neighbourhood of those strange mountains. It is the back suction, caused, as I have already told you, by the rising of the heated air on the sunny side of the planet. It may play the deuce with us when we get into the midst of it. I shall have to be cautious."

He immediately reduced the speed to not more than ten miles an hour, and at once we noticed the wind of which he had spoken. It came now in great gusts from behind, rapidly increasing in frequency and fury. Soon it was strong enough to drive the sleds without any pull upon the cable, and sometimes they were forced directly under the car, and even ahead of it, the natives clinging to one another in the utmost terror. Edmund managed to govern the motions of the car for a time, holding it back against the storm, but as he confessed, this was a contingency he had made no provision for, and eventually we became almost as helpless as a ship in a typhoon.

"Of course I could cut loose from the sleds and run right out of this," said Edmund, "but that would never do. I've taken them into my service and I'm bound to look out for them. If there was room for them in the car it would be all right. Let's see. Yes! I've got it. I'll fetch up the sleds and fasten them underneath the car, like baskets to a balloon, and so carry the whole thing. There's plenty of power; it's only room that's wanting."

No sooner said than done with Edmund. By this time we were getting into the ice, huge hills of which surrounded us. Edmund dropped the car in the lee of one of these strange hummocks. Here the force of the wind was broken, and the sky directly over us was free from clouds, but a short distance ahead we could see them whirling and tumbling in mighty masses of tumultuous vapour. Lashing the two sleds together we attached them about ten feet below the bottom of the car. Then the natives, who had been unbound, and had stood looking on in utter bewilderment, were securely fastened on the sleds. We entered the car and the power was turned on.

"We'll rise straight up," said Edmund, "and as soon as we are out of the wind current we will sail over the mountains and come down on the other side as nice as you please. Strange that I didn't think of carrying the sleds in this way to begin with."

It was a beautiful program that Edmund had outlined, and we had complete confidence in our leader's ability to carry it through; but it didn't work as expected. Even his genius had met its match this time.

No sooner had we risen out of the protection of the hill of ice than the hurricane caught us. It was a blast of such power and ferocity that in an instant it had the car spinning like a *teetotum*, and then it shot us ahead, banging the sleds against the car as if they had been tassels. It is a wonder of wonders that the poor creatures on them were not flung off, but fortunately we had taken particular pains with their lashings, and as for knocks, they could stand them like so many bears.

In the course of twenty minutes we must have travelled twice as many miles, perfectly helpless to arrest our mad rush because, Edmund said, the atomic reaction partly refused to work, and he could not rise as he had expected to do. We were pitched hither and thither, and were sprawling on the floor more than half the time. The noise was awful, and nobody tried to speak after Edmund had shouted his single communication about the power, which would have filled us with dismay if we had had leisure to think.

The shutters were open, and suddenly I saw through one of the windows a sight which I thought must surely be my last. The car had been sweeping through a dense cloud of boiling vapours, and these had without warning split open before my eyes—and there, almost in contact with the car, was a glittering precipice of solid ice, gleaming with wicked blue flashes, and we were rushing upon it as if shot out of a cannon!

The next instant came a terrific shock, which I thought must have crushed the car like an eggshell, and down we fell—down and down!

CHAPTER 6

Lost in the Crystal Mountains

If we had seen the danger earlier, and had not been so tumbled about by the pitching of the car, it is possible that Edmund would have prevented the collision, in spite of the partial disablement of his apparatus. The blow against the precipice of ice was not as severe as it had seemed to me, and the car was not smashed; but the fall was terrible! There was only one thing which saved us from destruction. At the base of the mighty cliff against which the wind had hurled the car an immense deposit of snow had collected, and into this we plunged. We were all thrown together in a heap, the car and the sleds being entangled with the wire ropes.

Fortunately the stout glass windows were not broken, and after we had struggled to our feet Edmund managed to open the door. Before emerging he bade us put on our furs, but even with them we found the cold outside all but unendurable. Yet the natives paid no attention to it. Not one of them was seriously hurt, although they were firmly attached to the sleds, and unable to undo their fastenings. We set them loose, and then began seriously to examine the situation.

Above us towered the vertical precipice disappearing in the whirling clouds, and the wind drove square against it with the roar of Niagara. The air was filled with snow and ice dust, and at intervals we could not see objects three feet away from our noses. Our poor furry companions huddled together, and being of no use to themselves or us, suffered more from the noise, and from the terror inspired by the snow than from any injuries that they had received.

"We've got to get out of this mighty quick," shouted Edward. "Hustle now and repair ship."

We got to work at once, Juba aiding us a little under Edmund's direction, and soon we had the sleds out of the tangle and properly attached. Then we replaced the natives on their seats, and entered the car. Edmund began to fumble with his apparatus. After some ten minutes' work he said, in an evasive way, that the damage was not serious enough to prevent the working of the car, but I thought I caught an expression of extreme anxiety in his face. Still, his manner indicated that he considered himself master of the situation.

"You notice," he said, "that this wind is variable, and there lies our chance. When the blasts weaken, the air springs back from the face of the cliff and then whirls round to the right. I've no doubt that there is a passage in that direction through which the wind finds its way behind this icy mountain, and if we can get there, too, we shall undoubtedly find at least partial shelter. I'm going to take advantage of the first lull."

It worked out just as he had predicted. As the wind surged back after a particularly vicious rush against the great blue cliff, we cut loose and went sailing up into it, rushing past the glittering wall so swiftly that it made our heads swim. In two or three minutes we rounded a corner, and then found ourselves in a kind of atmospheric eddy, where the car simply spun round and round, with the sleds whirling below it.

"Now for it!" shouted Edmund. "Hang on!"

He touched a knob, and instantly we rose with immense speed. We must have shot up a couple of thousand feet, when the wind, coming over the top of the icy barrier we had just flanked, caught us again, and swept us off on a horizontal course. Then, suddenly, the air cleared all round about, as if a magic broom had swept away the clouds. The spectacle that was revealed—but why try to describe it! No language could do it. Yet I must tell you what we saw.

We were in the heart of the *Crystal Mountains!* They towered round us on every side, and stretched away in interminable ranges of shining pinnacles. Such shapes! Such colours! Such flashing and blazing of gigantic rainbows and prisms! There were mountains that looked to my amazed eyes as lofty as Mont Blanc, and as massive, every solid mile of which was composed of crystalline ice, refracting and reflecting the sunbeams with iridescent splendour. For now we could begin to see a part of the orb of the sun itself, prodigious in size, and poised on the edge of the gem-glittering horizon, where the jewelled summits split its beams into a thousand haloes.

There was one mighty peak, still ahead of us, but toward which we were rushed sidewise by the wind, which surpassed all the others in marvelousness. It towered majestically above our level—a superb, stupendous, coruscating *Alp of Light!* On every side it darted blinding rays of a hundred splendid hues, as if a worldful of emeralds, rubies, sapphires, and diamonds had been heaped together in one gigantic pile and transfused with a sunburst. Even Edmund was for a moment speechless with astonishment at this wildly magnificent sight. But presently he spoke, very calmly, though what he said changed our amazement to terror.

"The trouble with the apparatus is very serious. I am unable to make the car rise higher. It will no longer react against an obstacle. We are entirely at the mercy of the wind. If it carries us against that glittering devil no power under heaven can save us."

If my hair had not whitened before it surely would have whitened now!

When we were swept against the first icy precipice the danger had come unexpectedly, out of a concealing cloud, and anticipation was swallowed up in the event. But now we had to bear the fearful strain of expectation, with the paralyzing knowledge that nothing that we could do could aid us in the least. I thought that even Edmund's face paled with fear.

On we rushed, still borne sidewise, so that the spectacle was burned into our eyes, as, with the fascination of impending death, we gazed helpless out of the window. Now we were upon it! Instinctively I threw myself backward; but the blow did not come. Instead there was a wild rush of ice crystals sweeping the thick glass.

"Look!" shouted Edmund. "We are safe! See how the particles of ice are swept from the face of the peak by the tempest. They leap toward us, and are then whirled round the mountain. The compacted air forms a buffer. We may yet touch the precipice, but the wind, having free vent on both sides, will carry us one way or the other without a serious shock."

He had hardly finished speaking, in a voice that had risen to a shriek with the effort to make himself heard, when the crisis came. We did just touch a projecting ridge, but the wind, howling past it, carried us in an instant round the obstruction.

"Scared ourselves for nothing," said Edmund, in a quieter voice, as the roar died down. "We were really as safe all the time as a boat in a deep rapid. The velocity of the current sheered us off."

Our hearts beat more steadily again, but there was a greater danger, of which he had warned us, but which we had not had time to contemplate. I, at least, began to think of it with dismay when the scintillant peak was left behind, and I saw Edmund again working away at his machinery. Presently it was manifest that we were rapidly sinking.

"What's the matter?" I cried. "We seem to be going down."

"So we are," he replied quietly, "and I fear that we shall not go up again very soon. The power is failing all the time. It will be pretty hard to have to stop indefinitely in this frightful place, but I am afraid that that is our destiny."

Lost and helpless in these mountains of ice and this world of gloom and storm! The thought was too terrible to be entertained. Yet it was forced into our minds even more by our leader's manner than by his words. Not one of us failed to comprehend its meaning, and it was characteristic that, while talkative Jack now said not a word, uncommunicative Henry burst into a brief fury of denunciation. I was startled by the energy of his words:

"Edmund Stonewall," he cried, agitating his arms, "you have brought me to my death with your infernal invention! May you be——"

But he never finished the sentence. His face turned as white as a sheet, and he sank in a heap upon the floor.

"Poor fellow," said Edmund, pityingly. "Would to God that he instead of Church had remained at home. But I'll get him and all of us out of this trouble; only give me a little time."

In a few minutes Jack and I had restored Henry to his senses, but he was as weak as a child, and remained lying on one of the cushioned benches. In the meantime the car descended until at last it rested upon the snow in a deep valley, where we were protected from the wind. In this profound depression a kind of twilight prevailed, for the sun, which we had glimpsed when we were on the level of the peaks, was at least thirty degrees below our present horizon. Henry having recovered his nerve, we all got out of the car, unloosed the natives, and began to look about us.

The scene was more disheartening than ever. All about towered the crystal mountains, their bases leaden-hued and formless in the ghostly gloom, while their middle parts showed deep gleams of ultramarine, brightening to purple higher up, and a few aspiring peaks behind us sparkled brilliantly where the sunlight touched them. It was such a spectacle as the imagination could not have conceived, and I have often tried in vain to reproduce it satisfactorily in my own mind.

Was there ever such a situation as ours? Cast away in a place wild and wonderful beyond description, millions of miles from all human aid and sympathy, millions of miles from the world that had given us birth! I could, in bitterness of spirit, have laughed at the suggestion that there was any hope for us. And yet, at that very moment, not only was there hope, but there was even the certainty of deliverance.

But, unknown to us, it lay in the brain of the incomparable man who had brought us hither.

I have told you that it was twilight in the valley where we lay. But when, as frequently happened, tempests of snow burst over the mountains, and choked the air about us, the twilight turned to deepest night, and we had to illumine the lamps in the car. By great good fortune, Edmund said, enough power remained to furnish us with light and heat, and now I looked upon those mysterious black-tusked muzzles in the car with a new sentiment, praying that they would not turn to mouths of death.

The natives, being used to darkness, needed no artificial illumination. In fact, we had observed that whenever the sunlight had streamed over them their great eyes were almost blinded, and they suffered cruelly from an affliction so completely outside of all their experience. Edmund now began to speak to us of this, saying that he ought to have foreseen and provided against it.

"I shall try to find some means of affording protection to their eyes when we arrive in the sunlit hemisphere," he said. "It must be my first duty."

We heard these words with a thrill of hope.

"Then you think that we shall escape?" I asked.

"Of course we shall escape," he replied cheerfully. "I give you my word for it, but do not ask me for any particulars yet. The exact means I have not yet found, but find them I will. We may have to stay where we are for a considerable time, and our companions must be made comfortable. Even under their furry skins they'll suffer from this kind of weather."

Following his directions we took a lot of extra furs from the car, and constructed a kind of tent, under which the natives could huddle on the sleds. There being but little wind in the valley, this was not so difficult an undertaking as it may seem. And the poor fellows were very glad of the shelter, for some of them were shivering, since, not knowing what to do, they were less active than ourselves. No sooner were they housed than they fell to eating ravenously. Both the car and the sleds had been abundantly provisioned, so that there was no immediate fear of a famine among us.

Inside the car we soon had things organized very much as they were during our voyage from the earth. We read, talked, and smoked to our hearts' content, almost forgetting the icy mountains that tottered over us, and the howling tempest which, with hardly an intermission, tore through the cloud-choked air a thousand or two thousand feet above our heads. We talked of our adventure with the meteors, which seemed an event of long ago, and then we talked of home—home twenty-six million miles away! In fact, it may have been thirty millions by this time, for Edmund had told us that Venus, having passed conjunction while we were at the caverns, was now receding from the earth.

But while we thus strove to kill the time and banish thoughts of our actual situation, Edmund sat apart much of the time absorbed in thought, and we respected his privacy, knowing that our only chance of escape lay in him. One day (I speak always of "days," because we religiously counted the passage of time by our clock) he issued alone from the car and was absent a long time, so that we began to be concerned, and, going outside looked everywhere for signs of him. At length, to our infinite relief, he appeared stumbling and crawling along the foot of an icy mountain. As he drew nearer we saw that he was smiling, and as soon as he was within easy earshot he called out:

"It's all right. I've found the solution."

Then upon joining us he continued:

"We'll get out all right, but we shall have to be patient for a while longer."

"What is it?" we asked eagerly. "What have you found out?"

"Peter," he said, turning to me, "you know what libration means; well, it's libration that is going to save us. As Venus travels round the sun she turns just once on her axis in making a complete circuit, the consequence being, as you already know, that she has one side on which the sun never rises while the other half is in perpetual daylight. But, since her orbit is not a perfect circle, she travels a little faster than the average during about half of her year and a little slower during the other half, but, at the same time, her steady rotation on her axis never varies. This produces the phenomenon that is called libration, the result of which is that, along the border between the day and night hemispheres there is a narrow strip where the sun rises and sets once in each of her years, which are about two hundred and twenty-five of our days in length. Within this strip the sun shines continuously for about sixteen weeks, gradually rising during eight weeks and sinking during the following eight. Then, during the next sixteen weeks, the strip lies in unceasing night.

"Now the kind fates have willed that we should fall just within this lucky strip. By the utmost good fortune after we passed the blazing peak which so nearly wrecked us, we were carried on by the wind so far, before the ascensional power of the car gave out, that we descended on the sunward side of the crest of the range. The sun is now just beginning to rise on the part of the strip where we are, and it will get higher for several weeks to come. The result will be that a great melting of ice and snow will occur here, and in this deep valley a river will form, flowing off toward the sunward hemisphere, exactly where we want to go. I shall take advantage of the torrent that will flow here and float down with it until we are out of the labyrinth. It's our only chance, for we couldn't possibly clamber over the hummocky ice and drag the car with us."

"Why not leave the car here?" asked Henry.

Edmund looked at him and smiled.

"Do you want to stay on Venus all your life?" he asked. "I thought you didn't like it well enough for that. How could we ever get back to the earth without the car? I can repair the mechanism as soon as I can find certain substances, which I am sure exist on this planet as well as on the earth. But it is no use looking for them in this icy wilderness. No, we can never abandon the car. We must take it with us, and the only possible way to transport it is with the aid of the coming river."

"But how will you manage to float?" I asked.

"The car, being air-tight, will float like a buoy."

"But the natives, will you abandon them?"

"God forbid. I'll contrive a way for them."

The effects of libration on Venus were not new to me, but they were to Jack and Henry, who had never studied such things, and they expressed much doubt about Edmund's plan, but I had confidence in it from the beginning, and it turned out just as he had predicted, as things always did. Every twenty-four hours we saw, with thankful hearts, that the sun had perceptibly risen, and as it rose, the sky gradually cleared, while the sunbeams, falling uninterruptedly, grew hotter and hotter. Soon we no longer had any use for furs, or for artificial heat. At the same time the melting of the ice began. It formed, in fact, a new danger, by bringing down avalanches into the valley, yet we watched the process joyously, since it fell so entirely within Edmund's program. While we were awaiting the flood, Edmund had prepared screens to protect the eyes of the natives.

We were just at the bottom of the trough of the valley, near its head. It wound away before us, turning out of sight beyond an icy bulwark. Streams were soon pouring down from the heights all around, and uniting, they formed a little torrent, which flowed swiftly over the smooth, hard ice. Edmund now completed his plan.

"I'll take Juba in the car with us," he said. "There's just room for him. As for the others, we'll fasten the sleds on each side of the car, which will be buoyant enough to float them, and they'll have to take their chances outside."

We made the final arrangements while the little torrent was swelling to a river. Before it became too broad and deep we managed to place the car across the centre of its course, the sleds forming outriders. Then all took their places and waited. Higher and higher rose the waters, while avalanches, continually increasing in size and number, thundered down the heights, and vast cataracts leaped and poured from the precipices. It was a mercy that we were so situated that the avalanches could not reach the car. But we received some pretty hard knocks before the stream became deep and steady enough to float us off. Shall I ever forget that moment?

There came a sudden wave, forced onward by a great slide of ice, which lifted car and sleds on its crest, and away we went! The car proved more buoyant than I had believed possible. The sleds, fastened on each side, tended to give it extra stability, and it did not sink deeper than the middle of the windows. The latter, though formed of very thick glass, might have been broken by the tossing ice if they had not been divided into small panes separated by bars of steel, which projected a few inches outside.

"I made that arrangement for meteors," said Edmund, "but I never thought that they would have to be defended against ice."

The increasing force of the current sent us spinning down the valley with accelerated speed. We swept round the nearest ice peak on the left, and as we passed under its projecting buttresses a fearful roar above informed us that an avalanche of unexampled magnitude had been unchained. We could not withdraw our eyes from the window on that side of the car, and almost instantly immense masses of ice appeared crashing into the water, throwing it over us in floods and half drowning the unfortunate wretches on the sleds. Still, they clung on, fastened together, and we could do nothing to aid them. The uproar grew worse, and the ice came plunging down faster and faster, accompanied with a deluge of water from the heights above. The car pitched and rolled until we were all flung off our feet. Poor Juba was a picture of abject terror. He hung moaning to a bench, his huge eyes aglow with fright.

Suddenly the car seemed to be lifted clear from the water, and then it fell back again and was submerged, so that we were buried in night. Slowly we rose to the surface, and Edmund, springing to a window, shouted:

"They're gone! Heaven have pity on them—and on me!"

In spite of their fastenings the water had swept every living soul from the sled on the left. We rushed to the other window. It was the same story there—the sled on that side was also empty. I saw a furry body tossed in the torrent alongside, but in a second it disappeared beneath the raging water. At the same time Edmund exclaimed:

"God forgive us for bringing those poor creatures here only to meet their death!"

CHAPTER 7

The Children of the Sun

But the situation was too critical to permit us to think of the unfortunates whose death we had undoubtedly caused. There seemed less than an even chance of our getting through with our own lives. As we tossed and whirled onward the water rose yet higher, and blocks of ice assailed us on all sides. First the sled on the left was torn loose; then the other followed it, leaving the car to fight its battle alone. But the loss of the sleds was a good thing now that their occupants were gone, for it eased off the weight and the car rose much higher in the water. Moreover, it gave way more readily when pressed by the ice. To be sure, it rolled more than before, but still, being well ballasted, it did not turn turtle, and most of the time we were able to keep on our feet by holding fast to the inside window bars.

Once we took a terrible plunge, over a vertical fall of not less than twenty or thirty feet. But the water below the fall was very deep, a profound hole having been quickly scooped out in the unfathomable ice beneath, so that we did not strike bottom, as I had feared, but came bobbing to the top again like a cork. Below this fall there was a very long series of rapids, extending, it seemed, for miles upon miles, and we shot down them with the speed of an express train, lurching from side to side, and colliding with hundreds of ice floes. It must not be supposed that we went through this experience without suffering any injuries. On the contrary, our hands were all bleeding, our faces cut, Henry had one eye closed by a blow, and our clothing, for we were not wearing our Arctic outfit, was badly used up. Yet none of our injuries was really serious, although we looked as if we had just come out of the toughest kind of a street brawl.

But there is no use in prolonging the story of this awful ride. It seemed to us to last for days upon days, though, in fact, the worst of it was over within twelve hours after we were lifted from our moorings in the valley. The tumbling stream gradually broadened out as it left the region of the high mountains, and then we found ourselves in a district covered with icy hills of no great elevation. But we could still see, by glances, as the stream curved this way and that, the glittering peaks behind. It was an appalling thing to watch many of the nearer hills as they suddenly sank, collapsed, and disappeared, like pinnacles of loaf sugar melting and falling to pieces in a basin of water.

Edmund said that all of the ice-hills and mounds through which we were passing no doubt owed their existence to pressure from behind, in the belt where the sun never rose, and where the ice was piled up in actual mountains. These foothills were, in fact, enormous glaciers thrust out toward the sunward hemisphere.

After a long time the now broad river widened yet more until it became a great lake, or bay. The surface of the planet around appeared nearly level, and, as far as we could see, was mostly covered by the water. Here vast fields of ice floated, and the water was not muddy, as it would have been if it had passed over soil, but of crystal purity and wonderfully blue in places where shafts of sunlight penetrated to great depths—for now the sun was high above the horizon ahead, and shining in an almost clear sky. Presently we began to notice the wind again. It came fitfully, first from one quarter and then another, rapidly increasing until, at times, it rose into a tempest. It lifted the water in huge combing waves, but the car rode them like a lifeboat.

"There is peril for us in this," said Edmund, at last. "We are being carried by the current into a region where the contending winds may play havoc. It is the place where the hot air from the sunward side begins to be chilled and to descend, meeting the colder air from the night side. It must form a veritable belt of storms, which may be as difficult to pass, circumstanced as we are, as the crystal mountains themselves."

"Suppose it should turn out that there is nothing but an ocean on this side of the planet," I suggested.

"That I believe to be impossible," Edmund responded. "This hemisphere must be, as a whole, broken up into highlands and depressions. The geological formation of the other side, as far as I could make it out from the appearance of the rocks in the caverns, indicates that Venus has undergone the same experience of upheavals and fracturings of the crust that the earth has been through. If that is true of one side it must be true of the other also, for during a large part of these geological changes she undoubtedly rotated rapidly on her axis like the earth."

"But we travelled five thousand miles on the other side without encountering anything but a frozen prairie," I objected.

"True enough, and yet I would lay a wager that all of that side of the planet is not equally level. Remember the vast plains of Russia and Siberia."

"Well," put in Jack, whose spirits were beginning to revive, "if there's a shore somewheres, let's find it. I want to see the other kind of inhabitants. These that we've met don't accord with my ideas of Venus."

"We shall find them," responded Edmund, "and I think I can promise you that they will not disappoint your expectations."

Yet there seemed to be nothing in our present situation to warrant the confidence expressed by our leader's words and manner. The current that had carried us out of the crystal mountains gradually disappeared in a vast waste of waters, and we were driven hither and thither by the tempestuous wind. Its force increased hour by hour, and at last the sky, which at brief intervals had been clear and exquisitely blue, became choked with black clouds, sweeping down upon the face of the waters, and often whirled into great *trombes* by the tornadic blasts. Several times the car was deluged by waterspouts, and once it was actually lifted up into the air by the mighty suction. An ordinary vessel would not have lived five minutes in that hell of winds and waters. But the car, if it had been built for this kind of navigation, could not have behaved better.

I do not know how long all this lasted. It grew worse and worse. Sometimes a flood of rain fell, and then would come a storm of lightning, and a downpour of gigantic hailstones that rattled upon the steel shell of the car like a rain of bullets from a battery of machine guns. Half the time one window or the other was submerged by the waves, and when we got an opportunity to glance out, we saw nothing but torn streamers of cloud whipping the face of the waters. But when the change came at last, it was as sudden as the dropping of a curtain. The clouds broke away, a soft light filled the atmosphere, the waves ceased to break and rolled in long undulations, and a marvellous dome appeared overhead.

That dome, at its first dramatic appearance, was one of the most astonishing things that we saw in the whole course of our adventures. It was not a cerulean vault like that which covers the earth in halcyon weather, but an indescribably soft, pinkish-grey concavity that seemed nearer than the sky and yet farther than the clouds. Here and there, far beneath it, but still at a vast elevation, floated delicate gauzy curtains, tinted like sheets of mother-of-pearl. The sun was no longer visible, but the air was filled with a delicious luminousness, which bathed the eyes as if it had been an ethereal liquid.

Below each window was a steel ledge, broad enough to stand on, with convenient hold-fasts for the hands. These had evidently been prepared for some such contingency, and Edmund, throwing open the windows, invited us to go outside. We gladly accepted the invitation, and all, except Juba, issued into the open air. The temperature was that of an early spring day, and the air was splendidly fresh and stimulating. The rolling of the car had now nearly ceased, and we had no difficulty in maintaining our positions. For a long while we admired, and talked of, the great dome overhead, which drew our attention, for the time, from the sea that had so strangely brought us hither.

"There," said Edmund, pointing to the dome, "is the inside of the shell of cloud whose exterior, gleaming in the sunshine, baffles our astronomers in their efforts to see the surface of Venus. I believe that we shall find the whole of this hemisphere covered by it. It is a shield for the inhabitants against the fervours of an unsetting sun. Its presence prevents their real world from being seen from outside."

"Well," said Jack, laughing, "I never heard before that Venus was fond of a veil."

"Not only can they not be seen," continued Edmund, "but they cannot themselves see beyond the screen that covers them."

"Worse and worse!" exclaimed Jack. "The astronomers have certainly made a mistake in naming this bashful planet Venus."

We continued for a long time to gaze at the great dome, admiring the magnificent play of iridescent colours over its vast surface, until suddenly Jack, who had gone to the other side of the car, called out to us:

"Come here and tell me what this is."

We hurried to his side and were astonished to see a number of glittering objects which appeared to be floating in the atmosphere. They were arranged in an almost straight row, at an elevation of perhaps two thousand feet, and were apparently about three miles away. After a few moments of silence, Edmund said, in his quiet way:

"Those are air ships."

"Air ships!"

"Yes, surely. An exploring expedition, I shouldn't wonder. I anticipated something of that kind. You know already how dense the atmosphere of Venus is. It follows that balloons, and all sorts of machines for aerial navigation, can float much more easily here than over the earth. I was prepared to find the inhabitants of Venus skilled in such things, and I'm not surprised by what we see."

"Venus with wings!" cried Jack. "Now, Edmund, that sounds more like it. I guess we've struck the right planet after all."

"But," I said, "you spoke of an exploring expedition. How in the world do you make that out?"

"It seems perfectly natural to me," replied Edmund. "Remember the two sides of the planet, so wonderfully different from one another. If we on the earth are so curious about the poles of our planet, simply because they are unlike other parts of the world, don't you think that the inhabitants of Venus should be at least equally curious concerning a whole hemisphere of their world, which differs *in toto* from the half on which they live?"

"That does seem reasonable," I assented.

"Of course it's reasonable, and I imagine that we, ourselves, are about to be submitted to investigation."

"By Jo!" exclaimed Jack, running his hands through his hair, and smoothing his torn and rumpled garments, "then we must make ready for inspection. But I'm afraid we won't do much honour to old New York. Can I get a shave aboard your craft, Edmund?"

"Oh, yes," Edmund replied, laughing. "I didn't forget soap and razors."

But Jack would have had no time to make his toilet even if he had seriously thought of it. The strange objects in the air approached with great rapidity, and we soon saw that Edmund had correctly divined their nature. They were certainly air ships, and I was greatly interested in the observation that they seemed to be constructed somewhat upon the principles upon which our inventors were then working on the earth. But they were neither aeroplanes nor balloons. They bore a resemblance to mechanical birds, and seemed to be sustained and forced ahead by a wing-like action.

This, of course, did not escape Edmund's notice.

"Look," he said admiringly, "how easily and gracefully they fly. Perhaps with our relatively light atmosphere we shall never be able to do that on the earth; but no matter," he added, with a flush, "for with the inter-atomic energy at our command, we shall have no need to imitate the birds."

"Perhaps they have made that discovery here, too," I suggested.

"No, it is evident that they have not, else they would not be employing mechanical means of flight. Once let me get the car fixed up and we'll give them a surprise."

"Yes, and if you had used common sense," growled Henry, nursing his injured eye, "you would not be here fooling away your time and ours, and risking our lives every minute, but you'd be making millions and revolutionizing life at home."

"And where'd the Columbus of Space be then?" demanded Jack. "Hanged if Edmund is not right! I'd rather be here meeting these doves of Venus than grinding out dollars on the earth. And can't we go back and scoop in the money when we get ready?"

The discussion went no further, for, by this time, two of the air ships were close at hand. And now we perceived, for the first time, the beings that they carried. Our surprise at the sight was even greater than that which we had experienced upon meeting the inhabitants of the dark hemisphere. The latter were extraordinary—but we were looking for extraordinary things. Indeed they were, except for certain peculiarities, much more like some members of our own race than we should have deemed possible. How great, then, was our astonishment upon seeing the two air ships apparently in charge of *real human beings!*

At least that was our first impression. In the midst of the strange apparatus, which evidently fulfilled the function of wings for the air ships, we saw decks, spacious enough to contain twenty persons, and surmounted with deck houses, and along the railings inclosing the decks were gathered the crews, among whom we believed that we could recognize their officers. The two vessels had approached within a hundred yards before being suddenly arrested. Then they settled gracefully down upon the water, where they floated like swans.

At first, as I have said, the resemblance of their crews to inhabitants of the earth seemed complete. One would have said that we had met a yachting party, composed of tall, well-formed, light-complexioned, yellow-haired Englishmen, the pick of their race. At a distance their dress alone appeared strange, though it, too, might easily be imitated on the earth. As well as I can describe it, it bore some resemblance, in general effect, to the draperies of a Greek statue, and it was specially remarkable for the harmonious blending of soft hues in its texture.

During a space of at least five minutes we gazed at them, and they at us. Probably their surprise was greater than ours, because we had been on the lookout for strange sights, being, of our own volition, in a foreign world, while they could have had no expectation of such an encounter, even if, as Edmund had conjectured, they were engaged in exploration. We could read their astonishment in their gesticulations. Slowly the car and the nearer of the two air ships drifted closer together. When we were within less than fifty yards of one another, Jack suddenly called out:

"A woman! By Jo, it's Venus herself!"

His excited voice rang like a rattle of musketry in the heavy air, and the beings on the air ship started back in alarm. But although, like the inhabitants of the dark hemisphere, they were, evidently, unaccustomed to hearing sounds of such forcefulness issue from a living creature no larger than themselves, they were not faint-hearted, and the air ship did not, as we half expected it would, take flight. The momentary commotion was quickly quieted, and our visitors continued their inspection. All of us immediately recognized the personage whom Jack had singled out as the subject of his startling exclamation. It was clear that he had rightly guessed her sex, and she appeared worthy of his admiring designation. Even at the distance of a hundred feet we could see that she was very beautiful. Her complexion was light, with a flame upon the cheeks; her hair a chestnut blond; and her large, round eyes were sapphire blue, and seemed to radiate a light of their own. This last statement (about the eyes) must not be taken for a conventional exaggeration, such as writers of fiction employ in describing heroines who never existed. On the contrary, it expresses a literal fact; and moreover, as the reader will see further on, this peculiarity of the eyes was shared, in varying degrees, by all these people of Venus, and was connected with the most amazing of all our discoveries on that planet. I should say here that, while the eyes of the inhabitants of the day side were larger than ours, they did not, in respect of size, resemble the extraordinary organs of vision possessed by the compatriots of Juba.

In a few minutes we became aware that the beautiful creature we had been admiring was not the only representative of the female sex on the air ship. Several others surrounded her, and the fact quickly became manifest that they recognized her as a superior. Still more surprising was the discovery, which we were not long in making, that she was actually the commander of the craft. We could see that the orders which determined its movements emanated from her.

"Amazons!" exclaimed Jack, taking pains this time to moderate his voice. "And what a queen they've got!"

During all this time the car and the air ship were slowly drifting nearer to one another, drawn by that strange attraction which seems to affect inanimate things when in close neighbourhood, and when they were not more than fifteen yards apart the personage we had been watching slowly lifted her arm, revealing a glittering bracelet, and, with an ineffably winning smile, made a gesture which said plainer than any words could have done:

"Welcome, strangers."

CHAPTER 8

Language Without Speech

"That breaks the ice," said the irrepressible Jack. "We're introduced! Now for the conquest of Venus."

We had all instinctively returned the smile of our beautiful interlocutor, with bows and gestures of amity, and it looked as though we might soon be within touch of her hand, for the vessels continued to drift nearer, when suddenly Juba clambered out of the window and stood beside us, his moon eyes blinking in the unaccustomed light. The greatest agitation was immediately manifest among the crowd on the deck of the air ship. They seemed to be even more startled than they had been by the sound of Jack's voice. They interchanged looks, and, apparently, a few words, spoken in very low voices, and glanced from Juba to us in a way which plainly showed that they were astonished at our being together.

Edmund, whose perspicacity never deserted him, immediately penetrated their thoughts.

"It is clear," he said, "that these people recognize Juba as an inhabitant of the dark hemisphere, while, as to us, they are puzzled, and all the more so now that Juba has made his appearance. I think it certain that they have never actually met any representative of Juba's race before, but no doubt he bears, to their eyes, ethnological characteristics which escape our discernment, and it is likely that tradition has handed down to them facts about the inhabitants of the other side of their planet which accord with his appearance."

"Then, they must conclude that we have come from the other side, and brought Juba along as a captive," I said.

"Undoubtedly."

"And what must they think of us—that we are inhabitants of the dark hemisphere also?"

"What else can they think?"

I do not know into what train of speculation this might have led us if a new incident had not suddenly changed the current of our thoughts. Unnoticed by us the second air ship had drawn near. Signals were interchanged between it and the first, and we observed that she who seemed to be the commander in chief gave orders that the second air ship should lay us aboard. The order was no sooner given than executed, and we found ourselves face to face with a dozen of the blond-haired natives, led by one who was clearly their captain. The deck of the air ship touched the side of the car, and, as if instinctively recognizing our leader, the captain laid his hand on Edmund's arm, but with a smile which gave assurance that no violence was intended.

"Come," said Edmund, in a low voice, "it is best that we should go aboard their craft. We are in their hands, and luckily so, for they will take us where we want to go."

Accordingly, all, including Juba, passed upon the deck of the air ship. You will readily imagine the intensity of interest with which we studied the faces and forms of those whom I will call our captors. Now that we were in contact with them we could better observe their resemblances to, and differences from, ourselves. In all the main features of body they were human beings, but of a somewhat superior stature. Noses and mouths were small and delicate; hair long, silken, and either light gold or rich chestnut in colour; skin white and smooth; ears small and peculiarly formed, with a curious mobility; and eyes large, round, invariably light blue, and possessing that strange luminousness of which I have already spoken. One could not look directly into these eyes without a certain shrinking, for some wonderful power seemed to radiate from them, and one had the feeling that the intelligence behind them could dip to the bottom of his mind. We were gently treated and could perceive no indication of peril to ourselves. Nevertheless, we were glad to feel our pistols in our pockets. There were seats on the deck to which we were civilly conducted, but Edmund refused to sit.

"I must see the commander herself," he whispered. "These are only subordinates, and I cannot deal with them. It will not do to leave the car here at the mercy of the waves. I must find the means of making them understand that it is to go with us."

Accordingly, he approached the captain, and we watched him with beating hearts, not being able to divine what an attempt to dictate terms on our part might lead to. Jack shook his head, and put his hand on his pistol, which Edmund had restored to him while we were in the ice mountains.

"I'll drop the jackanapes in his tracks if he shows up ugly," he said.

"You'd better keep quiet," I whispered, "and don't let them see your weapon. They appear to have no arms, and you should trust to Edmund to manage the affair. When he gives the word it will be time enough to begin shooting."

Jack grumbled, but kept the pistol in his pocket, although he did not withdraw his hand from it.

I have already told you how, at the caverns, Edmund had discovered that the inhabitants there possessed a means of converse which he likened to telepathy, and from what I had seen of the people here I was convinced that they had the same mysterious power, and probably in a higher degree. To be sure, they used words occasionally, but for the most part they communed together in some other way. I felt sure that Edmund was now about to apply what he had learned, and his actions quickly demonstrated that my conjecture was well founded. Just what he did, I do not know, but the result of his conference was promptly apparent.

The first air ship had withdrawn a short distance when the other boarded the car, but now the two mutually approached until it was possible to step from one deck to the other. As soon as they touched, Edmund was conducted by the captain, at whose side he had remained standing, to the presence of the important personage whom Jack had begun to designate as the queen. We remained where we were, watching with all eyes, while Jack persisted in keeping his hand on the pistol in his pocket. A crowd immediately surrounded Edmund and we were unable to see exactly what went on, a fact that rendered Jack so much the more impatient. But it turned out that there was no cause for alarm. In about ten minutes the crowd opened and Edmund appeared. Uninterfered with, he came to the edge of the deck, close by us, and said:

"It is all arranged. The car will be towed by one of the air ships. I am to stay here and you will remain where you are until we reach our destination."

"Have you had a talk with her?" asked Jack.

"Not in any language that you understand," Edmund responded, smiling. "But I have made good use of what I learned in the caverns. These people are intellectually vastly superior to the others, and, as I guessed, they possess a more perfect command of the sort of telepathy that I told you about. I have not found much difficulty in making my wish understood, and your Amazon is a very obliging person. It is only necessary to be discreet and we shall have no trouble."

"But why are you to be separated from us?" asked Jack anxiously. "That looks bad, for it is exactly what they would do if they meant to kill us one at a time."

"Why should they kill us?" retorted Edmund.

"And why should we be separated?" persisted Jack. "I tell you, Edmund, I don't like it."

"Very well, then," Edmund said, after a moment's thought; "if that's the way you feel about it, I'll see what I can do. It will be another exercise for me in this new kind of language. But, mark this, if I succeed in persuading the chieftainess to keep us together, you will have to acknowledge that your fears were groundless. Perhaps it's worth trying on that very account."

He disappeared from our eyes again—for as soon as he approached their leader the people of the air ship crowded close around as if to afford her protection—and, after another ten minutes' conference, came back smiling to the edge of the deck.

"Dismiss your fears, friend Jack," he said cheerfully. "You are all to come aboard here with me. So you see there could have been no thought of treachery; but I'm glad that we are not to be separated, and I thank you for your solicitude on my account. I'm sure that the original arrangement was made only because of lack of room aboard this craft, and you'll see that that was the reason."

He was right, for immediately half a dozen of the crew of the principal air ship were sent aboard ours while we were transferred to take their place.

We now had an opportunity to study the countenance of the "Amazon" commander, and we found her to be an even more remarkable personage than she had appeared at a distance. Of the beauty of her features and form I shall say no more, but about her eyes I could write a chapter. The pupils, widely expanded amidst their circles of sky-blue iris, seemed to speak. I can describe the impression that they made in no other way. I no longer wondered at Edmund's ability to converse with her, for I felt that, with a little instruction, and more of our leader's mental penetration, I could do it myself. At times I shrank from encountering her gaze, for I verily believed that she read my inmost thoughts. And I could see that *thought came out of her eyes*, but it escaped all my efforts to grasp it; it was too evanescent, or I was too dull. Sometimes I imagined that the meaning was at the threshold of comprehension, but yet it evaded me, like forgotten words whose general sense dimly irradiates the mind, while they refuse to take a definite shape, and keep flitting just beyond the reach of memory. Still, charity and good will shone out so plainly that anybody could read them, and I do not know how to express the feeling that came over me at this evidence of friendliness exhibited by an inhabitant of a world so far from our own. It was as if a dim sense of ultimate fraternity bound her to us. Jack's enthusiasm, as you may guess, was without bounds, and strangely enough it rendered him almost speechless.

"By Jo!" he kept repeating to himself in an undertone, without venturing upon any further expression of his feelings.

Henry, as usual, was silent, but I know that he felt the influence no less than the rest of us. Edmund, too, said nothing, but it was plain that he was continually studying the phenomenon, and I felt sure that his analytic mind would find a more complete explanation than we yet possessed. Of course you are not to suppose that the power that I have been trying to describe was peculiar to this woman. On the contrary, as I have already intimated, it was common to all of them; but with her it seemed to have reached a higher development, and, what was of special interest, she alone exhibited a marked benevolence toward us.

The car was attached by a cable to the air ship that we had just quitted, and our voyage into a new unknown began. The other air ships, which had been hovering about, moved up into line, and, with the exception of the one which towed the car, all rose to an elevation of perhaps a thousand feet, and moved rapidly away from a row of dark clouds which we could now see low on the horizon behind. We found the air ship splendidly fitted up, with everything that could contribute to the comfort of its inmates. And what a voyage it was! "Yachting on Venus," as Jack called it. We sat on the deck, with a pleasant breeze, produced by the swift, steady motion, fanning our faces; the temperature was delightful; the air was wonderfully stimulating; the light, softly and evenly diffused from the great shell-like dome of the sky, seemed to bewitch the eyesight; and the sea beneath us, reflecting the dome, was a marvel of refluent colours.

We had left the calendar clock in the car, but, with our watches, which we had never ceased to wind up regularly, we were able to measure the time. The voyage lasted about seventy-two hours, but could, perhaps, have been performed in less time if we had not been somewhat delayed by the towing of the car. They had on the air ship ingenious clocks, driven by weights, and governed by pendulums, but the divisions of time were unlike ours, and there was nothing corresponding to our days. This, of course, arose from the fact that there was never any night, and, being unable to see either sun or stars, they had no measure of the year. With them time was simply endless duration, with no return in cycles.

"What interests me most," said Edmund, "is the fact that they should have established any chronological measure at all. It would puzzle some of our metaphysicians on the earth to account for the origin of their sense of time. To me it seems evident that the consciousness of duration is fundamental in all intelligent life, and does not necessarily demand natural recurrences, like the succession of day and night, and the passage of sun and stars across the meridian, to give it birth. Did you ever read St. Augustine's reply to the question, 'What is time'—'I know if you don't ask me'?"

"If they haven't any years," said Jack, "how do they know when they are old enough to die?"

"They have the years, but no measure for them," replied Edmund, and then added quizzically, "Perhaps they *don't* die."

"Well, I shouldn't wonder," Jack returned, "for this seems to me to be Paradise for sure."

When we felt sleepy, we imitated the natives themselves, and, just as we had done during the voyage from the earth, created an artificial night by shutting ourselves up in the cabins that had been assigned to us. Rest was taken by all of them in this manner as regularly as it is taken at night on the earth.

One subject which we frequently discussed during the voyage was the astonishing resemblance of our hosts to the *genus homo*. Influenced by speculations which I had read at home about the probable unlikeness to one another of the inhabitants of different planets, I was particularly insistent upon this point, and declared that the facts as we found them were utterly inexplicable.

"Not at all," Edmund averred. "It is perfectly natural, and quite as I expected. Venus resembles the earth in composition, in form, in physical constitution, and in subordination to the sun, the great ruler of the entire system. Here are the same chemical elements, and the same laws of matter. The human type is manifestly the highest possible that could be developed with such materials to work upon. Why, then, should you be surprised to find that it prevails here as well as upon our planet? Intelligent life could find no more suitable abode than in a human body. The details are simply varied in accordance with the environment—a principle that works on the earth also."

I was not altogether satisfied with the reasoning—but as to the facts, we had to believe our eyes.

Palatable food was served to us, and during the waking time Edmund was frequently engaged in his mysterious conversation with the "queen." Within forty-eight hours after we had set out in the air ship, he came to us, wearing one of his enigmatic smiles, and said:

"I've got another aphroditic word for you to remember. It is the name of our hostess—Ala."

We were not so much surprised by this news as we should have been but for what had occurred at the caverns, where he had discovered the patronymic of Juba.

"Good!" cried Jack, "it's a fine name. I was going to call her Aphrodite, myself, but this is better as well as shorter."

"But, Edmund," I said, "how does it happen that these people, if they converse by 'telepathy' as you say, and as I fully believe, nevertheless occasionally use sounds and words? I should think it would be all one thing or all the other."

"Think a moment," he replied. "Is it so with us? Do we not use signs and gestures as well as words? And what do we mean by 'silent converse,' when mind speaks to mind and soul to soul without the intervention of spoken language? We have the potentiality of telepathic intercommunication, but we have not yet developed it into a kinetic form as these people have done. Ah, when will men begin to appreciate *what mind means?*"

I made no reply, and after a moment's musing, he continued:

"I suspect that here, too, speech preceded the higher form of converse, and that the spoken language remains only as a survival, presenting certain advantages for particular cases. But we shall learn more as time goes on."

There was no disputing Edmund's conclusions. He was the greatest accepter and defender of facts as he found them that I have ever known.

It was written that before this voyage ended we should have another phase of language without speech presented for our wonderment. It came about near the end of the trip. We were standing apart in a group, greatly interested and excited by the discovery, which had just been made, of land ahead. Far in advance we could see a curving, yellow shore line, and, dim in the distance behind it, a range of mountains. Edmund had just called our attention to these, with the remark that now I must admit that he had reasoned correctly about the existence of elevated regions on this side of Venus, when Jack, always the first to note a new phenomenon, exclaimed:

"Hurrah! Here they come! We're going to have a royal reception."

He pointed toward the land in a different direction from that in which we had been gazing, and immediately we beheld an extraordinary assemblage of air ships, perhaps ten miles off, but rapidly making toward us. More were coming up from behind, as if rising out of the land, and soon they resembled flocks of large birds all converging to a common centre. In a little while they became almost innumerable, but their number soon ceased to be as great a cause of surprise to us as their peculiar appearance. Viewed with our binoculars they showed an infinite variety of shapes and sizes. Chinese kites could not, for a moment, be compared in grotesqueness with the forms which many of them presented. Some soared in vast circles at a great height, with the steady flight of eagles; others spread out to right and left, as if to flank us on either hand; and in the centre, directly ahead, about a hundred advanced in column deployed in a semicircle, each keeping its place with the precision of a soldier in line of battle.

As we continued to gaze, fascinated by the splendour and strangeness of the spectacle, suddenly the air was filled with fluttering colours. I do not mean flags and streamers, but *colours in the air itself!* Colours the most exquisite that ever the eye looked upon! They changed, flickered, melted, brightened, flowed over one another in iridescent waves, mingled, separated, turned the whole atmosphere into a spectral kaleidoscope. And it was evident that, in some inexplicable way, the approaching squadrons were the sources of this marvellous display. Presently from the craft that carried us, answering colours flashed out, as if the air around us had suddenly been changed to crystal with a thousand quivering rainbows shot through it, their beautiful arches shifting and interchanging so rapidly that the eye could not follow them.

Then I began to notice that all this incessant play of colours was based upon an unmistakable rhythm. I can think of no better way to describe it than to say that it was as if a great organ should send forth from its keys harmonic vibrations consisting not of concordant sounds but of even more perfectly related undulations of colour. The permutations and combinations of this truly chromatic scale were marvellous and magical in their infinite variety. It thrilled us with awe and wonder. But none was so rapt as Edmund himself. He gazed as if his soul were in his eyes, and finally he turned to us, with a strange look, and said, almost under his breath:

"This, too, is language, and more than that—it is music!"

"Impossible!" I exclaimed.

"No, not impossible, since it *is*. They are not only exchanging intelligence in this way, but we are being greeted with a great anthem played in the heaven itself!"

There was the force of enthusiastic conviction in Edmund's words, and we could only look at him, and at one another, in silent astonishment.

"Oh, what a people! What a people!" he muttered. "And yet I am not surprised. I dimly fore-read this in Ala's eyes."

Even Jack's levity was subdued for the time, but after a while he said to me with a shrug, half in earnest, half in derision:

"Well, this Yankee-doodling in the air gets me! I'd prefer a little plain English and the Old Folks at Home."

After about ten minutes the display ceased as suddenly as it had begun, and the nearer of the approaching air craft began to circle around us. Finally one of them ran so close alongside that an officer of high rank, for such he seemed to be, leaped aboard us, and was quickly at Ala's side. There was a rapid interchange of communications between them, and then the newcomer was, I may say, presented. Ala led him to where we were standing, and I could read in his eyes the astonishment that the sight of such strangers produced in him.

CHAPTER 9

An Amazing Metropolis

If I should undertake to describe in detail all the events that now followed in rapid succession, this history would take a lifetime to write. I must choose only the more significant facts.

The newcomer, whose remarkable face had immediately impressed me, and not altogether favourably, proved to be a personage of very great importance, second only, as we could see, to Ala herself. And, what was particularly important for us, he showed none of her friendly disposition. I do not mean to suggest that he seemed inclined to any active hostility, but evidently we were, in his eyes, no better than savages, and consequently entitled to no special consideration, and especially to no favours. Jack, who, with all his careless ways, had a penetrating mind for the perception of character, whispered to me, within five minutes after the fellow came aboard:

"If that galoot had his way, we'd make our entry in irons. Mark my words, there's mischief in him. Hang him! I'm going to keep my pistol handy when he's around."

Edmund, who happened to overhear Jack's remark, interposed:

"See here, Master Jack, this is no time to be talking of pistols. I trust that we are done with shooting."

We were not done with it; but that comes later.

It was not long before Edmund had discovered a name for the newcomer also; he called him Ingra. It was singular, he said, that all the names seemed to be characterized by the prevalence of vowels sounds, but he thought it likely that this arose from the greater ease with which they could be enunciated. They were like Spanish words, which are the easiest of all for foreigners, and probably also for natives, to pronounce.

After we reached the coast we descended to the ground, at Edmund's request, I believe, because he wished to superintend the load-

ing of the car upon one of the largest air ships, and it was an unforget-
table sight to watch him managing the work as coolly and effectively
as if he had been in charge of a gang of workmen at home! And, while
I looked, I found myself again doubting if, after all, this was not a
dream. The workers hurrying about, Edmund following them, pointing, objecting, urging and directing, with his derby hat, which had
come through all our adventures (though somewhat damaged), stuck
on the back of his head—and all this on the planet Venus! No! I could
not be awake. But yet I was.

When we started again, we were escorted by a hundred air ships,
forming a complete circle about us. Now I noticed, what had escaped
attention during the extraordinary atmospheric display, viz., that these
craft were painted in colours that I should call gorgeous if they had
not been so perfectly harmonious and pleasing. Every one looked like
the careful creation of an artist, and the variety of tints exhibited was
incredible. Our own air ship, and its consorts, on the other hand, were
very plain in their decorations. I called Edmund's attention to this and
immediately he said:

"Remember what I told you—this has been an exploring expedition, and the craft taking part in it have been fitted up for rough work.
That reminds me that I have not yet made the inquiries that I intended on that subject. I shall go to Ala now and see what I can learn."

She was standing on the deck near the other end, with Ingra beside
her. As Edmund approached them, Jack nudged me:

"Look at that fellow," he said. "Wasn't I right?"

There was no doubt about it; Ingra scowled and showed every sign
of displeasure at Edmund's presence. But Ala greeted him graciously,
and, apparently, Ingra did not dare to interfere. I could see that Jack
was grasping his pistol again, but I did not anticipate that there would
be any occasion to use it. Nevertheless, I watched them closely for a
time, hoping to discover Edmund's method of reading her meaning; as
to her comprehension of his I had no question about that. But I got
no light on the subject, and, as it soon became evident, even to Jack,
that there was no danger this time, we fell to examining the land over
which we were passing.

We flew at a height of about two thousand feet, so that the range
of vision was very wide. The sea behind us curved into the land in
three great scallops, separated by acuminate promontories, whose ter-
minal bluffs of sand were as yellow as gold. Away ahead the line of
mountains, that we had noticed before, appeared as a dark sierra, and
between it and the sea the country seemed to be very little broken by

hills. Large forests were visible, but from our elevation it was impossible to tell whether the trees composing them bore any resemblance to terrestrial forms. The open land was about equally divided in area between bare yellowish soil (or what we took to be soil) and bright green expanses whose colour suggested vegetation. Scattered here and there we saw what appeared to be habitations, but we could not be sure of their nature; and, upon the whole, the land seemed to us to be very thinly populated.

Many birds accompanied us in our flight, frequently alighting on the deck and other parts of the air ship. They were remarkably tame, allowing us to approach them closely, and we were delighted by their beautiful plumage and their singular forms. This reminds me to say that the motion of the craft was extremely curious—a kind of gentle rising and falling, which was very agreeable when once we were accustomed to it, and which resembled what one would suppose to be the movement of a bird in flight. This, of course, arose from the structure of the air ship, which, as I have before said, seemed to be modelled, as far as its motive parts were concerned, upon the principle of wings rather than of simple aeroplanes. But the mechanism was very complicated, and I never arrived at a full comprehension of it.

Edmund remained a long time in conference with Ala, Ingra staying constantly with them, and when he had apparently finished his "conversation" we were surprised to see them begin a tour of inspection of the air ship, finally descending into the interior. This greatly excited Jack, who was for following them at once.

"I can't be easy," he declared. "Nobody can tell what may happen to him if they get him alone."

But I succeeded in persuading him that there could be no danger, and that we ought to trust to Edmund's discretion. They were gone so long, however, that at last I became anxious myself, and was on the point of suggesting to Jack that we try to find them, when they reappeared, and Edmund at once came to us, his face irradiated with smiles.

"I have plenty of news for you," he said, as soon as he had joined us. "Never in my life have I spent two hours more delightfully. In the first place, I have found out practically all that I wished to know about this expedition, and, second, I have thoroughly examined the mechanism of the ship. Its complication is only apparent, and the management of it is so simple that a single man can pilot it easily. I could do it myself."

We did not appreciate at the time what the knowledge that Edmund had thus acquired meant for us.

"Well, what about the expedition?" asked Jack. "And where are we going?"

"From what I can make out," replied Edmund musingly, "Ala is really what you called her, Jack, a queen. But such a queen! If we had some like her on the earth, monarchy might not be such a bad thing after all. She is a *savant.*"

"Bluestocking," put in Jack. "This is a new kind of Amazon."

Edmund did not smile.

"I am in earnest," he continued. "Of course you understand that most of my conclusions are really based upon inference. I cannot grasp all that she tries to tell me, but her gestures are so speaking, and her eyes so full of a kind of meaning which seems to force its way into my mind, I cannot tell how, that I am virtually sure of the correctness of my interpretation. The expedition, which I am certain was planned by her, was intended to explore the outskirts of the dark hemisphere. Perhaps they meant to penetrate within it, but, if so, the stormy belt that we crossed was too serious an obstacle for them to overcome. Our encountering them was the greatest stroke of good fortune that we have yet had. It places us right at the centre of affairs."

"Where are they going now?"

"Evidently back to their starting point; which is likely to be a great city—the capital and metropolis, most probably. The more I think of it the stronger becomes my conviction that Ala is really, at least in power and influence, a queen. And you can see for yourselves that it must be a great and rich empire that she rules, for remember the extraordinary reception with which she was greeted, the innumerable air ships, the splendour of everything."

"But are we to be well treated? Is there no danger for us in accompanying them?"

"If there were danger, it would be hard for us to escape from it now; but why should there be danger? We did not kill the Eskimo that our polar explorers brought from the Arctic regions, and for these people, we are a greater curiosity than ever the Eskimo, or the Pygmies of Africa, were for us. Instead of encountering any danger, I anticipate that we shall be very well treated."

"Perhaps they'll put us in a cage," said Jack, with a ludicrous grimace, "and tote us about as a great moral show for children. If there's a Barnum on Venus, our fate is sealed."

Jack's humorous suggestion struck home, for there seemed to be probability behind it, and Henry groaned, while, for my part, I confess that I felt rather uncomfortable over the prospect. But Edmund did not pursue the conversation, and soon we fell to regarding again the landscape beneath and far around us. We were gradually nearing the mountains, although they were still distant, and presently we caught sight of what resembled, as much as anything, gigantic cobwebs glittering with dew, and rising out of the plain between us and the mountains.

"There, Edmund," said Jack, "there's another chance to exercise your genius for explaining mysteries. What are those things?"

Edmund watched the objects for several minutes before replying. At length he said, with the decision characteristic of him:

"Palaces."

Jack burst out laughing.

"Castles in Spain, I reckon," he said. "But, really, Edmund, what do you think they can be?"

"I have already told you, palaces, or castles, if you prefer."

"You are serious?" I asked.

"Perfectly so. They cannot be anything else."

Seeing our astonishment and incredulity, Edmund added:

"Since they retain their places, it is evident that they are edifices of some kind, attached to the ground. But their great height and aerial structure indicate that they are erected in the air—floating, I should say, but firmly anchored at the bottom. Really, I cannot see anything astonishing about it; it accords with everything else that we have seen. Your minds are too hidebound to terrestrial analogies, and you do not give your imaginations sufficient play with the new materials that are here offered.

"This atmosphere," he continued, after a pause, "is exactly suited for such things. It is a region of atmospheric calm. If we were not moving, you would hardly feel a breeze, and I doubt if there is ever a high wind here. To build their habitations in the air and make them float like gossamers—could any idea be more beautiful than that, or more in harmony with the nature of this planet, which is the favourite of the sun, for first he inundates it with a splendour unknown to the earth, and then generously covers it with a gorgeous screen of cloud which cuts off his scorching beams but suffers the light to pass, filtered to opalescent ether?"

When Edmund spoke like that, as he sometimes did, suffusing his words with the fervour of his imagination, even Henry, I believe, felt his soul lifted to unaccustomed heights. We hung upon his lips, and, without a word, waited for him to continue. Presently he murmured, in an undertone:

"Yes, all this I foresaw in my dream. A world of crystal, houses that seemed not made with hands, reaching toward heaven, and a people, beautiful beyond compare, dwelling in the aerial home of birds"; and then, addressing us, in his ordinary tones: "You will see that the capital, which we are unquestionably approaching, is to a large extent composed of this airy architecture."

And it turned out to be as he had said—when, indeed, was it ever otherwise? As we drew nearer, the aerial structures which we had first seen began to tower up to an amazing height, just perceptibly swaying and undulating with the gentle currents of air that flowed through their traceried lattices, while behind them began to loom an immense number of floating towers, rising stage above stage, like the steel monsters of New York before they have received their outer coverings, but incomparably lighter in appearance, and more delicate and graceful; truly fairy constructions, bespangled with countless brilliant points. Yet nearer, and we could see cables attached to the higher structures, and running downward as if anchored to the ground beneath, but the ground itself we could not see, because now we had dropped lower in the air, and a long hill rose between us and the fairy towers, whose slight sinuous motion, affecting so many together, produced a trifling sense of dizziness as we gazed. Still nearer, and we believed that we could see people in the buoyant towers. A minute later there was no doubt about their presence, for the *colours* broke forth, and that marvellous interchange of chromatic signals, which had so astonished us as we drew near the coast, was resumed.

"It is my belief," said Edmund, "that, notwithstanding the buoyancy of the heavy atmosphere, those structures cannot be maintained at such elevations without mechanical aid. You will see when we get nearer that every stage is furnished with some means of support, probably vertical screws reacting upon the air."

Again he had guessed right, for in a little while we were near enough to see the screws, working in a maze of motion, like the wings of a multitude of insects. The resemblance was increased by their gauzy structure, and, as they turned, they flashed and glittered as if enamelled. (The supernatant structures that they maintained were, as we afterwards ascertained, framed of hollow beams and trusses—a kind of bamboo, of great strength and lightness.)

Now we rose over the intervening hill, and as we did so a cry burst from our lips. A vast city made its appearance as by magic, a magnified counterpart of the aerial city above it. Put all the glories of Constantinople, Damascus, Cairo, and Bombay, with all their spires, towers, minarets, and domes together, and multiply their splendour a thousand times, and yet your imagination will be unable to picture the scene of enchantment on which our eyes rested.

"It is the capital of Venus," exclaimed Edmund. "There can be nothing greater than this!"

It must, indeed, be the capital, for in the midst of it rose an edifice of unparalleled splendour, which could only be the palace of a mighty monarch. Above this magnificent building, which gleamed with metallic reflections, although it was as light and airy in construction as frostwork, rose the loftiest of the aerial towers, a hundred, two hundred—I cannot tell you how many stories in height, for I never succeeded in counting them.

The other air ships now dropped back, and ours alone approached this stupendous tower, making apparently for its principal landing stage. Along the sides of the tower a multitude of small air ships ran up and down, stopping at various stages to discharge their living cargoes.

"Elevators," said Edmund.

Glancing round we saw that similar scenes were occurring at all the towers. They were filling up with people, and the continual rising and descending of the little craft that bore them, the holiday aspect of the gay colours everywhere displayed, and the brilliancy of the whole spectacle moved us beyond words. But the most astonishing scene still awaited us.

Just before our vessel reached the landing stage, the enormous tower, from foot to apex, broke out with all the hues of the rainbow, like an enchanted rose tree covered with millions of brilliant flowers at the touch of a wand. The effect was overwhelming. The air became tremulous with rippling colours, whose vibrant waves, with quick succession of concordant tints afforded to the eye an exquisite pleasure akin to that which the ear receives from a carillon of bells. Our companions, and the people crowded on the towers, seemed to be transported with ecstatic delight.

"Again the music of the spectrum!" cried Edmund. "The diapason of colour! It is their national hymn, or the hymn of their race, written on a prismatic, instead of a sonometric, staff. And, mark me, this has a significance beyond your conjectures!"

I believe that our enjoyment of this astonishing spectacle was hardly less than that of the natives themselves, but the pleasure was suddenly broken off by a tragedy that struck cold to our hearts.

We had nearly touched the landing, when we observed that a discussion was going on between Ala and Ingra, and it quickly became evident that we were the subject of it. Before we could exchange a word, they approached us, and Ingra, in a threatening manner, laid his hand on Edmund's shoulder. In a second Jack had his pistol covering Ingra. Edmund saw the motion, and struck Jack's arm aside, but the weapon exploded, and, clutching her breast, Ala fell at our feet!

CHAPTER 10

Imprisonment and a Wonderful Escape

The shock of this terrible accident, the full import of which must have flashed simultaneously through the mind of every one of us, drove the blood from Edmund's face, while Jack staggered, uttering a pitiful moan, Henry collapsed, and I stood trembling in every limb. The report of the pistol produced upon the natives the effect that was to have been expected. Ingra sprang backward with a cry like that of a startled beast, and many upon the deck fell prostrate, either through terror or the effect of collision with one another in their wild flight. What occurred among the waiting crowd on the tower I do not precisely know, but a wind of fear seemed to pass through the air—a weird, heart-quaking *shadow of sound*.

For a few moments, I believe, no one but ourselves understood what had happened to Ala. Ingra may have thought, if he thought at all in his terror and surprise, that she had fallen as the result of nervous shock. This moment of paralysis on the part of those whom we had now to regard as our enemies, whatever they may have been before, afforded the opportunity for escape—if there had been any way to escape. But we were completely trapped; there was no direction in which we could flee. Yet I doubt if the thought of flight occurred to any of us. Certainly it did not to Edmund, who was the first to recover his self-command.

"We have shot down our only friend!" he said with terrible emphasis, and, as he spoke, he lifted Ala in his arms and laid her on a seat. Her breast was stained with blood.

At the sight of this, a flash of comprehension passed over the features of Ingra; then, instantly, his face changed to a look of fury, and he sprang upon Edmund. With trembling hand, I tried to draw my pistol, but before I could get it from my pocket there was a rush, a hairy form darted past me, and Ingra lay sprawling on his back. Over him, with foot planted on his breast, stood the burly form of Juba, with his muscular arms uplifted, and his enormous eyes blazing fire!

God only knows what would have happened next, but at this instant Ala—to my amazement, for I had thought that the bullet had gone through her heart—rose to an upright posture, and made a commanding gesture, which arrested those who were now hurrying to take a part in the scene. All, natives as well as ourselves, stood as motionless as stone. Her face was pale and her eyes were wonderful to look upon. With a gasp of thankfulness, I noticed that the blood on her breast was but a narrow streak Juba, staring at her, slowly withdrew his foot from his prostrate opponent, and Ingra first sat up, and then got upon his feet. Ala, who had been seated, rose at the same moment, and looked Ingra straight in the face. I saw Edmund glancing from one to the other, and I knew he was trying to follow the communication that was taking place between them.

The general sense of it I could follow, myself. Ingra, metaphorically, stormed and Ala commanded. That she was defending us was plain, and it was but natural that my admiration for this wonderful woman should rise to the highest pitch. I thanked God, in my heart, that her wound could be no more than a scratch—and yet it was a wound, inflicted upon the person of her who, there could be no doubt, was the ruler of a powerful empire. It was less majesty, or worse, and she, herself, might not be able to protect us against its consequences.

At last, it became evident that a decision had been made. Ala turned to us with a smile, which we took for an assurance of encouragement, at least, and started to leave the deck. Edmund instantly stepped in front of her, and pointed to the stain of blood, with a gesture and a look which meant, at the same time, an inquiry as to the nature of the wound and an expression of the wish to do something to repair the injury. She shook her head and smiled again, in a manner which clearly said that the hurt was not serious and that she understood that it was an accident. Then, surrounded by her female attendants, she passed out of our sight in the crowd on the landing. Edmund turned to us:

"We shall probably get out of it all right," he said, "but not without some difficulty. They will surely imprison us. Make no resistance. Leave all to me. Jack's pistol will, no doubt, be seized, but if the rest of you keep yours concealed, they may not search for them, as they know nothing about the weapons."

Edmund had spoken hurriedly, and had hardly finished when a dozen stout fellows, under Ingra's directions, took us in charge, Juba included, and we were led from the deck, through the vast throng on the platform, who made room for our passage, while devouring us with curious, though frightened eyes. In a minute we embarked on one of the "elevators," and made a thrillingly rapid descent. Arrived at the bottom, we were conducted, through long, stone-walled passages, into a veritable dungeon. And there they left us. I wondered if this had been done at Ala's order, or in defiance of her wishes. After all, I reflected, what claim have we upon her?

In the absolute darkness where we now found ourselves, we remained silent for a minute or two, feeling about for one another, until the quiet voice of Edmund said:

"Fortune still favours us."

As he spoke, a light dazzled our eyes. He had turned on a pocket electric lamp. We looked about and found that we were in a square chamber, about fifteen feet on a side, with walls of heavy stone.

"They make things solid enough down here," said Jack, with some return of his usual spirits, "however airy and fairy they may be above."

"All the better for us," returned Edmund enigmatically.

Henry sank upon the floor, the picture of dejection and despair. I expected another outbreak from him, but he spoke not a word. His heart was too full for utterance, and I pitied him so much that I tried to reanimate his spirits.

"Come, now," I said, "don't take it this way, man. Have confidence in Edmund. He has never yet been beaten."

"I reckon he's got his hands full this time," put in Jack. "What do you think, Edmund, can your atomic energy bore a hole through these walls?"

"If I had it here, you'd see," Edmund replied. "But there's no occasion to worry, we'll come out all right."

It was his unfailing remark when in difficulties, and somehow it always enheartened us. Juba, more accustomed to such situations, seemed the least disturbed member of the party. He rolled his huge eyes around the apartment once or twice, and then lay down on the floor, and seemed at once to fall asleep.

"That's a good idea of Juba's," said Edmund, smiling; "it's a long time since we have had a nap. Let's all try a little sleep. I may dream of some way out of this."

It was a fact that we were all exhausted for want of sleep, and, in spite of our situation, I soon fell into deep slumber, as peaceful as if I had been in my bed at home. Edmund had turned out the lamp, and the silence and darkness were equally profound.

I dreamt that I was at the Olympus Club on the point of trumping an ace, when a flash of light in the eyes awoke me. I started up and found Edmund standing over me. The others were all on their feet. Edmund immediately whispered:

"Come quietly; I've found a way out."

"What have you found?"

"Something extremely simple. This is no prison cell, but a part of what appears to be the engine rooms—probably it is an unused storeroom. They have put us here for convenience, trusting more to the darkness than to the lock, for the corridors outside are as black as Erebus and as crooked as a labyrinth."

"How do you know?"

"Because, while you were all asleep, I made an exploration. The lock was nothing; the merest tyro could pick it. Fortunately they never guessed that I had a lamp. In this world of daylight, it is not likely that pocket lamps have ever been thought of. Just around the corner, there is another door opening into a passage that leads by a power house. That passage gives access to a sort of garage of air craft, and when I stole into it five minutes ago, there was not a soul in sight. We'll simply slip in there, and if I can't run away with one of those fliers, then I'm no engineer. To tell the truth, I'm not altogether sure that it is wise for us to escape, for I have a feeling that Ala will help us; still, when Providence throws one a rope, it's best, perhaps, to test its strength. Come on, now, and make no noise."

Accompanied by Juba, we stepped noiselessly outside, extinguishing the light, and, led by Edmund, passed what he had called the power house, where we saw several fellows absorbed in their work, lighted somehow from above. Then we slipped into the "garage." Here light entered from without, through a large opening at the side. There may have been twenty small air ships resting on cradles. Edmund selected one, which he appeared to have examined in advance, and motioning us to step upon its little deck, he began to manipulate the mechanism as confidently as if it had been his own invention.

"You see that I did not waste my time in examining the air ship that brought us," he whispered, and never before had I admired and trusted him as I did now. In less than a minute after we had stepped aboard, we were circling in the air outside. We rose with stunning rapidity, swooping away in a curve like an eagle.

At this instant we were seen!

There was a quick flashing of signals, and two air craft shot into sight above us.

"Now for a chase!" cried Edmund, actually laughing with exultation.

We darted upward, curving aside to avoid the pursuers. And then they swooped after us. We rose so rapidly that within a couple of seconds we were skirting the upper part of the great tower. Then others saw us, and joined in the chase. Jack's spirits soared with the excitement:

"Sorry to take rogue's leave of these Venuses," he exclaimed. "But no dungeons for us, if you please."

"We're not away, yet," said Edmund over his shoulder; and, indeed, we were not!

The air ships swarmed out on every side like hornets; the atmosphere seemed full of them. I gave up all hope of escape, but Edmund was like a racer who hears the thud of hoofs behind him. He put on more and more speed until we were compelled to hang on to anything within reach in order to save ourselves from being blown off by the wind which we made, or whirled overboard on sharp turns.

Crash! We had run straight into a huge craft that persisted in getting in our way. She dipped and rolled like a floating log. I saw the fellows on her tumble over one another, as we shot by, and I glanced anxiously to see if any had gone overboard. We could afford to do no killing if we could avoid it; for, in case of recapture, that would be another indictment against us. I saw no one falling from the discomfited air ship, and I felt reassured. Occupied as he was, dodging and turning, Edmund did not cease to address a few words to us occasionally.

"There's just one chance to beat them," he said, "and only one. I'm going to try it as soon as I can get out of this press."

I had no notion of what he meant, but a few minutes later I divined his intention. I had observed that all the while he was working higher and higher, and this, as you will presently see, was the key to his plan.

Up and up we shot, Edmund making the necessary circles as short as possible, and so recklessly did he turn on the speed that it really began to look as if we might get away after all. Two thirds of our pursuers were now far below our level, but none showed a disposition to give up the chase, and those which were yet above tried to cross our bow. While I saw that Edmund's idea was to hold a skyward course, I was far from guessing the particular reason he had for doing so, and, finally, Jack, who comprehended it still less, exclaimed:

"See here, Edmund, if you keep on going up instead of running off in one direction or another, they'll corner you in the middle of the sky. Don't you see how they have circled out on all sides so as to surround us? Then when we get as high as we can go, they'll simply close in, and we'll be trapped."

"Oh, no, we won't," Edmund replied.

"I don't see why."

"Because they can't go as high as we can."

"The deuce they can't! I guess they understand these ships as well as you do."

"Can a fish live out of water?" asked Edmund, laughing.

"What's that got to do with it?"

"Why, it's plain enough. These people are used to breathing an atmosphere surcharged with oxygen and twice as dense as that of the earth. It doesn't trouble our breathing, simply giving us more energy; but we can live where they would gasp for breath. Air impossibly rare for them is all right for us, and that's what I am in search of, and we shall find it if we can get high enough."

The beauty and simplicity of this unexpected plan struck us all with admiration, and Jack, his doubts instantly turning to enthusiasm, cried:

"By Jo, Edmund, you're a trump! I'd like to get a gaff into the gills of that catfish, Ingra, when he begins to blow. By Jo, I'd pickle him and make a present of him to the Museum of Natural History. '*Cat-fishia Venusensis*, presented by Jack Ashton, Esq.'—how'd that look on a label, hey?"

And Jack hugged himself with delight over his conceit.

In a short time the accuracy of Edmund's conjecture became apparent. Our pursuers, one by one, dropped off. Their own strategy, to which Jack had called attention, was simply a playing into our hands. They had really thought to catch us in the centre of a contracting circle, when, to their amazement, we rose straight up into air so rare that they could not live in it. Edmund roared with laughter when he saw the assured success of his manoeuvre.

But there was one thing which even he had overlooked, and it struck to our hearts when we became aware of it. Poor, faithful Juba, who had so recently proved his devotion to us, could endure this rare air no better than our pursuers. Already, unnoticed in the excitement, he had fallen upon the deck, where he lay gasping.

"Good God, he's dying!" exclaimed Jack.

"He shall not die!" responded Edmund, setting his lips, and turning to his machinery.

"But, you're not going back down there!"

"I'll run beyond the edge of the circle, and drop down far enough to revive him. Then we can keep dodging up and down just out of their reach, and so be out of danger both ways."

No sooner said than done. We ran rapidly on a horizontal course until we had cleared the air ships below, and then dropped like a shot. Juba came to his senses in a few moments after we entered the denser air. But now our pursuers, thinking, no doubt, that we had found it impracticable to remain where they knew they could not go, began to close in upon us. I reflected that here was the only mistake that Edmund had made—I mean the bringing along with us of the natives of the dark hemisphere. It was only their presence that had prevented us from sailing triumphantly over the crystal mountains; it was because of them that we had wrecked the car; and now it was Juba who baffled our best chance of escape. And yet—and I am glad to be able to say it—I could not regret his presence, for had he not made himself one of us; had he not proved himself entitled to all the privileges of comradeship?

But Henry (I am sorry to write it) did not share these feelings.

"Edmund," he said, "why do you insist upon endangering our lives for the sake of this—this—animal here?"

Never have I beheld such a blaze of anger as that which burst from Edmund's eyes as he turned upon Henry:

"You cowardly brute!" he shouted. "I ought to throw you overboard!"

He seemed about to execute his threat, dropping the controller from his hand as he spoke, and Henry, with ashen face, ran from him like a madman. I caught him in my arms, fearing that he would tumble overboard in his fright, and Edmund, instantly recovering his composure, turned back to his work.

Finding Juba sufficiently recovered, although yet weak and almost helpless, he rose again, but more cautiously than before. And now our pursuers, plainly believing that these manoeuvres could have but one ending, began to set their net, and I could not help admiring their plan, which would surely have succeeded if they had not made a fundamental error in their calculations, but one for which they were not to blame. There was such a multitude of their craft, fresh ones coming up all the while, that they were able to form themselves into the shape of a huge bag net, the edge of which was carried as high as they dared to go, while the sides and receding bottom were composed of air ships so numerous that they were packed almost as closely as meshes. Edmund laughed again as he looked down into this immense net.

"No, no," he shouted. "We're no gudgeons! You'll have to do better than that!"

"See here, Edmund," Jack suddenly exclaimed, "why don't you make off and leave them? By keeping just above their reach we could easily escape."

"And leave the car?" was the reply.

"By Jo," returned Jack, "I never thought of that. But, then, what did you run away for at all?"

"Because," said Edmund quietly, "I thought it better to parley than to lie in prison."

"Parley! How are you going to parley?"

"That remains to be seen; but I guess we'll manage it."

We were now, as far as I could estimate, five or six miles high. When we were highest, the great cloud dome seemed to be but a little way above our heads, and I thought, at first, that Edmund intended to run up into it and thus conceal our movements. The highest of our pursuers were about half a mile below us. They circled about, and were evidently parleying on their own account, for waves of colour flowed all about them, making a spectacle so brilliant and beautiful that sometimes I almost forgot our critical situation in watching it.

"I suppose you'll play them a prismatic symphony," said Henry mockingly.

I looked at him in surprise. Evidently his fear of Edmund had vanished; no doubt because he knew in his heart the magnanimity of our great leader.

"Who knows?" Edmund replied. "I've no doubt the materials are aboard, and if I had been here a month, I'd probably try it. As things stand, we shall have to resort to other methods."

While we were talking, Edmund did not relax his vigilance, and two or three times, when he had dropped to a lesser elevation for Juba's sake, he baffled a dash of the enemy. At last we noticed a movement in the crowd which betokened something of importance, and in a moment we saw what it was. A splendid air ship, by far the most beautiful that we had yet seen, was swiftly approaching from below.

"It's the queen," said Edmund. "I thought she'd come."

The approaching ship made its way straight toward us, and, without the slightest hesitation, Edmund dropped down to meet it. Those who had been our pursuers now made no attempt to interfere with us; they recognized the presence of a superior authority. Soon we were so near that we could recognize Ala, who looked like Cleopatra in her barge on the charmed waves of Cydnus. Beside her, to the intense disappointment of Jack and myself, stood Ingra.

"Confound him!" growled Jack. "He's always got to have his oar in the puddle. Blamed if I'm not sorry Edmund spoiled my aim. I'd have had his scalp to hang up at the Olympus to be smoked at!"

Of what now occurred, I can give no detailed account, because it was all beyond my comprehension. We approached almost within touch, and then Edmund stood forth, fearless and splendid as Caesar, and conducted his "parley." When it was over, there was a flashing of aerial colours between Ala's ship and the others, and then all, including ours, set out to return to the capital. After a while Edmund, who had been very thoughtful, turned to us and said:

"You can make your minds easy. Of course you'll understand there is a certain amount of guesswork in what I tell you, but you can depend upon the correctness of my general conclusions. I believe that I have made it perfectly clear that we intended no harm, and that we are not dangerous characters. At least Ala understands it perfectly. As for Ingra, perhaps he doesn't want to understand it. I can't make out the cause of his enmity, but it is certain that he doesn't like us, and if it all depended upon him, it would go hard with us. I believe that we shall have to stand a trial of some kind, but remember that we've got a powerful advocate. I don't regret our running off, for, as I anticipated, it afforded us the opportunity to establish some sort of terms. The mere fact that we return willingly when they know that we might have fled beyond their reach should count in our favour, for, as I have always insisted, these are highly intelligent people, with civilized ideas. If I had not been sure of that I should have continued the flight and depended upon some other means of recovering the car—or constructing a new one."

We had become so much accustomed to accept Edmund's decisions as final that none of us thought of objecting to what he had done; unless it might have been Henry, but he kept his thoughts to himself.

CHAPTER 11

Before the Throne of Venus

While we were dropping down toward the city, with a great fleet of air ships attending, Edmund opened his mind upon another curious difficulty besetting us.

"You, of course, noted," he said, "how close we approached at one time to the cloud dome. The existence of that sky screen is a circumstance which may possibly be decisive in the determination of our fate."

"Favourable or unfavourable?" I asked.

"Unfavourable, for this reason. If these people could be made to understand that we are visitors from another world, and not inhabitants of the other side of their own planet, they might treat us with greater consideration, and even with a certain superstitious deference. The imagination is doubtless as active with them as with terrestrial beings, and if you can once touch the imagination, even of the most intelligent and instructed persons, you can do almost anything you choose with them. But how am I to convey to them any idea of this kind? Seeing neither sun, nor moon, nor stars, they can have no conception of such a thing as another world than their own."

"Couldn't you persuade them," said Jack, "that we come from the upper side of the cloud dome? You could pretend that it's very fine living up there—plenty of sunshine and good air."

Edmund laughed.

"I'm afraid, Jack, that they are too intelligent to believe that a person of your avoirdupois could walk on the clouds. You're not quite angelic enough for that. I'm sure that they know perfectly well what the dome consists of."

"The presence of Juba with us is another difficulty," I suggested. "If, as you suppose, they recognize certain racial characteristics in him, which convince them that he belongs to the other side of Venus, then they are sure to believe that we belong there, too."

"Certainly. But I must find some way round the difficulty. I depend upon the intelligence of Ala. If she had been killed, nothing could have saved us. We have had an unpleasant escape from something too closely resembling the misfortune of Oedipus."

In the meanwhile, we reached the capital and disembarked on the great tower. To our intense surprise and delight, instead of being re-conducted to prison, we were led into a magnificent apartment, with open arches facing toward the distant mountains, and a repast was spread before us. Juba, to our great contentment, was allowed to ac-company us. I think that Jack was the most pleased member of the party at the sight of the food. We sat at a round table, and I observed that the eatables consisted, as with Juba's people, exclusively of veg-etables, except that there were birds, of species unknown to us, but of most exquisite flavour, and a light, white wine, the most delicious that I ever tasted.

When we had finished eating, we fell to admiring the view, and Jack pulled out his pipe, and, aided by Edmund's pocket lamp, which possessed an attachment for cigar lighting, began to smoke, leaning back luxuriously in his seat, with as much nonchalance as if he had been in the smoking room at the Olympus. I think I may say that we all exhibited a *sang froid* amidst our novel surround-ings that would have astonished us if we had stopped to analyze our feelings, but in that respect Jack was often the coolest member of the party, although he had not the iron nerves of Edmund. On this occasion, he was not long in producing a sensation. No sooner had the smoke begun to curl from his lips than the attendants in the room were thrown into a state of laughable consternation. Evidently they thought, like the servant of Walter Raleigh, that the smoke must come from an internal fire. Their looks showed alarm as well as astonishment.

"Keep your pipe concealed," whispered Edmund. "Take a few strong whiffs, and hide it in your pocket before they observe whence the smoke really comes. This may do us some good; it will, at least, serve to awake their imagination, and that is what we need."

Jack did as requested, first filling his mouth with smoke, and then slowly letting it out in puffs that more and more astonished the on-lookers, who kept at a respectful distance, and excitedly discussed the phenomenon. Suddenly, Jack, with characteristic mobility of thought, turned to Edmund and demanded:

"Edmund, why didn't those fellows shoot us when we were running away? There were enough of them to bring us down with the wildest sort of shooting."

"They didn't shoot," was the reply, "because they had nothing to shoot with. I have made up my mind that they are an unwarlike people. I don't believe that they have the slightest idea what a gun is. Yet they are no cowards, and they'll fight if there is need of fighting, and no doubt they have weapons of some kind; only they are not natural slaughterers like ourselves, and I shouldn't be surprised if war is unknown on Venus.

"All the same," said Jack, "I wish I had my pistol back. I tried to hide it, but those fellows had their eyes on it, and it's confiscated. I'm glad you think they don't know how to use it."

"And I'm glad," returned Edmund, "that you haven't got your pistol. You've been altogether too handy with it. Now," he continued, "let us consider our situation. You see at a glance that we have gained a great deal as a result of the parley; the way we have just been treated here shows plainly enough that we shall, at least, have a fair trial, and we couldn't have counted on that before. You can never make people listen to reason against their inclination unless you hold certain advantages, and our advantage was that we clearly had it in our power to continue our flight. My only anxiety now is in regard to the means of holding them to the agreement—for agreement it certainly was—and of impressing them not only with a conviction of our innocence but with a sense of our reserve power, and the more mysterious I can make that power seem to them, the better. That is why I welcomed even the incident of Jack's smoking. We shall surely be arraigned before a court of some kind, and I imagine that we shall not have long to wait. What I wish particularly is that all of you shall desist from every thought of resistance, and follow strictly such instructions as I may have occasion to give you."

He had hardly ceased speaking when a number of official-looking persons entered the room where we were.

"Here come the cops," said Jack. "Now for the police court."

He was not very far wrong. We were gravely conducted to one of the little craft which served for elevators, and after a rapid descent, were led through a maze of passages terminating in a vast and splendid apartment, apparently perfectly square in plan, and at least three hundred feet on a side. It was half filled with a brilliant throng, in which our entry caused a sensation. Light entered through lofty windows on all four sides. The floor seemed to be of a rose-colored marble, with inlaid diapering of lapis lazuli, and the walls and ceiling were equally rich. But that which absolutely fascinated the eye in this great apartment was a huge circle high on the wall opposite the entrance door, like a great clock face, or the rose window of a cathedral, from which poured trembling streams of coloured light.

"Chromatic music, once more," said Edmund, in a subdued voice. "Do you know, that has a strange effect upon my spirits, situated as we are. It is a prelude that may announce our fate; it might reveal to us the complexion of our judges, if I could but read its meaning."

"It is too beautiful to spell tragedy," I said.

"Ah, who knows? What is so fascinating as tragedy for those who are only lookers-on?"

"But, Edmund," I protested, "why do you, who are always the most hopeful, now fall into despondency?"

"I am not desponding," he replied, straightening up. "But this soundless music thrills me with its mysterious power, and sometimes it throws me into dejection, though I cannot tell why. To me, when what I firmly believe was the great anthem of this wonderful race, was played in the sky with spectral harmonies, there was, underlying all its mystic beauty, an infinite sadness, an impending sense of something tragic and terrible."

I was deeply surprised and touched by Edmund's manner, and would have questioned him further, but we were interrupted by the officials, who now led us across the vast apartment and to the foot of a kind of throne which stood directly under the great clock face. Then, for the first time, we recognized Ala, seated on the throne. Beside her was a person of majestic stature, with features like those of a statue of Zeus, and long curling hair of snowy whiteness. The severity of his aspect struck cold to my heart, but Ala's countenance was smiling and full of encouragement. As we were led to our places a hush fell upon the throng of attendants, and the colours ceased to play from the circle.

"Orchestra stopped," whispered the irrepressible Jack. "Curtain rises."

The pause that followed brought a fearful strain upon my nerves, but in a moment it was broken by Ala, who fixed her eyes upon Edmund's face as he stood a little in advance of the rest of us. He returned her regard unflinchingly. Every trace of the feeling which he had expressed to me was gone. He stood erect, confident, masterful, and as I looked, I felt a thrill of pride in him, pride in his genius which had brought us hither, pride in our mother earth—for were we not her far-wandering children?

I summoned all my powers in the effort to understand the tongue-less speech which I knew was issuing from Ala's eyes. And I did understand it! Although there was not a sound, I would almost have sworn that my ears heard the words:

"Who and what are you, and whence do you come?"

Breathlessly I awaited Edmund's answer. He slowly lifted his hand and pointed upward. He was, then, going at once to proclaim our origin from another world; to throw over us the aegis of the earth!

The critical experiment had begun, and I shivered at the thought that here they knew no earth; here no flag could protect us. I saw perplexity and surprise in Ala's eyes and in those of the stern Zeus beside her. Suddenly a derisive smile appeared on the latter's lips, while Ala's confusion continued. God! Were we to fail at the very beginning?

Edmund calmly repeated his gesture, but it met with no response; no indication appeared to show that it awakened any feeling other than uncomprehending astonishment in one of his judges and derision in the other. And then, with a start, I caught sight of Ingra, standing close beside the throne, his face made more ugly by the grin which overspread it.

I was almost wild; I opened my mouth to cry I know not what, when there was a movement behind, and Juba stepped to Edmund's side, dropped on his knees, rose again, and fixed his great eyes upon the judges!

My heart bounded at the thoughts which now raced through my brain. Juba belonged to their world, however remote the ancestral connection might be; he possessed at least the elements of their unspoken language; and *it might be a tradition among his people, who we knew worshipped the earth-star, that it was a brighter world than theirs.* Had Edmund's gesture suddenly suggested to his mind the truth concerning us—a truth which the others had not his means of comprehending—and could he now bear effective testimony in our favour?

With what trembling anxiety I watched his movements! Edmund, too, looked at him with mingled surprise and interest in his face. Presently he raised his long arm, as Edmund had done, and pointed upward. A momentary chill of disappointment ran through me—could he do no more than that? But he *did* more. Half unconsciously I had stepped forward where I could see his face. *His eyes were speaking.* I knew it. And, thank God! there was a gleam of intelligence answering him from the eyes of our judges.

He had made his point; he had suggested to them a thought of which they had never dreamed!

They did not thoroughly comprehend him; I could see that, for he must have been for them like one speaking a different dialect, to say nothing of the fundamental difficulty of the idea that he was trying to convey, but yet the meaning did not escape, and as he continued his strange communication, the wonder spread from face to face, for it was not only the judges who had grasped the general sense of what he was telling them. Even at that critical moment there came over me a feeling of admiration for a language like this; a truly universal language, not limited by rules of speech or hampered by grammatical structure. At length it became evident that Juba had finished, but he continued standing at Edmund's side.

Ala and her white-headed companion looked at one another, and I tried to read their thoughts. In her face, I believed that I could detect every sign of hope for us. Occasionally she glanced with a smile at Edmund. But the old judge was more implacable, or more incredulous. There was no kindness in his looks, and slowly it became clear that Ala and he were opposed in their opinion.

Suddenly she placed her hand upon her breast, where the bullet must have grazed her, and made an energetic gesture, including us in its sweep, which I interpreted to mean that she had no umbrage against those who had unintentionally injured her. It was plain that she insisted upon this point, making it a matter personal to herself, and my hopes rose when I thought that I detected signs of yielding on the part of the other. At this moment, when the decision seemed to hang in the balance, a new element was introduced into the case with dramatic suddenness and overwhelming force.

For several minutes I had seen nothing of Ingra, but my thoughts had been too much occupied with more important things to take heed of his movements. Now he appeared at the left of the throne, leading a file of fellows bearing a burden. They went direct to the foot of the throne, and deposited their burden within a yard of the place where Edmund was standing. They drew off a covering, and I could not repress a cry of consternation.

It was the body of one of their compatriots, and a glance at it sufficed to show the manner in which death had been inflicted. It had been crushed in a way which could probably mean nothing else than a fearful fall. The truth flashed upon me like a gleaming sword. The victim must have been precipitated from the air ship which we had struck at the beginning of our flight!

And there stood our enemy, Ingra, with exultation written on his features. He had made a master stroke, like a skilful prosecutor.

"Hang him!" I heard Jack mutter between his teeth. "Oh, if I only had my pistol!"

"Then you would make matters a hundred times worse," I whispered. "Keep your head, and remember Edmund's injunction."

The behaviour of the latter again awoke my utmost admiration. Contemptuously turning his back upon Ingra, he faced Ala and old Zeus, and as their regards mingled, I knew well what he was trying to express. This time, since his meaning involved no conception lying utterly beyond their experience, he was more successful. He told them that the death of this person was a fact hitherto unknown to us, and that, like the injury to Ala, it had been inflicted without our volition. I believed that this plea, too, was accepted as valid by Ala; but not so with the other. He understood it perfectly, and he rejected it on the instant. My reason told me that nothing else could have been expected of him, for, truly, this was drawing it rather strong—to claim twice in succession immunity for evils which had undeniably originated from us.

Our case looked blacker and blacker, as it became evident that the opposition between our two judges had broken out again, and was now more decided than before. The features of the old man grew fearfully stern, and he rejected all the apparent overtures of Ala. He had been willing to pardon the injury and insult to her person, since she herself insisted upon pardon, but now the affair was entirely different. Whether purposely or not, we had caused the death of a subject of the realm, and he was not to be swerved aside from what he regarded as his duty. My nerves shook at the thought that we knew absolutely nothing about the social laws of this people, and that, among them, the rule of an eye for an eye, and blood for blood, might be more inviolable than it had ever been on the earth.

As the discussion proceeded, with an intensity which spoken words could not have imparted to it, Ala's cheeks began to glow, and her eyes to glitter with strange light. One could see the resistance in them rising to passion, and, at last, as the aged judge again shook his head, with greater emphasis than ever, she rose, as if suddenly transformed. The majestic splendour of her countenance was thrilling. Lifting her jewelled arm with an imperious gesture, she commanded the attendants to remove the bier, and was instantly obeyed. Then she beckoned to Edmund, and without an instant's hesitation, he stepped upon the lower stage of the throne. With the stride of a queen, she descended to his side, and, resting her hand on his shoulder, looked about her with a manner which said, as no words could have done:

"It is the power of my protection which encircles him!"

CHAPTER 12

More Marvels

It was not until long afterwards that we fully comprehended all that Ala had done in that simple act; but I will tell you now what it meant. By the unwritten law of this realm of Venus, she, as queen, had the right to interpose between justice and its victim, and such interposition was always expressed in the way which we had witnessed. It was a right rarely exercised, and probably few then present had ever before seen it put into action. The sensation which it caused was, in consequence, exceedingly great, and a murmur of astonishment arose from the throng in the great apartment, and hundreds pressed around the throne, staring at us and at the queen. The majestic look which had accompanied her act gradually faded, and her features resumed their customary expression of kindness. The old judge had risen as she stepped from her place beside him, and he seemed as much astonished as any onlooker. His hands trembled, he shook his head, and a single word came from his mouth, pronounced with a curious emphasis. Ala turned to him, with a new defiance in her eyes, before which his opposition seemed to wither, and he sank back into his seat.

But there was at least one person present who accepted the decision with a bad grace—Ingra. He had been sure of victory in his incomprehensible persecution of us, he had played a master card, and now his disappointment was written upon his face. With surprise, I saw Ala approach him, smiling, and I was convinced that she was trying to persuade him to cease his opposition. There was a gentleness in her manner—almost a deference—which grated upon my feelings, while Jack's disgust could find no words sufficient to express itself:

"Beauty and the beast!" he growled. "By Jo, if *he's* got any influence over her, I'm sorry for her."

"Well, well, don't worry about him," I said. "He's played his hand and lost, and if you were in his place, you wouldn't feel any better about it."

"No, I'd go and hang myself, and that's what he ought to do. But isn't *she* a queen, though!"

Ala now resumed her place upon the throne, and issued orders which resulted in our being conducted to apartments that were set aside for us in the palace. There were four connecting rooms, and Juba had one of them. But we immediately assembled in the chief apartment, which had been assigned to Edmund. There was much more deference in the manner of our attendants than we had observed before, and as soon as they left us we fell to discussing the recent events. Jack's first characteristic act was joyously to slap Juba on the back:

"Bully old boy!" he exclaimed. "Edmund, where'd we have been without Juba?"

"I ought to have foreseen that," said Edmund. "If I had been as wise as I sometimes think myself, I'd have arranged the thing differently. Of course it should have been obvious all the while that Juba would be our trump card. I dimly saw that, but I ought to have instructed him in advance. As it was, his own intelligence did the business. He understood my claim to an origin outside this planet, when they could not. It must have come over him all at a flash."

"But do you think that they understand it now?" I asked.

"To a certain extent, yes. But it is an utterly new idea to them, and all the better for us that it is so. It is so much the more mysterious; so much the more effective with the imagination. But this is not the end of it; they will want to know more—especially Ala—and now that Juba has broken the ice, it will be comparatively easy to fortify the new opinion which they have conceived of us."

"But Ingra nearly wrecked it all," I remarked.

"Yes, that was a stunning surprise. How devilish cunning the fellow is; and how inexplicable his antipathy to us."

"I believe that it is a kind of jealousy," I said.

"A kind of natural cussedness, *I* guess," put in Jack.

"Why should he be jealous?" asked Edmund.

"I don't know, exactly; but you know we are not simple barbarians in their eyes, and Ingra may have conceived a prejudice against us, somehow, on that very account."

"Very unlikely," Edmund returned, "but we shall find out all about it in time; in the meanwhile, do nothing to prejudice him further, for he is a power that we have got to reckon with."

The conversation then turned upon the mysterious language that had been employed at what we called the trial. I expressed the admiration which I had felt for such a means of communication when I had observed the effect that Juba had been able to produce.

"Yes," said Edmund, "it seems as wonderful as it is beautiful, but there is no reason why it should not have been acquired by the inhabitants of the earth. We have the elements, not merely in what we call telepathy, or mind reading, but in our everyday converse. Try it yourself, and you will be astonished at what the eyes, the looks, are able to convey. Even abstract ideas are not beyond their reach. Often we abandon speech for this better method of conveying our meaning. How many a turn in the history of mankind has depended upon the unspoken diplomacy of the eyes; how many a crisis in our personal lives is determined, not by words, but by looks."

"That's right," said Jack, "more matches are made with eyes than with lips."

Edmund smiled and continued: "There's nothing really mysterious about it. It has a purely physical basis, and only needs attention and development to become the most perfect mode of mental communication that intellectual beings could possibly possess."

"And the music and language of colour?" I asked. "How has that been developed?"

"As naturally as the silent speech. We have it, and we feel it, in pictures, in flower gardens, and in landscapes; only with us it is a frozen music. Living music exists on the earth only in the form of sonorous vibrations because we have not developed our sense of the harmony of colours except when they lie dead and motionless before us. A great painting by Raphael or Turner is to one of these colour hymns of Venus like a printed score, which merely suggests its harmonies, compared with the same composition when poured forth from a perfect instrument under the fingers of a master player."

"Well, Edmund," interposed Jack, "I've no doubt it's all as you say, and I'd like to know just enough of their speechless speech to tell Ingra what he ought to hear; and if I understood their music, I'd play him a dead march, sure."

"But," continued Edmund, disregarding Jack's interruption, "mark me, there's something else behind all this. I have a dim foreglimpse of it, and if we have luck, we'll know more before long."

I find that the enthusiasm which these wonderful memories arouse, as they flood back into my mind, is leading me to dwell upon too many details, and I must sum up in fewer words the story of the events which immediately followed our acquittal, although it involves some of the most astonishing discoveries that we made in the world of Venus.

As Edmund had surmised, Ala lost no time in seeking more light upon the mystery surrounding us. Within twenty-four hours after the dramatic scene in the hall of judgment, we were summoned before her, in a splendid apartment, which was apparently an audience chamber, where we found her surrounded by several of her female attendants, as well as by what seemed to be high officers of the court; and among them, to our displeasure, was Ingra. He, in fact, appeared to be the most respected and important personage there, next to the queen herself, and he kept close by her side. Edmund glanced at him, and half turning to us, shook his head. I took his meaning to be that we were not to manifest any annoyance over Ingra's presence.

The queen was very gracious, and seats were offered to us. Immediately she began to question Edmund, as I could see; but with all my efforts I could make out nothing of what was "said." But Juba evidently was able to follow much of the conversation, in which he manifested the liveliest interest. The conference lasted about an hour, and at its conclusion, we retired to our apartments. There we eagerly questioned Edmund concerning what had occurred.

He seemed to be greatly impressed and pleased. He told us that he had learned more than he had communicated, but that he had succeeded, as he believed, in making clearer to Ala our celestial origin. Still, he doubted if she fully comprehended it, while as for Ingra, he was sure that the fellow rejected our claim entirely, and persisted in regarding us as inhabitants of the dark hemisphere.

"Bosh!" cried Jack. "He's too stupid to understand anything above the level of his nose, and I'd like to flatten that for him!"

"No," said Edmund, "he's not stupid, but I'm afraid he's malicious. If he were a little more stupid, it would be the better for us."

"But does Ala comprehend the difference between us and Juba—I mean in regard to origin?" I asked.

"I think so. In fact Juba bears unmistakable signs that he is of their world, although so different in physical appearance. His remarkable comprehension of their method of mental communication is alone sufficient to stamp him as ancestrally one of them. And yet," Edmund continued, musing, "think of the vast stretch of ages that separates the inhabitants of the two sides of this planet, the countless eons of evolution that have brought about the differences now existing! I am delighted to find that Ala has some understanding of all this. She has had good teachers—do not smile—for what you have seen of their mechanical achievements proves that science exists and is cultivated here; and from her savants she has learned—what our astronomers have deduced—that formerly Venus turned rapidly on her axis, and had days and nights swiftly succeeding one another. But they do not know the scientific reasons as completely as we do. With them this is knowledge based largely upon tradition, 'ancestral voices' echoing down through periods of time so vast that our most ancient legends seem but tales of yesterday. Whatever may be the measure of man's antiquity on the earth, I am certain that here intellectual life has existed for millions upon millions of years, and its history stretches back beyond the time when the brake of tidal friction had so far destroyed the rotation of the planet that its surface became permanently divided between the reigns of day and night.'

I listened with amazement and could not help exclaiming:

"But, Edmund, how could you learn all this in so short a time?"

"Because," he replied, smiling, "the language of the mind, unhampered by dragging words and blundering sentences, plays back and forth with the quickness of thought. There is another thing, too, which I have learned, a thing so amazing that it daunts me. I have found, I believe, the explanation of that minor note of infinite sadness which, as I told you, I always feel, even in the most joyous-seeming paeans of their colour music. I think it is due to their forereaching science, which assures them that this world has entered upon the last stage of its existence which began with the arrest of its axial rotation, and which will end with the total extinction of life through the evaporation of all the waters under the never-setting sun, and the consequent complete desiccation of this now so beautiful land."

"But," I objected, "you have said that they never see the sun."

"That was, I believe, a mistake, I am sure that they never see the stars or the planets, but I think that sometimes they see the sun, or, at least that there is a tradition of its having been seen. The whole thing is yet obscure to me, but I have received an inkling of something very, very strange in that regard."

"Then, Ala may think that it is from the sun that we claim to come," I said, disregarding his last remark, which had a significance which even he could not then have appreciated.

"I am not sure; we must wait for further light. But I have still another communication not so instinct with mystery. We are to be shown the sources of their mechanical power—the means by which they run all their motors."

"Hurrah," cried Jack. "Now, that's something I like! I can understand a machine—if you don't ask me to run it—but as for this talking through the eyes, and playing Jim Crow with rainbows, it's too much for me."

It was not many hours later when we were conducted by Ala, accompanied as usual by the inevitable Ingra, and a brilliant cortège of attendants, upon our first excursion through the capital. We embarked in a gorgeous air ship, and flying low at first, skirted the roofs of the innumerable houses which constituted the bulk of the city resting on the ground. The oriental magnificence of the views which we caught in the winding streets and frequent squares crowded with people, excited our interest to the utmost. But we kept on without descending or stopping until, at length, we passed the limits of the immense metropolis, and, flying more rapidly, and at a greater elevation, soon approached what, at a distance, appeared to be a waterfall, greater than Niagara, pouring out of the air!

"What marvel can this be?" I asked.

"A fountain," responded Edmund.

"A cataract turned upside down," exclaimed Jack. "Well, I've ceased to be surprised at anything I see here. I wouldn't be astonished now to find that their whole old planet was hollow, and full of gnomes, or whatever you call 'em."

When we got nearer we saw that Edmund's description was substantially correct. The vast mass of water gushed from the top of a broad plateau, in the form of a gigantic vertical fountain, with a roar so stupendous that Ala and her attendants immediately covered their ears with protectors, and we should not have been sorry to follow their example, for our eardrums were almost burst by the billowing force of the sound waves. The water shot upward four or five hundred feet with geyser-like plumes reaching a thousand feet, and then descended in floods on all sides. But the slope of the ground was such that eventually it was all collected in a river, which flowed away with great swiftness, past the distant city, and disappeared in the direction of the sea from which we had come. The solid column of rising water must have been, at its base, three hundred feet in diameter!

But our amazement was redoubled when we recognized, at various points of vantage, squat, metallic towers of enormous strength, which caught the descending water, allowing it to issue in roaring torrents from their bases.

"Those," shouted Edmund in our ears, "are power houses. I knew already that these people had learned the mechanical uses of electricity; and if we have seen no electric lights as yet, it is because, in a world of perpetual daylight, they have little or no use for them. They employ the power for other purposes."

"But how do you account for this incredible fountain?" I asked.

"It must be due to geological causes, if I may use a terrestrial term. You observe that the land all has a slope hitherward from the distant range of mountains, and that between us and the sea there is a chain of hills. The metropolis lies at the lower edge of a vast basin, and it must be that the relatively porous surface, over many thousands of square miles, is underlain by an almost unbroken shell of rock, impermeable to water. The result is that the drainage of this whole immense region, after being collected under ground, flows together to this point, where the existence of a huge vent in the upper layer offers it a way of escape, and it comes spouting out of the great crater with the consequences which you behold."

Many objections to Edmund's theory occurred to my mind; but he spoke so confidently, the course of things on this strange planet had so often followed his indications, and I felt myself so incapable of suggesting a more satisfactory hypothesis, that I made no reply, as a geologist, perhaps, would have done. At any rate the wonderful phenomenon existed before our eyes, explanation or no explanation. We learned afterwards that the river formed by the giant fountain passed through a gap in the hills to the seaward, and the more I reflected upon Edmund's idea the more acceptable I found it.

A great deal of the water was led away from the foot of the plateau out of which the fountain issued by ditches constructed to irrigate the rich gardens surrounding the metropolis and the open agricultural country for many miles around. At the queen's invitation, although she did not accompany us, we inspected one of the power houses, and Edmund found the greatest delight in studying the details of the enormous dynamos and the system of cables by which, quite in our own manner, the electric power was conveyed to the city. We noticed that everywhere the most ingenious devices were employed for killing noise.

"I knew we should find all this," said Edmund—"although I did not precisely anticipate the form that the natural supply of energy would take—as soon as I saw the aerial screws that give buoyancy to the great towers. In fact, I foresaw it as soon as I found, in inspecting the machinery of the air ship which brought us from the sea, that their motors were driven by storage batteries. It was obvious, then, that they had some extraordinary source of energy."

"Oh, of course, you knew it all!" muttered Henry under his breath. "But if you were as omniscient as you think yourself, you'd not be in this fool's paradise."

"What's that you're saying?" demanded Jack, partly catching the import of Henry's remark, and beginning to ruffle his feathers.

"Oh, nothing," mumbled Henry, and I shook my head at Jack to keep quiet. We all felt at times Edmund's assumption of superiority, but Jack and I were willing to put up with it as one of the privileges of genius. If Edmund had not believed in himself, he would never have brought us through. And besides, we always found that he was right, and if he sometimes spoke rather boastingly of his knowledge and foresight, at least it was real knowledge and genuine foresight.

CHAPTER 13

We Fall Into Trouble Again

It was not long after our visit to the marvellous fountain when Jack proposed to me that he and I should make a little excursion on our own account in the city. Edmund was absent at the moment, engaged in some inquiries which interested him, under the guidance of Ala and her customary attendants. I forget why Jack and I had stayed behind, since both Juba and Henry had accompanied Edmund, but it was probably because we wished to make some necessary repairs to our garments for I confess that I shared a little of the coquettishness of Jack in that matter. At any rate, we grew weary of being alone, and decided to venture just a little way in search of adventure. We calculated that the tower of the palace, which was so conspicuous, would serve us as a landmark, and that there was no danger of getting lost.

Nobody interfered with us at our departure, as we had feared they might, and in a short time we had become so absorbed in the strange spectacles of the narrow streets, lined with shops and filled with people on foot, while small air ships continually passed just above the roofs, that we forgot the necessity of keeping our landmark constantly in view, and were lost without knowing it.

One thing which immediately struck us was the entire absence of beasts of burden—nothing like horses or mules did we see. There were not even dogs, although, as I have told you, some canine-like animals dwelt with the people of the caverns. Everybody went either on foot or in air ships. There were no carriages, except a kind of palanquin, some running on wheels and others borne by hand.

"I should think they would have autos," said Jack, "with all their science and ingenuity which Edmund admires so much."

But there was not a sign of anything resembling an auto; the silence of the crowded streets was startling, and made the scene more dreamlike. Everybody appeared to be shod with some noise-absorbing material. We strolled along, turning corners with blissful careless-ness, staring and being stared at (for, of course, everybody knew who we were), peering into open doors and the gaping fronts of bazaars, chattering like a couple of boys making their first visit to a city, and becoming every moment more hopelessly, though unconsciously, lost, and more interested by what we saw. The astonishing display of pleas-ing colours and the brilliancy of everything fascinated us. I had never seen anything comparable to this in beauty, variety, and richness. We passed a market where we saw some of the bright-plumaged birds that we had eaten at our first repast hung up for sale. They had a way of serving these birds at table with the brilliant feathers of the head and neck still attached, as if they found a gratification even at their meals in seeing beautiful colours before them.

Other shops were filled with birds in gilded cages, which we should have taken for songsters but for the fact that, although crowds gathered about and regarded them with mute admiration, not a sound issued from their throats—at least we heard none. A palanquin stopped at one of these shops, and a lady alighted and bought three beauti-ful birds which she carried away in their cages, watching them with every indication of the utmost pleasure, which we ascribed to the splendour of their plumage and the gracefulness of their forms. As a crowd watched the transaction without interference on the part of the shopkeeper, or evidence of annoyance on that of the lady, we took the liberty of a close look ourselves. Then we saw their money.

"Good, yellow gold," whispered Jack.

Such, indeed, it seemed to be. The lady took the money, which consisted of slender rings, chased with strange characters, from a gold-en purse, and the whole transaction seemed so familiar that we might well have believed ourselves to be witnessing a purchase in a bazaar of Cairo or Damascus. This scene led to a desire on Jack's part to buy something himself.

"If I only had some of their money," he said, "I'd like to get some curiosities to carry home. I wonder if they'd accept these?" and he drew from his pocket some gold and silver coins.

"No doubt they'd be glad to have a few as keepsakes," I said.

"By Jo! I think I'll try it," said Jack, "but not here. I'm not a bird fancier myself. Let's look a little farther."

We wandered on, getting more and more interested, and followed by a throng of curious natives, who treated us, I must say, much more respectfully than we should have been treated in similar circumstances at home. Many of the things we saw, I cannot describe, because there is nothing to liken them to, but all were as beautiful as they were strange. At last we found a shop whose contents struck Jack's fancy. The place differed from any that we had yet seen; it was much larger, and more richly fitted up than the others, and there were no counters, the things that it contained being displayed on the inner walls, while a single keeper, of a grave aspect, and peculiarly attired, all in black, occupied a seat at the back. The objects on view were apparently ornaments to be hung up, as we hang plaques on the wall. They were of both gold and silver, and in some the two metals were intermixed, with pleasing effects. What seemed singular was the fact that the *motif* of the ornaments was always the same, although greatly varied in details of execution. As near as I could make it out, the intention appeared to be to represent a sunburst. There was invariably a brilliant polished boss in the centre, sometimes set with a jewel, and surrounding rays of crinkled form, which plunged into a kind of halo that encircled the entire work. The idea was commonplace, and it did not occur to me amidst my admiration of the extreme beauty of the workmanship that there was any cause for surprise in the finding of a sunburst represented here. Jack was enthusiastic.

"That's the ticket for me," he said. "How would one of those things look hanging over the fireplace of old Olympus? You bet I'm going to persuade the old chap to exchange one for a handful of good solid American money."

I happened to glance behind us while Jack was scooping his pocket, and was surprised to see that the crowd of idlers, which had been following us, had dispersed. Looking out of the doorway, I saw some of them furtively regarding us from a respectful distance. I twitched Jack by the sleeve:

"See here," I said, "there's some mistake about this. I don't believe that this is a shop. You'd better be careful, or we may make a bad break."

"Oh, pshaw!" he replied; "it's a shop all right, or if it isn't exactly a shop that old duffer will be glad to get a little good money for one of his gimcracks."

My suspicion that all was not right was not allayed when I noticed that the old man, whose complexion differed from the prevailing tone here, and who was specially remarkable by the possession of an eagle-beaked nose, a peculiarity that I had not before observed among these people, began to frown as Jack brusquely approached him. But I could not interfere before Jack had thrown a handful of coin in his lap, and, reaching up, had put his hand upon one of the curious sunbursts, saying:

"I guess this will suit; what do you say, Peter?"

Instantly the old fellow sprang to his feet, sending the coins rolling over the polished floor, and with eyes ablaze with anger, seized Jack by the throat. I sprang to his aid, but in a second four stout fellows, darting out of invisible corners, grappled us, and before we could make any effective resistance, they had our arms firmly bound behind our backs! Jack exerted all his exceptional strength to break loose, but in vain.

"I tried to stop you, Jack—" I began, in a tone of annoyance, but immediately he cut me off:

"This is on *me*, Peter; don't you worry. *You* haven't done anything."

"I'm afraid it's on all of us," I replied. "The whole party, Edmund and all, may have to suffer for our heedlessness."

"Fiddlesticks," he returned. "I haven't got his old ornament, but he's got my coin. This looks like a skin game to me. What in thunder did he hang the things up for if he didn't want to sell 'em?"

"But I told you this wasn't a shop."

"No, I see it isn't; it's a trap for suckers, I guess."

Jack's indignation grew hotter as we were dragged out into the street, and followed by a crush of people drawn to the scene, were hurried along, we knew not whither. In fact, his indignation swallowed up the alarm which he ought to have experienced, and which I felt in full force. I beat my brains in vain to find some explanation for the merciless severity with which we were treated so out of all proportion to the venial fault that had unconsciously been committed, and my perplexity grew when I saw in the faces of the crowd surrounding us, and running to keep up, a look of horror, as if we had been guilty of an unspeakable crime. We were too much hurried and jolted by our captors to address one another, and in a short time we were widely separated, Jack being led, or rather dragged, ahead, as if to prevent any communication between us. Once in a while, to my regret, I observed him exerting all his force to break his bonds and slinging his custodians about; but he could not get away, and at last, to my infinite comfort, he ceased to struggle, and went along as quietly as the rapid pace would permit.

Presently an air ship swooped down from above, and alighted in a little square which we had just entered. Immediately we were taken aboard, with small regard to our comfort, and the air ship rose rapidly, and bore off in the direction of the great tower of the palace which we could now see. Upon our arrival we were taken through the inevitable labyrinth of corridors, and finally found ourselves in a place that was entirely new to us.

It was a round chamber, perhaps two hundred feet in diameter, lighted, like the Roman Pantheon, by a huge circular opening in the vaulted roof, through which I caught a glimpse of the pearl-tinted cloud dome, which seemed infinitely remote. No opposition was made when I pushed ahead in order to be at Jack's side, and as a throng quickly hedged us round, our conductors released their hold, although our arms remained bound. When at last we stood fast we were in front of a rich dais, containing a throne-like seat occupied by a personage attired in black, the first glimpse of whose face gave me such a shock as I had not experienced since the priest of the earth-worshipers seized me for his prey. I have never seen anything remotely resembling that face. It was without beard, and of a ghastly paleness. It was seen only in profile, except when, with a lightning-like movement, it turned, for the fraction of a second, toward us, and was instantly averted again. It made my nerves creep to look at it. The nose was immense, resembling a huge curved beak, and the eyes, as black and glittering as jet, were roofed with shaggy brows, and seemed capable of seeing crosswise.

Sometimes one side of the face and sometimes the other was presented, the transition being effected by two instantaneous jerks, with a slight pause between, during which the terrible eyes transfixed us. At such moments the creature—though he bore the form of a man—seemed to project his dreadful countenance toward the object of his inspection like a monstrous bird stretching forth its neck toward its prey. The effect was indescribable, terrifying, paralyzing! The eyes glowed like fanned embers.

"In God's name," gasped Jack, leaning his trembling shoulder upon me, "what is it?"

I was, perhaps, more unmanned than he, and could make no reply.

Then there was a movement in the throng surrounding us, and the old man of the sunbursts appeared before the throne, and, after dropping on his knees and rising again, indicated us with his long finger, and, as was plain, made some serious accusation. The face turned upon us again with a longer gaze than usual, and we literally shrank from it. Then its owner rose from his seat, towering up, it seemed, to a height of full seven feet, shot his hand out with a gesture of condemnation, and instantly sat down again and averted his countenance. There seemed to have been a world of meaning in this brief act to those who could comprehend it. We were seized, even more roughly than before, and dragged from the chamber, and at the end of a few minutes found ourselves thrown into a dungeon, where there was not the slightest glimmer of light, and the door was locked upon us.

It was a long time before either of us summoned up the courage to speak. At length I said faintly:

"Jack, I'm afraid it's all over with us. We must have done something terrible, though I cannot imagine what it was."

But Jack, after his manner, was already recovering his spirits, and he replied stoutly:

"Nonsense, Peter, we're all right, as Edmund says. Wait till he comes and he'll fix it."

"But how can he know what has happened? And what could he do if he did? More likely they will all be condemned along with us."

Jack felt around in the dark and got me by the hand, giving it a hearty pressure.

"Remember Ala," he said. "She's our friend, or Edmund's, and they'll bring us out of this. You want to brace up."

"Remember Ingra!" I responded with a shiver, and I could feel Jack start at the words.

"Hang him!" he muttered. "If I'd only finished him when I had the drop!"

After that neither spoke. If Jack's thoughts were blacker than mine he must have wished for his pistol to blow out his own brains. At no time since our arrival on the planet had I felt so depressed. I had no courage left; could see no lightening of the gloom anywhere. In the horror of the darkness which enveloped us, the *horror of space* came over my spirit. One feels a little of that sometimes when the breadth of an ocean separates him from home, and from all who really care for him—but what is the Atlantic or the Pacific to millions upon millions of leagues of interplanetary space! To be cast away among the inhabitants of another world than one's own! To have lost, as we had done (for in that moment of despair I was *sure* Edmund could never repair the car), the only possible means of return! To have offended, just *because* we were strangers, and *could* not know better, some incomprehensible social law of this strange people, who owned not a drop of the blood of our race, or of any race whatsoever dwelling on the earth! To lie under the condemnation of that goblin face, without the possibility of pleading even the mercy that our hearts instinctively grant to the smallest mite of fellow life on our own planet! To be alone! friendless! forsaken! condemned!—in a far-off, kinless world! I could have fallen down in idolatry before a grain of sand from the shore of the Atlantic!

In the murkiest depth of my despair a sound roused me with a shock that made my heart ache. In a moment the door opened, light streamed in, and Edmund stood there.

CHAPTER 14

The Sun God

Strangely enough, I, who have an exceptional memory for spoken words, cannot, by any effort, recall what Edmund said, as his face beamed in upon us. I have only a confused recollection that he spoke, and that his words had a marvellous effect upon my broken spirit. But I can see, as if it were yet before me, the smile that illumined his features. My heart bounded with joy, as if a messenger had come straight from the earth itself, bearing a reprieve whose authority could not be called in question.

Jack's joy was no less than mine, although he had not suffered mentally as I had done. And the sight of Ala was hardly less reassuring to us, but to find Ingra, too, present was somewhat of a shock to our confidence in speedy delivery from trouble. And, in fact, we were not at once delivered. We had to spend many weary hours yet in our dark prison, but they were rendered less gloomy by Edmund's assurance that he would save us. The confidence that he always inspired seems to me to have been another mark of his genius. We had an instinct that he could do in any circumstances what was impossible to ordinary men.

At last the welcome moment came, and we were led forth, free, and rejoined Edmund, Henry, and Juba in our apartments. Then, for the first, we learned what we had done, and how narrow had been our escape from a terrible doom. It was a new chapter of wonder that Edmund opened before us. I shall tell it in his own words.

"When I returned to the palace and found you missing I was greatly wrought up. Immediately I applied to Ala for aid in finding you. She was quickly informed of all the circumstances of your arrest, and I saw at once, by the expression of her features, that it was a matter of the utmost gravity. I was not reassured by Ingra's evident joy. I could read in his face the pleasure that the news gave him, and I perceived that there was again opposition between him and Ala, and that she was trying, with less success than I hoped for, to bring him round to her view.

"With no little trouble I finally discovered the nature of your offence. I understood it the more readily because I had already begun to suspect the existence among these people of a strange form of idolatry, in some respects akin to the earth-worship of the cavern dwellers. I have told you that certain things had led me to think that they occasionally see the sun here. It is a phenomenon of excessive rarity, and whole generations sometimes pass without its recurrence. It is due to an opening which at irregular periods forms for a brief space of time in the cloud dome. I imagine that it may be in some way connected with sunspots, but here they have no notion of its cause, and look upon it as entirely miraculous.

"Whenever this rare event occurs it gives rise to extraordinary religious excitement, and ceremonies concerning which there is some occult mystery that I have not yet penetrated. I suspect that the ceremonies are not altogether unlike the Bacchanalian festivals of ancient Greece. At any rate the momentary appearance of the sun at these times is regarded as the avatar of a supreme god, and their whole religious system is based upon it. So universal and profound is the superstition to which it gives rise that the most instructed persons among them are completely under its dominion. The eagle-beaked individual who condemned you, and whom I have since seen, is the chief priest of this superstition, and within his sphere his power is unlimited. It is solely to the belief—which, through Ala, I have succeeded in impressing upon him—that we are *children of the sun* that I owe the success of my efforts in your behalf. Without that you would surely have been sacrificed, and we with you.

"One of the forms which this superstition takes is a belief that the anger of the sun god can be mollified by offerings of images, made in his likeness, which are first consecrated by the chief priest, and then hung up on the walls of certain small temples, which are scattered through the city, and are always kept open to the air under the guard of a minor priest and his attendants. A whole family, as I understand it, deems itself protected by one of these images, which are made by artists who never touch any other work, and which are only granted to those who have undergone a painful series of purifications in the great temple. The preliminary ceremonies finished, the images are suspended, and at certain times those to whom they belong go and kneel and pray before them, as before their guardian saints."

"What a fool I was not to understand it," I murmured.

"You will understand now," Edmund continued, "how serious was Jack's offence in insulting a priest, and laying impious hands upon a sacred image, belonging, no doubt, to a family whose antiquity of descent would make our oldest pedigrees on the earth seem as ephemeral as the existence of a May fly; for I am convinced that here life has gone on, uninterrupted by wars and changes of dynasty, for untold ages.

"It is a marvel that you escaped, for already they were preparing the awful sacrifice. The chief priest was amazed when an interposition was made on your behalf. Such a thing had never been known, and, as I have said, it was only by acting upon his superstition that I succeeded, with Ala's assistance, in obtaining a reprieve. As the case stands, we find ourselves occupying a dangerous eminence, which it may be difficult for us to maintain. I must beseech you to be on your guard, and to act only under my direction. It is all the more serious for us because I am convinced that Ingra has no faith whatever in the legend which protects us. He persists in believing that we are simply interlopers from the dark hemisphere, and the opposition between him and Ala has now become so sharp that he would gladly witness our destruction. I am sure that he will do his utmost to unmask us, and thus send us to our death."

"But—" I began.

"Wait a moment," said Edmund, "I have not yet finished. I must now tell you who Ingra is. *He is the destined consort of Ala.* That explains his influence over her. From what I can make out, it appears that he is of the royal blood, and that the marriage of the queen is arranged, not by her preference, but by an unwritten law, administered by the chief priest. She has no choice in the matter."

"I should say not," broke in Jack. "She never would have chosen that jackanapes! If you hadn't spoiled my aim I'd have relieved her of the burden."

"Not another word of that!" said Edmund severely. "In no manner, not even by a look, are you ever to express your dislike of him. And remember, you must govern your very thoughts, for here they lie open, as legible as print."

"Hang me," growled Jack, "if I like a world where a man can't even think his own thoughts because his mind goes bare! Take me back where you have to speak before you are understood."

"When you have wicked thoughts don't look them in the eyes," said Edmund, half smiling, "and then you will run no danger. It is through the eyes that they read. Now, to resume what I was saying, I am more than ever anxious to recover the car, and to find the materials that will enable me to repair its machinery. With it in our possession, and in good shape, we shall be in a position to run away whenever it may seem necessary to do so, and in the meantime to impose our legend upon them by the possession of so apparently miraculous a means of conveying ourselves through space. It will be overwhelming proof of the truth of our assertion of an origin outside their world, and perhaps, upon the whole, it is just as well that they should think that we belong to the sun, of whose existence they have some knowledge, rather than to the earth, of which they know nothing, in spite of the inkling that Juba succeeded in conveying to them."

"The car is here, isn't it?" I asked.

"Yes, it is in the great tower, but it is useless in its present condition."

"And what materials do you want to find?"

"Primarily nothing but uranium. They understand chemistry here. They have the apparatus that I need, but they do not know how to use it as I do. The uranium certainly exists somewhere. They mine gold and silver, and other things, and when I can find their mines, without exciting their suspicion, and can get the use of a laboratory in secret, I shall soon have what I need. But I must be very circumspect, for it would not do to let them perceive that chemistry really lies at the basis of our miracle. It is this necessity for secrecy which troubles me most. But I shall find a way."

"For God's sake, find it quick," Henry burst out. "And then get away from this accursed planet."

Edmund looked at him a moment before replying:

"We shall go when the necessity for going arises, and not before. We have not yet seen all the interesting things of this world."

I believe that even Jack and I shared to some extent Henry's disappointment on hearing this announcement. We should have been glad to know that we were to start on the return journey as soon as the car was in shape to transport us. But the event proved that Edmund's instinct was, as usual, right, and that the things which were yet to be seen and experienced were well worth the fearful risk we ran in remaining.

While Edmund undertook the delicate inquiries which were necessary in order to determine the direction that his search for uranium should take, and to enable him to conduct his chemical processes without awaking suspicion as to his real purpose, we were left much of the time in charge of a party of attendants who, by his intercession, had been selected to act as our guides when we wished to examine the wonders of the palace and the capital. Sometimes he accompanied us; but more often he was with Ala and her suite, including her uneludable satellite, Ingra.

"I bless my stars that he doesn't favour *us* with his delightful company," was Jack's comment, when he saw Ingra tagging along after Ala and Edmund.

I privately believed that Ingra had his spies among our attendants, but I was careful not to mention my suspicions to Jack.

But, oh, the delight of those excursions! Those streets; and those aerial towers, which rose like forests of coral in a gulf of liquid ether! They shine often in my dreams. A thousand times I have tried to put into words, simply for my own satisfaction, a description of the things that we saw, and the impressions that they made on my mind—but it is impossible. I understand now why the tales of travellers into strange lands never convey a tithe of what is in the writers' minds; they simply cannot; the necessary words and analogies do not exist. I can only use general terms, ransacking the vocabulary of adjectives—*beautiful, wonderful, fascinating, marvellous, indescribable, magical, enchanting, amazing, inexplicable, sans pareil*—what you will—but all that says nothing except to my own mind. Only the language of Venus could describe the charms and the wonders of Venus!

There was one thing, however, which was sufficiently comprehensible—*the great library*. Edmund was not with us when we paid our first visit to it; but he had predicted its existence during one of our conversations, when we were talking of the silent language.

"This people," he had said, "has a great history behind it, extending over periods which would amaze our disinterers of human antiquity, but an intelligent race cannot make history without also keeping records of it. Tradition alone, handed on from mind to mind, would not answer their requirements. The possession of the power to communicate thought without spoken language does not presuppose a power of memory any more perfect than we have. The brain forgets, the imagination misleads, with them as with us, and consequently they must have books of some kind—which implies a written or printed language. It is probable that this language does not correspond with the very meagre one of which we occasionally hear them pronounce a few words. The latter is, I am convinced, used only for names and interjections, and sometimes to call the attention of the person addressed, while the former must be a rich and carefully elaborated system of literary expression, which may not be phonetic at all. We shall find that this is so; and there are unquestionably libraries—probably a great imperial library—devoted to history and science. There must be schools also."

Thus Edmund had spoken, and thus we found it to be. The great library was in a building separate from the palace. It was admirably lighted from without, and its nature was apparent the moment we were led into it. The "books" were long scrolls, which might have been taken for parchment or papyrus, and the characters written on them resembled those of the Chinese language, but worked out in exquisite colours, which might themselves have had a meaning. The rolls were kept in proper receptacles under the charge of librarians, and we saw many grave persons at desks poring over them. Absolute silence reigned, and as I gazed at the scene I found admiration for this extraordinary people taking the place of the prejudice which I had recently been led to feel against them.

Jack, unusually impressed, whispered to me that Edmund must have been playing us some Hindu bedevilment trick, for he could not believe that we were actually in a foreign world. The same impression came over me. This was too earth-like; too much as if, instead of being on the planet Venus, we had been transported to some land of antique civilization in our own world. But, after all, we *knew where we were*, and as the realization of that fact came to us we could only stare with increasing astonishment at the scene before us. I may say here that Edmund subsequently visited this great library, and also some of the schools, and I know that he made notes of what he discovered and learned in them, with the purpose, as I supposed, of writing upon the subject after his return. But the expected book, which would have supplemented and clarified much of what I have undertaken to tell, with but a half understanding of what we saw, never appeared.

Our wonderful excursions came to an end when Edmund at length announced that he had obtained the information he needed, and that we were about to make a trip to some of the mines of Venus.

"I have discovered," he said, "that Venus is exceedingly rich in the precious metals, as well as in iron and lead. They mine them all, and we shall visit the mines under Ala's escort. My real purpose, of course, is to find uranium, of whose properties, strangely—and for us luckily—enough, they seem to have no knowledge. Nevertheless, they are capital chemists as far as they go, and possess laboratories provided with all that I shall need. They refine the metals at the mines themselves, so that I am sure of finding everything necessary to do my work right on the ground. The substance which I obtain from uranium is so concentrated that I can carry in my pocket all that will be required to repair the damage done to the transformers in the car. A careful examination, which I have made of the car, proves that the terrific shocks the machinery suffered in the crystal mountains caused an atomic readjustment which destroyed the usefulness of the material in the transformers, and while I might, by laboratory treatment, possibly restore its properties, I think it safer to obtain an entirely fresh supply. We shall start with the queen's ship within a few hours; so you had better make your preparations at once."

CHAPTER 15

At the Mercy of Fearful Enemies

If we could have foreseen what was to happen during this trip, even Edmund, I believe, would have shrunk from undertaking it. But we all embarked upon it gladly, because we had conceived the highest expectations of the delight that it would afford us; and at the news that we were to visit mines of gold richer than any on the earth, Henry exhibited the first enthusiasm that he had shown since our departure from home.

Embarked on Ala's splendid "yacht," as Jack called it, and attended by her usual companions, we rapidly left the city behind, and sped away toward the purple mountains, so often seen in the distance. The voyage was a long one, but at length we drew near the foot-hills, and beheld the mountains towering into peaks behind. Lofty as they looked, there was no snow on their summits. We now descended where plumes of smoke had for some time attracted our attention, and found ourselves at one of the mines. It was a gold mine. The processes of extracting the ore, separating the metal, etc., were conducted with remarkable silence, but they showed a knowledge of metallurgy that would have amazed us if we had not already seen so much of the capacity of this people. Yet similarly to the scene in the library, its earth-likeness was startling.

"This sort of thing is uncanny," said Jack, as we were led through the works. "It makes me creep to see them doing things just as we do them at home, except that they are so quiet about it. If everything was different from our ways it would seem more natural."

"Anyhow," I replied, "we may take it as a great compliment to ourselves, for it shows that we have found out ways of doing things which cannot be improved even in Venus."

I should like to describe in detail the wonders of this mine, but I have space for only a few words about it. It was, Edmund learned, the richest on the planet, and was the exclusive property of the government, furnishing the larger part of its revenues, which were not comparable with those of a great terrestrial nation because of the absence of all the expenditures required by war. No fleets and no armies existed here, and no tariffs were needed where commerce was free. This great mine was the Laurium of Venus. The display of gold in the vaults connected with it exceeded a hundredfold all that the most imaginative historian has ever written of the treasures of Montezuma and Atahualpa. Henry's eyes fairly shone as he gazed upon it, and he could not help saying to Edmund:

"You might have had riches equal to this if you had stayed at home and developed your discovery."

Edmund contemptuously shrugged his shoulders, and turned away without a word.

We were afterwards conducted to a silver mine, which we also inspected, and finally to a lead mine in another part of the hills. This was in reality the goal at which Edmund had been aiming, for he had told us that uranium was sometimes found in association with lead. Our joy was very great when, after a long inspection, he informed us that he had discovered uranium, and that it now remained only to submit it to certain operations in a laboratory in order to prepare the substance that was to give renewed life to those Lilliputian monsters in the car, which fed upon men's breath and begot power illimitable.

"I must now contrive," said Edmund, "to get admission to the laboratory connected with the mine, and to do my work without letting them suspect what I am about."

He managed it somehow, as he managed all things that he undertook, and within forty-eight hours after our arrival he was hard at work, evidently exciting the admiration of the native chemists by the knowledge and skill which he displayed. At first they crowded around him so that he was hampered in his efforts to conceal the real object of his labours; but at last they left him comparatively alone, and I could see by his expression whenever I visited the laboratory that things were going to his liking. But the work was long and delicate. Edmund had to fabricate secretly some of the chemical apparatus he needed, destroying it as fast as it served its purpose, so that weeks of time rolled by before he had what he called the "thimbleful of omnipotence" that was to make us masters of our fate. As fast as he produced it he put it in a metal box, shaped like a snuffbox, and covertly he showed it to us. It consisted of brilliant black grains, finer than millet seeds.

"Every one of those minute grains," he told us, "is packed with as much potential energy as that of a ton's weight suspended a mile above the earth."

But while the little box was being gradually filled with crystallized powder, we, who could lend no aid in the fabrication of Edmund's miracle, improved the opportunity to make acquaintance with the beauties of the surrounding country. Ala had returned to the capital, leaving an air ship at our disposal, and, of all persons in the world, *Ingra in command!* We refused all invitations to accompany him in the air ship, preferring to make our excursions on foot, accompanied at first by some of the attendants that Ala had left. Edmund did not share our fears that Ingra meditated mischief.

"He doesn't dare," was his reply to all our representations. But nothing could induce Jack and me to trust to Ingra's tender mercies.

Among the favourite spots which we had found to visit in the neighbourhood of the mine was a little knoll crowned with a group of the most beautiful trees that I ever saw, and washed at its base by a brook of exquisitely transparent water which tinkled over a bed of white and clear-yellow pebbles, sparkling like jewels. More than once at the beginning I fished some of them out in the belief that they were nuggets of pure gold polished by the water. In a pool under the translucent shadow of the overhanging trees played small fish so splendid in their varied hues that they looked like miniature rainbows darting about beneath the water. Birds of vivid colour sometimes flitted among the branches overhead. There was but one "rainy day" while we were at the mine; all the rest of the time not a cloud appeared under the great dome, and a scented zephyr continually drew down from the mountains and fanned us. Here, then, we passed many hours and many days, chatting of our adventures and our chances, drowsily happy in the pure physical enjoyment which this charming spot afforded.

When at last Edmund informed us that his box was full, and he was ready to return to the capital, we would not let him go without first conducting him to our little paradise. All together, then, with the exception of Juba, who, by some interference of an overlooking providence, was left at the mine, we set out in the highest spirits to be for once our leader's leaders in the exploration of some of the charms of Venus. Edmund was no less delighted than we had been with the place, and yielding to its somnolent influences we were soon stretched side by side on the spreading roots of a giant tree, and sleeping the sleep of sensuous languor.

Our waking was as terrible as it was sudden. I heard a cry, and at the same instant felt an irresistible hand grasping me by the throat. As I opened my eyes I saw that the whole party were prisoners. Nearby an air ship was quivering, as, held in leash, it lightly touched the ground; and a dozen gigantic fellows, whipping our hands behind our backs, hurried us aboard, the great mechanical bird, which instantly rose, describing a circle that carried us above the treetops. I did not try to struggle, for I felt how vain would be any effort that I could make.

Glancing about me, the very first features I recognized were those of Ingra. At last he had us in his power!

I looked at Edmund, but his face was set in thought, and he did not return my glance. Henry, as usual, had plunged into silent hopelessness, and Jack was a picture of mingled rage and despair. Although we were loosely fastened side by side to a rail on the deck, neither of us spoke for perhaps half an hour. In the meantime the air ship rose to a height greater than that of the nearby mountains, and then more slowly approached them. At last it began to circle, as if an uncertainty concerning the route to be chosen had arisen, and I observed, for we could look all about in spite of our bonds, that Ingra and one who appeared to be his lieutenant were engaged in an animated discussion. They pointed this way and that, and the debate grew every moment more earnest. This continued for a long time, while the ship hovered, running slowly in the wide circles. We could not then know how much this hesitation meant for us. If Ingra had been as rapid in his decision now as he was in the act of taking us prisoners, this history would never have been written. I watched Edmund, and saw that his attention was absorbed by what our captors were about, and even in that emergency I felt a touch of comfort through my unfailing confidence in our leader.

Finally a decision seemed to have been reached, and we set off over the crest of the range. As its huge peaks towered behind us and we descended nearer the ground, my heart sank again, for now we were cut off from the world beyond, and in the improbable event of any pursuit, how could the pursuers know what course we had taken, or where to look for us? And, then, who would pursue? Juba could do nothing, Ala was far away at the capital, even supposing that she should be disposed to set out in search of us, and hours, perhaps days, must elapse before she could be informed of what had happened. Not even when Jack and I were in the dungeon had our case seemed so desperate.

But how the gods repent when they have sunk men in the blackest pit of despair, sending them a messenger of hope to steady their hearts!

Good fortune had willed that we should be so placed upon the deck that we faced most easily sternward. Suddenly, as I gazed despondently at the serrated horizon receding in the distance, a thrill ran through my nerves at the sight of a dark speck in the sky, which seemed to float over one of the highest peaks. A second look assured me that it was moving; a third gave birth to the wild thought that it was in chase. Then I turned to Edmund and whispered:

"There is something coming behind us."

"Very well, do nothing to attract attention," he returned. "I have seen it. They are following us."

I said nothing to Jack or Henry, who had not yet caught sight of the object; but I could not withdraw my eyes from it. Sometimes I persuaded myself that it was growing larger, and then, with the intensity of my gaze, it blurred and seemed to fade. At last Jack spied it, and instantly, in his impetuous way, he exclaimed:

"Edmund! Look there!"

His voice drew Ingra's attention, and immediately the latter observed the direction of our glances, and himself saw the growing speck. He turned with flushed face to his lieutenant and in a trice the vessel began fairly to leap through the air.

"Ah, Jack," said Edmund reproachfully, but yet kindly, "if only you could always think before you speak! It is certain from Ingra's alarm that we are pursued by somebody whom he does not wish to meet. Most likely it is the queen, although it seems impossible that she could so quickly have learned of our mishap. Peter and I have been watching that object, which is unquestionably an air ship, in silence for the last twenty minutes, during which it has perceptibly gained upon us. But for your lack of caution it might have come within winning distance before it was discovered by Ingra, but now—"

The rebuke was deserved, perhaps, but yet I wished that Edmund had not given it, so painful was the impression that it made upon Jack's generous heart. His countenance was convulsed, and a tear rolled down his cheek—all the more pitiful to see because his arms were pinioned, and he could do nothing to conceal his agitation. Edmund was stricken with remorse when he saw the effect of his words.

"Jack," he said, "forgive me; I am sorry from the bottom of my heart. I should not have blamed you for a little oversight, when I alone am to blame for the misfortunes of us all."

"All right, Edmund, all right," returned Jack in his usual cheerful tones. "But, see here, I don't admit that you are to blame for anything. We're all in this boat together and hanged if we won't get out of it together, too, and you'll be the man to fetch us out."

Edmund smiled sadly, and shook his head.

Meanwhile Ingra, with the evident intention of concealing the movements of the vessel, dropped her so low that we hardly skipped the tops of the trees that we were passing over, for now we had entered a wide region of unbroken forest. Still that black dot followed straight in our wake, and I easily persuaded myself that it was yet growing larger. Edmund declared that I was right, and expressed his surprise, for we were now flying at the greatest speed that could be coaxed out of the motors. Suddenly a shocking thought crossed my mind. I tried to banish it, fearing that Ingra might read it in my eyes, and act upon it. Suppose that he should hurl us overboard! It was in his power to do so, and it seemed a quick and final solution. But he showed no intention to do anything of the kind. He may have had good reasons for refraining, but, at the time I could only ascribe his failure to take a summary way out of his difficulty to a protecting hand which guarded us even in this extremity.

On we rushed through the humming air, and still the pursuing speck chased us. And minute by minute it became more distinct against the background of the great cloud dome. Presently Edmund called our attention to something ahead.

"There," he said, "is Ingra's hope and our despair."

I turned my head and saw that in front the sky was very dark. Vast clouds seemed to be rolling up and obscuring the dome. Already there was a twilight gloom gathering about us.

"This," said Edmund, "is apparently the edge of what we may call the temperate zone, which must be very narrow, surrounding in a circle the great central region that lies under the almost vertical sun. The clouds ahead indicate the location of a belt of contending air currents, resembling that which we crossed after floating out of the crystal mountains. Having entered them, we shall be behind a curtain where our enemy can work his will with us."

Was it knowledge of this fact which had restrained Ingra from throwing us overboard? Was he meditating for us a more dreadful fate?

It was, indeed, a land of shadow which we now began to enter, and we could see that ahead of us the general inclination of the ground was downward. I eagerly glanced back to see if the pursuers were yet in sight. Yes! There was the speck, grown so large now that there could be no doubt that it was an air ship, driven at its highest speed. But we had entered so far under the curtain that the greater part of the dome was concealed, the inky clouds hanging like a penthouse roof far behind. We could plainly perceive the chasers; but could they see us? I tried to hope that they could, but reason was against it. Still they were evidently holding the course.

But even this hope faded when Ingra cunningly changed our course, turning abruptly to the left in the gloom. He knew, then, that we were invisible to the pursuers. But not content with one change, he doubled like a hunted fox. We watched for the effect of these manoeuvres upon those behind us, and to our intense disappointment, though not to our surprise, we saw that they were continuing straight ahead. They surely could not have seen us, and even if they anticipated Ingra's ruse, how could they baffle it, and find our track again? At last the spreading darkness swallowed up the arc of illuminated sky behind, and then we were alone in the gloom.

This, you will understand, was not the deep night of the other side of the planet; it was rather a dusky twilight, and as our eyes became accustomed to it, we could begin to discern something of the character of our surroundings. We flew within a hundred yards of the ground, which appeared to be perfectly flat, and soon we were convinced by the pitchy-black patches which frequently interrupted the continuity of the umbrageous surface beneath, that it was sprinkled with small bodies of water—in short, a gigantic Dismal Swamp, or Everglade. I need hardly say that it was Edmund who first drew this inference, and when its full meaning burst upon my mind I shuddered at the hellish design which Ingra evidently entertained. Plainly, he meant to throw us into the morass, either to drown in the foul water, whose miasma now assailed our nostrils, or to starve amidst the fens! But his real intention, as you will perceive in a little while, was yet more diabolical.

The bird ship stooped lower, just skimming the tops of strange trees, the most horrible vegetable forms that I have ever beheld. And then, without warning, we were seized and pushed overboard, while the vessel, making a broad swoop, quickly disappeared. Henry alone uttered a loud cry as we fell.

We crashed through the clammy branches and landed close together in a swamp. Fortunately the water was not deep, and we were able to struggle upon our feet and make our way to a comparatively dry open place, perhaps half an acre in extent. No sooner were we all safe on the land than I noticed Edmund struggling violently and then he exclaimed:

"Here, quick! Hold a hand here!"

As he spoke he backed up to me.

"Take a match from this box which I have twisted out of my pocket, and while I hold the box, scratch it, and hold the flame against the bonds around my wrists."

I managed to get out a match, and scratched it. But the match broke. Edmund, with the skill of a prestidigitator, got out another match, and pushed it into my fingers. It failed again.

"It's got to be done!" he said. "Here, Jack, you try."

Again he extracted a match, as Jack backed up in my place. Whether his hands happened to be less tightly bound, or whether luck favoured him, Jack, on a second attempt, succeeded in illuminating a match.

"Don't lose it," urged Edmund, as the light flashed out; "burn the cord."

Jack tried. The smell of burning flesh arose, but Edmund did not wince. In a few seconds the match went out.

"Another!" said Edmund, and the operation was repeated. A dozen separate attempts of this kind had been made, and I believe that I felt the pain inflicted by them more than Edmund did, when, making a tremendous effort, he burst the charred cord. His hands and wrists must have been fearfully burned, but he paid no attention to that. In a flash he had out his knife and cut us all loose. It was a mercy that they had not noticed the flame of the matches from the air ship, for if they had, unquestionably Ingra would have returned and made an end of us.

After our release we stood a few moments in silence, awaiting our leader's next move. Presently a sonorous sign startled us, followed by a sticky, tramping sound.

"In God's name, what's that?" exclaimed Jack.

"We'll see," said Edmund quietly, and threw open his pocket lantern.

As the light streamed out there was a rustle in the branches above us, and the form of an air ship pushed into view.

Ingra!

No, it was not Ingra! Thank God, there was the bushy head of Juba visible on the deck as the ship drifted over us! And near him stood Ala and a half dozen attendants.

As one man we shouted, but the sound had not ceased to echo when, out of the horrible tangle about us, rose, with a swift, sinuous motion, a monstrous anaconda-like arm, flesh pink in the electric beam, but covered with spike-edged spiracles! It curled itself over the edge of the hovering air ship and drew it down.

CHAPTER 16

Dreadful Creatures of the Gloom

The deck of the air ship was tipped up at an angle of forty-five degrees by the pressure, and with inarticulate cries most of those on board tumbled off, some falling into the water and some disappearing amidst the tangled vegetation. Ala was visible, as the machine sank lower, and crashed through the branches, clinging to an upright on the sloping deck, while Juba, who hung on like a huge baboon, was helping her to maintain her place.

Almost at the same moment I caught sight of the head of the monstrous animal which had caused the disaster. It was as massive as that of an elephant or mammoth; and the awful arm resembled a trunk, but was of incredible size. Moreover, it was covered with sucking mouths or disks. The creature apparently had four eyes ranged round the conical front of the head where it tapered into the trunk, and two of these were visible, huge, green, and deadly bright in the gleam of the lantern.

For a moment we all stood as if petrified; then the great arm was thrown with a movement quick as lightning round both Ala and Juba as they clung to the upright! My heart shot into my mouth, but before the animal could haul in its prey, a series of terrific reports rattled like the discharge of a machine gun at my ear. The monstrous arm released the victims, and waved in agony, breaking the thick, clammy branches of the vegetation, and the vast head disappeared. Edmund had fired all the ten shots in his automatic pistol with a single pressure of the double trigger and an unvarying aim, directed, no doubt, at one of the creature's eyes.

"Quick!" he shouted, as the air ship, relieved from the stress, righted itself; "climb aboard."

The vessel had sunk so low, and the vegetation was so crowded about it, that we had no great difficulty in obeying his commands. He was the last aboard, and instantly he grasped the controlling apparatus, and we rose out of the tangle. We could hear the wounded monster thrashing in the swamp, but saw only the reflection of its movements in the commotion of the branches.

I had expected that Edmund would immediately fly at top speed away from the dreadful place, but, instead, as soon as we were at a safe elevation, he brought the air ship to a hover, circling slowly above the comparatively open spot of dry ground at the edge of the swamp.

"We cannot leave the poor fellows who have fallen overboard," he said, as quietly as if he had been safely aboard his own car. "We must stay here and find them."

Soon their cries came to our ears, and turning down the light of the lantern we saw five of them collected together on the solid ground, and gesticulating to us in an agony of terror. Edmund swept the ship around until we were directly over the poor fellows, and then allowed it to settle until it rested on the ground beside them. I trembled with apprehension at this bold manoeuvre, but Edmund was as steady as a rock. Ala instantly comprehended his intention, and encouraged her followers, who were all but paralyzed with fright, to clamber aboard. A momentary communication of the eyes took place between Edmund and Ala, and I understood that he was demanding if all had been found.

There was another—and not a trace of him could be seen.

"We must wait a moment," said Edmund, reloading the chamber of his pistol while he spoke. "I'll look about for him."

"In God's name, Edmund! You don't think of going down there!"

"But I do," he said firmly, and before I could put my hand on his arm he had dropped from the deck. The gigantic creature that he had wounded was still thrashing about a little distance off, occasionally making horrible sounds, but Edmund seemed to have no fear. We saw him, with amazement, walk collectedly round the ground encircled by the swamp, peering into the tangle, and frequently uttering a call. But his search was vain, and after five minutes of the most intense nervous strain that I ever endured, I thanked Heaven for seeing him return in safety, and come slowly aboard. There was another consultation with Ala, which evidently related to the ability of the engineer of the ship to resume his functions. This had a satisfactory result, for the fellow took his place, and the vessel finally quitted the ground. But, at Edmund's request, it rose only to a moderate height, and then began again to circle about. He would not yet give up the search.

We flew in widening circles, Edmund keeping his lantern directed toward the ground, and the full horror of these interminable morasses now became plain. I was in a continual shudder at the evidence of Ingra's pitiless scheme for our destruction. He had meant that we should be the prey of the unspeakable inhabitants of the fens, and had believed that there was no possibility of escape from them. We became aware that there was a great variety of them in the swamps and thickets beneath through the noises that they made—heart-quaking cries, squealing sounds, gruntings, and, most trying of all, a loud, piercing whistle whose sibilant pulsations penetrated the ear like thrusts of a needle. I pictured to myself a colossal serpent as the most probable author of this terrifying sound, but the error of my fancy was demonstrated by a tragedy which shook even Edmund's iron nerves.

Always circling, and always watching what was below by the light of the lantern, which was of extraordinary power for so small an instrument, we saw occasionally a curling trunk uplifted above the vegetation, as if its owner imagined that the strange light playing on the branches was some delicate prey that could be grasped, and sometimes a gliding form whose details escaped detection, when, upon passing over a relatively open place, like that where our adventure had occurred, a blood-curdling sight met our eyes.

Directly ahead, in the focus of the reflector of the lantern, and not more than a hundred feet distant, stood a prodigious black creature, on eight legs, rolling something in its mandibles, which were held close to what seemed to be its mouth.

"Good Lord!" cried Jack. "It's a tarantula as big as a buffalo!"

"It has caught the missing man!" said Edmund. "Look!"

He pointed to a shred of garment dangling on a thorny branch. I felt sick at heart, and I heard a groan from Jack. After all, these people were like us, and our feelings would not have been more keenly agitated if the victim had been a descendant of Adam.

"He is beyond all help," I faltered.

"But he can be avenged," said Edmund, in a tone that I had never heard him use before.

As he spoke he whipped out his pistol, and crash! crash! crash! sounded the hurrying shots. As their echo ceased, the giant arachnid dropped his prey, and then there came from him—clear, piercing, quivering through our nerves—that arrowy whistle that had caused us to shudder as we unwillingly listened to it darting out of the gloom of the impenetrable thickets.

Then, to our horror, the creature, which, if touched at all by the shots, had not been seriously injured, picked up its prey and bounded away in the darkness. Edmund instantly turned to Ala, and I knew as well as if he had spoken, what his demand was. He wished to follow, and his wish was obeyed. We swooped ahead, and in a minute we saw the creature again. It had stopped on another oasis of dry land, and it still carried its dreadful burden. Its head was toward us, and it appeared to be watching our movements. Its battery of eyes glittered wickedly, and I noticed the bristle of stiff hairs, like wires, that covered its body and legs.

Again Edmund fired upon it, and again it uttered its stridulous pipe of defiance, or fear, and leaped away in the tangle. We sped in pursuit, and when we came upon it for the third time it had stopped in an opening so narrow that the bow of the air ship almost touched it before we were aware of its presence. This time its prey was no longer visible. There was no question now that its attitude meant defiance. Cold shivers ran all over me as, with fascinated eyes, I gazed at its dreadful form. It seemed to be gathering itself for a spring, and I shrank away in terror.

Crash! bang! bang! bang! sounded the shots once more, and in the midst of them there came a blinding tangle of bristled, jointed legs that thrashed the deck, a thud that shook the air ship to its centre, and a cry from Jack, who fell on his back with a crimson line across his face.

"Give me your pistol!" shouted Edmund, snatching my arm.

I hardly know how I got it out of my pocket, I was so unnerved, but it was no sooner in Edmund's hand than he was leaning over the side of the deck and pouring out the shots. When the pistol was emptied he straightened up, and said simply:

"*That* devil is ended."

Then he turned to where Jack lay on the deck. We all bent over him with anxious hearts, even Ala sharing our solicitude. He had lost his senses, but a drop from Edmund's flask immediately brought him round, and he rose to his feet.

"I'm all right," he said, with a rather sickly smile; "but," drawing his hand across his brow and cheek, "he got me here, and I thought it was a hot iron. Where is he now?"

"Dead," said Edmund.

"Jo, I'd have liked to finish him myself!"

We were worried by the appearance of the wound, like a long, deep scratch, on Jack's face, but, of course, we said nothing about our worriment to him. Edmund bound it up, as best he could, and it afterwards healed, but it took a long time about it, and left a mark that never disappeared. There was probably a little poison in it.

Edmund himself needed the attention of a surgeon, for his wrists had been cruelly burned by the matches, but he would not allow us to speak of his sufferings, and putting on some slight bandages, he declared that it was time now to get out of this wilderness of horrors. He communicated with Ala, and in a few minutes we were speeding, at a high elevation, toward the land of the opaline dome. So far above the morasses we no longer heard the brute voices of its terrible inhabitants, nor saw the swaying of the branches as they looked about in search of prey.

"This," said Edmund, "exceeds everything that I could have imagined. I do not know in what classification to put any of the strange beasts that we have seen. They can only be likened to the monsters of the early dawn on the earth, in the age of the dinosaurs. But they are *sui generis*, and would make our anatomists and palaeontologists stare. I am only surprised that we have encountered no flying dragons here."

"But was it really a—a giant spider that captured Ala's man?" I asked with a shudder.

"God knows what it was! It had the form of a spider, and it leaped like one. If it had been armoured I could never have killed it. I think the shock of its impact against the air ship helped to finish it."

It was only after we had issued from under the curtain of twilight that we learned the story of the chase which had brought our salvation. Edmund first obtained it from Ala and Juba, filling out the outlines of their wordless narrative with his ready power of interpretation, and then he told it to us."

"We owe our lives to Juba," he said. "Ala had just returned to the mine from the capital when our abduction took place. Juba, who had wandered out on our track, saw from a distance the seizure, and a few minutes afterwards Ala's air ship arrived. He instantly communicated the facts to her, and without losing an instant the chase was begun. Ingra's delay in choosing his course was the thing that saved us. They knew that they must not lose sight of us for an instant, and their motors were driven to their highest capacity. Fortunately, Ala's vessel is one of the speediest, and they were able to gain on us from the start. Slowly they drew up until the border of the twilight zone was reached. Then as we entered under the clouds we were swallowed from the sight of all except Juba. But for his wonderful eyes, there would have been no hope of continuing the chase. He had lived all his life in a land of darkness and now he began to feel himself at home. Throwing off the shades which he has worn since our arrival, he had no difficulty in following the movements of Ingra, even after our vessel had completely faded from the view of all the others. So, without abating their fearful speed, they plunged into the gloom straight upon our track. The nose of the bloodhound is not more certain in the chase than were Juba's eyes in that terrible flight through the darkness. When Ingra changed his course and doubled, Juba saw the manoeuvre and turned the dodge against its inventor, for now Ingra could not see them, and did not know that they were still on his track. They cut off the corners, and gained so rapidly that they were close at hand when Ingra rose from the swamp after pitching us overboard. They had heard Henry's cry, which served to tell them what had happened, and to direct them to the spot. But even Juba could not discern us in the midst of the vegetation, and it was the sudden flashing out of our lamp which revealed our location when they were about to pass directly over us."

I need not say with what breathless attention we listened to this remarkable story, which Edmund's scientific imagination had constructed out of the bones of fact that he had been able to gather.

"Jo," said Jack, "our luck is simply outlandish!"

Then he broke out in one of his fits of enthusiasm. Slapping Juba on the shoulder, he danced around him, laughing joyously, and exclaiming:

"Bully old boy! Oh, you're a trump! Wait till I get you in New York, and I'll give you the time of your life! Eh, Edmund, won't we make him a member of Olympus? Golly, won't he make a sensation!"

And Jack hugged himself again with delight. His reference to home threw us into a musing. At length I asked:

"Shall we ever see the earth again, Edmund?"

"Why, of course we shall," he replied heartily. "I have the material I need, and it only remains to repair the car. I shall set about it the moment we reach the capital. Do you know," he continued, "this adventure has undoubtedly been a benefit to us."

"How so?"

"By increasing our prestige. They have seen the terrible power of the pistols. They have seen us conquer monsters that they must have regarded as invincible. When they see what the car can do, even Ingra will begin to fear us, and to think that we are more than mortal."

"But what will Ala think of Ingra now?"

"Ah, I cannot tell; but, at any rate, he cannot have strengthened himself in her regard, for it is plain that she, at least, has no desire to see us come to harm. But he is a terrible enemy still, and we must continue to be on our guard against him."

"I should think that he would hardly dare to show himself now," I remarked.

"Don't be too sure of that. After all, we are interlopers here, and he has all the advantages of his race and his high rank. Ala is interested in us because she has, I believe I may say, a philosophical mind, with a great liking for scientific knowledge. It was she who planned and personally conducted the expedition toward the dark hemisphere. From me she has learned a little. She appreciates our knowledge and our powers, and would ask nothing better than to learn more about us and from us. Her prompt pursuit and interference to save us when she must have understood, perfectly, Ingra's design, shows that she will go far to protect us; but we must not presume too much on her ability to continue her protection, nor even on her unvarying disposition to do so. For the present, however, I think that we are safe, and I repeat that our position has been strengthened. Ingra made a great mistake. He should have finished us out of hand."

"His leaving us to be devoured by those fearful creatures showed an inexplicable cruelty on his part; he chose the most horrible death he could think of for us," I said.

"Oh, I don't know," replied Edmund. "Did you ever see a laughing boy throw flies into a spider's den? It is my idea that he simply wished to have us disappear mysteriously, and then *he* would never have offered an explanation, unless it might have been the malicious suggestion that we had suddenly decamped to return to the world we pretended to have come from. And but for Ala's unexpected return to the mine he would have succeeded. No doubt his crew were pledged to secrecy."

CHAPTER 17

Earth Magic on Venus

We were no sooner installed again at the capital than Edmund began his "readjustment of the atomic energies."

"Blessed if I know what he means," said Jack; "but he gets the goods, and that's enough for me."

In reality I did not understand it any better than Jack did, only I had more knowledge than he of the nature of the forces that Edmund employed. We went with him to the place in the great tower where the car had been stored, and where it seemed to be regarded with a good deal of superstitious awe. But they had not yet the least idea of its marvellous powers.

We were preparing for them the greatest surprise of their lives, and our impatience to see the effect that would be produced when we made our first flight grew by day, while Edmund, shut up alone in the car, laboured away at his task.

"I wonder what they think he is doing in there," I said, the third day after our return, as we sat on a balcony of the floating tower, with our feet nonchalantly elevated on a railing, and our eyes drinking in the magnificent prospect of the vast city, as brilliant in variegated colours as a flower garden, while a soft breeze, that gently swayed the gigantic gossamer, soothed us like a perfumed fan.

"Worshipping the sun god, I reckon," laughed Jack. "But, see here, Peter, what do you make of this religion of theirs, anyway?"

"I don't know what to make of it," I replied. "But if the sun really does appear to them once in a lifetime, or so, as Edmund thinks, it seems to me natural enough that they should worship it. We have done more surprising things of the kind on the earth."

"Not civilized people like these."

"Oh, yes. The Egyptians were civilized, and the Romans, and they worshipped all sorts of strange things that struck their fancy.

And what can you say to the Greeks—they were civilized enough, and look what a collection of gods they had."

"But the wise heads among them didn't really believe in their gods."

"I'm not sure of that; at any rate they had to pretend that they believed. No doubt there were some who secretly scoffed at the popular belief, and it may be the same here. I shouldn't wonder if Ingra were one of the scoffers. Edmund has a great opinion of his intelligence, and if he really doesn't believe in the thing, he is all the more dangerous for us, because you know that now we are depending a good deal on their superstition for our safety."

"But Ala is very intelligent, a regular wonder, I should think, from what Edmund says; and yet she accepts their superstition as gospel."

"Lucky for us that she does believe," I said. "But there's some great mystery behind all this; Edmund has convinced me of that. We don't begin to understand it yet, and there are moments when I think that Edmund is afraid of the whole thing. He seems dimly to foresee some catastrophe connected with it, though what it may be I cannot imagine, and I think he doesn't know himself."

Henry listened to our conversation without proffering a remark—quite the regular thing with him—and at this point Jack, yielding to the overpowering sense of well-being, and the soothing influence of the delicious air and delightful view, closed his eyes for a nap.

Presently Edmund came and roused us all up with the remark that he had finished his work. Jack was instantly on his feet:

"Hurrah!" he exclaimed. "Now for another trip that will open the eyes of these Venusians. Where shall we go, Edmund?"

"We shall go nowhere just at present. I want first to make sure by a trial trip that everything is in perfect shape. For that purpose I shall wait for the hours of repose when there will be nobody to watch us."

I must here explain more fully what I have already said—that in this land of unceasing daylight, everybody took repose as regularly as on the earth. That is a necessity for all physical organisms. When they slept, they retired into darkened chambers, and passed several hours in peaceful slumber. We had learned the time when this periodical need for sleep seized upon the entire population, and although, naturally, there were a few wide-awakes who kept "late hours," yet within a certain time after the habitual hour for repose had arrived it was a rare thing to see anybody stirring. We had, then, only to wait until "the solemn dead of night" came on in order that Edmund might try his experiment with almost a certainty of not being observed. This was the easier, since latterly there had been no guard kept over our movements. We were not confined in any way, and could go and come as we pleased. Evidently, if anybody thought of such a thing as an attempt to escape on our part, they trusted to the fact that we had no means of getting away, for after our first exploit of that kind, all the air ships were carefully guarded, and placed beyond our reach. As to the car, there was nothing about it to suggest that it could fly, and probably they took it simply for some kind of boat, since they had seen us employ it only in navigating the sea. I have often thought, with wonder, of their unsuspiciousness in permitting Edmund to spend so much time alone and undisturbed in the car. Possibly, there was something in Jack's suggestion, that they supposed it to be connected with our religious observances. Anyhow, so it was; and I can only ascribe the fact to the kindness of that overlooking Power which so often interfered in our behalf, making it no disparagement of our claim upon its protection that we had abandoned our mother earth and ventured so far away into space!

One thing decidedly in our favour was that, since our return from the mine (the adventure in the land of bogs and monsters was, as far as Edmund could ascertain, unknown at the capital, except by those who had taken part in it), we had been accustomed to pass the hours of repose in the tower. We should thus be close to the car when we got ready to start. Another equally favourable circumstance—and perhaps it was even more important—was the absence of Ingra, who, either because he did not care just now to face Ala, or because he had gone off somewhere after throwing us to the animals and was not yet aware of our escape, had not shown himself. If he had been present it might not have been so easy for Edmund to make his preparations.

Never had the great city seemed to me so long in quieting down for its periodical rest as on this occasion. After all was deserted in the streets below, people were still moving about on the tower, and it did seem as if they had taken a fit of wakefulness expressly to annoy us and interfere with our plans. We kept stealing out of our sleeping room, and looking cautiously about, for at least two hours, but always there was some one stirring in the immediate neighbourhood. At last a tall fellow, who had been standing an interminable time at the rail directly in front of the storage place of the car, and whom Jack had half seriously threatened to throttle if he stood there any longer, turned and went yawning away. No sooner was he out of sight than Edmund led the way, and with the slightest possible noise, aided by Juba, who was as strong as three men, we got the car out on the platform. I was in a fever lest there should be a squeak from the little wheels that carried it. But they ran as still as rubber.

"Get in," whispered Edmund; and we obeyed him with alacrity.

Would it go?

Even Edmund could not answer that question. He pulled a knob, and I held my breath. There was the slightest perceptible tremor. Was it going to balk? No, thank Heaven! It was under way. In a few seconds we were off the tower in the free air. Edmund pressed a button, and the speed instantly increased. The gorgeous tower seemed to be flying away from us like a soap bubble. Jack, in ecstasy, could hardly repress a cheer.

"Hurrah, if you want to,'" said Edmund.

"They won't hear you, and now I don't care if they do. The apparatus is all right, and we'll give them something to wake up for. My only anxiety was lest they should witness a failure, which might have led to disagreeable consequences. There must be no dropping of knives in our juggling."

"Good!" cried Jack. "Then let's give 'em a salute."

Edmund smiled and nodded his head:

"The guns are in the locker," he said.

Jack had one of the automatic rifles out in a hurry.

"Shoot high," said Edmund, "and off toward the open country. The projectiles fly far, and I guess we can take the risk."

He threw both windows open, and Jack aimed skyward and began to pull the trigger.

Bang! bang! bang! Heavens, what a noise it was! The car must have seemed a flying volcano. And it woke them up! The sleeping city poured forth its millions to gaze and wonder. Surely they had never heard such a thundering. Within five minutes we saw them on the roofs and in the towers. Many were staring at us through a kind of opera glasses which they had. Then from a dozen aerial pavilions the colours broke forth and quivered through the air.

"Saluting us!" exclaimed Jack, delighted.

"Asking one another questions, rather," said Edmund.

They certainly asked enough of them, and I wondered what answers they returned.

"Probably they think we're off for good," said I.

"And aren't we?" asked Henry anxiously.

"Not yet," Edmund replied, and Henry's countenance fell.

The car turned and approached the great tower again. We swept round it within a hundred yards, and could see the amazement in the faces that watched us. But if they were astonished they were not terror-stricken. Within ten minutes twenty air ships were swiftly approaching us. Edmund allowed them to come within a few yards, and then darted away, rushed round the whole city like a flying cloud, and finally rose straight up with dizzying velocity, which made the vast metropolis shrink to a coloured patch, as if we had been viewing it through the wrong end of a telescope.

"I'll go right up through the cloud dome now," he said. "Nothing could more impress them with a sense of our power than that; and when we come back again they will know that we have no fear, and the very act will be a proof of origin from the sky."

When we were in the midst of the mighty curtain of vapour, I was interested in noticing the peculiar quality of the light that surrounded us. We seemed to be immersed in a rose-pink mist.

"I do not understand," I said to Edmund, "how this dome is maintained at so great an elevation, and in apparent independence of the rain clouds which sometimes form beneath. No rain ever falls from the dome itself, and yet it consists of true clouds."

"I think," he replied, "that the dome is due to vapours which assemble at a general level of condensation, and do not form raindrops, partly because of the absence of dust to serve as nuclei at this great height, and partly because of some peculiar electrical condition of the air, arising from the relative nearness of Venus to the sun, which prevents the particles of vapour from gathering into drops heavy enough to fall. You will observe that there is a peculiar inner circulation in the vapour surrounding us, marked by ascending and descending currents which are doubtless limited by the upper and lower surfaces of the dome. The true rain clouds form in the space beneath the dome, where there seems to be an independent circulation of the winds."

On entering the cloud vault Edmund had closed the windows, explaining that it was not merely the humidity which led him to do so, but the diminishing density of the air which, when we had risen considerably above the dome, would become too rare for comfortable breathing. In a little while his conjecture about a peculiar electrical condition was justified by a pale-blue mist which seemed to fill the air in the car; but we felt no effects and the mechanism was not disturbed. Owing to our location on Venus, still at a long distance from the centre of the sunward hemisphere, the sun was not directly overhead, but inclined at a large angle to the vertical, so that when we began to approach the upper surface of the vault, and the vapour thinned out, we saw through one of the windows a pulsating patch of light, growing every moment brighter and more distinct, until as we shot out of the clouds it instantly sharpened into a huge round disk of blinding brilliance.

"The sun! The sun!" we cried.

We had not seen it for months. When it had gleamed out for a short time during our drift across the water from the land of ice into the belt of tempests, we had been too much occupied with our safety to pay attention to it; but now the wonder of it awed us. Four times as large and four times as bright and hot as it appears from the earth, its rays seemed to smite with terrific energy. Juba, wearing his eye shades, shrank into a corner and hid his face.

"It is well that we are protected by the walls of the car and the thick glass windows," said Edmund, "for I do not doubt that there are solar radiations in abundance here which scarcely affect us on the earth, but which might prove dangerous or even mortal if we were exposed to their full force."

Even at the vast elevation which we had now attained there was still sufficient air to diffuse the sunlight, so that only a few of the brightest stars could be glimpsed. Below us the spectacle was magnificent and utterly unparalleled. There lay the immense convex shield of Venus, more dazzling than snow, and as soft in appearance as the finest wool. We gazed and gazed in silent admiration, until suddenly Henry, who had shown less enthusiasm over the view than the rest of us, said, in a doleful voice:

"And now that we are here—free, free, where we can do as we like—with all means at our command—oh! why will you return to that accursed planet? Edmund, in the name of God, I beseech you, go back to the earth! Go now! For the love of Heaven do not drag us into danger again! Go home! Oh, go home!"

The appeal was pitiful in its intensity of feeling, and a shade of hesitation appeared on Edmund's face. If it had been Jack or I, I believe that he would have yielded. But he slowly shook his head, saying in a sympathetic tone:

"I am sorry, Henry, that you feel that way. But I *cannot* leave this planet yet. Have patience for a little while and then we will go home."

I doubt whether afterwards, Edmund himself did not regret that he had refused to grant Henry's prayer. If we had gone now when it was in our power to go without interference, we should have been spared the most tragic and heart-rending event of all that occurred during the course of our wandering. But Edmund seemed to feel the fascination of Venus as a moth feels that of the candle flame.

When we emerged again on the lower side of the dome we were directly over the capital. We had been out of view for at least three hours, but many were still gazing skyward, toward the point where the car had disappeared, and when we came into sight once more there were signs of the utmost agitation. The prismatic signals began to flash from tower to tower, conveying the news of the reappearance of the car, and as we drew near we saw the crowds reassembling on every point of vantage. We went out on the window ledges to watch the display.

"Perhaps they think that we have been paying a visit to the sun," I suggested.

"Well, if they do I shall not undeceive them," said Edmund, "although it goes against the grain to make any pretence of the kind. Ala, particularly, is so intelligent, and has so genuine a desire for knowledge, that if I could only cause her to comprehend the real truth it would afford me one of the greatest pleasures of my life."

"I hope old Beak Nose is getting his fill of this show," put in Jack. "He'll be likely to treat us with more respect after this. By the way, I wonder what's become of my money. I think I'll sue out a writ of replevin in the name of the sun to recover it."

Nobody replied to Jack's sally, and the car rapidly approached the great tower.

"Are you going to land there?" I asked.

"I certainly shall," Edmund responded with decision.

"But they'll seize the car!" exclaimed Henry in affright.

"No, they won't. They are too much afraid of it."

Any further discussion was prevented by a sight which arrested the eyes of all of us. On the principal landing of the tower, whence we had departed with the car, stood Ala with her suite, and by her side was Ingra!

His sudden apparition was a great surprise, as well as a great disappointment, for we had felt sure that he was not in the city, and I, at least, had persuaded myself that he might be in disgrace for his attempt on our lives. Yet here he was, apparently on terms of confidence with her whom we had regarded as our only sure friend.

"Hang him!" exclaimed Jack. "There he is! By Jo, if Edmund had only invented a noiseless gun of forty million atom power, I'd rid Venus of *him*, in the two-billionth part of a second!"

"Keep quiet," said Edmund, sternly, "and remember what I now tell you; in no way, by look or act, is any one of us to indicate to him the slightest resentment for what he did. Ignore him, as if you had never seen him."

By this time the car had nearly touched the landing. Edmund stepped inside a moment and brought it completely to rest, anchoring it, as he whispered to me, by "atomic attraction." When the throng on the tower saw the car stop dead still, just in contact with the landing, but manifestly supported by nothing but the air—no wings, no aeroplanes, no screws, no mechanism of any kind visible—there arose the first *voice of a crowd* that we had heard on the planet. It fairly made me jump, so unexpected, and so contrary to all that we had hitherto observed, was the sound. And this multitudinous voice itself had a quality, or timbre, that was unlike any sound that had ever entered my ears. Thin, infantine, low, yet multiplied by so many mouths to a mighty volume, it was fearful to listen to. But it lasted only a moment; it was simply a universal ejaculation, extorted from this virtually speechless people by such a marvel as they had never dreamed of looking upon. But even this burst of astonishment, as Edmund afterwards pointed out, was really a tribute to their intelligence, since it showed that they had instantly appreciated both the absence of all mechanical means of supporting the car and the fact that here was something that implied a power infinitely exceeding any that they possessed. And to have produced in a world where aerial navigation was the common, everyday means of conveyance, such a sensation by a performance in the *air* was an enormous triumph for us!

No sooner had we gathered at the door of the car to step out upon the platform than an extraordinary thing occurred. The front of the crowd receded into the form of a semicircle, of which the point where we stood marked the centre, and in the middle of the curve, slightly in advance of the others, stood forth the tall form of the eagle-beaked high priest with the terrible face, flanked on one side by Ala and on the other by the Jove-like front of the aged judge before whom our first arraignment had taken place. Directly behind Ala stood Ingra. The contrast between the three principal personages struck my eye even in that moment of bewilderment—Ala stately, blonde, and beautiful as a statue of her own Venus; the high priest ominous and terrifying in aspect, even now when we felt that he was honouring us; and the great judge, with his snow-white hair and piercing eyes, looking like a god from Olympus.

"Do you note the significance of that arrangement?" Edmund asked, nudging me. "Ala, the queen, yields the place of honour to the high priest. That indicates that our reception is essentially a religious one, and proves that our flight sunward has had the expected effect. Now we have the head of the religious order on our side. Human nature, if I may use such a term, is the same in whatever world you find it. Touch the imagination with some marvel and you awaken superstition; arouse superstition and you can do what you like."

It would be idle for me to attempt to describe our reception because Edmund himself could only make shrewd guesses as to the meaning of what went on, and you would probably not be particularly interested in his conjectures. Suffice it to say that when it was over, we felt that, for a time at least, we were virtually masters of the situation.

Only one thing troubled my mind—what did Ingra think and what would he do? At any rate, he, too, for the time being, seemed to have been carried away with the general feeling of wonder, and narrowly as I watched him I could detect in his features no sign of a wish to renew his persecution.

CHAPTER 18

Wild Eden

The next day after our return from the trip above the cloud dome, and our astonishing reception (you will, of course, understand the sense in which I use the term "day"), Edmund sprang another surprise upon us.

"I have persuaded Ala," he said, "to make a trip in the car."

"You don't mean it!"

"Oh, yes, and I am sure she will be delighted."

"But she is not going alone?"

"Surely no; she will be accompanied by one of her women—and by Ingra."

"Ingra!"

"Of course. Did you suppose that he would consent to be left behind? Ala herself would refuse to go without him."

"Then," I said, with deep disappointment, "he has resumed all his influence over her."

"I'm not sure he ever lost it," returned Edmund. "You forget his rank, and his position as her destined consort. Whatever we do we have got to count him in."

Jack raged inwardly, but said nothing. For my part, I almost wished Jack's bullet had not gone astray at that first memorable shooting.

"Now," Edmund continued, "the car, as you know, has but a limited amount of room. I do not wish to crowd it uncomfortably, but I can take six persons. Ala's party comprises three, so there is room for just two besides myself. You will have to draw lots."

"Is Juba included in the drawing?"

"Yes, and I'm half inclined to take him anyway, and let you three draw for the one place remaining."

"You can count me out," said Henry. "If there is another to stay with me I prefer to remain."

"Very well," said Edmund, "then Peter and Jack can draw lots."

"Since we can't all go," said Jack, "and since that fellow is to be of the party, I'll stay with Henry."

So it was settled without an appeal to chance, and I went with Edmund and Juba. As usual Edmund immediately put his project into execution. It showed an astonishing confidence in us that Ala should consent to make such a trip, and that her people, and especially Ingra, should assent to it, and I could not sufficiently wonder at the fact. But we were now at the summit of favour and influence, and it is impossible to guess what thoughts may have been in their minds. At any rate, it showed how completely Edmund had established himself in Ala's esteem, and I suspect that her woman's curiosity had played a large part in the decision. There was another thing which astonished me yet more, and, in fact, awakened a good deal of apprehension in my mind. I could not but wonder that Edmund, after all the precautions that he had previously taken, should now think of admitting these people into the car, where they could witness his manipulations of the mechanism. I spoke to him about it. "Rest your mind easy about that," he said. "Now that everything goes like a charm, they will suspect nothing. It will be all a complete mystery to them. Even the gods used natural agencies when they visited the earth without shaking the belief of mankind in them. I employ no force of which they have the least idea, and if they see me touch a button, or pull a knob, what can that convey to their minds except an impression of mysterious power?"

I said no more, but I was not convinced, and the sequel proved that, for once, Edmund had made a serious mistake, the more amazing because he had been the first to detect the exceptional intelligence and shrewdness of Ingra. But, no doubt, in the exultation of his recent triumph, he counted upon the strength of the superstitious regard in which we were held.

Our departure from the tower was the signal for the assembling of great crowds of spectators again, and we sailed away with the utmost *éclat*. Ala at once showed all the eager excitement of a child over so novel and enjoyable an experience. The motion of the car was entirely unlike that of the air ships. Perfectly steady, it skimmed along at a speed which filled her with amazement and delight. The city, with its towers, seemed to fly away from us by magic, and the trees and fields beneath ran into streaming lines. The windows were thrown wide open, and all stood by them, watching the scene. Finally Ala wished to go out on the window ledges, where one was perfectly secure if he kept a firm hold on the supports. Edmund was most of the time with us outside, only stepping within when he wished to change the course. I thought that he showed a disposition to conceal his manipulations as much as possible, as if what I had said had made an impression. But all were so much occupied with their novel sensations that, for the time at least, there was no danger of their taking note of anything else.

I believe that it must have been some intimation from Ala which finally led Edmund to hold his course toward the mountains, but in a direction different from that which led to the mines. When he had once chosen this direction he worked up the speed to fully a hundred miles an hour, and all were compelled to go inside on account of the wind created by our rush through the air. We held on thus for five hours. During this time Edmund spread a repast made up of dishes chosen from the supplies in the car, and, of course, utterly strange to our guests. They found them to their taste, however, and were delighted with Edmund's entertainment. We spent a long time at our little table, and I was surprised at the variety of delicious things which Edmund managed to extract from his stores. There was even some champagne, and I noticed that Edmund urged it upon Ingra, who, nothing loath, drank enough to make him decidedly tipsy, a fact which was not surprising since we had found that the wines of Venus were very light, and but slightly alcoholised.

At length we began to approach what proved to be the goal of our journey. Before us spread a vast extent of forest composed of trees of the most beautiful forms and foliage. Some towered up to a great height, spreading their pendulous branches over the less aspiring forms, like New England elms; others were low and bushy, and afire with scarlet blossoms, whose perfume filled the air; a few resembled gigantic grasses or great timothy stems, surmounted with nodding plumes of golden leaves, streaming out like gilt gonfalons in the breeze; but there was one species, as tall and massive as oaks, and scattered everywhere through the forest, that I could liken to nothing but enormous rose bushes in the full bloom of June. When we began to pass above this strange woodland, Ala made some communication to Edmund which caused him to slow down the movement of the car. By almost imperceptible touches he controlled the motive power, and presently we came to rest above a delightful glade, where a small stream ran at the foot of a gravelly slope, crowned with grass and overhung by trees.

Here the car was allowed to settle gently upon the ground, and all alighted. Ingra, over whom the influence of the champagne had been growing, tottered on his legs in a way that would have filled Jack with uncontrollable delight, but Edmund gravely helped him out of the car and steadied him to a seat on the soft turf under the tree. I saw Ala regarding Ingra with a puzzled look, and no wonder, for Edmund had been careful that no one else should take enough of the wine to produce more than the slightest exhilaration of spirits. It is possible that Edmund had plied Ingra with the idea of rendering him less observant, and it probably had that effect; but it resulted, as you will see presently, in a revelation which finally put Edmund on guard against the very danger to which he had seemed so insensible when I mentioned it to him before our start.

The place where we now were was, beyond comparison, the most charming that we had yet seen. A very Eden it seemed, wild, splendid, and remote from all cultivation. The air was loaded with indescribable fragrance shed from the thousands of strange blossoms that depended from trees and shrubs, and starred the rich grass. I learned afterwards from Edmund, who had it from Ala, that the spot was famous for its beauty and other attractions, and was sometimes visited in air ships from the capital. But for them, what took us but a few hours was a trip extending over several days of time. One would have said that the forest was imbedded in a garden of the most extraordinary orchids. The shapes of some of the flowers were so fantastic that it seemed impossible that Nature could have produced them. And their colours were no less unparalleled, inimitable, and incredible.

The flowery bank on which we had chosen our resting place was removed a few yards from the spot where the car rested, and the latter was hidden from view by intervening branches and huge racemes of gorgeous flowers, hanging like embroidered curtains about us. A peculiarity of the place was that little zephyr-like breezes seemed to haunt it, coming one could not tell whence, and they stirred the hanging blossoms, keeping them in almost continual rhythmic motion. The effect was wonderfully charming, but I observed that Ala was especially influenced by it. She sat with her maid beside her, and fixed her eyes, with an expression of ecstasy, upon the swinging flowers. I whispered to Edmund to regard her singular absorption. But he had already noticed it, and seemed to be puzzling his brain with thoughts that it suggested to him.

Thus as we sat, the leaves of a tree over our heads were lightly stirred, and a bird, adorned with long plumes more beautiful than those of a bird of paradise, alighted on a branch, and began to ruffle its iridescent feathers in a peculiar way. With every movement waves of colour seemed to flow over it, merging and dissolving in the most marvellous manner. As soon as this bird appeared, Ala gave it all her attention, and the pleasure which she experienced in watching it was reflected upon her countenance. She seemed positively enraptured. After a few moments the conviction came to me that she was *listening!* Her whole attitude expressed it. And yet not an audible sound came from the bird. At last I whispered to Edmund:

"Edmund, I believe that Ala hears something which we do not."

"Of course she does," was his reply. "There is music here, such music as was never heard on earth. That bird is *singing*, but our ears are not attuned to its strain. You know the peculiarity of this atmosphere with regard to sound, and that all of these people have a horror of loud noises. But their ears detect sounds which are beyond the range of the vibrations that affect ours. If you will observe the bird closely you will perceive that there is a slight movement of its throat. But that is not the greatest wonder, by any means. I am satisfied that there *is a direct relation here between sounds and colours.* The swaying of the flowers in the breeze and the rhythmic motion of the bird's plumage produce harmonious combinations and recombinations of colours which are transformed into sounds as exquisite as those of the world of insects. A cluster of blossoms, when the wind stirs them, shake out a kind of Aeolian melody, and it was that which so entranced Ala a few moments ago. She hears it still, but now it is mastered by the more perfect harmonies that come from the bird, partly from its throat but more from the agitation of its delicate feathers."

You may imagine the wonder with which I listened to this. It immediately recalled what Jack and I had observed at the shop of the bird fancier, and when the lady carried off her seemingly mute pets in the palanquin.

"But," I said, after a moment of reflection, "how can such a thing be? To me it seems surely impossible."

"I can only try to explain it by an analogy," said Edmund. "You know how, by a telephone, sounds are first transmuted into electric vibrations and afterwards reshaped into sonorous waves. You know, also, that we have used a ray of light to send telephonic messages, through the sensitiveness of a certain metal which changes its electric resistance in accord with the intensity of the light that strikes it. Thus with a beam of light we can reproduce the human voice. Well, what we have done awkwardly and tentatively by the aid of imperfect mechanical contrivances, Nature has here accomplished perfectly through the peculiar composition of the air and some special adjustment of the auditory apparatus of this people.

"Light and sound, colour and music, are linked for them in a manner entirely beyond our comprehension. It is plain to me now that the music of colour which we witnessed at the capital, was something far more complete and wonderful than I then imagined. Together with the pleasure which they derive from the harmonic combinations of shifting hues, they drink in, at the same time, the delight arising from sounds which are associated with, and, in many cases, awakened by, those very colours. It is probable that all their senses are far more fully, though more delicately, developed than ours. The perfume of these wonderful flowers is probably more delightful to Ala than to us. As there are sounds which they hear though inaudible to us, and colours visible to them which lie beyond the range of our vision, so there may be vibrations affecting the olfactory nerves which make no impression upon our sense of smell."

"Well, well," I exclaimed, "this seems appropriate to Venus."

"Yes," said Edmund with a smile, "it is appropriate; and yet I am not sure that some day we may not arrive at something of the kind on the earth."

I was about to ask him what he meant when there came an exciting interruption. Ingra, who had fallen more and more under the influence of the champagne, had stumbled to the other side of the little glade, virtually unnoticed, and Juba had wandered out of sight. Suddenly there came from the direction of the car the sound of a struggle mingled with inarticulate cries. We sprang to our feet, and, running to the car, found both Ingra and Juba inside it. The former had his hands on one of the knobs controlling the mechanism, and Juba had grasped him round the waist and was trying to drag him away. Ingra was resisting with all his strength, and uttering strange noises, whose sense, if they had any, we, of course, did not comprehend. Just as we reached the door, Juba succeeded in wrenching his opponent from his hold, and immediately gave him a fling which sent him clear out of the car, tumbling in a heap at our feet. Juba's eyes were ablaze with a dangerous light, but the moment he encountered Edmund's gaze he quietly walked away and sat down on the bank. Ala was immediately by our side, and I thought that I could read embarrassment as well as surprise in her looks. Fortunately the knob that Ingra had grasped had been thrown out of connection; else he and Juba might have made an involuntary voyage through space.

We picked up Ingra, found a seat for him, and Edmund, going down to the brook, filled a pocket flask with water and flung it in the fellow's face. This was repeated several times with the effect of finally straightening out his muddled senses sufficiently to warrant us in embarking for the return trip. All the way home Ingra was in a sulky mood, like any terrestrial drunkard after a debauch, but he kept his eyes on all Edmund's movements with an expression of cunning, which he had not sufficient self-command to conceal, and which could leave no doubt in our minds as to the nature of the quest which had led him into the car. As to Juba—although his interference had been of no practical benefit, since Ingra, especially in his present state, could surely have made no discovery of any importance—the devotion which he had again shown to our interests endeared him the more to us. Ala's manner showed that she was deeply chagrined, and thus our trip, which had opened so joyously, ended in gloom, and we were glad when the car again touched the platform, and our guests departed.

CHAPTER 19

The Secret of the Car

Jack and Henry were overjoyed to see us again, for after our departure they had fallen into a despondent mood, and began to imagine all sorts of evil.

"Jo!" was Jack's greeting; "I never was so glad to see anybody in my life. Edmund, don't you ever go off and leave any of us alone again."

"I'll never leave you again," responded Edmund. "You can count on that."

Then we told them the story of what we had seen, and of what had happened in the wild Eden that we had visited. They were not so much interested in the most wonderful thing of all—the combination of sound and colour—as they were in the conduct of Ingra. Jack laughed until he was tired over Ingra's drunkenness, but he drew a long face when he heard of the adventure in the car.

"Edmund," he said earnestly, "I am beginning to be of Henry's opinion; you had better get away from here without losing a moment."

"No," said Edmund, "we'll not go yet. The time hasn't come to run away. What difference does it make even if Ingra does suspect that the car is moved by some mechanism instead of by pure magic? He could not understand it if I should explain it to him."

"But you have said that he is extraordinarily intelligent."

"So he is, but his intelligence is limited by the world he lives in, and while there are many marvellous things here, nobody has the slightest conception of inter-atomic force. They have never heard even of radioactivity. At the same time I don't mean that they shall go nosing about the car. I'll take care of that."

"But," said Jack, "it grinds me to see that brute Ingra get off scot-free after trying to murder us. And what has he got against us, anyway? But for him we should never have had any trouble. He was against us from the beginning."

"I don't think he was particularly *against* us at the start," said Edmund. "Only he was for treating us with less consideration than Ala was disposed to show. But after the first accidental shooting, and the drubbing that Juba gave him, naturally his prejudices were aroused, and he could hardly be blamed for thinking us dangerous. Then, when he found himself defeated, and his wishes disregarded, on all sides, he began to hate us. It is easy enough to account for his feelings. Now, since our recent astonishing triumph, being himself incredulous about our celestial origin, he will try to undermine us by showing that our seeming miracle is no miracle at all."

"And you gave him the chance by taking him in the car!" I could not help exclaiming.

"Yes," said Edmund, with a smile. "I admit that I made a mistake. I counted too much upon the influence of the sense of mystery. But it will come out all right."

"I doubt it," I persisted. "He will never rest now until he has found out the secret."

Nothing more was said on the subject, but Edmund was careful not to leave the car unguarded. It was always kept afloat, though in contact with the landing. The expenditure of energy needed to keep it thus anchored without support was, Edmund assured us, insignificant in comparison with the quantity stored in his mysterious batteries.

We were not long in finding, on all sides, evidence that our trip up through the cloud dome had been a master stroke, and that the presumable incredulity of Ingra with regard to our claims was not shared by others. He might have his intimates, who entertained prejudices against us resembling his own, but if so we saw nothing of them. In fact, Ingra was much less in evidence than before, but I did not feel reassured by that; on the contrary, it made me all the more fearful of some plot on his part, and Jack was decidedly of my opinion.

"Hang him!" he said, "he's up to some mischief, and I know it. Much as I detest him, I'd rather have him *in* sight than *out*, just now. He makes me feel like a snake in a bush; if he'd only show his ugly head, or spring his rattle, I'd be more comfortable."

But the kindness and deference with which we were treated, and the new wonders that were shown to us in the capital, gradually drove Ingra from our minds. Now we were permitted to enter the temples without opposition, our presence there according with our new character of "children of the sun." We saw the worship that was offered before the solar images by family parties, and attended, as favoured guests, the periodical ceremonies in the great temple. Edmund confessed that the high priest greatly embarrassed him by staring into his eyes, and plainly assuming that he knew things of which he was profoundly ignorant.

"The hardest thing I ever undertook," he said, "is to hold my mind in suspense during these trying interviews, when he endeavours to read the depths of my soul, and I to throw a veil over them which he cannot penetrate."

In some way, Edmund discovered that the high priest and all the priests connected with the sun worship (and they certainly bore a family likeness) belonged to a special race, whose roots ran back into the most remote antiquity, and about whose persons clung a sacredness that placed them, in some respects, above the royal family itself. We frequently visited the great library, where Edmund undertook a study of the language of the printed rolls, though what he made of it I never clearly understood. I do not think that he succeeded in deciphering any of it. He also spent much time studying their mechanics and engineering, for which he professed great admiration.

But most interesting of all to us was what Edmund himself accomplished. I have told you of his remark about the colour-sound music, viz., that he thought it not impossible that even human senses might be enabled to appreciate it. Well, he actually realized that wildly improbable dream! He fitted up a laboratory of his own in which he laboured sometimes for twenty hours at a stretch, and at last he brought to us the astonishing invention he had made.

I can make no pretence of understanding it; although Edmund declared that, in substance, it was no more wonderful than a telephone. The machine consisted of a little metal box. (He made three of them, and I have mine yet, but it will not work on the earth, and it lies on my table as I write, serving for the most wonderful paper weight that a man ever possessed.) When this box was pressed against the ear in front of one of the revolving disks that threw out blending colours, or in the presence of a "singing" bird, the most divine harmonies seemed to awake *in the brain*. I cannot make the slightest approach to a description of the marvellous phenomenon. One felt his whole being infused with ecstatic joy. It was the very soul of music itself, celestial, ineffable! The wonder-box also enabled us to catch many sounds peculiar to the atmosphere of Venus, formed of vibrations, as Edmund had explained, that lie outside our gamut. But to these, apart from the music, I could never listen. They were *too* abnormal, filling one with inexplicable terror, as if he had been snatched out of nature and compelled to listen to the sounds of a preternatural world. The only sound that I ever heard with my natural ear which bore the slightest resemblance to these was the awful piercing whistle of the monster that killed Ala's man.

Yet we derived immense pleasure from the possession of those little boxes. With their aid, we could appreciate the exquisite melodies that were played everywhere—in great halls where thousands were assembled, in the temples great and small, and in the homes of the people, to which we were often admitted. In every house there was on one of the walls a "musical rose," whose harmonies entranced the visitor. And the variety of musical *motifs* seemed to be absolutely without limit. One was never tired of the entertainment because there was so little repetition.

On one ever-memorable occasion we heard the great national, or, as Edmund preferred to call it, "racial" hymn, played in the air from the principal tower. When we had only beheld the play of colours characterizing this composition we had found it altogether delightful, although, as I have said, Edmund detected, even then, some underlying tone of sadness or despair; but when its *sounds* broke into the brain the effect was overwhelming. The entire thing seemed to have been "written in a minor key," of infinite world-embracing pathos. The listener was plunged into depths of feeling that seemed unfathomable, eternal—and unendurable.

"Heavens!" whispered Jack to me in an awed voice, dropping the box from his ear, "I can't *stand* it!"

I saw tears running down his face, and felt them on my own. Edmund and Henry were equally affected, and could not continue to listen. Edmund said nothing, but I recalled his words about the traditional belief of this people that their world had entered upon the last stage of its existence. Then I watched the countenances about us; they wore an expression of solemnity, and yet there was something which spoke of an uplifting pride, awakened by the great paean, and swelling the heart with memories of interminable ages of past glory.

"Come," said Edmund at last, turning away, "this is not for us. The measureless sadness we feel, but the triumphant reflection of ancestral greatness is for them alone. Heavens! what an artist he must have been who composed this!—if it be not like the Iliad, the work of an age rather than of a man."

We almost forgot the passage of time in the enjoyment of our now delightful and untroubled existence, but there came at last a rude awakening from this life, which had become for us like a dream.

As I have said, we had ceased to worry about Ingra, whom we seldom saw, and who, when we did see him, gave no indication of continued enmity. At first we had kept the car under continual surveillance, but as time went on we became careless in this respect, and at last we did not guard it at all.

One day, during the time of repose, I happened to be, with Juba, in our room on that stage of the great tower where the car was anchored, while Edmund and the others were below in the palace. Juba was already asleep, and I was lying down and courting drowsiness, when a slight noise outside attracted my attention. I stepped softly to the door and looked out. The door of the car was open! Supposing that Edmund was there I approached to speak to him. By good fortune I was wearing the soft slippers worn by everybody here, and which we had adopted, so that my footsteps made no sound.

As I reached the car door and looked in, I nearly dropped in the intensity of my surprise and consternation. There, at the farther end, was Ingra, on his knees before the mechanical mouths which swallowed the invisible elements of power from the air; and beside him was another, also on his knees, and busy with tools, apparently trying to detach the things. The explanation flashed over my mind; Ingra had brought a skilled engineer to aid him in discovering the secret of the car, and, no doubt, to rob it of its mysterious mechanism. They seemed to fear no interruption, because Ingra had undoubtedly informed himself of the fact that for a day or two past we had abandoned the use of our room in the tower, and taken our repose in our apartments in the palace. It was by mere chance that Juba and I had, on this occasion, remained so long aloft that I had decided to take our sleep in the tower room.

Anticipating no surveillance, Ingra was not on his guard, and had no idea that I was behind him. Instinctively I grasped for my pistol but instantly remembered that it was with my coat in the room. I tiptoed back, awoke Juba, making him a sign to be noiseless, got the pistol, and returned, without a sound, to the open door of the car with Juba at my heels. They were yet on their knees, with their heads under the shelf, and I heard the slight grating made by the tool that Ingra's assistant was using. The pistol was in my hand. What should I do? Shoot him down without warning, or trust to the strength of Juba to enable us to overcome them both and make them prisoners?

While I hesitated, and it was but a moment, Ingra suddenly rose to his feet and confronted us. An exclamation burst from his lips, and the other sprang up. I covered Ingra with the pistol and pulled the trigger. There was not a sound! The sickening remembrance then burst over me that I had not reloaded the pistol since Edmund had emptied its whole chamber in the closing fight with the tarantula of the swamps. Ingra, followed by his man, sprang upon me like a tiger. In a twinkling I lay on my back, and before I could recover my feet, I saw Juba and Ingra in a deadly struggle, while the other ran away and disappeared. Jumping up I ran to Juba's assistance, but the fight was so furious, and the combatants whirled so rapidly, that I could get no hold. I saw, however, that Juba was more than a match for his opponent, and I darted into the car to get one of the automatic rifles, thinking that I could use it as a club to put an end to the struggle if the opportunity should offer. But the locker was firmly closed and I could not open it. After a minute of vain efforts I returned to the combatants and found that Juba had nearly completed his mastery. He had Ingra doubled over his knee and was endeavouring to pinion his hands.

At this instant, when the victory seemed complete, and our enemy in our power, Juba uttered a faint cry and fell in a heap. Blood instantly stained the floor around him, and Ingra, with a bound, dropping a long knife, attained the door of a nearby chamber, and was out of sight before I could even start to pursue him. Nevertheless, I ran after him, but quickly became involved in a labyrinth where it was useless to continue the search, and where I nearly lost my way.

I then returned to see how seriously Juba had been wounded. He had crawled into the car. I bent over him—he was dead! The knife had inflicted a fearful wound, and it seemed wonderful that he could have made his way unassisted even over the short distance from where he was struck down to the door of the car.

Juba dead! I felt faint and sick! But the critical nature of the emergency helped to steady my nerves by giving me something else to think of and to do. Edmund must be called at once. There were no "elevators" running regularly during the general hours of repose, and I did not know the way up and down the tower by the ladder-like stairways which connected the stages. But there were signals by which the little craft that served as elevators could be summoned in case of necessity, and I pulled one of the signal cords. It seemed an age before the air ship came, and another before I could reach Edmund.

His great self-control enabled him to conceal his grief at my news, but Jack was overcome. He had really loved Juba almost as if he had been human and a brother. The big-hearted fellow actually sobbed as if his heart would break. Then came the reaction, and I should never have believed that Jack Ashton could exhibit such malevolent ferocity. His lips all but foamed, as he fairly shouted, striking his big fists together:

"This'll be *my* job! Edmund! Peter! You hear me! Don't either of you dare to lay a hand on *that devil! He's mine!* Oh! I'll—" But he could not finish his sentence for gnashing his teeth.

We calmed him as best we could and then summoned an air ship. While we waited, Edmund suddenly put his hand in his pocket, and withdrawing it quickly, said, with a bitter smile:

"What a fool I have been in my carelessness. Ingra has had the key abstracted from my pocket by some thief. That explains how he got the car open."

The moment the ship came we hurriedly ascended to the platform. When Edmund saw poor Juba's body lying in the car and learned how he had made his way there to die, he was more affected than when he first heard of his death.

"He has died for us," he said solemnly; "he has crawled here as to a refuge, and here he shall remain until I can bury him among his people in his old home. Would to God I had never taken him from it!"

"Then you will start at once for the dark hemisphere?" I asked.

"At the earliest possible moment; and it shall be on the way to our own home."

But we were not to depart before even a more terrible tragedy had darkened over us, for now the tide of fate was suddenly running at flood.

The Corybantia of the Sun

I have several times mentioned Edmund's half-formed impression that there was some very remarkable ceremony connected with the cyclical apparition of the sun before the eyes of its worshipers. He had said, you may recall, that it seemed probable that the religious rites on these rare occasions bore some resemblance to the *bacchanalia*, or *dionysia*, of ancient Greece. How he had derived that idea I do not know, but it proved to have been but too well founded—-only he had not guessed the full truth. The followers of Dionysus made themselves drunken with the wine of their god and then indulged in the wildest excesses. Here, as we were now to learn, the worshipers of the sun were seized with another kind of madness, leading to scenes that I believe, and hope, have never had their parallel upon the earth.

With our hearts sore for Juba, we had completed our preparations for departure within six hours after his tragic death. Ala had been informed of the tragedy, and had visited the car and looked upon the dead form, which I thought greatly affected her. Edmund held little communication with her, but it was evidently with her cooperation that he was able to procure a kind of coffin, in which we placed Juba's body. I do not know whether Edmund informed her of his purpose to quit the planet, but she must have known that we were going to convey our friend somewhere for interment.

We were actually on the point of casting loose the car, Ala and a crowd of attendants watching our movements, when there came the second great sound of united voices which we had heard in this speechless world. It rose like a sudden wail from the whole city. There was a rushing to and fro, Ala's face grew as pale as death, and her attendants fell upon their knees and began to lift their hands heavenward, with an expression of terror and wild appeal.

At the same time we noticed a sudden brightening about us, and Edmund stepping out on the platform, immediately beckoned, with the first signs of uncontrollable excitement that I had ever seen him display. I was instantly at his side, and a single glance told the story.

High in the heavens, the sun had burst forth in all its marvellous splendour!

A vast rift was open in the cloud dome, through which the gigantic god of day poured down his rays with a fierceness that was inconceivable. The heat was like the blast of a furnace, and I felt my head beginning to swim.

"Quick!" cried Edmund, grasping my sleeve and pulling me into the car. "These rays are fatal! My God, what a sight!"

As by magic the atmosphere had become crowded with air ships, and throngs of thousands were pouring from them upon the great platform and the other stages, as well as upon the surrounding towers. Every available space was filling up with people hastening from below. As fast as they arrived they threw themselves into the most extraordinary postures of adoration, lifting hands and eyes to the sun. I remember thinking, in a flash, that the intense glare of light must burn to the very sockets of their eyes—but they did not flinch. It was evident, however, that those who looked directly in the sun's face were blinded.

I looked round for Ala, and noticed with a thrill that her beautiful eyes were wide open and glancing with an expression that I cannot describe, over her kneeling people. Beside her was the towering form of the great priest, who was staring straight at the sun—and yet, although his eyes were open, it was evident that they were not rendered altogether sightless even by that awful light. They burned like coals. He was making strange gestures with his long arms, and in unison with his every movement a low, heart-thrilling sound came from the throats of the multitude.

Edmund, at my shoulder, muttered under his breath:

"Shall I try to save her from this?—But to what good?"

For a moment he seemed to hesitate, and I thought that he was about to rush out upon the platform and seize Ala in order to rescue her from some danger that he foresaw; when, all at once, the multitude rose to its feet, staggering, and began to rush to and fro, colliding with one another, falling, rising again, grappling, struggling, uttering terrible cries—and then I saw the flash of knives.

"Good heavens!" shouted Edmund. "It is the ultraviolet rays! They have gone mad!"

In the meantime the gigantic high priest whirled upon his heel, swinging his arms abroad and uttering a kind of chant which was audible above the dreadful clamour of the rabid multitude. Though he had no weapon, he seemed the inspirer of this Aceldama, and around him its fury raged. Presently he drew close to Ala, who still stood motionless, as if petrified by the awful scene. I felt Edmund give a violent start, and before I comprehended his intention, he had dashed from the car, and was forcing his way through the struggling throng toward the queen.

"Edmund!" I shouted. "For God's sake, come back!"

Jack started to follow him, but I held him back with all my strength.

"Let me go!" he yelled. "Edmund will be killed!"

"And you, too!" I answered. "Break open the locker and get the guns!"

Jack threw himself upon the door of the locker, and strove to wrench it open. Meanwhile, half paralyzed with excitement, I remained standing at the door. I saw Edmund hurl aside those who attacked him, and push on toward his goal. But a minute later a knife reached him, and he fell.

"Quick, Jack, quick!" I shouted; "Edmund is down!"

He had not got the locker open, but he darted to my side, and together we rushed out into the press. Shall I ever forget that moment! We were pushed, hustled, struck, hurled to and fro; but we had only a few steps to go, and we reached our leader where he lay. Seizing him, we succeeded somehow in carrying him into the car. Our clothes were torn, our hands and faces were bleeding, and there was blood on Jack's shoulder. Edmund was alive. We placed him on a bench, and then the fascination of the spectacle without again enchained us.

Suddenly my eyes fell upon Ingra, who had not previously made his appearance. He was as insane as the others, and like many of them had a knife in his hand. In a moment he pushed his way toward Ala, and my heart rose in my throat, for I did not know what mad thought might be in his mind. If I had had a weapon, I believe I should have shot him, but before he had arrived within three yards of the queen there came an explosion of flame—I do not know how else to describe it, for it was so sudden—and the great platform was instantly wrapped in licking tongues of fire.

The wickerwork caught like tinder, and the gauzy screws threw off streams of sparks like so many Fourth of July pinwheels. The gush of heat from the conflagration was terrible, and I turned my eyes in horror from the stricken multitude which seemed to have been shocked back into sanity by the sudden universal danger only to find itself a helpless prey to the flames.

"It's all over with them!" cried Jack.

His words awoke me to our own danger. We must get away instantly. Knowing the proper button to touch to throw the mechanism into action, I pushed it forcibly and pulled out a knob which I had often seen Edmund manipulate in starting the car. It responded immediately, and in a second we were afloat, and clear of the tower. Seeing that the direction which the car was taking would remove us from the reach of the flames, and that there was nothing ahead to obstruct its progress, and knowing that Edmund often left it to run of itself when the speed was slow, and there was no occasion to change its course, I now hurried with Jack to Edmund's side. Henry all this time had been lying on a bench like one in a trance.

Jack and I stripped off Edmund's coat, and at once saw the nature of his wound. A knife had penetrated his side, and there was considerable effusion of blood, but I was surgeon enough to feel sure that the wound was not mortal. He roused up as he felt us working over him, and opening his eyes, said faintly:

"You will find bandages under the locker. What has happened? We are moving."

"The tower is all in flames!" exclaimed Jack, before I could interrupt him, for I should have preferred not to tell Edmund the real situation just at that moment.

Jack's words roused him like an electric shock. He pushed us aside, and struggled to his feet. Then he sprang to a knob, and brought the car to rest.

We had been moving slowly, and had not gone more than a quarter of a mile from the tower. The car had swung round so that the fire was not visible from the open door, but now, as Edmund arrested its progress, it swayed back again and the spectacle burst into view. The heat smote us in the face even at this distance. In the few minutes since I had last seen the tower the flames had made incredible progress. The whole of the immense structure was blazing. Spires of flame leaped and swayed from its summit, partitions were falling, platforms giving way, and hundreds of air ships caught by the sheets of fire were crumpling and falling in swooping curves like birds whose wings had been seared. I was thankful that we could not see the unfortunates who were perishing in that furnace. It was but too evident that not a soul on the tower could have escaped.

I glanced at Edmund's face. It was pale and set—the face of a man gazing upon an awful tragedy with which he is absolutely powerless to interfere. His breath came quick, but he did not utter a word. Then came the reaction, and, staggering, he leaned on my shoulder, and I led him to the bench from which he had risen. For a moment I thought he had fainted, but when I put a flask to his lips he swallowed a mouthful and immediately recovered sufficient strength to sit up, resting his head on his hand.

"Had we not better go on?" I asked.

"Ye-es," he replied, after a moment's hesitation. "We can do nothing. They are all gone; the queen has perished with the rest! Pull out that knob on the right, but gently, and then push this button. We must circle round the outskirts until we see whether the fire will seize upon the other towers and extend to the city below."

I followed his directions, and, as we started our circuit, the vast tower suddenly swayed aside, and then, tumbling in upon itself, it went down in a whirl of smoke and eddying sparks.

As far as we could see none of the other aerial structures had caught fire. The entire absence of wind was no doubt the favourable circumstance that saved them. But all the towers were swaying under the impulse imparted to them by the excited multitudes that crowded their platforms. Although the light of the conflagration faded as soon as the principal tower fell, the others continued to shine brilliantly in the solar rays, but suddenly, as we watched, the splendour failed, and the subdued illumination characteristic of the endless daylight under the great dome took its place. The rift in the clouds above had closed as unexpectedly as it had recently opened, and the sun was no longer visible. It had been in view less than an hour, but in that brief space what scenes had been enacted!

Presently Edmund, shaking his head sadly, said:

"It is useless to stay longer. Even if the conflagration should spread we could do nothing to help the unfortunates. They must depend upon themselves."

He then gave me directions for changing our course to a direct line away from the city, at the same time increasing the speed. In the meantime he himself aided in binding up his wound.

"If there were the slightest chance that Ala could have escaped," he said, after a few minutes, "I would remain here, and search for her, but it is only too clear what her fate has been. She was really our only friend, and now that she is gone, we must get away from the sight and memory of these things as quickly as possible."

Seeing that his strength was gradually coming back to him, and secretly rejoicing that he bore this terrible blow so stoically, I felt that we might now converse about the catastrophe which we had witnessed.

"What do you think was the cause of the sudden outburst of fire?" I asked.

"It could hardly have been the direct action of the sunlight," he replied. "It must have resulted from some accidental concentration of the solar rays upon an inflammable substance by a mirror."

"I recall seeing a large concave glass on the principal platform in which they were fond of looking at their magnified images," I said.

"Yes, and no doubt that was the instrument chosen by fate to bring about this terrible end. The power of the sunbeams is twice as great here as upon the earth, and the heat in the focus of a mirror a couple of feet in diameter would suffice to set fire to the flimsy materials which abounded on the tower. Once started in such a place it ran like sparks in a train of gunpowder."

"But the madness that seized the multitude before the catastrophe—what did you mean by saying that it was the ultraviolet rays?"

"I used the term," Edmund replied slowly, "without attaching a very clear meaning to it. It simply expressed the general thought that was in my mind. It may be some other form of solar radiation to which we are not accustomed on the earth, but which is specially effective here when the sun is uncovered because of the greater nearness of Venus. This atmosphere, notwithstanding its density, may well be diaphanous to the ultraviolet rays, owing to some peculiarity in its composition which I have not had time to study. At any rate, it is evident, from what we have seen, that the rays of the unclouded sun almost instantly affect the brain. I, myself, felt them as if a thousand needles had been thrust through my skull; and I believe that they are responsible, rather than the shock of the wound in my side, for my present weakness."

"And did you foresee the consequences of the uncovering of the sun?"

"Not altogether. I had been led to think that something extraordinary must accompany the periodical appearances of the great orb, and if I could have known that an apparition was at hand I might have made preparations for it and we might have been able to save Ala. When I saw what was going on, I tried to reach her, and you know the result."

"But is it not incredible that a people of so peaceable a disposition should be seized with such murderous instincts when driven out of their senses by the effect of the rays?"

"No, it does not seem so to me. You know the general tendency of sudden madness, which usually produces a complete reversal of the ordinary instincts of the demented persons, making them dangerous to their dearest friends. But why talk longer of this? It is too painful—too overwhelming. What can man do against the great forces of Nature? At this moment I solemnly declare to you that I regret that I ever entered upon this expedition."

While we had been talking, the car had receded to a great distance from the city, and now all but the tops of a few of the airy pinnacles were lost to our sight forever. But as we gazed, straining our sight for a last look, we perceived a familiar flickering of prismatic lightning on the horizon. We glanced at each other meaningly. It was the colour speech again. But, oh, what must be the burden of their communications now! Suddenly, Edmund, whose eyes were fixed with intensity upon the scene, remarked, half shuddering:

"It is the great Paean."

Seized with curiosity, I pressed the magic box to my ear, and faintly there echoed in my brain a few disconnected strains of that solemn music. But now, more than ever, it was insufferable to me, and I dropped the box with a crash.

As Edmund recovered his strength he once more took charge of the car, and in a little while he had risen to a great height in order to take advantage of the easier going in the lighter atmosphere above. Thus we ran on for several hours until we began to catch sight of the sea, which was soon beneath us, while far ahead we saw the tumbling clouds marking the location of the belt of tempests behind which we knew lay the range of the crystal mountains. At length we issued from beneath the cloud dome, and then we saw the sun again, and the storms whipping the waters, whose waves occasionally flashed up at us through rifts in the streaming clouds beneath. And at last the icy peaks began to glitter on the horizon, and we knew that we were nearing the world of eternal night and frost. It was with strange feelings that we once more beheld the crystal mountains, for our minds were filled with the recollection of the scenes that had occurred among them when we were helpless in the grasp of their tempests. But now there was a certain exhilaration in the thought that this time we could safely sail over their summits. As we passed over them we looked eagerly for landmarks that might show where our former passage had occurred, and as Edmund purposely dropped as close to their summits as it was safe to go, I at last believed that I recognized the mighty peak of rainbows that had so nearly wrecked us.

When we had left the mountains behind and entered into the region of night, I asked Edmund how he would proceed in order to find the location of the caverns.

"I shall go by the stars," he said. "I noted the bearing of the place, and I have no doubt that I can find it again."

The Earth

Edmund's reference to the stars instantly drew my attention to the heavens. They were ablaze with amazing gems, but at first I could not see the earth among them.

"I know what you are looking for," said Edmund. "Here, look through the peephole in the bow. From our present position the earth appears but little elevated above the horizon, but when we reach the caverns, which are in the centre of the dark hemisphere, we shall see her overhead."

I knelt at the peephole, and my heart was in my throat. There was our glorious planet, oh, so bright! and close beside her the moon. At the sight, an irrepressible longing arose in me to be once more at home. Jack and Henry took their turns at looking, and they were no less affected than I had been. But Edmund retained a perfect self-command:

"Do you know," he asked with an odd smile (for now the lamps were glowing, and we had plenty of light in the car), "how long we have been absent from home?"

Not one of us had kept a record.

"It is just six hundred and four days," he continued, "since we left New York. We were sixteen days on our way to Venus; six days after our arrival at the caverns occurred the conjunction of the earth, and the ceremonies that Peter will not forget as long as he refrains from hair dye; two days later we departed for the sun lands; and since then five hundred and eighty days have passed. Now, between one conjunction of the earth and Venus to the next, five hundred and eighty-four days elapse. Already five hundred and eighty-two of those days have passed, so that within two days another conjunction will occur, and if we are then at the caverns we shall doubtless witness another sacrifice to the earth and the moon."

"God forbid!" I exclaimed.

"I feel as you do," said Edmund. "We have seen enough of such things. In order, then, to hasten our arrival at the caverns, where we must bury Juba, for on that I insist, I am going to rise up out of the atmosphere, in order that we may fly with planetary speed. We can thus reach the caverns, traversing the five thousand miles of distance that yet remain, in something like an hour, for some time must be lost in rising out of and returning into the atmosphere, and in the meantime I must make observations to determine our location. Having found the caverns we will complete our rites at Juba's grave, and get away for good before the sacrificial ceremonies begin."

It was a programme that suited us all, and it was quickly carried out. I had not thought that my admiration of Edmund's ability could be increased, but it was carried a notch higher when I saw how easily, guiding himself by the ever-visible stars, he located the caverns. When he knew that he was directly over them he dropped the car swiftly, and we could not repress a cry as we saw directly beneath us the familiar shafts of light issuing from the ground.

"We may have to do a little searching," said Edmund, as we approached the lights, "for, of course, my observations are not accurate enough to enable me to locate the exact spot where we landed before."

But fortune favoured us marvellously, and the very first opening that we approached was at once recognized, for there stood the sacrificial altar.

We anchored the car near the shaft, and carried out Juba's coffin.

"Wait here," said Edmund, "while I descend."

"No, you're not going alone," exclaimed Jack. "I'll go with you."

Edmund made no objection and he and Jack descended the steps. Half an hour elapsed before they returned, accompanied by a dozen of the natives, stolid, and not exhibiting the signs of surprise over our return which I had expected to see. Edmund had now made so much progress in their strange means of communication that he had little difficulty in causing them to comprehend what was wanted. They easily carried the coffin, and all of us followed down into the depths. It was the strangest funeral procession that ever a man saw!

While the grave was being prepared in the underground cemetery where we had witnessed the interment of the first victim of our pistols, Henry and I remained as a sort of guard of honour for Juba in the lower of the two great chambers which have been described in the earlier chapters of this history, and there a most singular thing occurred. We were startled by a low whining, and looking about saw one of the doglike creatures which appeared to be the only inhabitants of the caverns except the natives seated on its haunches close to the coffin, and exhibiting exactly the signs of distress that a dog sometimes displays over its dead master. That we were taken aback by this scene I need not assure you. We had never observed, during our former visit, that either Juba or any of his people was followed by these creatures; in fact, they had always fled at our approach, and we had paid little attention to them.

But now, if the poor animal could have spoken, he could not more plainly have told us that, by means of the mysterious instinct which beings of his kind possess, he had recognized the presence of his old master, and was mourning for him. It was truly a touching spectacle, and Henry was hardly less moved by it than I. When Edmund and Jack came back, having superintended the preparations, Jack was cut to the heart by the sight. Immediately he declared that the "dog" must accompany us in the car, and Edmund assented by a grave inclination of the head. The animal followed us to the grave, and remained there watching us intently. He seemed to have dismissed his fear, as if he comprehended that we were friends of his master.

There were not more than twenty of the natives present at the interment, and none of them showed signs of sorrow. And when the grave was closed and we turned away, the little creature followed at our heels. Edmund had carved on a flat stone the word "JUBA," and left it lying on the grave, and Jack, having nothing else, threw a silver dollar on top of it. The natives probably regarded these things as talismans, or religious symbols, for they treated them with the greatest deference, and no doubt they lie there yet, and will continue to lie there through all the eons, for in those dry caverns the progress of decay can hardly be perceptible even after the passage of ages. It was a singular fact, noted by Edmund, that the natives exhibited not the slightest curiosity concerning their comrades who had been lost in the crystal mountains, and I really doubt whether they knew what the coffin contained.

When we had paid the last honours to Juba, we began to think of our final departure. This place had become disagreeable to us. After the brilliant scenes that we had witnessed on the other side of the planet, the gloom here, and the absence of all that had made the land of perpetual daylight seem a paradise of beauty, were intensely oppressive to our spirits. But Edmund still wished to make some investigations, and we were compelled to await his movements. What the nature of his investigations was I do not know, for I was devoured by the desire to get away, and did not inquire. But fully twenty-four hours had elapsed before our leader was ready to depart. In the meanwhile "Juba's dog" had become firmly attached to Jack, who petted it as probably no creature of its race had ever been petted before. It was a strange-looking animal; about as large as a terrier, with a big square head, covered with long black hair, while, in startling imitation of the hirsute adornment of the natives themselves, its body was clothed with a golden-white pelt of silky texture. It would eat anything we offered it, and seemed immensely pleased with its new master, as it had every reason for being.

During the last hours of our stay we noticed unmistakable indications of preparation for the dreaded ceremonies of the conjunction, and our departure was hastened on that account. The priests, whom Edmund had been compelled to put out of the way of further mischief on the former occasion, had been replaced by others, and we thought that, perhaps, this being the first opportunity for the display of their functions, they would try to make it memorable—which presented a still stronger reason why we should not delay. But, with one thing and another, we were held back until the very eve of the ceremonies.

When we finally stood ready to enter the car, with Juba's dog at Jack's heels, the procession up the steps had already begun. Edmund decided to wait until the multitude had all assembled. They came trooping up into the starlight, and I am sure that they had no idea of what we intended to do. Undoubtedly they must have recalled what had happened on the other occasion, but they showed no sign of either regret or anxiety on that account. They arranged themselves in a dense circle, as before, and the priests took their place in the centre. At this moment Edmund gave the word to enter the car. We sprang into it, and immediately Jack and I went out on a window ledge in order to get a better view of the scene. Edmund started the car, and we rose straight toward the earth which glowed in the zenith. Our movement was unexpected, and we at once arrested the attention even of the priests. The beginning of the ceremony was stopped short. All eyes were evidently drawn to us, and when they saw the direction that we were taking a low murmur arose.

"Let me give them a parting salute," said Jack.

Edmund thought a moment, and then said:

"Very well, take a gun, but don't fire at them. If it terrifies them into abandoning their sacrifice we shall have done one good thing in this world."

Jack instantly had the gun roaring, and although we were now high above their heads, we could see that they were seized with consternation, rising from their knees, and running wildly about. Whether the noise and the sight of us flying toward the earth, had the effect which Edmund had hoped for, will never be known; but the last sight we had of living beings on Venus was the spectacle of those white forms darting about in the starry gloom.

Our long journey home was interrupted by one more almost tragic episode. When we had been ten days in flight, and the earth had become like a round moon of dazzling brilliance, Juba's dog, which had grown feeble and refused to eat, died. Jack was broken-hearted, and protested when Edmund said that the body of the animal must be thrown out. He would have liked to try to stuff the skin, but Edmund was firm.

"But if you open a window," I said, "the air will escape."

"Some of it will undoubtedly escape," Edmund replied. "But, luckily, this is the air of Venus which we are carrying, and being very dense, we can spare a little of it without serious results. I shall be quick, and there will be no danger."

It was as he had said. When the window was partially opened, for only a second or two, we distinctly felt a lowering of the atmospheric pressure that made us gasp for a moment, but instantly Edmund had the window closed again, and we were all right. As we shot away we saw the little white body gleaming in the sunlight like a thistledown, and then it disappeared forever.

"It is a new planet born," said Edmund, "and the law of gravitation will pay it as much attention as if it were a Jupiter. It may wander in space for untold ages, and sometime it may even fall within the sphere of the earth's attraction, and then Jack's wish will have been fulfilled; but it will be but a flying spark, flashing momentarily in the heavens as it shoots through the air."

* * * * * * * *

Our home-coming was a strange one. For some reason of his own Edmund did not wish to take the car to New York. He landed in the midst of the Adirondack woods, far from any habitation, and there, concealed in a swamp, he insisted upon leaving the car. We made our way out of the wilderness to the nearest railway station, and our first care was to visit a barber and a clothing merchant. Probably, as we carried some of the guns, they took us for a party of hunters who wished to furbish up before revisiting civilization.

On reaching New York, we went, in the evening, straight to the Olympus Club, where our arrival caused a sensation. We found Church in the old corner, staring dejectedly at a newspaper. He did not see who was approaching him. Jack slapped him on the shoulder, and as he looked up and recognized us he fell back nearly fainting, and with mouth open, unable to utter a word.

"Come, old man," said Jack, "so we've found you! What did you run away for? Let me introduce you to the Columbus of Space, and don't you forget that I'm one of his lieutenants."

I don't think that Church has ever fully believed our story. He thinks, to this day, that we lost our "balloon," as he calls it, and invented the rest. We purposely allowed the newspaper reporters to take the same view of the case, but when we four were alone we unburdened our hearts, and relived the marvellous life of Venus. I use the past tense, because I have yet to tell you most disquieting news.

Edmund has disappeared.

Within three months after our return he bade us good night at an unusually early hour and we have never seen him since, although more than a year has now elapsed since he went out of the room at the Olympus. Jack and I have made every effort to find a trace of him, without avail. Led by a natural suspicion, we have ransacked the Adirondack woods, but we could never satisfy ourselves that we had found the place where the car was left. Henry persists in the belief that Edmund is trying in secret to develop his invention, with the intention of "revolutionizing industry and making himself a multibillionaire." But Jack and I know better! Wherever he may be, whatever may occupy his wonderful powers, we feel that the ordinary concerns of the earth have no interest for him. Yet we are sure that if he is alive he often thinks of us.

Last night as Jack and I were walking to the club with my completed manuscript under my arm, a falling star shot across the sky.

"Do you know what that recalls to me?" asked Jack, with a far-off expression in his eyes.

"What?"

"Juba's dog."

Neither of us spoke again before we reached the clubhouse steps, but I am certain that through both our minds there streamed a glittering procession of such memories as life on this planet could never give birth to. And they ended with a sigh.

The Moon Metal

CHAPTER 1

South Polar Gold

When the news came of the discovery of gold at the south pole, nobody suspected that the beginning had been reached of a new era in the world's history. The newsboys cried "Extra!" as they had done a thousand times for murders, battles, fires, and Wall Street panics, but nobody was excited. In fact, the reports at first seemed so exaggerated and improbable that hardly anybody believed a word of them. Who could have been expected to credit a despatch, forwarded by cable from New Zealand, and signed by an unknown name, which contained such a statement as this:

"A seam of gold which can be cut with a knife has been found within ten miles of the south pole."

The discovery of the pole itself had been announced three years before, and several scientific parties were known to be exploring the remarkable continent that surrounds it. But while they had sent home many highly interesting reports, there had been nothing to suggest the possibility of such an amazing discovery as that which was now announced. Accordingly, most sensible people looked upon the New Zealand despatch as a hoax.

But within a week, and from a different source, flashed another despatch which more than confirmed the first. It declared that gold existed near the south pole in practically unlimited quantity. Some geologists said this accounted for the greater depth of the Antarctic Ocean. It had always been noticed that the southern hemisphere appeared to be a little overweighted. People now began to prick up their ears, and many letters of inquiry appeared in the newspapers concerning the wonderful tidings from the south. Some asked for information about the shortest route to the new goldfields.

In a little while several additional reports came, some via New Zealand, others via South America, and all confirming in every respect what had been sent before. Then a New York newspaper sent a swift steamer to the Antarctic, and when this enterprising journal published a four-page cable describing the discoveries in detail, all doubt vanished and the rush began.

Some time I may undertake a description of the wild scenes that occurred when, at last, the inhabitants of the northern hemisphere were convinced that boundless stores of gold existed in the unclaimed and uninhabited wastes surrounding the south pole. But at present I have something more wonderful to relate.

Let me briefly depict the situation.

For many years silver had been absent from the coinage of the world. Its increasing abundance rendered it unsuitable for money, especially when contrasted with gold. The "silver craze," which had raged in the closing decade of the nineteenth century, was already a forgotten incident of financial history. The gold standard had become universal, and business all over the earth had adjusted itself to that condition. The wheels of industry ran smoothly, and there seemed to be no possibility of any disturbance or interruption. The common monetary system prevailing in every land fostered trade and facilitated the exchange of products. Travellers never had to bother their heads about the currency of money; any coin that passed in New York would pass for its face value in London, Paris, Berlin, Rome, Madrid, St. Petersburg, Constantinople, Cairo, Khartoum, Jerusalem, Peking, or Yeddo. It was indeed the "Golden Age," and the world had never been so free from financial storms.

Upon this peaceful scene the south polar gold discoveries burst like an unheralded tempest.

I happened to be in the company of a famous bank president when the confirmation of those discoveries suddenly filled the streets with yelling newsboys. "Get me one of those 'extras'!" he said, and an office-boy ran out to obey him. As he perused the sheet his face darkened.

"I'm afraid it's too true," he said, at length. "Yes, there seems to be no getting around it. Gold is going to be as plentiful as iron. If there were not such a flood of it, we might manage, but when they begin to make trousers buttons out of the same metal that is now locked and guarded in steel vaults, where will be our standard of worth? My dear fellow," he continued, impulsively laying his hand on my arm, "I would as willingly face the end of the world as this that's coming!"

"You think it so bad, then?" I asked. "But most people will not agree with you. They will regard it as very good news."

"How can it be good?" he burst out. "What have we got to take the place of gold? Can we go back to the age of barter? Can we substitute cattle-pens and wheat-bins for the strong boxes of the Treasury? Can commerce exist with no common measure of exchange?"

"It does indeed look serious," I assented.

"Serious! I tell you, it is the deluge!"

Thereat he clapped on his hat and hurried across the street to the office of another celebrated banker.

His premonitions of disaster turned out to be but too well grounded. The deposits of gold at the south pole were richer than the wildest reports had represented them. The shipments of the precious metal to America and Europe soon became enormous—so enormous that the metal was no longer precious. The price of gold dropped like a falling stone, with accelerated velocity, and within a year every money centre in the world had been swept by a panic. Gold was more common than iron. Every government was compelled to demonetize it, for when once gold had fallen into contempt it was less valuable in the eyes of the public than stamped paper. For once the world had thoroughly learned the lesson that too much of a good thing is worse than none of it.

Then somebody found a new use for gold by inventing a process by which it could be hardened and tempered, assuming a wonderful toughness and elasticity without losing its non-corrosive property, and in this form it rapidly took the place of steel.

In the mean time every effort was made to bolster up credit. Endless were the attempts to find a substitute for gold. The chemists sought it in their laboratories and the mineralogists in the mountains and deserts. Platinum might have served, but it, too, had become a drug in the market through the discovery of immense deposits. Out of the twenty odd elements which had been rarer and more valuable than gold, such as uranium, gallium, etc., not one was found to answer the purpose. In short, it was evident that since both gold and silver had become too abundant to serve any longer for a money standard, the planet held no metal suitable to take their place.

The entire monetary system of the world must be readjusted, but in the readjustment it was certain to fall to pieces. In fact, it had already fallen to pieces; the only recourse was to paper money, but whether this was based upon agriculture or mining or manufacture, it gave varying standards, not only among the different nations, but in successive years in the same country. Exports and imports practically ceased. Credit was discredited, commerce perished, and the world, at a bound, seemed to have gone back, financially and industrially, to the dark ages.

One final effort was made. A great financial congress was assembled at New York. Representatives of all the nations took part in it. The ablest financiers of Europe and America united the efforts of their genius and the results of their experience to solve the great problem. The various governments all solemnly stipulated to abide by the decision of the congress.

But, after spending months in hard but fruitless labour, that body was no nearer the end of its undertaking than when it first assembled. The entire world awaited its decision with bated breath, and yet the decision was not formed.

At this paralyzing crisis a most unexpected event suddenly opened the way.

CHAPTER 2

The Magician of Science

An attendant entered the room where the perplexed financiers were in session and presented a peculiar-looking card to the president, Mr. Boon. The president took the card in his hand and instantly fell into a brown study. So complete was his absorption that Herr Finster, the celebrated Berlin banker, who had been addressing the chair for the last two hours from the opposite end of the long table, got confused, entirely lost track of his verb, and suddenly dropped into his seat, very red in the face and wearing a most injured expression.

But President Boon paid no attention except to the singular card, which he continued to turn over and over, balancing it on his fingers and holding it now at arm's-length and then near his nose, with one eye squinted as if he were trying to look through a hole in the card.

At length this odd conduct of the presiding officer drew all eyes upon the card, and then everybody shared the interest of Mr. Boon. In shape and size the card was not extraordinary, but it was composed of metal. What metal? That question had immediately arisen in Mr. Boon's mind when the card came into his hand, and now it exercised the wits of all the others. Plainly it was not tin, brass, copper, bronze, silver, aluminium—although its lightness might have suggested that metal—nor even base gold.

The president, although a skilled metallurgist, confessed his inability to say what it was. So intent had he become in examining the curious bit of metal that he forgot it was a visitor's card of introduction, and did not even look for the name which it presumably bore.

As he held the card up to get a better light upon it a stray sunbeam from the window fell across the metal and instantly it bloomed with exquisite colours! The president's chair being in the darker end of the room, the radiant card suffused the atmosphere about him with a faint rose tint, playing with surprising liveliness into alternate canary colour and violet.

The effect upon the company of clear-headed financiers was extremely remarkable. The unknown metal appeared to exercise a kind of mesmeric influence, its soft hues blending together in a chromatic harmony which captivated the sense of vision as the ears are charmed by a perfectly rendered song. Gradually all gathered in an eager group around the president's chair.

"What can it be?" was repeated from lip to lip.

"Did you ever see anything like it?" asked Mr. Boon for the twentieth time.

None of them had ever seen the like of it. A spell fell upon the assemblage. For five minutes no one spoke, while Mr. Boon continued to chase the flickering sunbeam with the wonderful card. Suddenly the silence was broken by a voice which had a touch of awe in it:

"It must be the metal!"

The speaker was an English financier, First Lord of the Treasury, Hon. James Hampton-Jones, K.C.B. Immediately everybody echoed his remark, and the strain being thus relieved, the spell dropped from them and several laughed loudly over their momentary aberration.

President Boon recollected himself, and, colouring slightly, placed the card flat on the table, in order more clearly to see the name. In plain red letters it stood forth with such surprising distinctness that Mr. Boon wondered why he had so long overlooked it.

"DR. MAX SYX."

"Tell the gentleman to come in," said the president, and thereupon the attendant threw open the door.

The owner of the mysterious card fixed every eye as he entered. He was several inches more than six feet in height. His complexion was very dark, his eyes were intensely black, bright, and deep-set, his eyebrows were bushy and up-curled at the ends, his sable hair was close-trimmed, and his ears were narrow, pointed at the top, and prominent. He wore black moustaches, covering only half the width of his lip and drawn into projecting needles on each side, while a spiked black beard adorned the middle of his chin. He smiled as he stepped confidently forward, with a courtly bow, but it was a very disconcerting smile, because it more than half resembled a sneer. This uncommon person did not wait to be addressed.

"I have come to solve your problem," he said, facing President Boon, who had swung round on his pivoted chair.

"The metal!" exclaimed everybody in a breath, and with a unanimity and excitement which would have astonished them if they had been spectators instead of actors of the scene. The tall stranger bowed and smiled again:

"Just so," he said. "What do you think of it?"

"It is beautiful!"

Again the reply came from every mouth simultaneously, and again if the speakers could have been listeners they would have wondered not only at their earnestness, but at their words, for why should they instantly and unanimously pronounce that beautiful which they had not even seen? But every man knew he had seen it, for instinctively their minds reverted to the card and recognized in it the metal referred to. The mesmeric spell seemed once more to fall upon the assemblage, for the financiers noticed nothing remarkable in the next act of the stranger, which was to take a chair, uninvited, at the table, and the moment he sat down he became the presiding officer as naturally as if he had just been elected to that post. They all waited for him to speak, and when he opened his mouth they listened with breathless attention.

His words were of the best English, but there was some peculiarity, which they had already noticed, either in his voice or his manner of enunciation, which struck all of the listeners as denoting a foreigner. But none of them could satisfactorily place him. Neither the Americans, the Englishmen, the Germans, the Frenchmen, the Russians, the Austrians, the Italians, the Spaniards, the Turks, the Japanese, or the Chinese at the board could decide to what race or nationality the stranger belonged.

"This metal," he began, taking the card from Mr. Boon's hand, "I have discovered and named. I call it 'artemisium.' I can produce it, in the pure form, abundantly enough to replace gold, giving it the same relative value that gold possessed when it was the universal standard."

As Dr. Syx spoke he snapped the card with his thumb-nail and it fluttered with quivering hues like a humming-bird hovering over a flower. He seemed to await a reply, and President Boon asked:

"What guarantee can you give that the supply would be adequate and continuous?"

"I will conduct a committee of this congress to my mine in the Rocky Mountains, where, in anticipation of the event, I have accumulated enough refined artemisium to provide every civilized land with an amount of coin equivalent to that which it formerly held in gold. I can there satisfy you of my ability to maintain the production."

"But how do we know that this metal of yours will answer the purpose?"

"Try it," was the laconic reply.

"There is another difficulty," pursued the president. "People will not accept a new metal in place of gold unless they are convinced that it possesses equal intrinsic value. They must first become familiar with it, and it must be abundant enough and desirable enough to be used sparingly in the arts, just as gold was."

"I have provided for all that," said the stranger, with one of his disconcerting smiles. "I assure you that there will be no trouble with the people. They will be only too eager to get and to use the metal. Let me show you."

He stepped to the door and immediately returned with two black attendants bearing a large tray filled with articles shaped from the same metal as that of which the card was composed. The financiers all jumped to their feet with exclamations of surprise and admiration, and gathered around the tray, whose dazzling contents lighted up the corner of the room where it had been placed as if the moon were shining there.

There were elegantly formed vases, adorned with artistic figures, embossed and incised, and glowing with delicate colours which shimmered in tiny waves with the slightest motion of the tray. Cups, pins, finger-rings, earrings, watch-chains, combs, studs, lockets, medals, tableware, models of coins—in brief, almost every article in the fabrication of which precious metals have been employed was to be seen there in profusion, and all composed of the strange new metal which everybody on the spot declared was far more splendid than gold.

"Do you think it will answer?" asked Dr. Syx.

"We do," was the unanimous reply. All then resumed their seats at the table, the tray with its magnificent array having been placed in the centre of the board. This display had a remarkable influence. Confidence awoke in the breasts of the financiers. The dark clouds that had oppressed them rolled off, and the prospect grew decidedly brighter.

"What terms do you demand?" at length asked Mr. Boon, cheerfully rubbing his hands.

"I must have military protection for my mine and reducing works," replied Dr. Syx. "Then I shall ask the return of one per cent, on the circulating medium, together with the privilege of disposing of a certain amount of the metal—to be limited by agreement—to the public for use in the arts. Of the proceeds of this sale I will pay ten per cent. to the government in consideration of its protection."

"But," exclaimed President Boon, "that will make you the richest man who ever lived!"

"Undoubtedly," was the reply.

"Why," added Mr. Boon, opening his eyes wider as the facts continued to dawn upon him, "you will become the financial dictator of the whole earth!"

"Undoubtedly," again responded Dr. Syx, unmoved. "That is what I purpose to become. My discovery entitles me to no less. But, remember, I place myself under government inspection and restriction. I should not be allowed to flood the market, even if I were disposed to do so. But my own interest would restrain me. It is to my advantage that artemisium, once adopted, shall remain stable in value."

A shadow of doubt suddenly crossed the president's face.

"Suppose your secret is discovered," he said. "Surely your mine will not remain the only one. If you, in so short a time, have been able to accumulate an immense quantity of the new metal, it must be extremely abundant. Others will discover it, and then where shall we be?"

While Mr. Boon uttered these words, those who were watching Dr. Syx (as the president was not) resembled persons whose startled eyes are fixed upon a wild beast preparing to spring. As Mr. Boon ceased speaking he turned towards the visitor, and instantly his lips fell apart and his face paled.

Dr. Syx had drawn himself up to his full stature, and his features were distorted with that peculiar mocking smile which had now returned with a concentrated expression of mingled self-confidence and disdain.

"Will you have relief, or not?" he asked in a dry, hard voice. "What can you do? I alone possess the secret which can restore industry and commerce. If you reject my offer, do you think a second one will come?"

President Boon found voice to reply, stammeringly:

"I did not mean to suggest a rejection of the offer. I only wished to inquire if you thought it probable that there would be no repetition of what occurred after gold was found at the south pole?"

"The earth may be full of my metal," returned Dr. Syx, almost fiercely, "but so long as I alone possess the knowledge how to extract it, is it of any more worth than common dirt? But come," he added, after a pause and softening his manner, "I have other schemes. Will you, as representatives of the leading nations, undertake the introduction of artemisium as a substitute for gold, or will you not?"

"Can we not have time for deliberation?" asked President Boon.

"Yes, one hour. Within that time I shall return to learn your decision," replied Dr. Syx, rising and preparing to depart. "I leave these things," pointing to the tray, "in your keeping, and," significantly, "I trust your decision will be a wise one."

His curious smile again curved his lips and shot the ends of his moustache upward, and the influence of that smile remained in the room when he had closed the door behind him. The financiers gazed at one another for several minutes in silence, then they turned towards the coruscating metal that filled the tray.

CHAPTER 3

The Grand Teton Mine

Away on the western border of Wyoming, in the all but inaccessible heart of the Rocky Mountains, three mighty brothers, "The Big
Tetons," look perpendicularly into the blue eye of Jenny's Lake, lying at the bottom of the profound depression among the mountains
called Jackson's Hole. Bracing against one another for support, these
remarkable peaks lift their granite spires from 12,000 to nearly 14,000
feet into the blue dome that arches the crest of the continent. Their
sides, and especially those of their chief, the Grand Teton, are streaked
with glaciers, which shine like silver trappings when the morning sun
comes up above the wilderness of mountains stretching away eastward
from the hole.

When the first white men penetrated this wonderful region, and
one of them bestowed his wife's name upon Jenny's Lake, they were
intimidated by the Grand Teton. It made their flesh creep, accustomed
though they were to rough scrambling among mountain gorges and
on the brows of immense precipices, when they glanced up the face of
the peak, where the cliffs fall, one below another, in a series of breathless descents, and imagined themselves clinging for dear life to those
skyey battlements.

But when, in 1872, Messrs. Stevenson and Langford finally reached
the top of the Grand Teton—the only successful members of a party
of nine practised climbers who had started together from the bottom—they found there a little rectangular enclosure, made by piling
up rocks, six or seven feet across and three feet in height, bearing evidences of great age, and indicating that the red Indians had, for some
unknown purpose, resorted to the summit of this tremendous peak
long before the white men invaded their mountains. Yet neither the
Indians nor the whites ever really conquered the Teton, for above the
highest point that they attained rises a granite buttress, whose smooth

vertical sides seemed to them to defy everything but wings. Winding across the sage-covered floor of Jackson's Hole runs the Shoshone, or Snake River, which takes its rise from Jackson's Lake at the northern end of the basin, and then, as if shrinking from the threatening brows of the Tetons, whose fall would block its progress, makes a detour of one hundred miles around the buttressed heights of the range before it finds a clear way across Idaho, and so on to the Columbia River and the Pacific Ocean.

On a July morning, about a month after the visit of Dr. Max Syx to the assembled financiers in New York, a party of twenty horsemen, following a mountain-trail, arrived on the eastern margin of Jackson's Hole, and pausing upon a commanding eminence, with exclamations of wonder, glanced across the great depression, where lay the shining coils of the Snake River, at the towering forms of the Tetons, whose ice-striped cliffs flashed lightnings in the sunshine. Even the impassive broncos that the party rode lifted their heads inquiringly, and snorted as if in equine astonishment at the magnificent spectacle.

One familiar with the place would have noticed something, which, to his mind, would have seemed more surprising than the pageantry of the mountains in their morning sun-bath. Curling above one of the wild gorges that cut the lower slopes of the Tetons was a thick black smoke, which, when lifted by a passing breeze, obscured the precipices half-way to the summit of the peak.

Had the Grand Teton become a volcano? Certainly no hunting or exploring party could make a smoke like that. But a word from the leader of the party of horsemen explained the mystery.

"There is my mill, and the mine is underneath it."

The speaker was Dr. Syx, and his companions were members of the financial congress. When he quitted their presence in New York, with the promise to return within an hour for their reply, he had no doubt in his own mind what that reply would be. He knew they would accept his proposition, and they did. No time was then lost in communicating with the various governments, and arrangements were quickly perfected whereby, in case the inspection of Dr. Syx's mine and its resources proved satisfactory, America and Europe should unite in adopting the new metal as the basis of their coinage. As soon as this stage in the negotiations was reached, it only remained to send a committee of financiers and metallurgists, in company with Dr. Syx, to the Rocky Mountains. They started under the doctor's guidance, completing the last stage of their journey on horseback.

"An inspection of the records at Washington," Dr. Syx continued, addressing the horsemen, "will show that I have filed a claim covering ten acres of ground around the mouth of my mine. This was done as soon as I had discovered the metal. The filing of the claim and the subsequent proceedings which perfected my ownership attracted no attention, because everybody was thinking of the south pole and its gold-fields."

The party gathered closer around Dr. Syx and listened to his words with silent attention, while their horses rubbed noses and jingled their gold-mounted trappings.

"As soon as I had legally protected myself," he continued, "I employed a force of men, transported my machinery and material across the mountains, erected my furnaces, and opened the mine. I was safe from intrusion, and even from idle curiosity, for the reason I have just mentioned. In fact, so exclusive was the attraction of the new gold-fields that I had difficulty in obtaining workmen, and finally I sent to Africa and engaged negroes, whom I placed in charge of trustworthy foremen. Accordingly, with half a dozen exceptions, you will see only black men at the mine."

"And with their aid you have mined enough metal to supply the mints of the world?" asked President Boon.

"Exactly so," was the reply. "But I no longer employ the large force which I needed at first."

"How much metal have you on hand? I am aware that you have already answered this question during our preliminary negotiations, but I ask it again for the benefit of some members of our party who were not present then."

"I shall show you to-day," said Dr. Syx, with his curious smile, "2500 tons of refined artemisium, stacked in rock-cut vaults under the Grand Teton." "And you have dared to collect such inconceivable wealth in one place?"

"You forget that it is not wealth until the people have learned to value it, and the governments have put their stamp upon it."

"True, but how did you arrive at the proper moment?"

"Easily. I first ascertained that before the Antarctic discoveries the world contained altogether about 16,000 tons of gold, valued at $450,000 per ton, or $7,200,000,000 worth all told. Now my metal weighs, bulk for bulk, one-quarter as much as gold. It might be reckoned at the same intrinsic value per ton, but I have considered it preferable to take advantage of the smaller weight of the new metal, which permits us to make coins of the same size as the old ones, but only one-quarter as heavy, by giving to artemisium four times the value per ton that gold had. Thus only 4000 tons of the new metal are required to supply the place of the 16,000 tons of gold. The 2500 tons which I already have on hand are more than enough for coinage. The rest I can supply as fast as needed."

The party did not wait for further explanations. They were eager to see the wonderful mine and the store of treasure. Spurs were applied, and they galloped down the steep trail, forded the Snake River, and, skirting the shore of Jenny's Lake, soon found themselves gazing up the headlong slopes and dizzy parapets of the Grand Teton. Dr. Syx led them by a steep ascent to the mouth of the canyon, above one of whose walls stood his mill, and where the "Champ! Champ!" of a powerful engine saluted their ears.

CHAPTER 4

The Wealth Of the World

An electric light shot its penetrating rays into a gallery cut through virgin rock and running straight towards the heart of the Teton. The centre of the gallery was occupied by a narrow railway, on which a few flat cars, propelled by electric power, passed to and fro. Black-skinned and silent workmen rode on the cars, both when they came laden with broken masses of rock from the farther end of the tunnel and when they returned empty.

Suddenly, to an eye situated a little way within the gallery, appeared at the entrance the dark face of Dr. Syx, wearing its most discomposing smile, and a moment later the broader countenance of President Boon loomed in the electric glare beside the doctor's black framework of eyebrows and moustache. Behind them were grouped the other visiting financiers.

"This tunnel," said Dr. Syx, "leads to the mine head, where the ore-bearing rock is blasted."

As he spoke a hollow roar issued from the depths of the mountain, followed in a short time by a gust of foul air.

"You probably will not care to go in there," said the doctor, "and, in fact, it is very uncomfortable. But we shall follow the next car-load to the smelter, and you can witness the reduction of the ore."

Accordingly when another car came rumbling out of the tunnel, with its load of cracked rock, they all accompanied it into an adjoining apartment, where it was cast into a metallic chute, through which, they were informed, it reached the furnace.

"While it is melting," explained Dr. Syx, "certain elements, the nature of which I must beg to keep secret, are mixed with the ore, causing chemical action which results in the extraction of the metal. Now let me show you pure artemisium issuing from the furnace."

He led the visitors through two apartments into a third, one side of which was walled by the front of a furnace. From this projected two or three small spouts, and iridescent streams of molten metal fell from the spouts into earthen receptacles from which the blazing liquid was led, like flowing iron, into a system of moulds, where it was allowed to cool and harden.

The financiers looked on wondering, and their astonishment grew when they were conducted into the rock-cut store-rooms beneath, where they saw metallic ingots glowing like gigantic opals in the light which Dr. Syx turned on. They were piled in rows along the walls as high as a man could reach. A very brief inspection sufficed to convince the visitors that Dr. Syx was able to perform all that he promised. Although they had not penetrated the secret of his process of reducing the ore, yet they had seen the metal flowing from the furnace, and the piles of ingots proved conclusively that he had uttered no vain boast when he said he could give the world a new coinage.

But President Boon, being himself a metallurgist, desired to inspect the mysterious ore a little more closely. Possibly he was thinking that if another mine was destined to be discovered he might as well be the discoverer as anybody. Dr. Syx attempted no concealment, but his smile became more than usually scornful as he stopped a laden car and invited the visitors to help themselves.

"I think," he said, "that I have struck the only lode of this ore in the Teton, or possibly in this part of the world, but I don't know for certain. There may be plenty of it only waiting to be found. That, however, doesn't trouble me. The great point is that nobody except myself knows how to extract the metal."

Mr. Boon closely examined the chunk of rock which he had taken from the car. Then he pulled a lens from his pocket, with a deprecatory glance at Dr. Syx.

"Oh, that's all right," said the latter, with a laugh, the first that these gentlemen had ever heard from his lips, and it almost made them shudder; "put it to every test, examine it with the microscope, with fire, with electricity, with the spectroscope—in every way you can think of! I assure you it is worth your while!"

Again Dr. Syx uttered his freezing laugh, passing into the familiar smile, which had now become an undisguised mock.

"Upon my word," said Mr. Boon, taking his eye from the lens, "I see no sign of any metal here!"

"Look at the green specks!" cried the doctor, snatching the specimen from the president's hand. "That's it! That's artemisium! But it's of no use unless you can get it out and purify it, which is my secret!"

For the third time Dr. Syx laughed, and his merriment affected the visitors so disagreeably that they showed impatience to be gone. Immediately he changed his manner.

"Come into my office," he said, with a return to the graciousness which had characterized him ever since the party started from New York.

When they were all seated, and the doctor had handed round a box of cigars, he resumed the conversation in his most amiable manner.

"You see, gentlemen," he said, turning a piece of ore in his fingers, "artemisium is like aluminium. It can only be obtained in the metallic form by a special process. While these greenish particles, which you may perhaps mistake for chrysolite, or some similar unisilicate, really contain the precious metal, they are not entirely composed of it. The process by which I separate out the metallic element while the ore is passing through the furnace is, in truth, quite simple, and its very simplicity guards my secret. Make your minds easy as to over-production. A man is as likely to jump over the moon as to find me out."

"But," he continued, again changing his manner, "we have had business enough for one day; now for a little recreation." While speaking the doctor pressed a button on his desk, and the room, which was illuminated by electric lamps—for there were no windows in the building—suddenly became dark, except part of one wall, where a broad area of light appeared. Dr. Syx's voice had become very soothing when next he spoke: "I am fond of amusing myself with a peculiar form of the magic-lantern, which I invented some years ago, and which I have never exhibited except for the entertainment of my friends. The pictures will appear upon the wall, the apparatus being concealed."

He had hardly ceased speaking when the illuminated space seemed to melt away, leaving a great opening, through which the spectators looked as if into another world on the opposite side of the wall. For a minute or two they could not clearly discern what was presented; then, gradually, the flitting scenes and figures became more distinct until the lifelikeness of the spectacle absorbed their whole attention.

Before them passed, in panoramic review, a sunny land, filled with brilliant-hued vegetation, and dotted with villages and cities which were bright with light-coloured buildings. People appeared moving through the scenes, as in a cinematograph exhibition, but with infinitely more semblance of reality. In fact, the pictures, blending one into another, seemed to be life itself. Yet it was not an earth-like scene. The colours of the passing landscape were such as no man in the room had ever beheld; and the people, tall, round-limbed, with florid complexion, golden hair, and brilliant eyes and lips, were indescribably beautiful and graceful in all their movements.

From the land the view passed out to sea, and bright blue waves, edged with creaming foam, ran swiftly under the spectator's eyes, and occasionally, driven before light winds, appeared fleets of daintily shaped vessels, which reminded the beholder, by their flashing wings, of the feigned "ship of pearl."

After the fairy ships and breezy sea views came a long, curving line of coast, brilliant with coral sands, and indented by frequent bays, along whose enchanting shores lay pleasant towns, the landscapes behind them splendid with groves, meadows, and streams.

Presently the shifting photographic tape, or whatever the mechanism may have been, appeared to have settled upon a chosen scene, and there it rested. A broad champaign reached away to distant sapphire mountains, while the foreground was occupied by a magnificent house, resembling a large country villa, fronted with a garden, shaded by bowers and festoons of huge, brilliant flowers. Birds of radiant plumage flitted among the trees and blossoms, and then appeared a company of gaily attired people, including many young girls, who joined hands and danced in a ring, apparently with shouts of laughter, while a group of musicians standing near thrummed and blew upon curiously shaped instruments.

Suddenly the shadow of a dense cloud flitted across the scene; whereupon the brilliant birds flew away with screams of terror which almost seemed to reach the ears of the onlookers through the wall. An expression of horror came over the faces of the people. The children broke from their merry circle and ran for protection to their elders. The utmost confusing and whelming terror were evidenced for a moment—then the ground split asunder, and the house and the garden, with all their living occupants were swallowed by an awful chasm which opened just where they had stood. The great rent ran in a widening line across the sunlit landscape until it reached the horizon, when the distant mountains crumbled, clouds poured in from all sides at once, and billows of flame burst through them as they veiled the scene.

But in another instant the commotion was over, and the world whose curious spectacles had been enacted as if on the other side of a window, seemed to retreat swiftly into space, until at last, emerging from a fleecy cloud, it reappeared in the form of the full moon hanging in the sky, but larger than is its wont, with its dry ocean-beds, its keen-spired peaks, its ragged mountain ranges, its gaping chasms, its immense crater rings, and Tycho, the chief of them all, shooting ray-like streaks across the scarred face of the abandoned lunar globe. The show was ended, and Dr. Syx, turning on only a partial illumination in the room, rose slowly to his feet, his tall form appearing strangely magnified in the gloom, and invited his bewildered guests to accompany him to his house, outside the mill, where he said dinner awaited them. As they emerged into daylight they acted like persons just aroused from an opiate dream.

CHAPTER 5

Wonders of the New Metal

Within a twelvemonth after the visit of President Boon and his fellow financiers to the mine in the Grand Teton a railway had been constructed from Jackson's Hole, connecting with one of the Pacific lines, and the distribution of the new metal was begun. All of Dr. Syx's terms had been accepted. United States troops occupied a permanent encampment on the upper waters of the Snake River, to afford protection, and as the consignments of precious ingots were hurried east and west on guarded trains, the mints all over the world resumed their activity. Once more a common monetary standard prevailed, and commerce revived as if touched by a magic wand.

Artemisium quickly won its way in popular favour. Its matchless beauty alone was enough. Not only was it gladly accepted in the form of money, but its success was instantaneous in the arts. Dr. Syx and the inspectors representing the various nations found it difficult to limit the output to the agreed upon amount. The demand was incessant.

Goldsmiths and jewellers continually discovered new excellences in the wonderful metal. Its properties of translucence and refraction enabled skilful artists to perform marvels. By suitable management a chain of artemisium could be made to resemble a string of varicoloured gems, each separate link having a tint of its own, while, as the wearer moved, delicate complementary colours chased one another, in rapid undulation, from end to end.

A fresh charm was added by the new metal to the personal adornment of women, and an enhanced splendour to the pageants of society. Gold in its balmiest days had never enjoyed such a vogue. A crowded reception room or a dinner party where artemisium abounded possessed an indescribable atmosphere of luxury and richness, refined in quality, yet captivating to every sense. Imaginative persons went so far as to aver that the sight and presence of the metal exercised a strangely soothing and dreamy power over the mind, like the influence of moonlight streaming through the tree-tops on a still, balmy night.

The public curiosity in regard to the origin of artemisium was boundless. The various nations published official bulletins in which the general facts—omitting, of course, such incidents as the singular exhibition seen by the visiting financiers on the wall of Dr. Syx's of-fice—were detailed to gratify the universal desire for information.

President Boon not only submitted the specimens of ore-bearing rock which he had brought from the mine to careful analysis, but also appealed to several of the greatest living chemists and mineralogists to aid him; but they were all equally mystified. The green substance contained in the ore, although differing slightly from ordinary chryso-lite, answered all the known tests of that mineral. It was remembered, however, that Dr. Syx had said that they would be likely to mistake the substance for chrysolite, and the result of their experiments justified his prediction. Evidently the doctor had gone a stone's-cast beyond the chemistry of the day, and, just as evidently, he did not mean to reveal his discovery for the benefit of science, nor for the benefit of any pockets except his own.

Notwithstanding the failure of the chemists to extract anything from Dr. Syx's ore, the public at large never doubted that the se-cret would be discovered in good time, and thousands of prospectors flocked to the Teton Mountains in search of the ore. And without much difficulty they found it. Evidently the doctor had been mistaken in thinking that his mine might be the only one. The new miners hurried specimens of the green-speckled rock to the chemical labo-ratories for experimentation, and meanwhile began to lay up stores of the ore in anticipation of the time when the proper way to extract the metal should be discovered.

But, alas! that time did not come. The fresh ore proved to be as refractory as that which had been obtained from Dr. Syx. But in the midst of the universal disappointment there came a new sensation.

One morning the newspapers glared with a despatch from Grand Teton station announcing that the metal itself had been discovered by prospectors on the eastern slope of the main peak.

"It outcrops in many places," ran the despatch, "and many small nuggets have been picked out of crevices in the rocks."

The excitement produced by this news was even greater than when gold was discovered at the south pole. Again a mad rush was made for the Tetons. The heights around Jackson's Hole and the shores of Jackson's and Jenny's lakes were quickly dotted with camps, and the military force had to be doubled to keep off the curious, and occasionally menacing, crowds which gathered in the vicinity and seemed bent on unearthing the great secret locked behind the windowless walls of the mill, where the column of black smoke and the roar of the engine served as reminders of the incredible wealth which the sole possessor of that secret was rolling up.

This time no mistake had been made. It was a fact that the metal, in virgin purity, had been discovered scattered in various places on the ledges of the Grand Teton. In a little while thousands had obtained specimens with their own hands. The quantity was distressingly small, considering the number and the eagerness of the seekers, but that it was genuine artemisium not even Dr. Syx could have denied. He, however, made no attempt to deny it.

"Yes," he said, when questioned, "I find that I have been deceived. At first I thought the metal existed only in the form of the green ore, but of late I have come upon veins of pure artemisium in my mine. I am glad for your sakes, but sorry for my own. Still, it may turn out that there is no great amount of free artemisium after all."

While the doctor talked in this manner close observers detected a lurking sneer which his acquaintances had not noticed since artemisium was first adopted as the money basis of the world.

The crowd that swarmed upon the mountain quickly exhausted all of the visible supply of the metal. Sometimes they found it in a thin stratum at the bottom of crevices, where it could be detached in opalescent plates and leaves of the thickness of paper. These superficial deposits evidently might have been formed from water holding the metal in solution. Occasionally, deep cracks contained nuggets and wiry masses which looked as if they had run together when molten.

The most promising spots were soon staked out in miners' claims, machinery was procured, stock companies were formed, and borings were begun. The enthusiasm arising from the earlier finds and the flattering surface indications caused everybody to work with feverish haste and energy, and within two months one hundred tunnels were piercing the mountain.

For a long time nobody was willing to admit the truth which gradually forced itself upon the attention of the miners. The deeper they went the scarcer became the indications of artemisium! In fact, such deposits as were found were confined to fissures near the surface. But Dr. Syx continued to report a surprising increase in the amount of free metal in his mine, and this encouraged all who had not exhausted their capital to push on their tunnels in the hope of finally striking a vein. At length, however, the smaller operators gave up in despair, until only one heavily capitalized company remained at work.

CHAPTER 6

A Strange Discovery

"It is my belief that Dr. Max Syx is a deceiver."

The person who uttered this opinion was a young engineer, Andrew Hall, who had charge of the operations of one of the mining companies which were driving tunnels into the Grand Teton.

"What do you mean by that?" asked President Boon, who was the principal backer of the enterprise.

"I mean," replied Hall, "that there is no free metal in this mountain, and Dr. Syx knows there is none."

"But he is getting it himself from his mine," retorted President Boon.

"So he says, but who has seen it? No one is admitted into the Syx mine, his foremen are forbidden to talk, and his workmen are specially imported negroes who do not understand the English language."

"But," persisted Mr. Boon, "how, then, do you account for the nuggets scattered over the mountain? And, beside, what object could Dr. Syx have in pretending that there is free metal to be had for the digging?"

"He may have salted the mountain, for all I know," said Hall. "As for his object, I confess I am entirely in the dark; but, for all that, I am convinced that we shall find no more metal if we dig ten miles for it."

"Nonsense," said the president; "if we keep on we shall strike it. Did not Dr. Syx himself admit that he found no free artemisium until his tunnel had reached the core of the peak? We must go as deep as he has gone before we give up."

"I fear the depths he attains are beyond most people's reach," was Hall's answer, while a thoughtful look crossed his clear-cut brow, "but since you desire it, of course the work shall go on. I should like, however, to change the direction of the tunnel."

"Certainly," replied Mr. Boon; "bore in whatever direction you think proper, only don't despair."

About a month after this conversation Andrew Hall, with whom a community of tastes in many things had made me intimately acquainted, asked me one morning to accompany him into his tunnel.

"I want to have a trusty friend at my elbow," he said, "for, unless I am a dreamer, something remarkable will happen within the next hour, and two witnesses are better than one."

I knew Hall was not the person to make such a remark carelessly, and my curiosity was intensely excited, but, knowing his peculiarities, I did not press him for an explanation. When we arrived at the head of the tunnel I was surprised at finding no workmen there.

"I stopped blasting some time ago," said Hall, in explanation, "for a reason which, I hope, will become evident to you very soon. Lately I have been boring very slowly, and yesterday I paid off the men and dismissed them with the announcement, which, I am confident, President Boon will sanction after he hears my report of this morning's work, that the tunnel is abandoned. You see, I am now using a drill which I can manage without assistance. I believe the work is almost completed, and I want you to witness the end of it."

He then carefully applied the drill, which noiselessly screwed its nose into the rock. When it had sunk to a depth of a few inches he withdrew it, and, taking a hand-drill capable of making a hole not more than an eighth of an inch in diameter, cautiously began boring in the centre of the larger cavity. He had made hardly a hundred turns of the handle when the drill shot through the rock! A gratified smile illuminated his features, and he said in a suppressed voice:

"Don't be alarmed; I'm going to put out the light."

Instantly we were in complete darkness, but being close at Hall's side I could detect his movements. He pulled out the drill, and for half a minute remained motionless as if listening. There was no sound.

"I must enlarge the opening," he whispered, and immediately the faint grating of a sharp tool cutting through the rock informed me of his progress.

"There," at last he said, "I think that will do; now for a look."

I could tell that he had placed his eye at the hole and was gazing with breathless attention. Presently he pulled my sleeve.

"Put your eye here," he whispered, pushing me into the proper position for looking through the hole.

At first I could discern nothing except a smoky blue glow. But soon my vision cleared a little, and then I perceived that I was gazing into a narrow tunnel which met ours directly end to end. Glancing along the axis of this gallery I saw, some two hundred yards away, a faint light which evidently indicated the mouth of the tunnel.

At the end where we had met it the mysterious tunnel was considerably widened at one side, as if the excavators had started to change direction and then abandoned the work, and in this elbow I could just see the outlines of two or three flat cars loaded with broken stone, while a heap of the same material lay near them. Through the centre of the tunnel ran a railway track.

"Do you know what you are looking at?" asked Hall in my ear.

"I begin to suspect," I replied, "that you have accidentally run into Dr. Syx's mine."

"If Dr. Syx had been on his guard this accident wouldn't have happened," replied Hall, with an almost inaudible chuckle.

"I heard you remark a month ago," I said, "that you were changing the direction of your tunnel. Has this been the aim of your labours ever since?"

"You have hit it," he replied. "Long ago I became convinced that my company was throwing away its money in a vain attempt to strike a lode of pure artemisium. But President Boon has great faith in Dr. Syx, and would not give up the work. So I adopted what I regarded as the only practicable method of proving the truth of my opinion and saving the company's funds. An electric indicator, of my invention, enabled me to locate the Syx tunnel when I got near it, and I have met it end on, and opened this peep-hole in order to observe the doctor's operations. I feel that such spying is entirely justified in the circumstances. Although I cannot yet explain just how or why I feel sure that Dr. Syx was the cause of the sudden discovery of the surface nuggets, and that he has encouraged the miners for his own ends, until he has brought ruin to thousands who have spent their last cent in driving useless tunnels into this mountain. It is a righteous thing to expose him."

"But," I interposed, "I do not see that you have exposed anything yet except the interior of a tunnel."

"You will see more clearly after a while," was the reply.

Hall now placed his eye again at the aperture, and was unable entirely to repress the exclamation that rose to his lips. He remained staring through the hole for several minutes without uttering a word. Presently I noticed that the lenses of his eye were illuminated by a ray of light coming through the hole, but he did not stir.

After a long inspection he suddenly applied his ear to the hole and listened intently for at least five minutes. Not a sound was audible to me, but, by an occasional pressure of the hand, Hall signified that some important disclosure was reaching his sense of hearing. At length he removed his ear.

"Pardon me," he whispered, "for keeping you so long in waiting, but what I have just seen and overheard was of a nature to admit of no interruption. He is still talking, and by pressing your ear against the hole you may be able to catch what he says."

"Who is 'he'?"

"Look for yourself."

I placed my eye at the aperture, and almost recoiled with the violence of my surprise. The tunnel before me was brilliantly illuminated, and within three feet of the wall of rock behind which we crouched stood Dr. Syx, his dark profile looking almost satanic in the sharp contrast of light and shadow. He was talking to one of his foremen, and the two were the only visible occupants of the tunnel. Putting my ear to the little opening, I heard his words distinctly:

"—end of their rope. Well, they've spent a pretty lot of money for their experience, and I rather think we shall not be troubled again by artemisium-seekers for some time to come."

The doctor's voice ceased, and instantly I clapped my eye to the hole. He had changed his position so that his black eyes now looked straight at the aperture. My heart was in my mouth, for at first I believed from his expression that he had detected the gleam of my eyeball. But if so, he probably mistook it for a bit of mica in the rock, and paid no further attention. Then his lips moved, and I put my ear again to the hole. He seemed to be replying to a question that the foreman had asked.

"If they do," he said, "they will never guess the real secret."

Thereupon he turned on his heel, kicked a bit of rock off the track, and strode away towards the entrance. The foreman paused long enough to turn out the electric lamp, and then followed the doctor.

"Well," asked Hall, "what have you heard?"

I told him everything.

"It fully corroborates the evidence of my own eyes and ears," he remarked, "and we may count ourselves extremely lucky. It is not likely that Dr. Syx will be heard a second time proclaiming his deception with his own lips. It is plain that he was led to talk as he did to the foreman on account of the latter's having informed him of the sudden discharge of my men this morning. Their presence within ear-shot of our hiding-place during their conversation was, of course, pure accident, and so you can see how kind fortune has been to us. I expected to have to watch and listen and form deductions for a week, at least, before getting the information which five lucky minutes have placed in our hands."

While he was speaking my companion busied himself in carefully plugging up the hole in the rock. When it was closed to his satisfaction he turned on the light in our tunnel.

"Did you observe," he asked, "that there was a second tunnel?"

"What do you say?"

"When the light was on in there I saw the mouth of a smaller tunnel entering the main one behind the cars on the right. Did you notice it?"

"Oh yes," I replied. "I did observe some kind of a dark hole there, but I paid no attention to it because I was so absorbed in the doctor."

"Well," rejoined Hall, smiling, "it was worth considerably more than a glance. As a subject of thought I find it even more absorbing than Dr. Syx. Did you see the track in it?"

"No," I had to acknowledge, "I did not notice that. But," I continued, a little piqued by his manner, "being a branch of the main tunnel, I don't see anything remarkable in its having a track also."

"It was rather dim in that hole," said Hall, still smiling in a somewhat provoking way, "but the railroad track was there plain enough. And, whether you think it remarkable or not, I should like to lay you a wager that that track leads to a secret worth a dozen of the one we have just overheard."

"My good friend," I retorted, still smarting a little, "I shall not presume to match my stupidity against your perspicacity. I haven't cat's eyes in the dark."

Hall immediately broke out laughing, and, slapping me good-naturedly on the shoulder, exclaimed:

"Come, come now! If you go to kicking back at a fellow like that, I shall be sorry I ever undertook this adventure."

Chapter 7

A Mystery Indeed!

When President Boon had heard our story he promptly approved Hall's dismissal of the men. He expressed great surprise that Dr. Syx should have resorted to a deception which had been so disastrous to innocent people, and at first he talked of legal proceedings. But, after thinking the matter over, he concluded that Syx was too powerful to be attacked with success, especially when the only evidence against him was that he had claimed to find artemisium in his mine at a time when, as everybody knew, artemisium actually was found outside the mine. There was no apparent motive for the deception, and no proof of malicious intent. In short, Mr. Boon decided that the best thing for him and his stockholders to do was to keep silent about their losses and await events. And, at Hall's suggestion, he also determined to say nothing to anybody about the discovery we had made.

"It could do no good," said Hall, in making the suggestion, "and it might spoil a plan I have in mind."

"What plan?" asked the president.

"I prefer not to tell just yet," was the reply.

I observed that, in our interview with Mr. Boon, Hall made no reference to the side tunnel to which he had appeared to attach so much importance, and I concluded that he now regarded it as lacking significance. In this I was mistaken.

A few days afterwards I received an invitation from Hall to accompany him once more into the abandoned tunnel.

"I have found out what that sidetrack means," he said, "and it has plunged me into another mystery so dark and profound that I cannot see my way through it. I must beg you to say no word to any one concerning the things I am about to show you."

I gave the required promise, and we entered the tunnel, which nobody had visited since our former adventure. Having extinguished our lamp, my companion opened the peep-hole, and a thin ray of light streamed through from the tunnel on the opposite side of the wall. He applied his eye to the hole.

"Yes," he said, quickly stepping back and pushing me into his place, "they are still at it. Look, and tell me what you see."

"I see," I replied, after placing my eye at the aperture, "a gang of men unloading a car which has just come out of the side tunnel, and putting its contents upon another car standing on the track of the main tunnel."

"Yes, and what are they handling?"

"Why, ore, of course."

"And do you see nothing significant in that?"

"To be sure!" I exclaimed. "Why, that ore—"

"Hush! hush!" admonished Hall, putting his hand over my mouth; "don't talk so loud. Now go on, in a whisper."

"The ore," I resumed, "may have come back from the furnace-room, because the side tunnel turns off so as to run parallel with the other."

"It not only may have come back, it actually has come back," said Hall.

"How can you be sure?"

"Because I have been over the track, and know that it leads to a secret apartment directly under the furnace in which Dr. Syx pretends to melt the ore!"

For a minute after hearing this avowal I was speechless.

"Are you serious?" I asked at length.

"Perfectly serious. Run your finger along the rock here. Do you perceive a seam? Two days ago, after seeing what you have just witnessed in the Syx tunnel, I carefully cut out a section of the wall, making an aperture large enough to crawl through, and, when I knew the workmen were asleep, I crept in there and examined both tunnels from end to end. But in solving one mystery I have run myself into another infinitely more perplexing."

"How is that?"

"Why does Dr. Syx take such elaborate pains to deceive his visitors, and also the government officers? It is now plain that he conducts no mining operations whatever. This mine of his is a gigantic blind. Whenever inspectors or scientific curiosity seekers visit his mill his mute workmen assume the air of being very busy, the cars laden with his so-called 'ore' rumble out of the tunnel, and their contents are ostentatiously poured into the furnace, or appear to be poured into it, really dropping into a receptacle beneath, to be carried back into the mine again. And then the doctor leads his gulled visitors around to the other side of the furnace and shows them the molten metal coming out in streams. Now what does it all mean? That's what I'd like to find out. What's his game? For, mark you, if he doesn't get artemisium from this pretended ore, he gets it from some other source, and right on this spot, too. There is no doubt about that. The whole world is supplied by Syx's furnace, and Syx feeds his furnace with something that comes from his ten acres of Grand Teton rock. What is that something? How does he get it, and where does he hide it? These are the things I should like to find out."

"Well," I replied, "I fear I can't help you."

"But the difference between you and me," he retorted, "is that you can go to sleep over it, while I shall never get another good night's rest so long as this black mystery remains unsolved."

"What will you do?"

"I don't know exactly what. But I've got a dim idea which may take shape after a while."

Hall was silent for some time; then he suddenly asked:

"Did you ever hear of that queer magic-lantern show with which Dr. Syx entertained Mr. Boon and the members of the financial commission in the early days of the artemisium business?"

"Yes, I've heard the story, but I don't think it was ever made public. The newspapers never got hold of it."

"No, I believe not. Odd thing, wasn't it?"

"Why, yes, very odd, but just like the doctor's eccentric ways, though. He's always doing something to astonish somebody, without any apparent earthly reason. But what put you in mind of that?"

"Free artemisium put me in mind of it," replied Hall, quizzically.

"I don't see the connection."

"I'm not sure that I do either, but when you are dealing with Dr. Syx nothing is too improbable to be thought of."

Hall thereupon fell to musing again, while we returned to the entrance of the tunnel. After he had made everything secure, and slipped the key into his pocket, my companion remarked:

"Don't you think it would be best to keep this latest discovery to ourselves?"

"Certainly."

"Because," he continued, "nobody would be benefited just now by knowing what we know, and to expose the worthlessness of the 'ore' might cause a panic. The public is a queer animal, and never gets scared at just the thing you expect will alarm it, but always at something else."

We had shaken hands and were separating when Hall stopped me. "Do you believe in alchemy?" he asked.

"That's an odd question from you," I replied. "I thought alchemy was exploded long ago."

"Well," he said, slowly, "I suppose it has been exploded, but then, you know, an explosion may sometimes be a kind of instantaneous education, breaking up old things but revealing new ones."

CHAPTER 8

More of Dr. Syx's Magic

Important business called me East soon after the meeting with Hall described in the foregoing chapter, and before I again saw the Grand Teton very stirring events had taken place.

As the reader is aware, Dr. Syx's agreement with the various governments limited the output of his mine. An international commission, continually in session in New York, adjusted the differences arising among the nations concerning financial affairs, and allotted to each the proper amount of artemisium for coinage. Of course, this amount varied from time to time, but a fair average could easily be maintained. The gradual increase of wealth, in houses, machinery, manufactured and artistic products called for a corresponding increase in the circulating medium; but this, too, was easily provided for. An equally painstaking supervision was exercised over the amount of the precious metal which Dr. Syx was permitted to supply to the markets for use in the arts. On this side, also, the demand gradually increased; but the wonderful Teton mine seemed equal to all calls upon its resources.

After the failure of the mining operations there was a moderate revival of the efforts to reduce the Teton ore, but no success cheered the experimenters. Prospectors also wandered all over the earth looking for pure artemisium, but in vain. The general public, knowing nothing of what Hall had discovered, and still believing Syx's story that he also had found pure artemisium in his mine, accounted for the failure of the tunnelling operations on the supposition that the metal, in a free state, was excessively rare, and that Dr. Syx had had the luck to strike the only vein of it that the Grand Teton contained. As if to give countenance to this opinion, Dr. Syx now announced, in the most public manner, that he had been deceived again, and that the vein of free metal he had struck being exhausted, no other had appeared. Accordingly, he said, he must henceforth rely exclusively, as in the beginning, upon reduction of the ore.

Artemisium had proved itself an immense boon to mankind, and the new era of commercial prosperity which it had ushered in already exceeded everything that the world had known in the past. School-children learned that human civilization had taken five great strides, known respectively, beginning at the bottom, as the "age of stone," the "age of bronze," the "age of iron," the "age of gold," and the "age of artemisium."

Nevertheless, sources of dissatisfaction finally began to appear, and, after the nature of such things, they developed with marvellous rapidity. People began to grumble about "contraction of the currency." In every country there arose a party which demanded "free money." Demagogues pointed to the brief reign of paper money after the de-monetization of gold as a happy period, when the people had enjoyed their rights, and the "money barons"—borrowing a term from nine-teenth-century history—were kept at bay.

Then came denunciations of the international commission for restricting the coinage. Dr. Syx was described as "a devil-fish suck-ing the veins of the planet and holding it helpless in the grasp of his tentacular billions." In the United States meetings of agitators passed furious resolutions, denouncing the government, assailing the rich, cursing Dr. Syx, and calling upon "the oppressed" to rise and "take their own." The final outcome was, of course, violence. Mobs had to be suppressed by military force. But the most dramatic scene in the tragedy occurred at the Grand Teton. Excited by inflammatory speeches and printed documents, several thousand armed men assem-bled in the neighbourhood of Jenny's Lake and prepared to attack the Syx mine. For some reason the military guard had been depleted, and the mob, under the leadership of a man named Bings, who showed no little talent as a commander and strategist, surprised the small force of soldiers and locked them up in their own guard-house.

Telegraphic communication having been cut off by the astute Bings, a fierce attack was made on the mine. The assailants swarmed up the sides of the canyon, and attempted to break in through the foundation of the buildings. But the masonry was stronger than they had anticipated, and the attack failed. Sharp-shooters then climbed the neighbouring heights, and kept up an incessant peppering of the walls with conical bullets driven at four thousand feet per second.

No reply came from the gloomy structure. The huge column of black smoke rose uninterruptedly into the sky, and the noise of the great engine never ceased for an instant. The mob gathered closer on all sides and redoubled the fire of the rifles, to which was now added the belching of several machine-guns. Ragged holes began to appear in the walls, and at the sight of these the assailants yelled with delight. It was evident that, the mill could not long withstand so destructive a bombardment. If the besiegers had possessed artillery they would have knocked the buildings into splinters within twenty minutes. As it was, they would need a whole day to win their victory.

Suddenly it became evident that the besieged were about to take a hand in the fight. Thus far they had not shown themselves or fired a shot, but now a movement was perceived on the roof, and the projecting arms of some kind of machinery became visible. Many marksmen concentrated their fire upon the mysterious objects, but apparently with little effect. Bings, mounted on a rock, so as to command a clear view of the field, was on the point, of ordering a party to rush forward with axes and beat down the formidable doors, when there came a blinding flash from the roof, something swished through the air, and a gust of heat met the assailants in the face. Bings dropped dead from his perch, and then, as if the scythe of the Destroyer had swung downward, and to right and left in quick succession, the close-packed mob was levelled, rank after rank, until the few survivors crept behind rocks for refuge.

Instantly the atmospheric broom swept up and down the canyon and across the mountain's flanks, and the marksmen fell in bunches like shaken grapes. Nine-tenths of the besiegers were destroyed within ten minutes after the first movement had been noticed on the roof. Those who survived owed their escape to the rocks which concealed them, and they lost no time in crawling off into neighbouring chasms, and, as soon as they were beyond eye-shot from the mill, they fled with panic speed.

Then the towering form of Dr. Syx appeared at the door. Emerging without sign of fear or excitement, he picked his way among his fallen enemies, and, approaching the military guard-house, undid the fastening and set the imprisoned soldiers free.

"I think I am paying rather dear for my whistle," he said, with a characteristic sneer, to Captain Carter, the commander of the troop. "It seems that I must not only defend my own people and property when attacked by mob force, but must also come to the rescue of the soldiers whose pay-rolls are met from my pocket."

The captain made no reply, and Dr. Syx strode back to the works. When the released soldiers saw what had occurred their amazement had no bounds. It was necessary at once to dispose of the dead, and this was no easy undertaking for their small force. However, they accomplished it, and at the beginning of their work made a most surprising discovery.

"How's this, Jim?" said one of the men to his comrade, as they stooped to lift the nearest victim of Dr. Syx's withering fire. "What's this fellow got all over him?"

"Artemisium! 'pon my soul!" responded "Jim," staring at the body. "He's all coated over with it."

Immediately from all sides came similar exclamations. Every man who had fallen was covered with a film of the precious metal, as if he had been dipped into an electrolytic bath. Clothing seemed to have been charred, and the metallic atoms had penetrated the flesh of the victims. The rocks all round the battle-field were similarly veneered. "It looks to me," said Captain Carter, "as if old Syx had turned one of his spouts of artemisium into a hose-pipe and soaked 'em with it."

"That's it," chimed in a lieutenant, "that's exactly what he's done."

"Well," returned the captain, "if he can do that, I don't see what use he's got for us here."

"Probably he don't want to waste the stuff," said the lieutenant. "What do you suppose it cost him to plate this crowd?"

"I guess a month's pay for the whole troop wouldn't cover the expense. It's costly, but then—gracious! Wouldn't I have given something for the doctor's hose when I was a youngster campaigning in the Philippines in '99?"

The story of the marvellous way in which Dr. Syx defended his mill became the sensation of the world for many days. The hose-pipe theory, struck off on the spot by Captain Carter, seized the popular fancy, and was generally accepted without further question. There was an element of the ludicrous which robbed the tragedy of some of its horror. Moreover, no one could deny that Dr. Syx was well within his rights in defending himself by any means when so savagely attacked, and his triumphant success, no less than the ingenuity which was supposed to underlie it, placed him in an heroic light which he had not hitherto enjoyed.

As to the demagogues who were responsible for the outbreak and its terrible consequences, they slunk out of the public eye, and the result of the battle at the mine seemed to have been a clearing up of the atmosphere, such as a thunderstorm effects at the close of a season of foul weather.

But now, little as men guessed it, the beginning of the end was close at hand.

CHAPTER 9

The Detective of Science

The morning of my arrival at Grand Teton station, on my return from the East, Andrew Hall met me with a warm greeting.

"I have been anxiously expecting you," he said, "for I have made some progress towards solving the great mystery. I have not yet reached a conclusion, but I hope soon to let you into the entire secret. In the meantime you can aid me with your companionship, if in no other way, for, since the defeat of the mob, this place has been mighty lonesome. The Grand Teton is a spot that people who have no particular business out here carefully avoid. I am on speaking terms with Dr. Syx, and occasionally, when there is a party to be shown around, I visit his works, and make the best possible use of my eyes. Captain Carter of the military is a capital fellow, and I like to hear his stories of the war in Luzon forty years ago, but I want somebody to whom I can occasionally confide things, and so you are as welcome as moonlight in harvest-time."

"Tell me something about that wonderful fight with the mob. Did you see it?"

"I did. I had got wind of what Bings intended to do while I was down at Pocotello, and I hurried up here to warn the soldiers, but unfortunately I came too late. Finding the military cooped up in the guard-house and the mob masters of the situation, I kept out of sight on the side of the Teton, and watched the siege with my binocular. I think there was very little of the spectacle that I missed."

"What of the mysterious force that the doctor employed to sweep off the assailants?"

"Of course, Captain Carter's suggestion that Syx turned molten artemisium from his furnace into a hose-pipe and sprayed the enemy with it is ridiculous. But it is much easier to dismiss Carter's theory than to substitute a better one. I saw the doctor on the roof with a gang of black workmen, and I noticed the flash of polished metal turned rapidly this way and that, but there was some intervening obstacle which prevented me from getting a good view of the mechanism employed. It certainly bore no resemblance to a hose-pipe, or anything of that kind. No emanation was visible from the machine, but it was stupefying to see the mob melt down."

"How about the coating of the bodies with artemisium?"

"There you are back on the hose-pipe again," laughed Hall. "But, to tell you the truth, I'd rather be excused from expressing an opinion on that operation in wholesale electro-plating just at present. I've the ghost of an idea what it means, but let me test my theory a little before I formulate it. In the meanwhile, won't you take a stroll with me?"

"Certainly; nothing could please me better," I replied. "Which way shall we go?"

"To the top of the Grand Teton."

"What! are you seized with the mountain-climbing fever?"

"Not exactly, but I have a particular reason for wishing to take a look from that pinnacle."

"I suppose you know the real apex of the peak has never been trodden by man?"

"I do know it, but it is just that apex that I am determined to have under my feet for ten minutes. The failure of others is no argument for us."

"Just as you say," I rejoined. "But I suppose there is no indiscretion in asking whether this little climb has any relation to the mystery?"

"If it didn't have an important relation to the clearing up of that dark thing I wouldn't risk my neck in such an undertaking," was the reply.

Accordingly, the next morning we set out for the peak. All previous climbers, as we were aware, had attacked it from the west. That seemed the obvious thing to do, because the westward slopes of the mountain, while very steep, are less abrupt than those which face the rising sun. In fact, the eastern side of the Grand Teton appears to be absolutely unclimbable. But both Hall and I had had experience with rock climbing in the Alps and the Dolomites, and we knew that what looked like the hardest places sometimes turn out to be next to the easiest. Accordingly we decided—the more particularly because it would save time, but also because we yielded to the common desire to outdo our predecessors—to try to scale the giant right up his face.

We carried a very light but exceedingly strong rope, about five hundred feet long, wore nail-shod shoes, and had each a metal-pointed staff and a small hatchet in lieu of the regular mountaineer's axe. Advancing at first along the broken ridge between two gorges we gradually approached the steeper part of the Teton, where the cliffs looked so sheer and smooth that it seemed no wonder that nobody had ever tried to scale them. The air was deliciously clear and the sky wonderfully blue above the mountains, and the moon, a few days past its last quarter, was visible in the southwest, its pale crescent face slightly blued by the atmosphere, as it always appears when seen in daylight.

"Slow westering, a phantom sail—The lonely soul of yesterday."

Behind us, somewhat north of east, lay the Syx works, with their black smoke rising almost vertically in the still air. Suddenly, as we stumbled along on the rough surface, something whizzed past my face and fell on the rock at my feet. I looked at the strange missile, that had come like a meteor out of open space, with astonishment.

It was a bird, a beautiful specimen of the scarlet tanagers, which I remembered the early explorers had found inhabiting the Teton canyons, their brilliant plumage borrowing splendour from contrast with the gloomy surroundings. It lay motionless, its outstretched wings having a curious shrivelled aspect, while the flaming colour of the breast was half obliterated with smutty patches. Stooping to pick it up, I noticed a slight bronzing, which instantly recalled to my mind the peculiar appearance of the victims of the attack on the mine.

"Look here!" I called to Hall, who was several yards in advance. He turned, and I held up the bird by a wing.

"Where did you get that?" he asked.

"It fell at my feet a moment ago."

Hall glanced in a startled manner at the sky, and then down the slope of the mountain.

"Did you notice in what direction it was flying?" he asked.

"No, it dropped so close that it almost grazed my nose. I saw nothing of it until it made me blink."

"I have been heedless," muttered Hall under his breath. At the time I did not notice the singularity of his remark, my attention being absorbed in contemplating the unfortunate tanager.

"Look how its feathers are scorched," I said.

"I know it," Hall replied, without glancing at the bird.

"And it is covered with a film of artemisium," I added, a little piqued by his abstraction.

"I know that, too."

"See here, Hall," I exclaimed, "are you trying to make game of me?"

"Not at all, my dear fellow," he replied, dropping his cogitation. "Pray forgive me. But this is no new phenomenon to me. I have picked up birds in that condition on this mountain before. There is a terrible mystery here, but I am slowly letting light into it, and if we succeed in reaching the top of the peak I have good hope that the illumination will increase."

"Here now," he added a moment later, sitting down upon a rock and thrusting the blade of his penknife into a crevice, "what do you think of this?"

He held up a little nugget of pure artemisium, and then went on:

"You know that all this slope was swept as clean as a Dutch housewife's kitchen floor by the thousands of miners and prospectors who swarmed over it a year or two ago, and do you suppose they would have missed such a titbit if it had been here then?"

"Dr. Syx must have been salting the mountain again," I suggested.

"Well," replied Hall, with a significant smile, "if the doctor hasn't salted it somebody else has, that's plain enough. But perhaps you would like to know precisely what I expect to find out when we get on the topknot of the Teton."

"I should certainly be delighted to learn the object of our journey," I said. "Of course, I'm only going along for company and for the fun of the thing; but you know you can count on me for substantial aid whenever you need it."

"It is because you are so willing to let me keep my own counsel," he rejoined, "and to wait for things to ripen before compelling me to disclose them, that I like to have you with me at critical times. Now, as to the object of this break-neck expedition, whose risks you understand as fully as I do, I need not assure you that it is of supreme importance to the success of my plans. In a word, I hope to be able to look down into a part of Dr. Syx's mill which, if I am not mistaken, no human eye except his and those of his most trustworthy helpers has ever been permitted to see. And if I see there what I fully expect to see, I shall have got a long step nearer to a great fortune."

"Good!" I cried. "*En avant*, then! We are losing time."

CHAPTER 10

The Top of the Grand Teton

The climbing soon became difficult, until at length we were going up hand over hand, taking advantage of crevices and knobs which an inexperienced eye would have regarded as incapable of affording a grip for the fingers or a support for the toes. Presently we arrived at the foot of a stupendous precipice, which was absolutely insurmountable by any ordinary method of ascent. Parts of it overhung, and everywhere the face of the rock was too free from irregularities to afford any footing, except to a fly.

"Now, to borrow the expression of old Bunyan, we are hard put to it," I remarked. "If you will go to the left I will take the right and see if there is any chance of getting up."

"I don't believe we could find any place easier than this," Hall replied, "and so up we go where we are."

"Have you a pair of wings concealed about you?" I asked, laughing at his folly.

"Well, something nearly as good," he responded, unstrapping his knapsack. He produced a silken bag, which he unfolded on the rock.

"A balloon!" I exclaimed. "But how are you going to inflate it?"

For reply Hall showed me a receptacle which, he said, contained liquid hydrogen, and which was furnished with a device for retarding the volatilization of the liquid so that it could be carried with little loss.

"You remember I have a small laboratory in the abandoned mine," he explained, "where we used to manufacture liquid air for blasting. This balloon I made for our present purpose. It will just suffice to carry up our rope, and a small but practically unbreakable grapple of hardened gold. I calculate to send the grapple to the top of the precipice with the balloon, and when it has obtained a firm hold in the riven rock there we can ascend, sailor fashion. You see the rope has knots, and I know your muscles are as trustworthy in such work as my own."

There was a slight breeze from the eastward, and the current of air slanting up the face of the peak assisted the balloon in mounting with its burden, and favoured us by promptly swinging the little airship, with the grapple swaying beneath it, over the brow of the cliff into the atmospheric eddy above. As soon as we saw that the grapple was well over the edge we pulled upon the rope. The balloon instantly shot into view with the anchor dancing, but, under the influence of the wind, quickly returned to its former position behind the projecting brink. The grapple had failed to take hold.

"'Try, try again' must be our motto now," muttered Hall.

We tried several times with the same result, although each time we slightly shifted our position. At last the grapple caught.

"Now, all together!" cried my companion, and simultaneously we threw our weight upon the slender rope. The anchor apparently did not give an inch.

"Let me go first," said Hall, pushing me aside as I caught the first knot above my head. "It's my device, and it's only fair that I should have the first try."

In a minute he was many feet up the wall, climbing swiftly hand over hand, but occasionally stopping and twisting his leg around the rope while he took breath.

"It's easier than I expected," he called down, when he had ascended about one hundred feet. "Here and there the rock offers a little hold for the knees."

I watched him, breathless with anxiety, and, as he got higher, my imagination pictured the little gold grapple, invisible above the brow of the precipice, with perhaps a single thin prong wedged into a crevice, and slowly ploughing its way towards the edge with each impulse of the climber, until but another pull was needed to set it flying! So vivid was my fancy that I tried to banish it by noticing that a certain knot in the rope remained just at the level of my eyes, where it had been from the start. Hall was now fully two hundred feet above the ledge on which I stood, and was rapidly nearing the top of the precipice. In a minute more he would be safe.

Suddenly he shouted, and, glancing up with a leap of the heart, I saw that he was falling! He kept his face to the rock, and came down feet foremost. It would be useless to attempt any description of my feelings; I would not go through that experience again for the price of a battleship. Yet it lasted less than a second. He had dropped not more than ten feet when the fall was arrested.

"All right!" he called, cheerily. "No harm done! It was only a slip."

But what a slip! If the balloon had not carried the anchor several yards back from the edge it would have had no opportunity to catch another hold as it shot forward. And how could we know that the second hold would prove more secure than the first? Hall did not hesitate, however, for one instant. Up he went again. But, in fact, his best chance was in going up, for he was within four yards of the top when the mishap occurred. With a sigh of relief I saw him at last throw his arm over the verge and then wriggle his body upon the ledge. A few seconds later he was lying on his stomach, with his face over the edge, looking down at me.

"Come on!" he shouted. "It's all right."

When I had pulled myself over the brink at his side I grasped his hand and pressed it without a word. We understood one another.

"It was pretty close to a miracle," he remarked at last. "Look at this."

The rock over which the grapple had slipped was deeply scored by the unyielding point of the metal, and exactly at the verge of the precipice the prong had wedged itself into a narrow crack, so firmly that we had to chip away the stone in order to release it. If it had slipped a single inch farther before taking hold it would have been all over with my friend.

Such experiences shake the strongest nerves, and we sat on the shelf we had attained for fully a quarter of an hour before we ventured to attack the next precipice which hung beetling directly above us. It was not as lofty as the one we had just ascended, but it impended to such a degree that we saw we should have to climb our rope while it swung free in the air!

Luckily we had little difficulty in getting a grip for the prongs, and we took every precaution to test the security of the anchorage, not only putting our combined weight repeatedly upon the rope, but flipping and jerking it with all our strength. The grapple resisted every effort to dislodge it, and finally I started up, insisting on my turn as leader.

The height I had to ascend did not exceed one hundred feet, but that is a very great distance to climb on a swinging rope, without a wall within reach to assist by its friction and occasional friendly projections. In a little while my movements, together with the effect of the slight wind, had imparted a most distressing oscillation to the rope. This sometimes carried me with a nerve-shaking bang against a prominent point of the precipice, where I would dislodge loose fragments that kept Hall dodging for his life, and then I would swing out, apparently beyond the brow of the cliff below, so that, as I involuntarily glanced downward, I seemed to be hanging in free space, while the steep mountain-side, looking ten times steeper than it really was, resembled the vertical wall of an absolutely bottomless abyss, as if I were suspended over the edge of the world.

I avoided thinking of what the grapple might be about, and in my haste to get through with the awful experience I worked myself fairly out of breath, so that, when at last I reached the rounded brow of the cliff, I had to stop and cling there for fully a minute before I could summon strength enough to lift myself over it.

When I was assured that the grapple was still securely fastened I signalled to Hall, and he soon stood at my side, exclaiming, as he wiped the perspiration from his face:

"I think I'll try wings next time!"

But our difficulties had only begun. As we had foreseen, it was a case of Alp above Alp, to the very limit of human strength and patience. However, it would have been impossible to go back. In order to descend the two precipices we had surmounted it would have been necessary to leave our life-lines clinging to the rocks, and we had not rope enough to do that. If we could not reach the top we were lost.

Having refreshed ourselves with a bite to eat and a little stimulant, we resumed the climb. After several hours of the most exhausting work I have ever performed we pulled our weary limbs upon the narrow ridge, but a few square yards in area, which constitutes the apex of the Grand Teton. A little below, on the opposite side of a steep-walled gap which divides the top of the mountain into two parts, we saw the singular enclosure of stones which the early white explorers found there, and which they ascribed to the Indians, although nobody has ever known who built it or what purpose it served.

The view was, of course, superb, but while I was admiring it in all its wonderful extent and variety, Hall, who had immediately pulled out his binocular, was busy inspecting the Syx works, the top of whose great tufted smoke column was thousands of feet beneath our level. Jackson's Lake, Jenny's Lake, Leigh's Lake, and several lakelets glittered in the sunlight amid the pale greys and greens of Jackson's Hole, while many a bending reach of the Snake River shone amid the wastes of sage-brush and rock.

"There!" suddenly exclaimed Hall, "I thought I should find it."

"What?"

"Take a look through my glass at the roof of Syx's mill. Look just in the centre."

"Why, it's open in the middle!" I cried as soon as I had put the glass to my eyes. "There's a big circular hole in the centre of the roof,"

"Look inside! Look inside!" repeated Hall, impatiently.

"I see nothing there except something bright."

"Do you call it nothing because it is bright?"

"Well, no," I replied, laughing. "What I mean is that I see nothing that I can make anything of except a shining object, and all I can make of that is that it is bright."

"You've been in the Syx works many times, haven't you?"

"Yes."

"Did you ever see the opening in the roof?"

"Never."

"Did you ever hear of it?"

"Never."

"Then Dr. Syx doesn't show his visitors everything that is to be seen."

"Evidently not since, as we know, he concealed the double tunnel and the room under the furnace."

"Dr. Syx has concealed a bigger secret than that," Hall responded, "and the Grand Teton has helped me to a glimpse of it."

For several minutes my friend was absorbed in thought. Then he broke out:

"I tell you he's the most wonderful man in the world!"

"Who, Dr. Syx? Well, I've long thought that."

"Yes, but I mean in a different way from what you are thinking of. Do you remember my asking you once if you believed in alchemy?"

"I remember being greatly surprised by your question to that effect."

"Well, now," said Hall, rubbing his hands with a satisfied air, while his eyes glanced keen and bright with the reflection of some passing thought, "Max Syx is greater than any alchemist that ever lived. If those old fellows in the dark ages had accomplished everything they set out to do, they would have been of no more consequence in comparison with our black-browed friend down yonder than—than my head is of consequence in comparison with the moon."

"I fear you flatter the man in the moon," was my laughing reply.

"No, I don't," returned Hall, "and some day you'll admit it."

"Well, what about that something that shines down there? You seem to see more in it than I can."

But my companion had fallen into a reverie and didn't hear my question. He was gazing abstractedly at the faint image of the waning moon, now nearing the distant mountain-top over in Idaho. Presently his mind seemed to return to the old magnet, and he whirled about and glanced down at the Syx mill. The column of smoke was diminishing in volume, an indication that the engine was about to enjoy one of its periodical rests. The irregularity of these stoppages had always been a subject of remark among practical engineers. The hours of labour were exceedingly erratic, but the engine had never been known to work at night, except on one occasion, and then only for a few minutes, when it was suddenly stopped on account of a fire.

Just as Hall resumed his inspection two huge quarter spheres, which had been resting wide apart on the roof, moved towards one another until their arched sections met over the circular aperture which they covered like the dome of an observatory.

"I expected it," Hall remarked. "But come, it is mid-afternoon, and we shall need all of our time to get safely down before the light fades."

As I have already explained, it would not have been possible for us to return the way we came. We determined to descend the comparatively easy western slopes of the peak, and pass the night on that side of the mountain. Letting ourselves down with the rope into the hollow way that divides the summit of the Teton into two pinnacles, we had no difficulty in descending by the route followed by all previous climbers. The weather was fine, and, having found good shelter among the rocks, we passed the night in comfort. The next day we succeeded in swinging round upon the eastern flank of the Teton, below the more formidable cliffs, and, just at nightfall, we arrived at the station. As we passed the Syx mine the doctor himself confronted us. There was a very displeasing look on his dark countenance, and his sneer was strongly marked.

"So you have been on top of the Teton?" he said.

"Yes," replied Hall, very blandly, "and if you have a taste for that sort of thing I should advise you to go up. The view is immense, as fine as the best in the Alps."

"Pretty ingenious plan, that balloon of yours," continued the doctor, still looking black.

"Thank you," Hall replied, more suavely than ever. "I've been planning that a long time. You probably don't know that mountaineering used to be my chief amusement."

The doctor turned away without pursuing the conversation.

"I could kick myself," Hall muttered as soon as Dr. Syx was out of earshot. "If my absurd wish to outdo others had not blinded me, I should have known that he would see us going up this side of the peak, particularly with the balloon to give us away. However, what's done can't be undone. He may not really suspect the truth, and if he does he can't help himself, even though he is the richest man in the world."

CHAPTER 11

Strange Fate of a Kite

"Are you ready for another tramp?" was Andrew Hall's greeting when we met early on the morning following our return from the peak.

"Certainly I am. What is your programme for to-day?"

"I wish to test the flying qualities of a kite which I have constructed since our return last night."

"You don't allow the calls of sleep to interfere very much with your activity."

"I haven't much time for sleep just now," replied Hall, without smiling. "The kite test will carry us up the flanks of the Teton, but I am not going to try for the top this time. If you will come along I'll ask you to help me by carrying and operating a light transit I shall carry another myself. I am desirous to get the elevation that the kite attains and certain other data that will be of use to me. We will make a detour towards the south, for I don't want old Syx's suspicions to be prodded any more."

"What interest can he have in your kite-flying?"

"The same interest that a burglar has in the rap of a policeman's night-stick."

"Then your experiment to-day has some connection with the solution of the great mystery?"

"My dear fellow," said Hall, laying his hand on my shoulder, "until I see the end of that mystery I shall think of nothing else."

In a few hours we were clambering over the broken rocks on the south-eastern flank of the Teton at an elevation of about three thousand feet above the level of Jackson's Hole. Finally Hall paused and began to put his kite together. It was a small box-shaped affair, very light in construction, with paper sides.

"In order to diminish the chances of Dr. Syx noticing what we are about," he said, as he worked away, "I have covered the kite with sky-blue paper. This, together with distance, will probably insure us against his notice."

In a few minutes the kite was ready. Having ascertained the direction of the wind with much attention, he stationed me with my transit on a commanding rock, and sought another post for himself at a distance of two hundred yards, which he carefully measured with a gold tape. My instructions were to keep the telescope on the kite as soon as it had attained a considerable height, and to note the angle of elevation and the horizontal angle with the base line joining our points of observation.

"Be particularly careful," was Hall's injunction, "and if anything happens to the kite by all means note the angles at that instant."

As soon as we had fixed our stations Hall began to pay out the string, and the kite rose very swiftly. As it sped away into the blue it was soon practically invisible to the naked eye, although the telescope of the transit enabled me to follow it with ease.

Glancing across now and then at my companion, I noticed that he was having considerable difficulty in, at the same time, managing the kite and manipulating his transit. But as the kite continued to rise and steadied in position his task became easier, until at length he ceased to remove his eye from the telescope while holding the string with outstretched hand.

"Don't lose sight of it now for an instant!" he shouted.

For at least half an hour he continued to manipulate the string, sending the kite now high towards the zenith with a sudden pull, and then letting it drift off. It seemed at last to become almost a fixed point. Very slowly the angles changed, when, suddenly, there was a flash, and to my amazement I saw the paper of the kite shrivel and disappear in a momentary flame, and then the bare sticks came tumbling out of the sky.

"Did you get the angles?" yelled Hall, excitedly.

"Yes; the telescope is yet pointed on the spot where the kite disappeared."

"Read them off," he called, "and then get your angle with the Syx works."

"All right," I replied, doing as he had requested, and noticing at the same time that he was in the act of putting his watch in his pocket. "Is there anything else?" I asked.

"No, that will do, thank you."

Hall came running over, his face beaming, and with the air of a man who has just hooked a particularly cunning old trout.

"Ah!" he exclaimed, "this has been a great success! I could almost dispense with the calculation, but it is best to be sure."

"What are you about, anyhow?" I asked, "and what was it that happened to the kite?"

"Don't interrupt me just now, please," was the only reply I received.

Thereupon my friend sat down on a rock, pulled out a pad of paper, noted the angles which I had read on the transit, and fell to figuring with feverish haste. In the course of his work he consulted a pocket almanac, then glanced up at the sky, muttered approvingly, and finally leaped to his feet with a half-suppressed "Hurrah!" If I had not known him so well I should have thought that he had gone daft.

"Will you kindly tell me," I asked, "how you managed to set the kite afire?"

Hall laughed heartily. "You though it was a trick, did you?" said he. "Well, it was no trick, but a very beautiful demonstration. You surely haven't forgotten the scarlet tanager that gave you such a surprise the day before yesterday."

"Do you mean" I exclaimed, startled at the suggestion, "that the fate of the bird had any connection with the accident to your kite?"

"Accident isn't precisely the right word," replied Hall. "The two things are as intimately related as own brothers. If you should care to hunt up the kite sticks, you would find that they, too, are now artemisium plated."

"This is getting too deep for me," was all that I could say.

"I am not absolutely confident that I have touched bottom myself," said Hall, "but I'm going to make another dive, and if I don't bring up treasures greater than Vanderdecken found at the bottom of the sea, then Dr. Syx is even a more wonderful human mystery than I have thought him to be."

"What do you propose to do next?"

"To shake the dust of the Grand Teton from my shoes and go to San Francisco, where I have an extensive laboratory."

"So you are going to try a little alchemy yourself, are you?"

"Perhaps; who knows? At any rate, my good friend, I am forever indebted to you for your assistance, and even more for your discretion, and if I succeed you shall be the first person in the world to hear the news."

CHAPTER 12

Better than Alchemy

I come now to a part of my narrative which would have been deemed altogether incredible in those closing years of the nineteenth century that witnessed the first steps towards the solution of the deepest mysteries of the ether, although men even then held in their hands, without knowing it, powers which, after they had been mastered and before use had made them familiar, seemed no less than godlike.

For six months after Hall's departure for San Francisco I heard nothing from him. Notwithstanding my intense desire to know what he was doing, I did not seek to disturb him in his retirement. In the meantime things ran on as usual in the world, only a ripple being caused by renewed discoveries of small nuggets of artemisium on the Tetons, a fact which recalled to my mind the remark of my friend when he dislodged a flake of the metal from a crevice during our ascent of the peak. At last one day I received this telegram at my office in New York:

San Francisco, May 16, 1940.
Come at once. The mystery is solved.
(Signed) Hall

As soon as I could pack a grip I was flying westward one hundred miles an hour. On reaching San Francisco, which had made enormous strides since the opening of the twentieth century, owing to the extension of our Oriental possessions, and which already ranked with New York and Chicago among the financial capitals of the world, I hastened to Hall's laboratory. He was there expecting me, and, after a hearty greeting, during which his elation over his success was manifest, he said:

"I am compelled to ask you to make a little journey. I found it impossible to secure the necessary privacy here, and, before opening my

388

experiments, I selected a site for a new laboratory in an unfrequented spot among the mountains this side of Lake Tahoe. You will be the first man, with the exception of my two devoted assistants, to see my apparatus, and you shall share the sensation of the critical experiment."

"Then you have not yet completed your solution of the secret?"

"Yes, I have; for I am as certain of the result as if I had seen it, but I thought you were entitled to be in with me at the death."

From the nearest railway station we took horses to the laboratory, which occupied a secluded but most beautiful site at an elevation of about six thousand feet above sea-level. With considerable surprise I noticed a building surmounted with a dome, recalling what we had seen from the Grand Teton on the roof of Dr. Syx's mill. Hall, observing my look, smiled significantly, but said nothing. The laboratory proper occupied a smaller building adjoining the domed structure. Hall led the way into an apartment having but a single door and illuminated by a skylight.

"This is my sanctum sanctorum," he said, "and you are the first outsider to enter it. Seat yourself comfortably while I proceed to unveil a little corner of the artemisium mystery."

Near one end of the room, which was about thirty feet in length, was a table, on which lay a glass tube about two inches in diameter and thirty inches long. In the farther end of the tube gleamed a lump of yellow metal, which I took to be gold. Hall and I were seated near another table about twenty-five feet distant from the tube, and on this table was an apparatus furnished with a concave mirror, whose optical axis was directed towards the tube. It occurred to me at once that this apparatus would be suitable for experimenting with electric waves. Wires ran from it to the floor, and in the cellar beneath was audible the beating of an engine. My companion made an adjustment or two, and then remarked:

"Now, keep your eyes on the lump of gold in the farther end of the tube yonder. The tube is exhausted of air, and I am about to concentrate upon the gold an intense electric influence, which will have the effect of making it a kind of cathode pole. I only use this term for the sake of illustration. You will recall that as long ago as the days of Crookes it was known that a cathode in an exhausted tube would project particles, or atoms, of its substance away in straight lines. Now watch!"

I fixed my attention upon the gold, and presently saw it enveloped in a most beautiful violet light. This grew more intense, until, at times, it was blinding, while, at the same moment, the interior of the tube seemed to have become charged with a luminous vapour of a delicate pinkish hue.

"Watch! Watch!" said Hall. "Look at the nearer end of the tube!"

"Why, it is becoming coated with gold!" I exclaimed.

He smiled, but made no reply. Still the strange process continued. The pink vapour became so dense that the lump of gold was no longer visible, although the eye of violet light glared piercingly through the coloured fog. Every second the deposit of metal, shining like a mirror, increased, until suddenly there came a curious whistling sound. Hall, who had been adjusting the mirror, jerked away his hand and gave it a flip, as if hot water had spattered it, and then the light in the tube quickly died away, the vapour escaped, filling the room with a peculiar stimulating odour, and I perceived that the end of the glass tube had been melted through, and the molten gold was slowly dripping from it.

"I carried it a little too far," said Hall, ruefully rubbing the back of his hand, "and when the glass gave way under the atomic bombardment a few atoms of gold visited my bones. But there is no harm done. You observed that the instant the air reached the cathode, as I for convenience call the electrified mass of gold, the action ceased."

"But your anode, to continue your simile," I said, "is constantly exposed to the air."

"True," he replied, "but in the first place, of course, this is not really an anode, just as the other is not actually a cathode. As science advances we are compelled, for a time, to use old terms in a new sense until a fresh nomenclature can be invented. But we are now dealing with a form of electric action more subtle in its effects than any at present described in the text-books and the transactions of learned societies. I have not yet even attempted to work out the theory of it. I am only concerned with its facts."

"But wonderful as the exhibition you have given is, I do not see," I said, "how it concerns Dr. Syx and his artemisium."

"Listen," replied Hall, settling back in his chair after disconnecting his apparatus. "You no doubt have been told how one night the Syx engine was heard working for a few minutes, the first and only night work it was ever known to have done, and how, hardly had it started up when a fire broke out in the mill, and the engine was instantly stopped. Now there is a very remarkable story connected with that, and it will show you how I got my first clew to the mystery, although it was rather a mere suspicion than a clew, for at first I could make nothing out of it. The alleged fire occurred about a fortnight after our discovery of the double tunnel. My mind was then full of suspicions concerning Syx, because I thought that a man who would fool people with one hand was not likely to deal fairly with the other.

"It was a glorious night, with a full moon, whose face was so clear in the limpid air that, having found a snug place at the foot of a yellow-pine-tree, where the ground was carpeted with odoriferous needles, I lay on my back and renewed my early acquaintance with the romantically named mountains and 'seas' of the Lunar globe. With my binocular I could trace those long white streaks which radiate from the crater ring, called 'Tycho,' and run hundreds of miles in all directions over the moon. As I gazed at these singular objects I recalled the various theories which astronomers, puzzled by their enigmatical aspect, have offered to a more or less confiding public concerning them.

"In the midst of my meditation and moon gazing I was startled by hearing the engine in the Syx works suddenly begin to run. Immediately a queer light, shaped like the beam of a ship's searchlight, but reddish in colour, rose high in the moonlit heavens above the mill. It did not last more than a minute or two, for almost instantly the engine was stopped, and with its stoppage the light faded and soon disappeared. The next day Dr. Syx gave it out that on starting up his engine in the night something had caught fire, which compelled him immediately to shut down again. The few who had seen the light, with the exception of your humble servant, accepted the doctor's explanation without a question. But I knew there had been no fire, and Syx's anxiety to spread the lie led me to believe that he had narrowly escaped giving away a vital secret. I said nothing about my suspicions, but upon inquiry I found out that an extra and pressing order for metal had arrived from the Austrian government the very day of the pretended fire, and I drew the inference that Syx, in his haste to fill the order—his supply having been drawn low—had started to work, contrary to his custom, at night, and had immediately found reason to repent his rashness. Of course, I connected the strange light with this sudden change of mind.

"My suspicion having been thus stimulated, and having been directed in a certain way, I began, from that moment to notice closely the hours during which the engine laboured. At night it was always quiet, except on that one brief occasion. Sometimes it began early in the morning and stopped about noon. At other times the work was done entirely in the afternoon, beginning sometimes as late as three or four o'clock, and ceasing invariably at sundown. Then again it would start at sunrise and continue the whole day through.

"For a long time I was unable to account for these eccentricities, and the problem was not rendered much clearer, although a startling suggestiveness was added to it, when, at length, I noticed that the periods of activity of the engine had a definite relation to the age of the moon. Then I discovered, with the aid of an almanac, that I could predict the hours when the engine would be busy. At the time of new moon it worked all day; at full moon, it was idle; between full moon and last quarter, it laboured in the forenoon, the length of its working hours increasing as the quarter was approached; between last quarter and new moon, the hours of work lengthened, until, as I have said, at new moon they lasted all day; between new moon and first quarter, work began later and later in the forenoon as the quarter was approached, and between first quarter and full moon the labouring hours rapidly shortened, being confined to the latter part of the afternoon, until at full moon complete silence reigned in the mill."

"Well! well!" I broke in, greatly astonished by Hall's singular recital, "you must have thought Dr. Syx was a cross between an alchemist and an astrologer."

"Note this," said Hall, disregarding my interruption, "the hours when the engine worked were invariably the hours during which the moon was above the horizon!"

"What did you infer from that?" "Of course, I inferred that the moon was directly concerned in the mystery; but how? That bothered me for a long time, but a little light broke into my mind when I picked up, on the mountain-side, a dead bird, whose scorched feathers were bronzed with artemisium, and sometime later another similar victim of a mysterious form of death. Then came the attack on the mine and its tragic finish. I have already told you what I observed on that occasion. But, instead of helping to clear up the mystery, it rather complicated it for a time. At length, however, I reasoned my way partly out of the difficulty. Certain things which I had noticed in the Syx mill convinced me that there was a part of the building whose existence no visitor suspected, and, putting one thing with another, I inferred that the roof must be open above that secret part of the structure, and that if I could get upon a sufficiently elevated place I could see something of what was hidden there.

"At this point in the investigation I proposed to you the trip to the top of the Teton, the result of which you remember. I had calculated the angles with great care, and I felt certain that from the apex of the mountain I should be able to get a view into the concealed chamber, and into just that side of it which I wished particularly to inspect. You remember that I called your attention to a shining object underneath the circular opening in the roof. You could not make out what it was, but I saw enough to convince me that it was a gigantic parabolic mirror. I'll show you a smaller one of the same kind presently.

"Now, at last, I began to perceive the real truth, but it was so wildly incredible, so infinitely remote from all human experience, that I hardly ventured to formulate it, even in my own secret mind. But I was bound to see the thing through to the end. It occurred to me that I could prove the accuracy of my theory with the aid of a kite. You were kind enough to lend your assistance in that experiment, and it gave me irrefragable evidence of the existence of a shaft of flying atoms extending in a direct line between Dr. Syx's pretended mine and the moon!"

"Hall!" I exclaimed, "you are mad!" My friend smiled good-naturedly, and went on with his story.

"The instant the kite shrivelled and disappeared I understood why the works were idle when the moon was not above the horizon, why birds flying across that fatal beam fell dead upon the rocks, and whence the terrible master of that mysterious mill derived the power of destruction that could wither an army as the Assyrian host in Byron's poem

"Melted like snow in the glance of the Lord."

"But how did Dr. Syx turn the flying atoms against his enemies?" I asked.

"In a very simple manner. He had a mirror mounted so that it could be turned in any direction, and would shunt the stream of metallic atoms, heated by their friction with the air, towards any desired point. When the attack came he raised this machine above the level of the roof and swept the mob to a lustrous, if expensive, death."

"And the light at night—"

"Was the shining of the heated atoms, not luminous enough to be visible in broad day, for which reason the engine never worked at night, and the stream of volatilized artemisium was never set flowing at full moon, when the lunar globe is above the horizon only during the hours of darkness."

"I see," I said, "whence came the nuggets on the mountain. Some of the atoms, owing to the resistance of the air, fell short and settled in the form of impalpable dust until the winds and rains collected and compacted them in the cracks and crevices of the rocks."

"That was it, of course."

"And now," I added, my amazement at the success of Hall's experiments and the accuracy of his deductions increasing every moment, "do you say that you have also discovered the means employed by Dr. Syx to obtain artemisium from the moon?"

"Not only that," replied my friend, "but within the next few minutes I shall have the pleasure of presenting to you a button of moon metal, fresh from the veins of Artemis herself."

CHAPTER 13

The Looting of the Moon

I shall spare the reader a recital of the tireless efforts, continuing through many almost sleepless weeks, whereby Andrew Hall obtained his clew to Dr. Syx's method. It was manifest from the beginning that the agent concerned must be some form of etheric, or so-called electric, energy; but how to set it in operation was the problem. Finally he hit upon the apparatus for his initial experiments which I have already described.

"Recurring to what had been done more than half a century ago by Hertz, when he concentrated electric waves upon a focal point by means of a concave mirror," said Hall, "I saw that the key I wanted lay in an extension of these experiments. At last I found that I could transform the energy of an engine into undulations of the ether, which, when they had been concentrated upon a metallic object, like a chunk of gold, imparted to it an intense charge of an apparently electric nature. Upon thus charging a metallic body enclosed in a vacuum, I observed that the energy imparted to it possessed the remarkable power of disrupting its atoms and projecting them off in straight lines, very much as occurs with a cathode in a Crookes's tube. But—and this was of supreme importance—I found that the line of projection was directly towards the apparatus from which the impulse producing the charge had come. In other words, I could produce two poles between which a marvellous interaction occurred. My transformer, with its concentrating mirror, acted as one pole, from which energy was transferred to the other pole, and that other pole immediately flung off atoms of its own substance in the direction of the transformer. But these atoms were stopped by the glass wall of the vacuum tube; and when I tried the experiment with the metal removed from the vacuum, and surrounded with air, it failed utterly.

"This at first completely discouraged me, until I suddenly remembered that the moon is in a vacuum, the great vacuum of interplanetary space, and that it possesses no perceptible atmosphere of its own. At this a great light broke around me, and I shouted 'Eureka!' Without hesitation I constructed a transformer of great power, furnished with a large parabolic mirror to transmit the waves in parallel lines, erected the machinery and buildings here, and when all was ready for the final experiment I telegraphed for you." Prepared by these explanations I was all on fire to see the thing tried. Hall was no less eager, and, calling in his two faithful assistants to make the final adjustments, he led the way into what he facetiously named "the lunar chamber."

"If we fail," he remarked with a smile that had an element of worriment in it, "it will become the 'lunatic chamber'—but no danger of that. You observe this polished silver knob, supported by a metallic rod curved over at the top like a crane. That constitutes the pole from which I propose to transmit the energy to the moon, and upon which I expect the storm of atoms to be centred by reflection from the mirror at whose focus it is placed."

"One moment," I said. "Am I to understand that you think that the moon is a solid mass of artemisium, and that no matter where your radiant force strikes it a 'cathodic pole' will be formed there from which atoms will be projected to the earth?"

"No," said Hall, "I must carefully choose the point on the lunar surface where to operate. But that will present no difficulty. I made up my mind as soon as I had penetrated Syx's secret that he obtained the metal from those mystic white streaks which radiate from Tycho, and which have puzzled the astronomers ever since the invention of telescopes. I now believe those streaks to be composed of immense veins of the metal that Syx has most appropriately named artemisium, which you, of course, recognize as being derived from the name of the Greek goddess of the moon, Artemis, whom the Romans called Diana. But now to work!"

It was less than a day past the time of new moon, and the earth's satellite was too near the sun to be visible in broad daylight. Accordingly, the mirror had to be directed by means of knowledge of the moon's place in the sky. Driven by accurate clockwork, it could be depended upon to retain the proper direction when once set.

With breathless interest I watched the proceedings of my friend and his assistants. The strain upon the nerves of all of us was such as could not have been borne for many hours at a stretch. When everything had been adjusted to his satisfaction, Hall stepped back, not without betraying his excitement in flushed cheeks and flashing eyes, and pressed a lever. The powerful engine underneath the floor instantly responded. The experiment was begun.

"I have set it upon a point about a hundred miles north of Tycho, where the Yerkes photographs show a great abundance of the white substance," said Hall.

Then we waited. A minute elapsed. A bird, fluttering in the opening above, for a second or two, wrenched our strained nerves. Hall's face turned pale.

"They had better keep away from here," he whispered, with a ghastly smile.

Two minutes! I could hear the beating of my heart. The engine shook the floor.

Three minutes! Hall's face was wet with perspiration. The bird blundered in and startled us again.

Four minutes! We were like statues, with all eyes fixed on the polished ball of silver, which shone in the brilliant light concentrated upon it by the mirror.

Five minutes! The shining ball had become a confused blue, and I violently winked to clear my vision.

"At last! Thank God! Look! There it is!"

It was Hall who spoke, trembling like an aspen. The silver knob had changed colour. What seemed a miniature rainbow surrounded it, with concentric circles of blinding brilliance.

Then something dropped flashing into an earthen dish set beneath the ball! Another glittering drop followed, and, at a shorter interval, another!

Almost before a word could be uttered the drops had coalesced and become a tiny stream, which, as it fell, twisted itself into a bright spiral, gleaming with a hundred shifting hues, and forming on the bottom of the dish a glowing, interlacing maze of viscid rings and circlets, which turned and twined about and over one another, until they had blended and settled into a button-shaped mass of hot metallic jelly. Hall snatched the dish away, and placed another in its stead.

"This will be about right for a watch charm when it cools," he said, with a return of his customary self-command. "I promised you the first specimen. I'll catch another for myself."

"But can it be possible that we are not dreaming?" I exclaimed. "Do you really believe that this comes from the moon?"

"Just as surely as rain comes from the clouds," cried Hall, with all his old impatience. "Haven't I just showed you the whole process?"

"Then I congratulate you. You will be as rich as Dr. Syx."

"Perhaps," was the unperturbed reply, "but not until I have enlarged my apparatus. At present I shall hardly do more than supply mementoes to my friends. But since the principle is established, the rest is mere detail."

Six weeks later the financial centres of the earth were shaken by the news that a new supply of artemisium was being marketed from a mill which had been secretly opened in the Sierras of California. For a time there was almost a panic. If Hall had chosen to do so, he might have precipitated serious trouble. But he immediately entered into negotiations with government representatives, and the inevitable result was that, to preserve the monetary system of the world from upheaval, Dr. Syx had to consent that Hall's mill should share equally with his in the production of artemisium. During the negotiations the doctor paid a visit to Hall's establishment. The meeting between them was most dramatic. Syx tried to blast his rival with a glance, but knowledge is power, and my friend faced his mysterious antagonist, whose deepest secrets he had penetrated, with an unflinching eye. It was remarked that Dr. Syx became a changed man from that moment. His masterful air seemed to have deserted him, and it was with something resembling humility that he assented to the arrangement which required him to share his enormous gains with his conqueror.

Of course, Hall's success led to an immediate recrudescence of the efforts to extract artemisium from the Syx ore, and, equally of course, every such attempt failed. Hall, while keeping his own secret, did all he could to discourage the experiments, but they naturally believed that he must have made the very discovery which was the subject of their dreams, and he could not, without betraying himself, and upsetting the finances of the planet, directly undeceive them. The consequence was that fortunes were wasted in hopeless experimentation, and, with Hall's achievement dazzling their eyes, the deluded fortune-seekers kept on in the face of endless disappointments and disaster.

And presently there came another tragedy. The Syx mill was blown up! The accident—although many people refused to regard it as an accident, and asserted that the doctor himself, in his chagrin, had applied the match—the explosion, then, occurred about sundown, and its effects were awful. The great works, with everything pertaining to them, and every rail that they contained, were blown to atoms. They disappeared as if they had never existed. Even the twin tunnels were involved in the ruin, a vast cavity being left in the mountain-side where Syx's ten acres had been. The force of the explosion was so great that the shattered rock was reduced to dust. To this fact was owing the escape of the troops camped near. While the mountain was shaken to its core, and enormous parapets of living rock were hurled down the precipices of the Teton, no missiles of appreciable size traversed the air, and not a man at the camp was injured. But Jackson's Hole, filled with red dust, looked for days afterwards like the mouth of a tremendous volcano just after an eruption. Dr. Syx had been seen entering the mill a few minutes before the catastrophe by a sentinel who was stationed about a quarter of a mile away, and who, although he was felled like an ox by the shock, and had his eyes, ears, and nostrils filled with flying dust, miraculously escaped with his life.

After this a new arrangement was made whereby Andrew Hall became the sole producer of artemisium, and his wealth began to mount by leaps of millions towards the starry heights of the billions.

About a year after the explosion of the Syx mill a strange rumour got about. It came first from Budapest, in Hungary, where it was averred several persons of credibility had seen Dr. Max Syx. Millions had been familiar with his face and his personal peculiarities, through actually meeting him, as well as through photographs and descriptions, and, unless there was an intention to deceive, it did not seem possible that a mistake could be made in identification. There surely never was another man who looked just like Dr. Syx. And, besides, was it not demonstrable that he must have perished in the awful destruction of his mill?

Soon after came a report that Dr. Syx had been seen again; this time at Ekaterinburg, in the Urals. Next he was said to have paid a visit to Batang, in the mountainous district of south-western China, and finally, according to rumour, he was seen in Sicily, at Nicolosi, among the volcanic pimples on the southern slope of Mount Etna.

Next followed something of more curious and even startling interest. A chemist at Budapest, where the first rumours of Syx's reappearance had placed the mysterious doctor, announced that he could produce artemisium, and proved it, although he kept his process secret. Hardly had the sensation caused by this news partially subsided when a similar report arrived from Ekaterinburg; then another from Batang; after that a fourth from Nicolosi!

Nobody could fail to notice the coincidence; wherever the doctor—or was it his ghost?—appeared, there, shortly afterwards, somebody discovered the much-sought secret.

After this Syx's apparitions rapidly increased in frequency, followed in each instance by the announcement of another productive artemisium mill. He appeared in Germany, Italy, France, England, and finally at many places in the United States.

"It is the old doctor's revenge," said Hall to me one day, trying to smile, although the matter was too serious to be taken humorously. "Yes, it is his revenge, and I must admit that it is complete. The price of artemisium has fallen one-half within six months. All the efforts we have made to hold back the flood have proved useless. The secret itself is becoming public property. We shall inevitably be overwhelmed with artemisium, just as we were with gold, and the last condition of the financial world will be worse than the first."

My friend's gloomy prognostications came near being fulfilled to the letter. Ten thousand artemisium mills shot their etheric rays upon the moon, and our unfortunate satellite's metal ribs were stripped by atomic force. Some of the great white rays that had been one of the telescopic wonders of the lunar landscapes disappeared, and the face of the moon, which had remained unchanged before the eyes of the children of Adam from the beginning of their race, now looked as if the blast of a furnace had swept it. At night, on the moonward side, the earth was studded with brilliant spikes, all pointed at the heart of its child in the sky.

But the looting of the moon brought disaster to the robber planet. So mad were the efforts to get the precious metal that the surface of our globe was fairly showered with it, productive fields were, in some cases, almost smothered under a metallic coating, the air was filled with shining dust, until finally famine and pestilence joined hands with financial disaster to punish the grasping world.

Then, at last, the various governments took effective measures to protect themselves and their people. Another combined effort resulted in an international agreement whereby the production of the precious moon metal was once more rigidly controlled. But the existence of a monopoly, such as Dr. Syx had so long enjoyed, and in the enjoyment of which Andrew Hall had for a brief period succeeded him, was henceforth rendered impossible.

CHAPTER 14

The Last of Dr. Syx

Many years after the events last recorded I sat, at the close of a brilliant autumn day, side by side with my old friend Andrew Hall, on a broad, vine-shaded piazza which faced the east, where the full moon was just rising above the rim of the Sierra, and replacing the rosy counter-glow of sunset with its silvery radiance. The sight was calculated to carry the minds of both back to the events of former years. But I noticed that Hall quickly changed the position of his chair, and sat down again with his back to the rising moon. He had managed to save some millions from the wreck of his vast fortune when artemisium started to go to the dogs, and I was now paying him one of my annual visits at his palatial home in California.

"Did I ever tell you of my last trip to the Teton?" he asked, as I continued to gaze contemplatively at the broad lunar disk which slowly detached itself from the horizon and began to swim in the clear evening sky.

"No," I replied, "but I should like to hear about it."

"Or of my last sight of Dr. Syx?"

"Indeed! I did not suppose that you ever saw him after that conference in your mill, when he had to surrender half of the world to you."

"Once only I saw him again," said Hall, with a peculiar intonation.

"Pray go ahead, and tell me the whole story."

My friend lighted a fresh cigar, tipped his chair into a more comfortable position, and began:

"It was about seven years ago. I had long felt an unconquerable desire to have another look at the Teton and the scenes amid which so many strange events in my life had occurred. I thought of sending for you to go with me, but I knew you were abroad much of your time, and I could not be certain of catching you. Finally I decided to go alone. I travelled on horseback by way of the Snake River canyon, and arrived early one morning in Jackson's Hole. I can tell you it was a gloomy place, as barren and deserted as some of those Arabian wadis that you have been describing to me. The railroad had long ago been abandoned, and the site of the military camp could scarcely be recognized. An immense cavity with ragged walls showed where Dr. Syx's mill used to send up its plume of black smoke.

"As I stared up the gaunt form of the Teton, whose beetling precipices had been smashed and split by the great explosion, I was seized with a resistless impulse to climb it. I thought I should like to peer off again from that pinnacle which had once formed so fateful a watchtower for me. Turning my horse loose to graze in the grassy river bottom, and carrying my rope tether along as a possible aid in climbing, I set out for the ascent. I knew I could not get up the precipices on the eastern side, which we were able to master with the aid of our balloon, and so I bore round, when I reached the steepest cliffs, until I was on the south-western side of the peak, where the climbing was easier.

"But it took me a long time, and I did not reach the rift in the summit until just before sundown. Knowing that it would be impossible for me to descend at night, I bethought me of the enclosure of rocks, supposed to have been made by Indians, on the western pinnacle, and decided that I could pass the night there.

"The perpendicular buttress forming the easternmost and highest point of the Teton's head would have baffled me but for the fact that I found a long crack, probably an effect of the tremendous explosion, extending from bottom to top of the rock. Driving my toes and fingers into this rift, I managed, with a good deal of trouble, and no little peril, to reach the top. As I lifted myself over the edge and rose to my feet, imagine my amazement at seeing Dr. Syx standing within arm's-length of me!

"My breath seemed pent in my lungs, and I could not even utter the exclamation that rose to my lips. It was like meeting a ghost. Notwithstanding the many reports of his having been seen in various parts of the world, it had always been my conviction that he had perished in the explosion.

"Yet there he stood in the twilight, for the sun was hidden by the time I reached the summit, his tall form erect, and his black eyes gleaming under the heavy brows as he fixed them sternly upon my face. You know I never was given to losing my nerve, but I am afraid I lost it on that occasion. Again and again I strove to speak, but it was impossible to move my tongue. So powerless seemed my lungs that I wondered how I could continue breathing.

"The doctor remained silent, but his curious smile, which, as you know, was a thing of terror to most people, overspread his black-rimmed face and was broad enough to reveal the gleam of his teeth. I felt that he was looking me through and through. The sensation was as if he had transfixed me with an ice-cold blade. There was a gleam of devilish pleasure in his eyes, as though my evident suffering was a delight to him and a gratification of his vengeance. At length I succeeded in overcoming the feeling which oppressed me, and, making a step forward, I shouted in a strained voice,

"'You black Satan!'

"I cannot clearly explain the psychological process which led me to utter those words. I had never entertained any enmity towards Dr. Syx, although I had always regarded him as a heartless person, who had purposely led thousands to their ruin for his selfish gain, but I knew that he could not help hating me, and I felt now that, in some inexplicable manner, a struggle, not physical, but spiritual, was taking place between us, and my exclamation, uttered with surprising intensity, produced upon me, and apparently upon him, the effect of a desperate sword thrust which attains its mark.

"Immediately the doctor's form seemed to recede, as if he had passed the verge of the precipice behind him. At the same time it became dim, and then dimmer, until only the dark outlines, and particularly the jet-black eyes, glaring fiercely, remained visible. And still he receded, as though floating in the air, which was now silvered with the evening light, until he appeared to cross the immense atmospheric gulf over Jackson's Hole and paused on the rim of the horizon in the east.

"Then, suddenly, I became aware that the full moon had risen at the very place on the distant mountain-brow where the spectre rested, and as I continued to gaze, as if entranced, the face and figure of the doctor seemed slowly to frame themselves within the lunar disk, until at last he appeared to have quitted the air and the earth and to be frowning at me from the circle of the moon."

While Hall was pronouncing his closing words I had begun to stare at the moon with swiftly increasing interest, until, as his voice stopped, I exclaimed,

"Why, there he is now! Funny I never noticed it before. There's Dr. Syx's face in the moon, as plain as day."

"Yes," replied Hall, without turning round, "and I never like to look at it."

LEONAUR

ALSO FROM LEONAUR

AVAILABLE IN SOFTCOVER OR HARDCOVER WITH DUST JACKET

THE COLLECTED SCIENCE FICTION AND FANTASY OF STANLEY G. WEINBAUM: INTERPLANETARY ODYSSEYS—Classic Tales of Interplanetary Adventure Including: A Martian Odyssey, its Sequel Valley of Dreams, the Complete 'Ham' Hammond Stories and Others.

THE COLLECTED SCIENCE FICTION AND FANTASY OF STANLEY G. WEINBAUM: OTHER EARTHS—Classic Futuristic Tales Including: Dawn of Flame & its Sequel The Black Flame, plus The Revolution of 1960 & Others.

THE COLLECTED SCIENCE FICTION AND FANTASY OF STANLEY G. WEINBAUM: STRANGE GENIUS—Classic Tales of the Human Mind at Work Including the Complete Novel The New Adam, the 'van Manderpootz' Stories and Others.

THE COLLECTED SCIENCE FICTION AND FANTASY OF STANLEY G. WEINBAUM: THE BLACK HEART—Classic Strange Tales Including: the Complete Novel The Dark Other, Plus Proteus Island and Others.

DARKNESS AND DAWN 1: THE VACANT WORLD *by George Allen England*—A Novel of a future New York.

DARKNESS AND DAWN 2: BEYOND THE GREAT OBLIVION *by George Allen England*—A Novel of a future America.

DARKNESS AND DAWN 3: THE AFTER GLOW *by George Allen England*—A Novel of a future America.

CARSON OF VENUS VOLUME 1: PIRATES OF VENUS & LOST ON VENUS—*by Edgar Rice Burroughs*—Two full length novels.

JOHN CARTER OF MARS VOLUME 1: THE PRINCESS OF MARS & THE GODS OF MARS—*by Edgar Rice Burroughs*—Two full length novels.

PELLUCIDAR - THE INNER WORLD VOLUME 1: AT THE EARTH'S CORE - PELLUCIDAR—*by Edgar Rice Burroughs*—Two full length novels.

BEFORE ADAM & OTHER STORIES—*by Jack London*—Includes the novel Before Adam + The Scarlet Plague A Relic of the Pliocene When the World Was Young and others.

THE IRON HEEL & OTHER STORIES—*by Jack London*—Includes the novel The Iron Heel + The Enemy of All the World The Shadow and the Flash The Strength of the Strong The Unparalleled Invasion The Dream of Debs.

LEONAUR

CLASSIC SF FROM LEONAUR
AVAILABLE IN SOFTCOVER OR HARDCOVER WITH DUST JACKET

SF4 CLASSIC SCIENCE FICTION SERIES
DARKNESS & DAWN 1: The Vacant World
by George Allen England

SOFTCOVER : **ISBN 1-84677-027-0**
HARDCOVER : **ISBN 1-84677-034-3**

New York City – the end of the 3rd millennium. Buildings in ruins. Central Park a jungle peopled by sub-humans. A huge black shape moving across the night sky. Civilization has vanished along with humankind. Into this hostile new world two survivors of our enlightened age awaken from 1000 years of slumber - to fall victims to a world gone wild? - or to give mankind a second chance?

SF5 CLASSIC SCIENCE FICTION SERIES
DARKNESS & DAWN 2: Beyond the Great Oblivion *by George Allen England*

SOFTCOVER : **ISBN 1-84677-028-9**
HARDCOVER : **ISBN 1-84677-036-X**

The distant future - exotic flora and fauna thrive - savage tribes of cannibalistic sub-humans fight for dominance. New York is a place of little hope! The last vestiges of humanity set out across America's devastated landscape in search of their dream, enticed onward by a mysterious and vast black chasm 500 miles deep - does the future threaten extinction for mankind? - or offer one last chance of redemption?

SF6 CLASSIC SCIENCE FICTION SERIES
DARKNESS & DAWN 3: The After Glow
by George Allen England

SOFTCOVER : **ISBN 1-84677-029-7**
HARDCOVER : **ISBN 1-84677-038-6**

Near the Great Lakes, 1000 years from now. Below our planet's surface tribes of albino warriors eke out an existence in a hostile environment. They tell stories of a golden age; but such tales are mere myths - until a man and a woman with god-like abilities arrive and promise to lead them towards the surface, towards the light and to a new life of plenty.

LEONAUR
CLASSIC SF FROM LEONAUR
AVAILABLE IN SOFTCOVER OR HARDCOVER WITH DUST JACKET

SF7 CLASSIC SCIENCE FICTION SERIES
INTERPLANETARY ODYSSEYS
by Stanley G. Weinbaum

Classic Tales of Interplanetary Adventure Including: A Martian Odyssey, its Sequel Valley of Dreams & Others

SOFTCOVER : **ISBN 1-84677-060-2**
HARDCOVER : **ISBN 1-84677-070-X**

SF8 CLASSIC SCIENCE FICTION SERIES
OTHER EARTHS
by Stanley G. Weinbaum

Classic Futuristic Tales Including: Dawn of Flame & its Sequel The Black Flame, plus The Revolution of 1960 & Others

SOFTCOVER : **ISBN 1-84677-062-9**
HARDCOVER : **ISBN 1-84677-072-6**

SF9 CLASSIC SCIENCE FICTION SERIES
STRANGE GENIUS
by Stanley G. Weinbaum

Classic Tales of the Human Mind at Work Including the Complete Novel The New Adam, the 'van Manderpootz' Stories & More

SOFTCOVER : **ISBN 1-84677-048-3**
HARDCOVER : **ISBN 1-84677-055-6**

SF10 CLASSIC SCIENCE FICTION SERIES
THE BLACK HEART
by Stanley G. Weinbaum

Classic Strange Tales Including: the Complete Novel The Dark Other, Plus Proteus Island and Others

SOFTCOVER : **ISBN 1-84677-049-1**
HARDCOVER : **ISBN 1-84677-054-8**

www.ingramcontent.com/pod-product-compliance
Lightning Source LLC
Chambersburg PA
CBHW020929020726
47495CB00002B/420